THE HOUSE OF DUST

NOAH BROYLES

Published by Inkshares, Inc., San Francisco, California
www.inkshares.com

Edited by Adam Gomolin, Barnaby Conrad, & Pamela McElroy
Cover design by Tim Barber
Interior design by Kevin G. Summers

ISBN: 9781947848870
e-ISBN: 9781947848887
LCCN: 2019930695

First edition

Printed in the United States of America

To my mom and dad.
Thank you for the typewriter.

There is the house whose people sit in darkness;
dust is their food. . . they are clothed like birds
with wings for covering, they see no light. . .
I entered the house of dust and saw the kings of the earth,
their crowns put away forever; rulers and princes,
all those who once. . . ruled the world in the days of old.

—The *Epic of Gilgamesh*

EDITOR'S NOTE

On June 4, 2018, a rental car registered to Bradley Ellison—*Southern Gothic*'s crime writer—was found in a McDonald's parking lot in Lexington, Tennessee. The driver's-side window was shattered, and the writer was inside, dead from a gunshot wound.

During the month prior to this tragedy, Mr. Ellison had been working with great enthusiasm on a project centered around a house in rural Tennessee. After we had expressed concern about the quality of his latest publications in this magazine, he assured us that this project would restore our faith in him.

Mr. Ellison certainly tells a fantastic tale in this—his last—article. But while *Southern Gothic* has been able to verify the locations, the events themselves are unverifiable. The locals Mr. Ellison interacted with proved reclusive, even hostile, when approached later by some of our colleagues. We trust, however, that when judging this piece, our readers will remember the caliber of Mr. Ellison's reporting on the Serene Flats murders.

Mr. Ellison expresses opinions in this article about the staff of this magazine, specifically myself, that may be shocking to our readers. We have decided not to edit these out for the sake of honesty and integrity. Mr. Ellison was entitled to his opinions, and we are entitled to ours—that his attacks are unfair and incorrect.

After carefully considering all of these factors, we have decided to publish the entire article, raw and unedited, as it was sent to us on that midsummer night last year, mere minutes before its author's death. Mr. Ellison did not consider it finished, and neither do we. We consider it a beginning, though to what future we cannot yet know. Awareness, perhaps, will make these types of tragedies less common. *Southern Gothic* has always embraced controversy, and with the publication of this piece we do so with a clear head. Even so, reader discretion is advised.

—*Heather Graff, Editor in Chief*

This issue of *Southern Gothic*
is dedicated to the memory of
Bradley Oswald Ellison
June 7, 1987–June 3, 2018

WHISPER FROM THE DUST

I got off the interstate to commit suicide.

I was supposed to interview a police chief in Jackson about a carjacking cold case, but my tire blew out with thirty miles to go. The delay killed the appointment, and the trouble I had swapping tires revealed my own inadequacy even more. The car rode unlevel on the spare, droning the prospect of another failed investigation into my bones. Heat pressed through the sunroof, pounding memories of my fiancée's screaming face through my sweaty scalp. Both those pillars of my life—collapsing. When I saw the next off-ramp, I put on my signal.

It was one of those dead, pointless exits in rural Tennessee that serves perhaps a dozen people a day. Left was the interstate underpass. Right was blank road. I wanted a quiet place to do it. I went right, out into the wilderness, leaving the world and all its weight behind.

But the weight followed me.

It was the end of April, but outside the grimy glass, the afternoon trees wore the tired green of late summer. I searched for a shady gravel patch along the shoulder. The broken driver's-side window control clicked beneath my forefinger as the rising pressure crushed open a primal place in my brain filled with flames and billowing smoke and the searing smell of raw oil. My eyes watered. I tried to still my finger but couldn't.

The clicking only stopped when I saw the sign. It leaned drunk-enly among thick honeysuckle at the far edge of the highway. My vision cleared. Buried beneath many spray-painted desecration attempts lay the official black lettering:

THREE SUMMERS—TWO MILES

Just beyond the sign, a leafy mouth opened in the wall of the woods, the shrouded access point to the forgotten town. It would do. I turned across the highway and stopped my car amid the brackish twilight.

An RIA .38 Special rode in the glove box. I took it out and braced it against my temple. The movements of my jaw, clenching and unclenching, translated along its length into my hand. I could already smell the sulfur, already feel the fiery track of the bullet through my brain. The window would shatter. The flies would come through the breach and settle on my body. Eventually, someone would happen down this road and find my car. Word would get out, swirl across local networks, then end up in Atlanta on the desk of my editor, Heather. My own death would be the last violent, mean-ingless story I provided her. I might just as well have stepped out in traffic while changing the car tire back on the interstate.

No, I did not want a violent death.

I replaced the gun and picked up an orange canister from the passenger-side floorboard. Ten milligrams would buoy me up. Lift the weight. Bring me back to the surface. But there was fire on the surface. The endless fight to stay afloat. The story I could never tell.

I gripped the canister. It would take about a dozen pills to get sleepy, a dozen more to soar from my body for good. But I couldn't swallow one pill dry, let alone twenty-four.

"Some water," I said aloud. "I need a drink of water."

—"The House of Dust"
Southern Gothic

BRAD STARTED THE car and stepped on the gas.

A winding kaleidoscope of fragmented sunlight and pavement sucked him into the breathless forest. The car lurched through potholes and tilted as the road slithered carelessly along a hillside. It felt like the roller coaster at the Enchanted Forest, back when he was a kid. *What if we die?* his dad had said. *Know what you'll say when you die, Brad? I know what I'll say: Amen.*

The leaves thickened overhead, and the branches hunched down and locked together, vines twisting around to secure them in place. The headlights blinked on automatically, and the dash display brightened. He was going almost fifty. But instead of the hum of tires, silence rose around his legs, filling up the car. Heavy. Squeezing. Dragging him down.

Brad screwed his hands tighter around the wheel. The headlights swept across a band of twilit forest as the car rounded another bend. Ahead, the trees ended abruptly. He pressed on the brakes. The glowing whiteness of the afternoon opened onto an ancient bridge.

It was barely wide enough for two cars, with low barriers on either side. Below the gray concrete span crawled a slow green river. A battered sign leaned nearby: LOCUST RIVER BRIDGE. Someone had spray-painted it with a different word: *Adamah.*

Something twisted inside him at the sight of it. He shook it off and rolled the Accord into the glare, across the bridge. Casting a sidelong glance at the water seventy feet below, he imagined stepping on the gas and giving the steering wheel a quick jerk. Down, down, into the—

No.

He just needed a drink.

As Brad crossed the bridge, the bleached bones of the town faded through the shimmering heat. Three Summers. The settlement occupied a half mile of shoreline. A main street connected to the bridge and cut through the heart of the silent town, between old brick buildings that lined the street with the slumping gallantry of veterans from some half-remembered war.

No birds perched along the town's uneven line of roofs. And no one was in sight. Just sunlight on the abandonment.

Immediately to his right as he bumped off the bridge stood a huge white house with faded green trim and wraparound porches on both floors. A small, high-grown yard and a rusted ironwork fence separated it from the street. A sign by the gate announced it as the Locust River Hotel. This time, the name had not been crossed out.

Brad's eyes turned. A placard on the side of the brick building opposite labeled the main street Adamah Road.

The dragging weight wavered.

Lifting the pill canister, he rattled it and pressed on the gas, following the street deeper into the town. All he needed was a glass of water.

Hazy-windowed drugstores, vacant warehouses, and four-story apartment buildings crept by outside. Shrouded windows. Empty alleys. Then an intersection. He stopped.

The street cutting in front of him was called Larkin Street, quiet as a cemetery path. A diner, the Theater Grill, occupied the first floor of a shuttered building out the passenger-side window. A silent cinema, the Adamah Theater, stood diagonally opposite, its sandstone façade rising in a worn art deco chevron, most of the large bulbs along its marquee sign shattered.

Somewhere in the back of his brain, curiosity clawed. Twisting around in his seat, he searched shop fronts along the cracked sidewalk for signs of life. Finding nothing, he leaned against the glass to examine the higher floors of the surrounding structures. Curtains stirred in several windows, as if faces had just withdrawn.

Where were the people? And the theater bulbs: Were they a tale of neglect or violence?

Violence.

Years spent chronicling it. Brutish and pointless.

The weight came rushing back, thick, cloaking him like oil.

He needed to escape. To rest. He drove on.

After a bit, the buildings ended, and two roads that bordered the edge of town curved in to join the main street. Beyond this intersection, the last few mundane structures buttressed the street. On the right, the decaying brick hulk of a building called Knowles Furniture Warehouse slid past to reveal Grammy's Grocery, a long, low, sundried shell from the fifties fronted by a flotilla of rusted shopping carts. To the left stood a Texaco gas station, its sign faded pink. He idled for a moment in the dead street, examining each.

In the grocery store parking lot, someone had poured tar across cracks in the cement, smothering the thirsty grass that grew there, leaving stiff black shoots that stretched like charred fingers toward the sky.

A woman with short silver hair, wearing a gray sweater and dirty cargo pants, had just climbed from a green seventies model Ford Falcon. She was barefoot, her grimy, gray-fleshed feet pressed unyieldingly against the sweltering pavement. She stared at him through dark sunglasses.

Brad opted for the gas station. Pulling into the shade under the awning by one of the pumps, he examined the storefront. There were no lights on inside, but a car—an eighties model Jeep Wagoneer with the wood paneling missing from the driver's-side door—sat by the icebox out front. A paper sign taped to the door of the icebox said: FREE WATER. RESTROOMS OUT OF ORDER.

Clutching the cylinder of pills in one hand, Brad opened the car door. The crumbly quality of the air struck him as he stepped out. The air was hot and gritty and prickled against his skin. Maybe there was a mine nearby, stirring up the bowels of the earth. He traversed the trailing gas pump hoses and walked to the front of the establishment.

Pulling open the icebox door, he reached inside and felt the clammy air wrap around his hand. Plastic water bottles floated in a dim, lukewarm pond. He glanced again at the windows of the store. They were obscured by banners advertising beer and cigarettes.

Well, it wouldn't matter if the water was corrupted. His dead stomach wouldn't care. He fished a bottle from the cooler and let the door fall shut. The slimy label came away in his hand. He tossed it into an overflowing trash can by the gas pump.

Hornets orbited the columns that supported the canopy, buzzing in the stillness. His mind was buzzing, too. His hand shook as he opened the car door. This was it.

In the quiet of the car, the weight wrapped him. Smothering. Binding. He cracked open the bottle and took a quick sip. It was briny, but it opened his throat. Lifting the canister, he sucked two pills into his mouth. As he lowered his hand, the stinging smell of grease caught in his nose. Bile rushed into his throat. For a moment, there was nothing but the horrible, thick sweetness of raw oil inside the car. For a moment, orange flickered in the corner of his vision. *Fire.*

Brad gulped another mouthful of brackish water to quench the sensations. Examining the back of his hand, he found it smeared with grease. Residue from changing the tire back on the interstate. Nothing to panic over. What did it matter, anyway? He pushed his sweaty hair back and let out a long breath.

Orange still danced at the edge of his right eye. It was his imagination. It should have gone away.

Brad turned his head.

A man was crossing the parking lot of Grammy's Grocery. He wore a bright orange jumpsuit, stained from head to foot with black smears. He walked with his right hand stretched out in front of him, and the slightest limp dragging at his right leg. He was just a hundred feet or so off and coming steadily. Coming toward the car. In the heat radiating from the pavement, his figure rippled.

The weight clenched around Brad's heart.

Water splashed as he set the bottle down. His fingers found the lock switch and pressed it. Facing forward, he shook the canister and downed two more pills. Blinking hard, he looked right again.

The man was crossing the barren street. Pebbles skittered before his heavy boots. The noonday sun pooled his shadow around his feet like an inverse halo.

Brad shut his eyes. He swallowed two more pills, then poured some of the water across his pounding head.

"Come on," he muttered. "Come on."

The frantic brain could play so many tricks to try to save itself. It was trying that now, throwing a rope to things he'd left in his wake, hauling them back into the light.

He forced two more pills into his mouth and opened his eyes.

The man was now on Brad's side of the road. Coming across the sidewalk. Coming toward the car. His arm bent at the elbow, palm open, rocking up and down. Beckoning.

Brad saw his face. Burned, blistered, peeling skin, glistening with black oil. Eyebrows scorched away. Steady gray eyes seared and shrunken to gravels.

He knew those eyes.

He tried to turn away, to flail, but couldn't. The weight was too pervasive, constricting his chest, dragging at his limbs, wringing even the color from his vision.

It was here.

The hand reached toward the passenger-side window. Thumping the glass. He *felt* it. Felt the car move.

His eyes winced shut. He forced the bottle to his lips, his head back, and downed the pills. That made six. No, eight.

The car rattled again. The hand was thumping against the window.

"Sir!" A muffled voice came through the glass. "Sir!"

Brad opened his eyes again. The heaviness hovered around him. The gray woman stood outside the window. The barefoot one who had looked at him across the parking lot. She was bent down, sunglasses pushed up on her head, peering in.

"Sir!"

Brad found the ignition and turned the key. He rolled the window down a crack.

The woman looked in at him. Her eyes were the same color as her hair. Her fingertips on the edge of the glass were painted with dry mud.

Brad stared at her.

"Are you the doctor?"

A portion of the pressure ebbed. He nodded faintly. "Yes. I'm the doctor."

"Then go!" the woman said. She pounded on the glass again and pointed up the avenue. "Keep going, then first road on your left. Cross a bridge, and you'll come to the house."

2

I don't know why I answered yes. To ease the weight, perhaps, forestall the inevitable.

The town petered out into abandoned lawns and weed-cracked drives running up to ivy-shrouded houses. I turned left at the first road I came to, still in sight of the town, still with the gray woman visible in my rearview mirror. Some part of me already itched to pull this thread.

The road was straight, and the woods formed a green tunnel around it, diffusing the light to an even emerald gloaming. The hazy catacomb of forest absorbed the sound and motion of my car, adding to my delirium.

Three miles later, I passed back into the sun, crossing a little clay-stained bridge that spanned a dark creek. The road that followed was in bad shape. Thick, empty fields appeared on my left. The fields ran down a mile or so to the glimmering green line of the river. The heat and the pills and budding nausea blurred my vision.

I would have sped right past the old place if my gaze had not been suddenly pulled to the passenger-side window by that mysterious, magnetic presence possessed by things that wait.

—"The House of Dust"
Southern Gothic

THE HOUSE WAS up among the trees.

Brad turned onto the strangled drive. The car crept through stripes of shadow and light, following a course that bent away from the house, then swooped around toward it again, bypassing what must have been in some past age a manicured front lawn, lost now beneath hordes of walnut and sycamore. Sticks and gravel popped beneath the tires. Curtains of Spanish moss drooped from the oaks along the drive, brushing across the roof, reaching through the open passenger window with a soft hiss as the car passed. A few pieces of moss clung to the border of the window as the car entered a clearing before the house.

Even here, the light was subdued. The trees pressed in on the dirt and gravel patch, allowing only scant groundcover that consisted mostly of tall, gangly weeds. Brad stopped the car in front of the house and turned off the engine. Stepping out, he glanced up at the circle of sky above the clearing and for a moment imagined he was at the bottom of a hole. At the far top of the hole, rain clouds were overwhelming the sun.

He could do it here, he thought. At least he would be out of the sun.

But someone was in need. And he'd claimed to be the doctor.

As Brad lowered his head, something mounted up between the eaves snagged his vision. It was a rusty circle with eight spokes that connected to a shape suspended in the center. An old wheel? Odd decoration. The shape at the center of the wheel looked almost human. He took off his glasses and cleaned them on the edge of his untucked dress shirt, then put them back on. The thing remained obscure, almost a part of the flaking wood behind it.

Again, the heaviness cloaking him pulsated.

He should take out his phone and snap a picture.

But all that was over. All the pictures and interviews and investigations he did led back to this same feeling. He grabbed the canister of pills and the water bottle from the seat and slammed the door.

Walking around the car, he looked up at the house. The architecture recalled other nineteenth-century plantation abodes: a huge front porch on the ground floor, and a second porch on the floor above, all supported by ivy-wrapped columns. The façade had been painted white at some point, then left to the mercy of the years and the secluded sunlight of the clearing, which had weathered it to a pale gray. The house rippled in the heat, a dead face beneath the surface of a pond. But it wasn't dead. The other houses he'd visited scattered around the South that shared its architecture and its age were corpses propped up behind mowed lawns and painted fences, bright-windowed and manicured and ready for visitation.

Here, the windows looked out from the back of the porches like deep-socketed eyes, panes hazy with a history of dusty summers, stained curtains for eyelids stitched shut with cobwebs. But not dead.

The house had been asleep for many years, he decided. Soon he would join it. Asleep. Eyelids closed forever in the dust. He shook another pill between his lips and climbed the front steps.

A rocking chair sat on the porch, between him and the front door. Its faded gray wood matched the house. Someone had once sat in this chair to rock slowly in the evening, to look over the breathless clearing and the gloomy trees. How would it be to sit down in that chair, to finish the pills, to drift off? He paused by the chair.

He had said he was the doctor. He *should* check on the person in the house. But what could he do? His forefinger trailed across the armrest.

A slow, cold tingle broke out on the finger. Pulling it away, he found dust clinging to the sweaty tip. Silvery. Sharp, almost. He rubbed it off and skirted the chair, avoiding nail heads that jutted from the shrunken floorboards.

The house's door was oak, swollen and weathered black. Brad knocked twice.

The moments dripped by, the rustle of leaves joined by the creak of withered timber. From the edge of his vision at least two dozen more rocking chairs ranged across the porch. He turned his head to study them. The nearest one leaned far forward. The next was leaned back. So down the line, all caught at the edge of movement.

Who had arranged them like that? Obviously no one besides the sick person lived here, otherwise the door would be opening. What would one person do with all those—

He stopped himself. He didn't need the beginning of another story. Just an ending.

Tipping his head back, he swallowed another pill.

Still staring down the porch, he reached up to knock again when the fog inside his brain thickened further. Dizziness erupted. His hand splayed out as he braced himself against the wood. How many pills was this? Ten? Eleven? It was time to lie down. Brad pushed himself away from the door.

Take a seat, Brad, he thought. *There are so many. Surely one must be for you.*

He felt it as his fingers left the wood: something cool and smooth.

It came into focus on the door like blood welling through a bandage: a tarnished metal symbol embedded in the wood. The same symbol he'd seen on the peak of the house. A circle, with a human body at the center. The figure reached out toward the circle with two legs and six arms. Its head was bald. It had no eyes.

Brad backed away from the door as grass sprouted from his spine. He couldn't stay on the porch. The thing wouldn't let him go to sleep. It would demand to be understood. It would demand that he open the door and enter the dark house.

Raking his hair back, he descended the steps to the clearing and walked quickly along the edge of the porch to the corner. A faint trail wandered along the side of the house through weeds and ivy. He stuffed the pill bottle into his breast pocket and followed the path. The air was swampy. The woods pressed in close on his left.

His hand snagged a vine as he walked, and he idly ripped it down. A portion of a window frame up on the second floor broke apart and rotten wood rained down. Brad paused.

The surest way to get someone's attention was to break something. But no barking dogs or angry voices disturbed the stillness.

Because the owner is inside, dead, he thought.

At the back of the house was a sunlit clearing where the moldering smell of the woods faded. Sugar rose around his knees, blown from the trumpets of hundreds of daffodils bursting in small yellow explosions from beds all across the yard. The land sloped gently beneath his feet, stretching down to the dark wall of the woods a hundred feet off. Milky air filled his lungs; that funeral smell of flowers.

Once more the weight dragged on his shoulders. So many flowers. Like the funeral this morning when his fiancée screamed at him. Like the funeral long ago when the awful load first came to settle across him.

This would be a good place to finish it.

He stopped somewhere near the middle of the garden and took the pills from his pocket. The water bottle crinkled in his left hand as he unscrewed the cap. Up above, the clouds were congealing, but down here the air was motionless. He closed his eyes. He opened his mouth. The canister's hard lip met his own.

A raspy sigh—long, low, crawling—entered his ear. A whisper. His hand froze.

The grease smears on his skin burned. Their scent filled his nose. With a sharp crack, the pill canister split in his hand. The water bottle thumped into the grass and the liquid chuckled softly as it drained away. Dizziness washed over him. His knees buckled. He slumped to the ground.

As he lifted his head and opened his eyes, he saw two bare feet protruding from a flower bed three yards away.

For a moment, his head cleared. *The person in need.* He crawled toward the feet. The daffodils filling the bed were different—yellow petals with tiny reddish trumpets. Clambering in among them, he pulled the stems and blossoms aside.

A body lay facedown in a little hollow in the dirt. It was a woman. Brilliant white hair spread across her shoulders and halfway down her back. A white dress shrouded her body, snug enough to be flattering and slack enough to be comfortable, a cross between a ballgown and a nightgown, with lacy sleeves and shoulders. A young woman's dress. But the bony feet peeping beneath the hem were dusty gray, laced by a patchwork of ruptured veins.

Still, it was her posture that drew his attention most. Her arms were thrown out before her, and her hands were buried in the dirt. Clawlike furrows extended behind her hands, and daffodils lay uprooted around her. She had been digging. Burrowing into the earth.

"Ma'am?" Brad said. "Can you hear me?"

Bending closer, he caught a glimpse of her face in profile, pressed against the dirt. She was certainly old, but she hadn't aged in the normal way. No wrinkles ran along her jaw or gathered around the visible eye. Her face had eroded, like a statue with the fine details rubbed away. The eye was open, the brow wrinkled slightly. Frustration. She hadn't finished the grave.

"Ma'am?" he said again. "Can you hear me?"

A sick twist of joy gripped part of him. The horrible part that lived for strange deaths and the circumstances surrounding them. The part that thrilled at the thought of a new investigation to lift his burden.

He straightened. It wasn't a good idea to disturb the body, but he needed to be sure she was gone. And he needed to see the rest of her face.

Trembling—from the drugs, of course—he reached for her shoulder.

"You dressed for the occasion, I see." The drawling, broken voice came from behind him.

Brad twisted around. Two men were coming through the garden. The leader, the one who had spoken, wore a black suit and shirt. He was reedy, and his head was reluctantly bald. His skin clung to his skull. His eyes were thin and black.

Brad bent stiffly to brush his own dark clothes: jeans and a dress shirt. He used the opportunity to locate the pill bottle among the flowers. "It's what I always wear." Slipping the bottle into his pocket, he stood. "I found her this way. She's dead."

The men stopped a few feet short of the flower bed. The second one, dressed in khakis and carrying a medical bag, tried to step past the first. The bony-faced man stuck out his arm. "No, no. If a fake doctor can tell she's dead, there's not much a real one can do."

His bright dark eyes stared at the woman for several seconds, then moved back to Brad. "You can head on out, now." He glanced at the doctor. "You too. Sorry for the inconvenience."

The doctor pulled a handkerchief from his pocket and nodded, wiping his face. "Of course, of course." He caught Brad's eyes for just a moment, then turned and hiked toward the house. Brad stepped out of the flowers. He glanced back as the man in black crouched beside the woman in white.

"Go on," the man said. As he bent farther over the body, Brad caught sight of a pistol strapped to his hip beneath the coat. Brad's pulse stumbled and he turned and walked away.

At the front of the house he watched the doctor toss his bag in the back seat of a silver Dodge pickup. He took a little brush out of the door pocket and proceeded to go over his clothes inch by inch. He looked at Brad as he stood, hands in his pockets, watching. "How'd you get this far out?"

Brad shrugged. "I was just driving. I ended up here."

The doctor tapped his head. "I mean up here. I saw the pill bottle you picked up back there. I see your posture now. You're in some pretty deep water."

Glancing up as wind stirred the treetops around the clearing, the doctor continued, "I know things can get kind of lonely in a rural community. Especially this one. I've been out here several times over the past year to check on that woman, all hours of the day and night. But the birds never sing. Nor the cicadas. It's eerie, almost. You can hear the dust falling. At least there's the wind."

"My dad used to say wind is the cousin of loneliness," Brad said absently. For an instant, there was a second hand in his pocket, wrapped around his own. His dad's hand as they wandered the Enchanted Forest, just the two of them, on a Tuesday afternoon. Never Mom, they'd already split. If Dad had cared about family time, she'd said, he wouldn't work a job where he was gone a month at a time. So they walked alone, listening to the wind move through the Enchanted Forest. *Wind is the cousin of loneliness, Brad. You learn that out there. Maybe you're already learning it here.*

His throat throbbed. He squeezed the canister in his pocket.

"That's interesting." The doctor had finished brushing off his shoes. "In that case, I'd advise you to get in your car and follow me out of here. GPS can't help you in these parts."

Brad withdrew his hands, folding his arms. "I'll take my chances. Thanks anyway."

The man climbed into his truck, pulled around through the weeds, and roared down the drive in a cyclone of dust.

Brad sat down on the porch steps. He drew the canister from his pocket and examined the cracks in the orange plastic. He could hear his labored heartbeat. The blood was moving sluggishly through his veins. A few more pills and it would all be over. He needed the water, though. It was lying back there by the flower bed. Near the body. Drained away. But perhaps a few drops remained.

He stood up and walked toward the corner of the house. His feet caught as the man in black appeared around the edge of the house. He was carrying the woman. Her white hair fell over his arm and stuck to his suit, clinging there as if by static, the individual strands standing out against the fabric like lightning across a dark sky.

The man's face reddened when he saw Brad. "I told you to leave. You're on my property now."

"I left something back there."

"Doesn't matter. Time to go."

Brad stopped a dozen feet from him and stared through the hazy lenses of his glasses. "I'm going to get it, and then I'll go. I see you've got a gun under that coat. If you want to shoot me while I'm walking back there, fine. I really don't care."

The man scowled. Something else moved in his eyes, though, as he examined Brad's careless stance. A hunger, almost. A gleam of admiration kindled by the frictional spark between them. Quickly, he quenched it and shifted the body in his arms. "Want to atone for your lie?"

"What?" Brad said.

"She needs a ride to the cemetery. We don't have a hearse."

The word uncloaked a gray memory. Brad, much younger, riding in a car, following one of those dark, distended vehicles along a January road. His mom, tapping the steering wheel, impatient at the procession's slowness. Then, the frigid graveyard.

"You want to use my car as a hearse?"

The man nodded slowly.

Brad stared at him. A thunderclap broke over some distant field and vibrated across the intervening miles and shook the air between them.

"Come on." The man stepped past him. "We need to bury her before the rain comes."

3

After crossing the clay-stained bridge, the darkness in the tunnel of trees was made heavier by the approaching storm. I switched on the headlights and discovered dozens of cars parked along both sides of the road, sitting crookedly in the depression edging the woods. Under the passing headlight beams, solemn, staring faces faded in and out of existence behind the windshield of each vehicle. The people of Three Summers had come to pay their respects.

"We've been expecting this," the man in black said by way of explanation.

"Why didn't they come to the house?" I asked.

"That island was her ground," he replied. "Invitation only."

—"The House of Dust"
Southern Gothic

IN THE BACK SEAT, the body lay quietly. In the back glass, headlights flashed as the cars turned to follow.

The bony-faced man rolled down his window and let the restless air wander in from beneath the canopy of trees. "So, what are you, exactly?"

Something itched on the back of Brad's neck. Her lifeless hand had brushed him there as they laid her in the car. He nodded toward the back seat, fighting the fog behind his eyes. "Tell me her name."

"So, a reporter type."

"I'm driving the woman to her final rest. Figured I could know."

"Final rest . . . " the man said contemplatively.

"What about you? What's your name?"

"Name's Sorrel. I'm the sheriff of this little backwater, doing my best to keep things quiet and peaceable. Your name?"

"Brad."

"Well, Brad, what pulled you down into our part of the world? Things getting tough for a writer out there?"

The man was studying him in the windshield reflection. Brad's temples throbbed as he caught sight of himself in the rearview mirror. Gaping pupils. Glassy eyes. Glistening forehead. Overdose. The symptoms were familiar.

"Dredging for a story, huh?" The sheriff spoke slowly. "Something impossible but true and with a happy ending."

"No." It came out unbidden as the car bumped along the ruptured road. "No happy endings in my field. Just justice. Sometimes."

"And what field is that?"

"True crime."

"Novelist?"

"Magazine. *Southern Gothic*."

"Pretty popular?"

It would be if you found a good story, his editor said in the back of his mind. He was grateful for the approaching mouth in the tree tunnel. "Right or left?"

"Left," Sorrel said. "We'll take her to the old Simmons Creek Cemetery."

Fat drops splattered heavily on the windshield as they turned out onto Adamah Road. Streetlamps glowed to life back toward Three Summers. Brad hit the defog, and Sorrel rolled up his window. On either side of the road, behind narrowing fields, the forest edged closer. His hands quivered on the wheel.

"You okay?" the sheriff said.

"What was your relationship to her?" Brad asked.

"I thought we dropped that subject, Brad."

"You mentioned back at the house that the property was yours now. I thought you two might be related."

Sorrel's knuckles tapped the glass. "So you are looking for a story."

Was he? That itch on his neck burned through the haze. He imagined the old woman's dead hand rising up from the back seat, her fingers burrowing beneath the headrest and coming out behind his neck, her dirty nails stroking his skin. Offering relief. A story.

The car bumped across a set of railroad tracks, rusted and weed-infested and desolate in both directions.

"Turn right up here on Simmons," Sorrel commanded.

They arrived at a road called Simmons Pike, bordering open fields. Across the road, in the distance, a house crouched on a low hill, silhouetted against the slate-gray sky.

Sorrel leaned over and punched the car horn.

Its startled bray broke the silence and Brad jerked. "I'm driving! Please don't touch the wheel when I'm—"

"That wasn't for you," Sorrel said. "It was for the folks out there. I want them to come. They need the closure."

Brad's gaze hovered on the field as he turned right onto Simmons Pike. The fading horn blast bounced like a pebble off the side of the lonely, distant house. And then, through the rain-streaked window, he saw figures coming out of the ground at the base of the hill. One after another, they appeared from the earth; they paused to look toward the road, then climbed toward cars and trucks parked on the slanted lawn before the house.

It was impossible to tell from this angle, but they must have clambered out of some sort of pit or ditch. A series of depressions or trenches must run across the field parallel to the road. Irrigation, maybe. But irrigation of what? It was a sea of empty grass.

The itching on his neck was maddening. He blinked, and they were past the field, trees enveloping the road. Sorrel turned and reached into the back seat.

Brad heard the flaps of a cardboard box parting. The man sat forward again, nose wrinkled, pinching a seven-by-ten-inch pulp paper booklet between two fingers. "*Southern Gothic*," he murmured. "My, my."

The cover painting depicted a lighthouse on a dark and stormy night, flashing its yellow beam on a capsized yacht. "The Breakwater Sirens," by Lamar Hughes.

Sorrel flipped through the pages. "You folks play up the supernatural, huh?"

Chewing down his annoyance, Brad said, "That was a Halloween issue. I only do real stuff."

"Huh." He examined the back cover. "What kind of circulation do you have?"

"Around three hundred thousand."

A church spire pierced the forest skyline on the right side of the road, tapering up toward the barren clouds. Adverse winds had stripped it, leaving flapping tar paper and dangling shingles. "Is that the place?"

Sorrel closed the magazine. "That's it."

The church and its cemetery sat on a peninsula above the Locust River.

Kudzu swarmed from the trees and the creek bank to the left of the church, blanketing the structure. Vines ringed the windows and clung to every inch of board and crawled across the roof. Only the spire had been spared. It strained upward like the arm of a drowning man pecked and flayed by seabirds.

None of the surrounding trees or ground had been swamped by the Kudzu; the invasive vines had been unusually selective.

Brad swung the car off the road, continuing on a gravel track that led through high grass, past the tilting headstones in the graveyard. A white wooden sign stood by the church doors: SIMMONS CREEK BAPTIST CHURCH.

Brad stopped near the church. The rest of the caravan filled the drive behind.

"Looks like you'll have to stick around for a few minutes," Sorrel observed. "I'm sure that's no problem." As he leaned toward the door, he paused and bent down to retrieve something from the floorboard. "Well, that's pretty. Belong to you?"

A ring. Four prongs on a white gold band clutching a solitaire diamond.

Her ring.

For an instant, it wasn't the sheriff in the passenger seat; it was his fiancée. Her wheezing filling the car. Her body crushed against the door, trying to get away. Her palms smearing down her face; her lips stretching toward a scream.

Brad leaned over and snatched the ring.

Sorrel's fingers hovered a moment. Then he got out and opened the back door and retrieved the body from the back seat. The rain had lightened. He laid the body in the grass outside Brad's window. All along the drive, people climbed from their vehicles. "Line up," Sorrel called. "Might as well show some respect." Then he turned and walked toward the church.

Brad opened the glove box and tossed the ring inside. It clinked softly against the RIA .38 Special cushioned atop the yellowed owner's manual. His fingers hovered for an instant before he slammed the hatch shut. Squirming the fractured pill bottle from his pocket, he threw it on the floor mat.

Outside, people filed around the car. Some stopped by the body, others processed out into the dripping grass and headstones. There were over a hundred of them, he guessed, and most were over fifty, though their sun-battered faces made age hard to judge.

It was their eyes. They weren't ragged eyes, blistered by grief like those he'd seen earlier in the day at the funeral with his fiancée, those eyes that withered what they looked at. They weren't even like those that had filed past him at a funeral much further in the past. The ones that had crinkled into sad smiles for his mother and then turned scornfully on him, a boy wearing headphones to the service. He'd had to. He'd needed to drown the feeling of gathering pressure. It didn't matter that he couldn't hear the pastor. It was better, in fact. His dad was dead. He wasn't coming back. Lies wouldn't lift the weight.

No, the eyes of the people in this cemetery were round and so wide open, they reminded him of those belonging to cave creatures, beings of perpetual darkness.

Too late he remembered that he had wanted to study the old woman's face.

The people had formed a double-sided line between the body and a spot two hundred feet away among the gravestones. Those nearest bent and lifted her between them. Together, they passed her slowly along the line, her body rising and falling along the row of arms like an item on a conveyor belt.

Sorrel came out of the church and walked briskly to the end of the line. He began to dig rapidly, tossing chunks of earth into a heap. By the time the body reached him, he already stood in a knee-deep trench. Maybe he was also the town undertaker, Brad mused.

Again, the buzzing sensation touched his neck. He reached back finally to scratch. But instead of giving relief, the tingling spread to his fingers. He brought them in front of his face.

His hand was smeared with pale dust. The same dust he had found on the rocking chair at the house.

Brad twisted around. His toes bunched together inside his shoes.

The rear seats were hazy where the body had lain. Reaching out, he scraped his fingers across the upholstery, gathering the dust under his nails. He examined it under the light of the windshield, rolling it between his fingers. The woman had been digging among flowers, so perhaps it was a garden chemical, like Sevin Dust. Or maybe a powder she had worn? That would reconcile with its presence on the arm of the rocking chair.

His arm tremored as he opened the car door. He stepped out and crouched down, rubbing his hands in the sodden grass. An erratic wind scraped the high stalks against the headstones and set the trees around the cemetery singing. Brad glanced up as a silent group of birds soared across the river. They swirled like leaves and came to rest on a derelict industrial tower on the far bank. It was gray, matching the clouds behind it, and streaked with rust. He imagined he could hear cries echoing up the side of that tower and being broadcast across the water—long hopeless cries.

Brad blinked. The sound was coming from this side of the river. It was coming from the people. He stood up.

The line of people had spread out among the graves, and a low murmur rose from the assembly. Hesitantly, he moved forward.

They were all talking among themselves. But none seemed to hear the other. Each was carrying on an intimate conversation with themselves. Delivering their own eulogy. Preaching their own sermon. The eyes, so wide a few minutes ago, drifting closed. The hard lines around the mouths were softening, melting each solemn expression into soft contentment. Lax lips forming words. One word. A sighing-sounding word.

His heartbeat lurched faster. As he moved through the murmuring mass, Brad tried to recall similar rituals in his ten years crisscrossing the South. This wasn't Full Gospel or Pentecostal. Was it some other fringe Christian sect? Yet the whole ceremony seemed somehow disconnected from the church. There was no pastor present, just the sheriff.

Sorrel was standing waist-deep in the grave. The shovel was stabbed in the mound of earth behind him. The body of the woman lay before him in the grass. He scooped the slender body in his arms and crouched down, disappearing into the earth.

Abruptly, the people around Brad began to sink to the ground. The younger ones dropped to their knees in the grass, while the older ones braced themselves on gravestones as they knelt. The silver-haired woman who had directed him to the house walked through their midst, eyes half-closed, holding a shovel.

Sorrel's head appeared above the surface. His face was down, mouth flat, as he examined the body beneath him. When the woman approached, he glanced up and took in the scene. "No!" It was like a gunshot in the quiet.

Scrambling from the hole, he spread his arms, black sleeves smeared orange with mud. "It's over! Y'all go home now. It's finished."

The murmuring stopped. The eyelids lifted. The faces hardened.

"You've paid your respects," Sorrel said a little more softly. "It's time to go."

Like disenchanted worshippers, the people rose to their feet. Their faces seemed to sag, burdened with weariness. They flashed glances at one another and gathered their plaids and denims around themselves tighter. For a moment, Brad felt it, too: A viscous chill seeping up from the ground. Warping the air. Seeming to stretch the sheriff's voice as he repeated his command: "Go."

Then, just as quickly, the aura was gone. Brad looked around.

The hiss of grass snaking around shoes was the only sound as the people departed. The silver-haired woman was the last to go. She threw her shovel down and stalked away.

When the last car and truck pulled out of the churchyard, Sorrel rubbed his brow, turned back to the hole, and began to shovel dirt. The shovel crunched. Rain splattered the leaves of the kudzu-shrouded church.

Blood hammered in Brad's skull. He couldn't leave. He stepped forward.

"You, too," Sorrel said over his shoulder as he approached. "Don't mind me. I can walk back."

Brad ignored him, picking up the fallen shovel. His muscles were jittery. His mind, too. He gripped the shaft and approached the grave. Ramming the shovel into the dirt, he hefted the loaded blade and turned toward the grave. He extended it out over the void and looked down.

The old woman lay at the bottom, her lower body obscured by dirt. The white dress was damp with rain. Her arms were at her sides, hands turned up—an almost plaintive posture. Slowly, he turned the shovel. The dirt fell.

And then her face moved. Her eyes.

They opened.

They turned toward him.

The pupils expanded like sudden sinkholes.

And then the dirt hit her face.

Brad stumbled forward. The slick edge of the grave crumbled beneath his feet.

As his shoes galloped on the collapsing brink, a hand grabbed his collar, yanking him away from the edge.

"You'll fall in!" Sorrel shouted in his ear. "Stay back!"

The sheriff released him. Brad collapsed, coughing into the grass. Loosening his collar, he tried to swallow the swarming mass of astonishment that filled his throat. The woman's gaping eyes burned like sunspots in his vision.

It couldn't be. It was the pills, so thick in his system, warping his mind. He could feel it coming from his stomach now, surging up his throat—stale water and dissolving chemicals.

He wretched it all out and stayed hunched on the grass for a while, fists clenching the stems, shivering as the weight evaporated. The endless cycle had reasserted itself. The aim that had driven him onward for ten years would not release him. He could not break free. He could not leave. He had to *know*.

When he sat up, a stooped, bald-headed man dressed in black was standing halfway out of one of the church doors. He was gripping the door to support himself, and he was staring at Sorrel. The sheriff, his face shedding sweat, was steadily refilling the grave.

Brad stood up. He walked over, cleaning his glasses on his shirt. When he spoke, the flat sound of his voice was startling against the stillness. "I want to rent out that house."

"Not for rent," the sheriff panted.

"Just a couple weeks. Maybe a month. I can give you five hundred dollars right now."

The flat of the shovel came down on the grave, packing the dirt. "What are you hoping to find?"

"I don't know," he said.

The sheriff straightened up and glanced back at the empty drive, rubbing the rainwater from his brow. Brad followed his glance to the church. The stooped man was gone.

"Look, I . . . " Brad imagined the woman beneath the soil, blinking back the mud, screaming into the smothering wet blackness. He replaced his glasses. "I'm sorry if this is an annoyance. It is to me, too, sometimes. But it's what I do. I've got to keep doing it. If you say no, then I'll get a hotel in the nearest town and come snooping around every day."

Sorrel slammed the shovel into the dirt and offered a bland smile. "That ring in the car . . ."

The rain fell between them.

"What about it?"

"There's two of you, isn't there? There'd be two of you in that house."

"There might be."

"There would be," Sorrel said. He stared heavily at the grave. "So, what's her name?"

HER FEET GO DOWN

4

In early February 2018, my editor, Heather, called me from Atlanta to complain. She did it in an unusually subtle way. Lily Verner, Heather explained, was a bright recent university grad who was writing a series of five true crime articles set in an allegedly haunted oil field in Alabama. After reading the first one, Heather had bought the series. They would serve for almost a full year's worth of issues. She let an ensuing silence tell me the rest: after eight months of nothing from me, *Southern Gothic* was seeking fresh blood.

When I called Heather in May, asking for money and promising a blockbuster, it took an hour to convince her. I told her the story of a strange town in which the kudzu came only for the church. I painted a picture of decay, of rot. Of our times. But in the end, it was reminiscing about my very first article that won her over. My fiancée took even more convincing. The prospect of a secluded life in western Tennessee did not initially appeal to her. But the financial and emotional extremes we were facing persuaded her that a strategic withdrawal from the world might do us both good.

So on the first Saturday in May, we exited the I-40 ramp, she in her Chevy pickup and I in my Accord. We followed the curvy single-lane road from the state highway to Three Summers, and then the tree tunnel road from Three Summers to the island that Sorrel called Angel's Landing. It was a very quiet two o'clock when we passed beneath the live oaks along the drive. It only occurred to me then that the trees were hundreds of miles beyond their natural coastal habitat.

—"The House of Dust"
Southern Gothic

"WHAT DO YOU think of that?" her fiancé asked.

They stood with their backs against the truck, looking up at the house.

"A real eyrie compared to our two-room Nashville nest, huh?"

Missy smiled halfway and tilted her head, jaw working. The two-hour drive had turned the gum in her mouth to a tacky-tasting lump. She dug the wrapper from her pocket while examining the house's sallow façade.

There was something sad about the crooked way the shutters hung. Something pitiful about the warped, shrunken boards around the windows. Something embarrassing about the vines clinging to the pillars like flies on the face of a dead loved one.

"Well?"

Spitting out the gum, she rolled it up in the piece of foil. "If it means you'll be around more, then I utterly adore it."

"That bad?"

His tone plummeted so much that she scooted over and kissed his cheek. "Course not. On second thought, I just adore it." Looking up, she added, "Seems kinda scrunched up, though, like it needs to breathe."

"Then here are the keys. Let's let it breathe."

Slipping the key ring around her ring finger, she advanced on the porch. He followed just behind, hand gentle, yet trembling, on her lower back, propelling her forward with almost childish excitement.

She examined the peeling railing of the second-floor porch and the cascades of wild grapevines falling from it. She fed a fresh piece of Wrigley's spearmint into her mouth as they reached the porch stairs. With him close behind, she placed her foot on the bottom step. It squealed beneath her weight. Quick fingers reached for her fiancé's shoulder and they chuckled together. The rest of the steps were spongy, too. Soft whines accompanied their climb.

At the top, behind the columns, a procession of listless rocking chairs ran to the far ends of the huge porch. What a social hub this place must have been. And how oddly they were arranged now: each one facing a slightly different direction.

At the door, she went through the keys. There were only three, but she made it seem a chore because his arms were around her, his breath on her neck. She turned into his embrace, and her shoulder blades thumped the dark wood.

The door moved.

"Huh?" Twisting again, her cheek near his, she slowly lifted her palm and pressed.

The door swung open. Air shifted around them, drawn in across the threshold. The hall was a dry throat and all the unseen rooms back through the old mansion were collapsed lungs, filling with fresh air after how many strangled years?

"Well . . ." She steadied herself on the doorframe. "And you're sure this house is ours? It's as secure as a tourist attraction."

"That's funny," her fiancé said. "I left it locked."

"Huh." Staring across the threshold, she could have sworn for a moment that she'd discerned movement. A black silhouette standing in the dimness and beckoning with a long left hand. Welcoming.

Slowly, grayness bled into her vision and the vestibule of the house became visible.

No, there was nothing there. Silly girl.

The smile from earlier expanded, and it felt pure now. *Our own house!* Tugging away from him, she stepped across the threshold. And burst out laughing.

"What? What now?" He stepped in quickly after her.

"I just got the strangest feeling walking in here."

"Really."

"Like I stepped off a sidewalk without looking."

"Well, the sheriff assured me the place is sound."

She turned, frustrated. "Look, you aren't bein' romantic at all." She walked back out onto the porch. "Get out here and carry me across this threshold. I don't care if it is bad luck the second time."

Shaking his head, he stepped out after her. "What way do you want to be carried?"

"Well, I suppose the normal way."

He scooped her up before looking into her eyes in a way that made her giggle, and then he walked into the house. A couple of feet inside the vestibule, he stopped, and they both craned their necks back. As they breathed, silk-curtain stillness fell around them.

Across the expanse of ceiling, clouds of cobwebs clustered around dusty light fixtures.

The hall extended to the rear of the house where a curtain masked the light from the back door. The corridor between was paneled in dark oak up to about waist height, and then flowery wallpaper took over and climbed to the ceiling, where painted wooden vines twisted together with leaves and fruits, forming the intricate crown molding.

A murmur of admiration escaped her gaping mouth as her eyes adjusted and a huge cascade of steps appeared from the gloom, jutting through a rectangular gap in the ceiling like a mummified arm and sagging toward the floor along the left side of the hall. More carved vines wrapped around the rungs of the bannister, creating the illusion of movement.

"What do you think now?" he whispered.

"I've never been in a house with such high ceilings."

"Yeah?"

"Yeah. It's so . . . "

"Perfect?" He kissed her exposed throat. "For a perfect woman."

"Your silly talk is sillier than most men's." She wriggled back onto her feet, shrieking as he tickled her. But even then she noticed how the sound of their laughter didn't carry down the hall.

Regaining her breath, she tugged his arm. "Come on, let's do the full tour."

Now it was his turn to slip free. He backed toward the door. "I have to get my desk in."

"Don't you wanna look around with me?"

"Seen it already. The sheriff showed me."

He seemed suddenly satisfied that she would fall in love with the place.

She sighed, scuffed her foot, and noticed the smeared tracks their shoes had left. "This place ain't been lived in for years."

"I'll need help in a minute," he called.

Perhaps he said something else, but he was outside now and sounds from outside had shifted out of focus, leaving a mournful whistle of air between her lips. She took a step deeper into the house. Yes, silence was nice. She would not have music playing in every room of her house like some people did in theirs. Especially not the horrible, noisy, thumping music that rattled your bones. No, there would be peace in their house.

Their house!

The floors would need a good cleaning, and that wallpaper would have to come down, but without too much work, it would be a place he would want to come home to. A place to *stay*.

The first task would be to take all the curtains down and get the house out of *The Twilight Zone*.

Two large doorways, framed by the same black oak, yawned on either side of her. She entered the door on her right, moving from hardwood to aged carpet. She'd have to get rid of that stuff, too—no carpet in her house to get stained and spilled on, smelling of mildew like the back rooms at the Club. The heels of her shoes went through it like lace underwear.

She dug around in her purse for a handkerchief, then went to the drapes that shrouded the front of the room. Holding the cloth to her face, she grabbed a handful of the heavy curtains and dragged backward, peeling the shadows away.

Light gushed in and flowed over the floor, churning around a table and six empty chairs, piling up against a huge sofa and coffee table, then splashing against yellow walls and sinking into alcoves where ancient books and antique vases rested. It drained into an empty fireplace near the back of the room and dripped off a strangely textured mantel.

Missy squinted. The mantel looked . . . flayed, almost. She crossed the room and gingerly touched the ledge of the mantel. It prickled. Dozens of tiny scratches had been cut into the wood, made with the tiniest blade. The accumulated dust in the cracks stuck to her fingers and she withdrew them after a moment, rubbing them together. The crumbly stuff clung to her skin.

Returning to the hall, she stood in the fresh air current from the open door and scrubbed her fingertips with the handkerchief. The powder seemed magnetic. She laughed to clear her throat, then stopped when she saw the arms.

The handkerchief floated from her grasp.

They were frail little things, reaching out from the dark wedge of floor behind the front door.

Missy approached and bent down. The lacy arms rose in her fingertips. Behind them, a dress unfolded. She stood and stepped back into the full light; she held the little arms wide and examined the garment.

It was silky and white. The arms would come to her elbows if she wore it, and the hem would trail behind her a bit. But it clearly wasn't for formal occasions. The sleeves were see-through, and the body wasn't much more substantial. This dress was sensual. Her fingers hardened.

Something for costume nights at the Club. Something the Boss would toss at her. *Hey, put this on.*

That almost made her throw it away. But as she lowered it, the filmy fabric felt so delicious on her hands that she gave it another glance. It wasn't really a Club dress after all. It was far more elegant. The embroidery work was exquisite, and the yellowing of age and smell of dust lent it a sense of sacredness. Something a great lady would wear. Perhaps this was the mistress's gown.

Missy pulled it closer. Who would leave something like this lying before the front door, to be pushed aside whenever it was opened next? She folded the dress across her arm and crossed the hall to the opposite doorway.

There were more curtains along the front of this room, but she forgot them as she looked across the dusty white expanse of floor. The room was huge, and the vastness drew her feet. Sixty feet long, at least, and thirty wide. A ceiling she couldn't reach if she was twice as tall. She remembered the dingy little Nashville flat they had vacated just that morning and tried to imagine how many times it would fit in this space. How many of its little windows would make one of the big windows that processed down the outer wall to her left.

All the room's furnishings were pushed against that outer wall, packed into cardboard boxes and draped in sheets. It was ghostly to have them lined up that way, swathed, still. The effect was amplified as her footsteps echoed off the peeling white wall opposite. Still, she liked the openness. She liked the chandelier hanging above the middle of the hall. She could feel it trying to sparkle through all that dust. She liked—

A shadowy form moved at the edge of her vision.

Missy stopped and turned her head.

A wide fireplace was set in the outer wall. A huge mirror hung over the mantel. It was angled down in such a way as to give her the impression of staring down on herself when she looked up.

Slowly, she smiled at her reflection. The smile split her face and stretched her eyes and she froze, staring at the hideous thing she'd become.

Something was wrong with the mirror. Something was distorting it. Hesitantly, she approached. The glass was grimy, but at its center a series of convex lines was discernible, forming a shape. As she moved, her reflection split and rippled, moving like ink through the warped glass.

She stopped beneath the mirror. A human form was at the center of the symbol. A ring formed the outer edge. Between the human form and the circle stretched six arms. It reminded her of something. A sketch in one of the encyclopedia volumes she'd read—Leonardo da Vinci's demonstration of movement. Perhaps the shape on the mirror was waving its arms.

"Dancing," she said suddenly. "This was a dance hall."

Eager to keep that thought, she turned and dropped her purse and spun out across the empty floor, spreading her arms and holding the dress so that it flapped softly. She imagined a piano played beneath one of those white sheets, dripping notes into the air that matched the click of her shoes. Dust rose from the boards, awakened by her tapping feet, and twirled up into the dress to form a phantom partner.

Her heart was racing. Yes, this was a dance hall. A place of music and people. She would clean these floors until they gleamed. She would invite dozens of people from the area and they would watch as she danced with her husband on endless summer nights. They would be envious of her house, and her husband, and *her*. No more hiding away. No more shame.

"There are lights, you know."

With a click, yellow radiance glared down from the chandelier. She dropped her arms and turned. The dress flopped to the floor. Through wobbly vision, she saw her fiancé standing at the front of the hall.

"Aw, don't turn on the lights." She took a tottering step. "It's not real in the light."

"What have you got there?"

"Just an old rag I found."

It's not a rag.

"Really?"

Why would you call it that, Missy?

"Look here." She picked up the dress and swayed toward the fireplace, pointing up. "What's this?"

He came over, placing one hand on her back. "Huh. There's one of those on the front door. Must be a family symbol."

"Like a coat of arms? That's medieval stuff."

"Maybe the people who lived here had an ancient bloodline."
He gazed at her with those murky eyes. "Come on. I need your help
with the desk."

Missy tossed the dress onto a box and followed.

When she saw the desk, she emptied her lungs. It was an heir-
loom piece, supposedly. Something his daddy had given him 'cause
he'd made him proud. Probably, Daddy had planned on papers lying
on the desk, not someone like her, legs apart, beckoning to his boy.

He'd managed to get the old thing through the door and to the
foot of the steps. A piece of soft foam had been attached by loops of
rope to the top of the desk. They would flip it over and slide it up, he
explained. At least she got to be on the uphill end.

Heaving it from the lip of one step to the next, they inched
upward. Their breath was loud in the silent house. The steps groaned.
The dust was slick beneath Missy's shoes. She paused halfway up
to take them off and throw them over the bannister. As her wrists
brushed the top of the bannister a familiar prickle danced through
them. She froze.

"What is it?" her fiancé huffed.

"Someone went wild with a razor blade in this house."

"What?"

"Look at the scratches. All down the railing."

He frowned at the delicate marks, then shrugged. "Nothing a
little sandpaper won't fix."

Her legs were shaking when the top stair came beneath her
wavering foot. She slumped back and looked down the dim corridor.
Light came from a curtained window at the end of the hall—the
front of the house—and it struck her that something had been moving around up here just before they came into view on the stairs; she
could see dust dancing beneath the window.

"Hey!" her fiancé called, still trapped in the stairwell by the desk.
"Come on, Missy, let's get it over with."

Grunting, she climbed to her feet and dragged the desk into the
hall. The ceiling was much lower up here, and the old wallpaper was
a pleasant green-and-white stripe. They pushed the desk down the

hall toward the window. At the end, he told her to kick open the door to the right. It swung easily open, and the air brightened as they wrestled the desk inside.

Once it was properly in place, Missy straightened, panting, and looked around the room. At the front, light came through two great windows shrouded by yellow curtains. Between the windows, a door led out onto the second-floor porch. A few strands of ivy clawed in through the crumbled seal along the threshold. Inside, books perched like abandoned cicada husks along shelves built into the entire right-side wall. The thick volumes, as well as the stacks of pamphlets and pocket-sized publications, were faded, almost from another time.

She crossed toward the yellow curtains, examining the titles as she went. None jumped out at her. Some were even in foreign languages. "My encyclopedias will look good on these shelves," she mentioned. "The next volume should be coming soon."

"Coming here?" It was spoken with that strained tone he'd used when they first met.

"Of course." She brushed the spine of a red-bound book, tracing the tarnished gold lettering: *The Daemonologie of King James*. "Nothing settles you into a home like havin' a package delivered there."

He breathed for a bit. "So, the old place is salvageable? The property shouldn't be condemned?"

"It's had a rough time." Missy pushed the curtain away from one of the cloudy windows, then pushed her hair away from her face. "But condemned? I'll find something grand under all this dirt."

"I'm sure you will."

Breath on her ear.

She stiffened, just a bit, as his finger came out of nowhere and followed a bead of sweat from her jaw down toward the base of her neck. His finger continued beneath her collar.

Missy turned to him quickly. "Which means I better get started! You bring the rest of our stuff inside"—she gave him a plentiful kiss—"and I'll start clearing out some of the rooms. How does chicken salad sound for dinner?"

He frowned, and she smiled at him and slipped from his arms. As she descended the creaking stairs, scraping the perspiration from her face with the back of her hand, it suddenly occurred to her that this wasn't the Nashville apartment in more ways than one. No one lived within earshot of the house. The only other people in the area were two humid miles of forest away, and they were strangers.

She shoved the thought away. They would all be her friends when she threw that dazzling party. *Yes!* She tried to recapture the magic of that thought as she reentered the dance hall.

The dust was still settling from her dancing. When she dragged the drapes off the windows, a fresh flurry of motes filled the air. She turned to examine the shrouded items along the wall, and something out in the middle of the floor caught her eye. It glimmered in the new light. A spot of yellow.

Missy approached. Her smile fractured as the thing emerged from the haze. A bright, fresh yellow daffodil. It stuck from a crevasse between the boards where she had danced, almost as if it had sprouted there.

The floor felt swishy. Unstable.

Leaning down, she plucked the flower. She held it at arm's length for a moment, until the delicate smell of its perfume entered her nostrils.

And with it the smell of rot. *Her* rot. Her own filthiness. It had followed her here.

She folded the daffodil into her fingers and crushed it.

5

The house's layout was fairly simple. Both floors were split down the middle by high-ceilinged hallways. Rooms opened off these halls, ribs branching from a spine. On the first floor, as you crossed the threshold, the doorway to the dance hall stood to the left and the parlor to the right.

Down the first-floor hall, the staircase, ornately carved, rose like a cornucopia toward the second floor. Past that, doorways let off to the wide kitchen and the dining room, the latter of which connected back to the dance hall.

Upstairs, a bathroom and three quiet bedrooms lined the western wing. The master bedroom and connecting master bathroom sprawled with royal abandon down the eastern side, capped near the front of the residence by a musty study and library. I set up base here, in the companionship of such titles as *The Coming Race*, *Justine*, and *Éloa*.

—"The House of Dust"
Southern Gothic

THE CARDBOARD BOX had ridden in the trunk of his car for ten years. The corners were blunted. The flaps hissed as Brad's trembling fingers pulled them apart.

The thing inside had last seen the light of day four years ago. That sweaty afternoon just before he started his final fruitful investigation that resulted in the "Scarlet Seven Miles" story. That afternoon, he'd read the reviews of his then most recent article, "The Glass Elephant," before finding out how many Prozac capsules he could down without water. That afternoon, he'd met his fiancée. June 8, 2014.

The box flaps fell limply open. As he dug down into the box, crumbling newspaper rustled around his arm and then boiled up as he lifted the treasure out. He held it before his face. The silver ball bearings suspended between taut plastic thread chattered together, frigid teeth in December air: *tap, tap, tap*.

The late Christmas gift. The last gift. And his father's last words to him still clearly visible, written neatly and quickly on the outside of the box. *It can't go on forever.*

He set the Newton's cradle on the desk, then stood back to examine it. *There.* His hands quivered on his waist. The thing had sat on the dash of his car four years ago, clicking loudly as he tried to choke down the pills.

How many more investigations? How many more years scraping up sins? How many more failed attempts to find peace? he'd asked himself.

Blinking hard, he bent forward and used his sleeve to clean off a patch in front of the high-back chair that loomed behind the desk. The gray grit showed up starkly on the black cloth, so he rolled his cuffs up. He unzipped his computer bag and placed his laptop in the clean spot.

He turned back toward his bag, and his fingers hesitated. Quivered. What if he just needed a little . . . ?

No. He thrust his hand inside and withdrew the crushed orange Prozac canister. He held it up to his face and shook it once. The pills *tap, tap, tapped* inside. They, too, had been a fixture in his car for over a decade, and in his life before that. Since winter of 2001. Since he was thirteen. Since his mom decided he was not recuperating from *the loss* properly and might be a danger to himself or others, and so he should see a psychiatrist.

Ten milligrams daily. Her gift to him.

He tossed the crushed container in a wastepaper basket beside the desk. No crutches. No contingencies. He'd dropped off last Sunday, after the funeral, and jitters had set in strong this morning. A tiny motor buzzed in the back of his skull, revving each time he turned his head, flushing energy down his arms. It was always tough while the stuff flushed from his system. But if this investigation was going to salvage anything, if it was going to stave off the gray drowning feeling, the hallucinations, then it would have to be conducted with a clear head. Like the one four years ago, that had revived his career for a bit. Like the one ten years ago, that had started it all.

The first thing to do was discover what the previous resident had left behind.

Brad rounded the desk. He lifted one of the cradle's beads and let it drop. The ensuing clicks followed him out of the study into the quiet upstairs hall. Because of the lower ceiling, the atmosphere felt closer here than in the bottom part of the house. Clingy. The air reticent to move, as in a stopped-up creek bed.

Brad drew out his phone and pointed it down the hall, capturing the lamps sprouting from the walls between the bedroom doorways, the sagging green-and-white wallpaper, and the wound-colored paint beneath. He looked down at the floors, gritty and gray. Failing health must have prevented the old woman from upkeeping the place. Or apathy. There were no signs of neighborly help. Why? Had she been a recluse? Sorrel had said this plantation was her ground. If her funeral had proved anything, it was that she held significance in the community.

Her funeral.

Her lonely corpse at the bottom of the hole. Her eyes, closed, then wide apart. Screaming. Pleading. Alive.

It wasn't real. *It was just your sick imagination.*

Tonight, he thought. Tonight he'd go back.

A door stood directly across the hall from the one leading into the study. Its metal knob was grooved and resembled a gourd, a pumpkin, perhaps. Agriculture would have been vital when this place was built. With his phone, he snapped a picture, then tried the door. Locked. He rattled the handle and applied pressure with his shoulder, but it would not give, so he moved down the hall to the next door.

This door opened easily and silently. Within, a window framed by floor-length floral curtains looked into the interlocking upper branches of the forest. Hazy light revealed a twin bed and companion nightstand. Stepping inside, he found a red velvet chair waiting out of sight behind the door. Otherwise, the room was bare. The only sign of past habitation was a rumpled spot near the head of the bed where someone might have sat. He photographed that, too.

Passing along the stairwell railing, he found the next door unlocked as well. He pushed it open. Almost identical. His fingers pulsed on the knob and the cavernous quiet brought back his "Glass Elephant" article again; brought him back to his walk through the old house on the edge of the salt marsh in Hyde County, North Carolina. In that case, too, the old woman who'd inhabited the house had recently died, leaving everything a frozen testament to her final day. *Dull*, readers had called it, because that was the plot: himself, Brad Ellison, pacing through the old house, piecing together its owner's possible history.

Sound interrupted the memory. Thumps from downstairs. His fiancée, moving around. Alone in one of the big rooms. Trying to tidy. He felt a twinge. He should go help. He would. But this came first. She understood his work.

The next door, the one at the back of the house, opened to the guest bathroom. A bowing floor and torn-out portions of the wall told a tale of water damage sometime in the recent past. Nothing related to the old woman, though.

A final unexplored doorway stood across the hall.

It was different from the rest. The wood was almost black, contrasting with the pale wallpaper. It was wider, too, with double doors mounted with latches instead of a knob.

He tested the latches, then pushed the doors inward.

Stale air, still tinged by the sour breath of the last inhabitant, hung heavily within. A window with white curtains looked out on the back garden. The wallpaper was white, gilded with twisting vines. The floorboards, like the door, were almost black. Daylight sunk into them.

He stepped deeper into the room.

A stand holding a porcelain washbasin, a great dresser with a cracked mirror, and a large vine-carved wardrobe were all made of the same black wood. Across the room, far enough from the window that the gloom could reassert itself, sat the dead woman's bed, shrouded by gauzy curtains.

Brad stopped and photographed the room, capturing the piled dishes by the side of the bed, and the skirts and shirts and underclothes strewn from the parted lips of the wardrobe, all reminiscent of a woman younger than the one laid in the ground last week.

No distinctive decorations, though. Nothing that told the woman's story.

Unless . . .

The nightstands. The place where people kept medications and journals and other relics from the innards of their lives. They should contain at least a few clues.

Pocketing the phone, he advanced to the nightstand on the left side of the bed, wrinkling his nose against the rancid smell that came through the cascade of yellowed bed curtains. He bent down and slid the top drawer open. Within, alone, lay a pocket-sized hardcover book, remarkably clean. Gold lettering on the spine read, *The Book of Common Prayer.*

Carefully lifting the cover, he examined the dedication page. In a tiny hand was written: *Presented to Walter Lloyd Collins on the occasion of his confirmation, July 27, 1947. "Do the first works." Revelation 2:5.*

He paged through it but discovered no further inscriptions.

Still, it was a name. It was someone who had perhaps lived in this house at one time, slept in this bed. Replacing the book, he closed the drawer and opened the lower ones. Nothing.

Standing, he rubbed his nose against the mossy smell radiating from the curtains. He started to turn away when something within the canopy caught his eye.

A dark form lay in the bed, just feet from where he stood.

For a second, his heart stalled. The form was utterly still.

Slowly, he extended a hand toward the curtain. His unsteady fingers rippled the gauze. He parted the cloth to stare down at the bed.

Earth. Rust-colored. Mounded on the near side of the naked mattress. A dry heap, granular with age, stretching from the head to the foot of the bed. And marked by a shallow horizontal indentation three-quarters of the way up. His eyes moved to the other side of the bed, where the mattress cratered, and then back.

An arm had made the impression in the mound of dirt. An arm extended by a sleeper nestled beside it.

The old woman had dug up a piece of the yard and brought it here to be her companion.

He clutched the curtain until he thought it might tear. Letting it fall, he backed away, cramming his hands into his pockets. His mind vibrated.

She was downstairs somewhere, but she would come up soon enough. She'd find this. She understood his job and the kind of places it brought him. But she wouldn't understand this. *He* didn't understand this.

He left the room, closed the door quietly, and descended to the first floor, pausing at the bottom of the staircase to listen. Gentle, plodding footfalls from the dance hall. He thought about going in and saying something cheerful and distracting.

Not now. Not yet.

He went up the hall to the kitchen, a room with stained yellow tile, scarred yellow countertops, and slack-jawed yellow cabinets. No garbage bags under the sink, though, or any other means of containing the dirt.

Returning to the hall, he pulled aside the curtain across the back door. The porch outside was only partially complete. Part of a failed addition, he guessed. Ineffectual mosquito netting stretched between the beams. A ceiling fan hung from the rafters. Nothing to remove the dirt with.

He restrained a sigh and turned back into the hall. At the far end, the front door was standing wide, and the slack late-afternoon heat was perceptible even here at the back of the house. Closer, halfway down the hall, was a door under the staircase. The way to the basement.

He might find a container down there that he could use to remove the dirt. Brad walked toward the door. He stepped into the nook beneath the stairs and resolutely grabbed the handle. The door squeaked open like a dry jaw.

Maybe in his article he could say that dread had filled him the moment he did that. Like the archeologists entering King Tut's tomb, he felt the curse descending. All nonsense, of course. Instead, what he really thought about was the shuffling whisper of his fiancée's footsteps on the other side of the wall. If they stopped, it would be time to come up.

Their gentle *hiss, hiss, hiss* followed him down into the dark.

The ceiling sloped with the stairs, always hovering a foot above his head. The passage was close, and the steps were oddly soft. They turned right, and it was cold at the bottom. He stepped off the last stair and smooth dirt pressed against his shoes. The damp smell, like the underbelly of a bridge, was strong in his face.

Drawing out his phone, he turned on the flashlight. The LED's cold glare cut through the nearby darkness. Bedposts and chairs and racks of suit coats and bookshelves and tables and a tube television and couches all crashed toward him like waves of a frozen sea. Finding a box should prove easy enough.

He stepped forward.

Something trickled across his scalp.

Quickly, he raised his flashlight and grabbed reflexively at the air with his other hand.

A vine, white as a bloodless vein, twined around his fingers. He tugged it and felt a gentle pop. It spiraled down, and he looked toward the ceiling.

The wooden rafters, what he could see of them, were bone gray. A writhing flesh of hundreds of pale vines had burst through the brick walls and flowed across the ceiling, wrapping rafters and burrowing between splits in the wood. The vines were smooth, lacking both root and leaf structure. Whatever plant produced them must have some connection to the surface and sunlight, but even so, what sustenance caused them to reach down here? And why cling to the ceiling? Only occasionally did a tendril break away and dangle toward the floor.

At least they had not broken through the dance hall floor. Their density, though, was such that it masked sound. Only vaguely were his fiancée's overhead footsteps audible through them.

His light jerked back to the floor when he stepped forward and rammed something with his foot. A cardboard box.

Perfect. He squatted down. The box lay on its side, the corners severely blunted, as if it had been hurled down the stairs. Parting the flaps, he began to shake the contents out. Tiny shirts, socks, and trousers tumbled onto the floor.

Not this box. He righted it and began to replace the items. The tags had been cut out, but they were a half-century old, at least, judging by the style and quality of the fabric. A child had been raised in this house during the fifties or sixties. At least for a little while. Straightening, he chewed his lip and stared through his dirty glasses at the mess.

Then he stepped into the forest of junk.

It was all a hopeless jumble. A gilt chair here, draped with once gaudy dresses now dry and stiff as last year's leaves. Over there, a circular gun rack with various late-eighteenth-century military rifles, each piece corroded by damp. Near the back wall, a collapsing harrow that must once have turned the fields above. All interspersed with hutches and cabinets and a large collection of tall mahogany Victrola record players.

Surprisingly few containers, though. This was a raw dumping ground for the closets and upper shelves and lower drawers of many generations.

A treasure trove, but without any contextual keys.

In reviews of "The Glass Elephant," they said he had invented too much of the context. Heather, his editor, had chastised him. Just because the old woman happened to place an order for a glass elephant each day that a body was found in that marsh, each day across decades, and then one last time on the day of her own death, did not mean the events were connected. Just because she was lonely did not mean she was a killer. Just because she was dead did not mean they could besmirch her name.

He stood at the back of the room and held out the flashlight, looking across the waves of refuse once more. And then he noticed something. A tangential pattern to the clutter. It was as tenuous a connection as he had drawn in his first "investigative" assignments at Poynter, but it was something.

It was the way clutter seemed to have been fed down the chute of the stairs in great gluts, shifting toward the back of the room by the accumulated pressure of the batch that followed. It was the fact that a poster stand stood beside the chair with old dresses. It was a battered casket, lid lifted, lying near the rifle rack. It was a series of coarse linen shirts and trousers, tacked up along the rear cinder-block wall above the harrow, all fragile with age and hazy with sweat and soil.

They were like props belonging to separate scenes of a play. Like rings dating a tree.

Panning the light, he clambered through the mess to the poster stand. He swiped the grime from the poster, and bright colors emerged, depicting a pert-mouthed woman in a white dress looking over her shoulder at a diminishing line of people in colorful party regalia. They followed her with smiles and tightly closed eyes. In the background, through a palatial parkland, a splendid house dumped yellow light through its windows. *This house.*

He moved the light down and found a title: MIRIAM LARKIN IN *THE SLEEPWALKERS.*

Shuffling backward, he found two more posters rolled up on the floor. He grabbed them and went to a nearby table. His hands shook as he unrolled them and pinned down the corners with a collection of floral-painted music boxes.

The first showed the same woman, Miriam Larkin, standing in a white dress among the trees before the house. But only the upper portion of her body was visible. Her legs were buried, and the dirt was mounded around her waist. Miriam's arms were crossed on her chest, and her eyes were closed. Short white bangs fringed across her forehead in an early-thirties Hollywood-style. The picture was titled *The Thin Land*.

The last poster was damaged. Water had blurred the ink, but he was able to make out things that at first looked like leaves tumbling down from heavy clouds toward the field in front of the house. Miriam Larkin stood in the field in the white dress and raised her hands to receive them. And then he realized they weren't leaves falling—they were people. The picture was called *Angel's Island*.

Brad leaned closer. Something about—

Of course. The dress. It was currently lying miles away in the cemetery, clothing the dead woman.

The latch on one of the music boxes gave, and the lid popped open. Brad jerked away, muscles taut. Tinny music squeaked out. Shaking his head, trying to dispel the tingles, he turned and shuffled over to the casket.

Dust had tarnished the pearlescent silk.

A book lay inside. Small, black, bound by a leather strap. Lifting it out, he propped it on the edge of the casket and unbound the strap. The spine creaked as he opened the cover. The paper was thick. The tinny melody from the music box continued as he examined the first page. A hurried hand had written: *The Utterances: A record of the things spoken by those anointed with Adamah. May 1, 1877.*

Adamah. The name of the main road through the town. The name of the theater at the town intersection: Adamah Theater. A tumbler fell into place. *Adamah*. The whispered word. The one the townsfolk had uttered sotto voce in the eerie reverie of their goodbye at her funeral.

He turned the page.

May 4, 1877. Words cannot manifest the utterance of my first patient; as near as I can approximate, the sound was thus expressed—
A ragged line crawled beneath the sentence, like the seismographic readout of an earthquake.

On the next page, another hasty sentence. *May 21, 1877. No words yet, but echoes. A voice in a well, far down.*

Next page.

June 12, 1877. At last! The breach has been opened. These words:
And below, in a more careful script, was written: *It's so dark.*

As he turned it, the page tingled between his fingers like a feather of ice.

June 25, 1877. In careful hand: *The air just trickles down here.*

July 3, 1877. How long is its arm?

July 11, 1877. It's coming through the cracks in the boards.

July 17, 1877. The floor is standing up.

A thud from above penetrated through the insulating vines.

His hands jostled. The book slid back into the casket as he raised his phone. The rusty music had cut off, the ancient mechanics giving out in the music box. He craned his head back. Silence rained down from the vine-smothered ceiling.

She had stopped moving. Lifting the book, he twined the strap around it and stumbled through the clutter to the staircase. At the top, the hall was empty.

The front door still stood wide. No sound of pacing from the next room over.

He hurried down the hall. The retreating drug had sapped him. He grabbed the bannister at the foot of the stairs and paused again to listen. Nothing. She must still be in the dance hall. He dropped the little book on the first stair, turned off his flashlight and pocketed his phone, and strode over to the dance hall doorway.

A ladder had been set up before the fireplace. She lay at its foot, small and pale in the deep room. She did not stir as he hurried to her. When he reached her, he stumbled down onto his knees. She did not look over. She was curled up on her side, hands drawn into her chest, staring at the empty mouth of the fireplace with the concentrated expression of impending nausea.

"Honey?" He switched to sitting and gently touched her shoulder. "You okay?"

"I just had one of those falling feeling moments. You know? Where everything just . . . "

He knew. He could feel his own unsteadiness against her shoulder and wished the words that flowed so readily in his articles would come at times like this. "You're okay."

She drew a slow breath, still staring into the fireplace "Someone died in here, didn't they?"

"No."

That stuff was still upstairs, in the bed. He couldn't let her see it. "No," he continued. "She went out back. Out to the garden."

"And she died in the garden."

"She . . . " Had she been dead? Those eyes in the grave.

Tonight, he thought.

"That's where I found her." He squeezed her shoulder gently. "You going to be all right?"

"I'm not afraid of dead people, Brad. What they leave behind, though . . . Listen to how quiet it is."

Not a sound from the front door. From the trees outside. From the house's ancient beams.

"I was trying to clean that mirror," his fiancée murmured. "But you can't clean quiet like that out of a house."

He knew what she was remembering. A story she'd never told. One he'd learned from the police chief in Jasper, Tennessee. How she'd come home late from work and found her mother and brother in the living room, sitting before the muted television, slumped, but not sleeping.

"We'll manage," he said. It was their mantra, the droll magnetism that had connected them across the counter of that muggy little diner in Jasper four years ago. Something in her smile as she tore off the receipt and handed it to him had revealed a soul struggling for buoyancy. It was the immediate companionship of finding in her face someone as desolate as himself. Someone whose eyes knew just as much failure.

"You're shaking, Brad."

He withdrew his hand and she sat up. She looked at his trembling fingers before gathering them between her own, cool and smooth. "You've stopped taking your medicine. You can't just drop it like that."

"I don't need it. I need this." He pointed his eyes around at the blank-faced walls and hovering ceiling. "I need to find out what it's seen. I need to work."

She turned his palms open and studied them. "So why'd you want me to come here? I sure hope it wasn't pity 'cause I know how to deal with pain. I've had plenty of practice."

"It wasn't pity." Bending down, Brad kissed the fingers that held him captive. "That day we met, when I came into the diner and asked for water—you knew why I wanted it. You saw I was in a black place. Work just wasn't enough to hold it off anymore. I needed you."

Her nose and lips came down to rest in his hair for a silent moment. Then, "I was sliding toward a black place, too. And I grabbed on to you. But . . . sometimes it feels inevitable."

"No." He straightened and saw memories moving in her eyes. "What happened to them won't happen to you. You're stronger. You're the one who didn't fall into the trap. And . . . " He knew he shouldn't continue; the wound was still too raw. "What happened last month wasn't your fau—"

She stood abruptly, letting go of him and pacing across the floor.

He squeezed empty air and held back further words.

Eventually, she turned and shrugged. "You're right. I'm okay. I'll be fine." She took a deep breath and squared her shoulders. "It's getting late. I'm gonna look for some light bulbs."

He sat on the floor a little longer before climbing to his feet and leaving the hall. On his way upstairs, he retrieved the book he had left on the step.

Slumped in the study, he eyed the motionless Newton's cradle, then the cardboard box filled with wadded newspaper. That would do to remove the soil from the bed.

His gaze returned to the desk, to the book. Opening it, he found the word again. The name he had seen repeated so often in the town. He pulled out his phone. The connection was sluggish, but he was able to load Google. He typed in *Adamah* and waited.

A Hebrew word returned.

It meant *ground. Dirt.*

6

I had, of course, conducted as much supplemental research as possible in the week before our arrival. It didn't result in much. No internet sites made reference to the town or the house. I located the practice of the doctor who had come to the house and pronounced the woman dead, but he refused to sway from the verdict. I also consulted the Register of Deeds at 17 Monroe Street in the county seat of Lexington. The last registered house owners were a couple named John and Ellen King, who purchased the property in 1946. After their abrupt demise, with no heirs and accumulating taxes due, the place fell to ownership by the town of Three Summers.

Finally, I went to the library in Lexington and asked for local records and writings about the community. But again, nothing was available. The woman who helped me, Brooke Carney, struck me as uncomfortable and slightly evasive. I left her my card and asked her to call should anything become available.

Thus, my initial knowledge was mainly geographical.

Three Summers lies a hundred miles west of Nashville in the northwestern corner of Henderson County, lost amid the woodlands bordering state route 104. At a width of approximately eight hundred feet, the Locust River flows flat and green past the settlement on its way toward the Mississippi. Due to the abundant distribution of sandy clay and gravelly silt loams, Henderson County has been described as inconducive to crop growth. This makes the plantation at Three Summers remarkable, not least because the quality of the soil is not discernibly superior to that of the surrounding county. On the contrary, it is gritty, crumbly, and quite gray in color.

—"The House of Dust"
Southern Gothic

"YOU SURE WE don't want to eat outside?" Missy asked.

She stood in the dining room doorway, a paper plate in each hand.

"When we've got a dining room like this?" Her fiancé was already sitting at the long dark walnut table. He smiled, gesturing to the deep green walls and the fireplace bordered by ivory tiles, and the gold drapes gathered away from the windows by a cord at their waist. "Course not."

"Meal doesn't really match the setting," she said, coming in and taking a seat just opposite. Behind her was a door to the dance hall.

A pair of unlit candelabras, fashioned like slender forearms with straining fingers, stood at the far end of the table, stiff and supplicant, right where she had scooted them. The musty smell that inhabited the whole house was heavy here, throbbing inside her nostrils. Evening light burrowed through the rear windows and cloaked him.

"No need for modesty." He grinned. "You've got chicken salad down to a science."

She pushed his plate across the table. "Grandmama grew me up on this stuff. It's always a safe bet, she said, in case no one shows up for dinner."

Preparing for a bite, he paused for a second.

She smiled back. "Anyway, what kept you upstairs all afternoon?"

"The case. Got to hit the ground running. It's . . . it might end up being the most important thing I've done."

"And what happens when it is done?"

He chewed, considering. "I guess then your project will be done, too."

"My project?"

"The restoration of this house."

"Oh."

"What?"

"Down here today, I was just wondering if it will be worth it. If we'll actually stay."

He took off his glasses and placed them on the table. "When it's fixed up, who would want to leave this place?"

Fixed up.

With flowers maybe.

Daffodils everywhere.

The heavy chair screeched as she stood up.

"What are you doing?"

"Just moving." She carried her plate to the end of the table, away from the weird candelabras. Away from the dance hall doorway. "Can't eat with all that empty space on my back."

Her fiancé shifted toward her new seat. "Hey. Honey. What's going on?"

"Do I seem off?" She sat down.

"All day you've seemed . . . suspicious."

"The house is beautiful. It's what I've dreamed of ever since . . ." She pinched pieces off her sandwich. "Still, it feels . . . deep, somehow. Like even if someone's just in another room, they're a long way off."

Her fingers stopped. He was looking at her. She looked at the table.

"You're remembering HUG. The Club, too. I'll bet you even threw our apartment into that mix. Grungy places. But this can be a real home, honey. Your dream to keep."

No. This wasn't about their apartment, or the Club, or even the Home for Underprivileged Girls in Atlanta. It was about the place before all those places. The place where daffodils grew thick as carpet in the backyard.

"You know how dreams can be," she said.

Pushing back his chair, he stood and came down the table. He bent and folded his arms across her chest. "How can they be?"

She leaned her cheek against his arm, but her gaze stayed in place on the table.

"What are you staring at?"

"Nothing."

"You didn't eat your dinner." He bent lower, nosing her neck, looking between her eyes and the table. "If the house isn't to your liking, perhaps the island will be."

At last she blinked, resuming her smile. "What do you mean 'island'?"

"We're on an island. The old plantation grounds. Dozens of acres, all of it ours."

Maybe it was just a trick of the dimness on the table; maybe her unease was making her imagine things. *Oh well.* It would be good to get out of the house, so she said, "Show me."

They walked down the drive.

Diminished seven-o'clock wind stirred the moss in the live oaks and Missy's hair. She let her head loll back, and the breeze slid across her neck.

They crossed the road at the end of the driveway and voyaged hand in hand into the field. Their voices were muffled by leaves and steam and dripping light and thick evening air.

"Wet spring," Missy remarked. It hadn't rained that afternoon, but the grass swishing around her legs was damp. "I bet I'll pull a thousand ticks off myself after this." Still, it felt delicious after the stuffy house.

"All this," her fiancé said, flinging out his arms. "All this is ours. Our northern shore is the Locust River, right here."

A few trees grew along the bank, but it was mostly clear. They arrived at the edge and looked down the weedy slope at the water. The gravel riverbed was visible for a good way out, and a pile of rocks was set up where the water became a deeper green. The far shore was completely forested and rose much higher, becoming the ridge that separated this slice of country from the state highway.

Her eyes lingered on that green barrier as they walked eastward along the bank.

"Look," she exclaimed, pointing across the water at clouds of fireflies rising from the trees.

"On this side, too," he said.

She watched them evaporate from the field and drift up, transforming the sky like the absinthe drinks she had mixed at the Club, morphing from clear emerald into something creamy and opalescent.

"Never really see those in the city," she breathed.

The little blinking points of light had become a canopy by the time the shoreline led them to the end of the island. The road that cut along its center terminated there, and a gentle slope of dark clay, rife with black-eyed Susans, led down to the water. An ancient wooden dock jutted into the shallows.

"This is where they'd ship the cotton and tobacco from, back when this was a plantation," he said. "In the early days, at least. Amazing: all these years and it hasn't rotted away."

"Mud can fossilize things, sometimes. Hold history in place."

"That from your encyclopedia?"

She grinned and they walked together down the slight incline, stopping on a marshy gravel patch near the water's edge. The air was faintly acrid. Algae swamped the shallows and clouds of miniscule flies danced above the scummy mud. Still, looking at the deepening sky, and the sky in the river, and the avenue of trees on either bank, fuzzing into darkness, Missy took a big breath and felt the tension in her back relax.

"The river flows toward us, and part of it catches on this point of land," he said. "It arcs around through a little channel to the south, creating a creek between us and the mainland." He swept his arm rightward, indicating the wooded half of the island and the invisible creek. "Then the water flows out under the clay-stained bridge at the other end and rejoins the river."

"And no one between here and the town," she said.

"That's right," he said with a relaxed sigh.

She bent down and pried a pebble from the boggy dirt. "Maybe when we get things all grand, we can invite some folks over. A little get-together." She tossed the pebble into the water and glanced back as a ripple crossed his contented face. "Nothing huge, just something to give us roots."

He shifted his feet, as if the pebble she'd tossed had gone inside his shoe instead of the river. "This place is rural. Folks out here might prefer to keep to themselves. Don't have to be the center of things, you know."

"Hey." Stepping against him, she kissed him lavishly, then traced a finger across his breast pocket. "There's only one thing I want to be the center of."

His lips puckered out a bit, and he looked at her with drowsy eyes. "You look good in yellow."

She watched the backs of his fingers brush her sleeveless blouse. When his hands became too heavy, she giggled and twisted away. Strolling off a couple feet, she picked up another pebble, examining it and waiting for him to follow. When he didn't, she glanced around. He was squinting up the island. "Your dream's coming true. Looks like our first guest is on the way."

The sound of a car faded into the quiet evening. Turning, she watched headlights journey toward them along the tired road.

"It's the sheriff." Her fiancé held out his hand. "Come on, you can meet him."

Missy tossed away the pebble and walked toward him. Only a dozen feet separated them. Halfway there, the ground beneath her right foot collapsed.

Balance fled. She reeled for a moment, then toppled forward. With a jolt, her splayed hands slapped against the ground. Like a blister, the soft earth broke apart. Sucking mud rose around her wrists as her hands disappeared into the ground.

The next instant, her fiancé was beside her. Grabbing her midriff, he hauled her up and pulled her away from the bank. As she straightened, he glanced uncertainly between her and the oncoming car. "What happened?"

"It's like it lunged at me." With a shaky laugh, she went over to a patch of Johnson grass and scrubbed her hands clean. The mucky smell clung to her skin. Dirt had darkened her sandal and made the sole slippery. "I can't meet him like this."

"Come on, it'll be fine." He didn't hold out his hand this time.

When they reached the top of the low incline, the sheriff was visible in the dusky light, sitting on the hood of his car, arms folded. "Stopped by the house, didn't see you folks," he called. "So I thought I'd check down here."

Missy's wet shoe scuffed as they crossed the pavement.

"This must be your lady."

"Yes," her fiancé said. "Here she is. This is Missy."

With a stiff, sort of restrained leap, the sheriff rose. His teeth were gleaming and grotesque, each one separated by a narrow black line. His voice was soft and sonorous, like a distant waterfall. "Name's Ezra. Three Summers's sheriff. Well, there's another guy, too, but . . . "

"Oh, I don't think we should," she said to his proffered hand. "I'm pretty dirty."

"I don't mind."

The palm that hugged hers was pleasantly arid. It stayed a little too long, though, and squeezed a little too tight, as if trying to extract something. Quickly, under its heat, she became aware of the gritty itch of residual dirt on her skin.

"Pleased to meet you," she said, backing up a bit.

"Do some wading?"

He smells me.

"No. Tripped. Down by the dock."

"Yeah, folks have commented on the soil in our part of the county. Kinda silty and unstable in places. Great for gardening, though, despite what you'd think. Don't suppose you care for gardening?"

"I . . . I've never really had the opportunity."

"Well, you will if you decide to stay. In the past, that garden behind the house has been full of the prettiest daffodils."

"I hate—" Her hands balled together. "I hate to say it, but I think I'll head back up to the house. Kinda want to get cleaned up."

"Let me give you a ride."

Her fiancé jumped in. "No need. We wouldn't want to get dirt in your car."

"It's just right up the road," Missy added. "Y'all stay and talk."

"In that case, it was a pleasure meeting you, Missy."

"Likewise, Sheriff."

"Ezra."

"*Ezra.*"

"I'll be right along," her fiancé said, and she nodded and slipped off into the dark.

The skin between her fingers was itching from the dirt and from his handshake. But she couldn't rub it out because her fingers were still locked fists.

The daffodil in the dance hall this afternoon—*he* had placed it there. He had come in and stuck it in the floorboards. He had left it where he knew she would find it. It meant her fiancé was innocent; that was a relief. But it also meant a stranger knew something. A sliver of darkness from more than a decade ago.

How?

He was a backwater lawman hundreds of miles from where she had grown up. No. Her fiancé didn't know, and he didn't know. Missy quickened her pace and soon reached the drive. As the house appeared through the bending oaks, her footsteps slowed. It was now fully night, and they had left no lights on inside.

Someone had placed the flower in there. A reminder of her wretchedness.

7

This night's activities had been caged in my mind for the past two weeks, clawing to get out.

—"The House of Dust"
Southern Gothic

LIGHT CAME THROUGH from the central hallway behind her. It stretched Missy's shadow out long and black as she stood before the dining room table. But it did not erase the thing lying in the murk of her silhouette.

She had noticed it first just before dinner, and then again while they ate. Maybe it was just the slant of the light, she had thought. But it remained after the light was gone. It lay there now. A human shape, five feet long, buried in the surface of the wood.

Not a shape. A stain.

Not a dust stain. She had already tried wiping the table down earlier. But perhaps something had been spilled on it at some point, removing the finish.

She looked down at the items in her hands and found them trembling, just a bit. The buzz from the riverbank lingered in her fingertips. She set the things on the table: a butter knife, an old can of varnish from beneath the sink, and a dry washrag.

Using the knife, she pried the lid off the can. As she had guessed from its weight, it was empty.

Still, some residue clung in the seam at the bottom. Scraping it up with the rag, Missy leaned out and smeared the varnish across the wood.

She was so intent on the scrubbing, her ears so filled by the hiss of the cloth, that she didn't notice when her shadow on the table changed. Swelled. Reached for her.

"Working kinda late, huh?" Hands crawled up her back.

She jerked up and turned. "Oh. Didn't hear you come in."

"Been upstairs and took a bath already." He was close, wearing his cobalt bathrobe. His wet hair was combed straight back. "What's going on?"

Reaching back, she pressed on the base of her spine to relieve the throb from crouching. "I wanted to . . . work on the table."

He took the rag from her and tossed it away, then clasped her hands. "I admire your dedication, but it's enough for today. You haven't even seen the bedroom yet."

She watched him examine her fingertips. "They feel funny. Since I fell at the riverbank."

"Funny?"

"Like . . . ants crawling all over them."

"Just tired, I bet." He massaged her knuckles.

"I wonder if there was something in the dirt by the water. Acid or something."

"But you washed them off. Though not the rest of you." He came in even closer, and she leaned back on the edge of the table as he kissed just below her ear.

"No, I'm dirty."

"I like it. You still smell like the river."

The odor of her soiled clothes mixing with the crisp scent of his aftershave churned her stomach.

Missy blinked as he touched her lips, tracing them into a smile. Their faces drifted nearer. Lips chanced together, then fused. He tasted warm and bland, like bathwater.

At the Club, she'd done enough kissing to perform the act with oblivion, and so she was aware of being nudged farther back until she was sitting on the table. Her right hand left his neck to grip the table's edge, preventing any farther movement toward the center.

Toward the shape.

When he moved from her lips to her neck, she let her other hand slip off his shoulder onto the edge, holding herself up, head back, giving him clear access as he unbuttoned the top of her blouse.

The room was dusky enough that the green walls were gray and the yellow drapes were green. She imagined it bright, for some reason. Searing. The roof gone and sun dumping in. As her hands skated back and forth on the table edge, she imagined the skin flaking away. The muscles and tendons drying up. Her hands shriveling like root clumps pulled from the dirt. Nothing but bone below the wrist where the muck had touched her.

The ground is cursed, Grandmama had said. *The ground is cursed. Cain shoulda known that.*

"Cain," she whispered.

"What?"

She hadn't meant to say it aloud. She opened her eyes and felt his kisses evaporating off her neck. "Cain," she repeated. "Cain was cursed."

Straightening, he combed back her hair. "What are you saying?"

"Cain and Abel. You went to church when you were little."

"What about it?"

"Cain wanted to sacrifice vegetables to God, but he was rejected. And then he was cursed. Sent away like he was nothing. He could never escape the curse no matter where he went in the entire empty world. He was marked. I always felt sorry for him."

"Where'd you get that? Did you read that in the encyclopedia?"

"My grandmama."

"Well, no one feels sorry for Cain. He was a real bastard." He unfastened the last button and cool air touched her belly as he pulled her blouse apart.

"But it wasn't fair."

A single finger climbed her navel. "It was the first and fairest trial ever."

"But it was God's fault the ground was cursed, so he shouldn't have rejected Cain."

The finger stopped below her bra. His drying hair had fallen around his temples. "God cursed the ground, but he didn't curse Cain for bringing fruit to offer. He told him he could do better. Cain's response? Murdered his brother so he wouldn't have to live with a reminder of his failure. And then the earth opened her mouth to receive his brother's blood. That means Cain buried him in the same ground his crops grew from. God's response? He didn't kill Cain; he exiled him. Pretty lenient, if you ask me."

"But he was marked." She could feel heat balling up in her throat. That feeling that would come right before Grandmama would call her petulant, a real chore. "The Mark of Cain. So everyone would know what he did. So it would stick to him always. Follow him. No peace."

Her fiancé smiled plastically, then shrugged. "I'm sorry you don't like the house."

"What?"

"It's simple. You've found something about this place you don't like and connected it to having the Mark of Cain."

"And you don't think something's going on? Why you're here is because something *is* going on!"

"And why are you here? Because you wanted more than what we had in Nashville."

"Because I wanted *you*. There, you were always going off. Coming around every few days: 'Time to let the dog out; gotta water the plant.'"

Something simmering moved in his eyes. "Well, here I am. God knows why you want me, but here I am."

Her breath hitched. "Back up."

Incredulous, he moved away. She slid off the table and walked down the length of it, then turned, flexing her finger once to ease the pressure before pointing. "Right there. See it?"

"See what?"

"The discoloration. See how the wood is grayer? Before dinner, I wiped the table down, but not all the dust would come off. While we were eating, I noticed the leftover stuff formed a pattern. I thought it was just the light, but then I polished it and it's still there."

He squinted. "Someone spilled something that removed the finish."

"No, it's part of the table." She bent out, scraping at the wood. "It's like a body. Like someone lying there on their back."

He was unfazed. His expression remained the same.

She straightened. "You don't care. You just came down here to lay me on this table."

He walked toward her, hand brushing the tops of the chairs as he passed them. When he reached her, he leaned in close, but then picked up his glasses where he had left them at dinner. "I just came for these." He put them on.

Deflated, she battled on. "Someone came in here earlier. While we were both upstairs, moving your desk. I found a flower right in there, right on the floor." She pointed to the dark dance hall doorway. "It had just been cut."

"I'll talk to the sheriff."

"You don't believe me."

He smiled ruefully at her, like she was a picture that each day hung obstinately crooked. "I do. This house was important to the community. Folks might poke around. But I don't want you alarmed." Nimbly, he buttoned up her blouse.

When he fastened the last button, he took her hands. "If you're concerned there may have been something in the river soil, I would in all seriousness recommend a bath. I left the tub full." He kissed her forehead lightly, tenderly. "I'll be in the study for a few hours. Don't wait up."

She drew breath to reply, but then swallowed it. She listened as he washed his hands in the kitchen. He was finished with her for the night. As his measured steps creaked up the stairs, she dug the tattered gum pack from her pocket and sucked the last piece from its wrapper, chewing it hard.

When his footsteps were gone, she followed their echoes down the hall. A switch by the staircase shut off the ceiling lights, casting the lower floor in darkness. A thrill she had felt when she was little, running from the bathroom to her bed to avoid the demons, brushed against her now. She didn't run.

Everyone thinks the same thing when they're little, Grandmama had told her tiredly.

And I thought I was so special, Missy thought to herself now as she steadily climbed the stairs, her palm skimming the rail, the slim scratches in the wood evoking the tingle of the river mud.

A bath wasn't a bad idea.

She went down the hall and found the doorway to the main bedroom. She walked in and stood in the center of the room for a minute, turning, chewing her gum, examining the furnishings and drapes. It was grand, even compared to the rest of the house, and tidy, as if specially prepared for her. Well, tidy except for the two black circles painted over the hall doorway like eyes. Paint would solve that. And the canopy bed looked luxurious. She'd always wanted a canopy bed.

The doorway to the bathroom was dark and dreamy with steam. Floorboards murmured as she crossed toward it.

The white tile floor would glare, so she decided against turning on the lights. The yellow glow from the bedroom would do.

A hanger stood beside the tub, the gallows for a bathrobe. She hung her clothes on it and stepped into the water, pausing to tie up her thick hair. A brief, toppling sensation touched her as she sat down, just like the one she had felt that afternoon when she first entered the house.

An almost smile twitched her lips as she lay back. Since he always drew it scalding, the water was just now cooling to something comfortable. The dimness was nice, and she could feel a window in the wall behind her. The night breathed on her neck.

The earth has opened its mouth to receive your brother's blood. She'd forgotten about that line until he'd referenced it. Now it returned, spoken in Grandmama's tired voice. Missy always wondered how long the earth kept its mouth open, and why it wanted to drink blood.

Leaning her head back, she extended her legs into the water until her feet encountered a hard nub at the end of the tub. The plug. She closed her eyes and listened to the water lap against the sides.

8

The house was still when I finally departed, and midnight was approaching.

—"The House of Dust"
Southern Gothic

BRAD LEFT THE lights in the study on. If she woke up and cared where he was, she could look down the hall and think he was working.

Carrying his shoes, he slipped down the stairs. Each careful step elicited a half-asleep animal whine from the planks, and he shifted as much weight as possible to the railing. The railing's strange scars pinched his palm, adding to the prickling sensation of the Prozac withdrawing from his body.

At the bottom of the stairs, his socked feet whispered across the floor to the front door. As he turned the lock, he noticed that the nose-parching smell of dust was gone, replaced by a thick, damp odor, like the underside of a rock.

Probably from the basement. It didn't matter; the hour he'd spent all week waiting for had finally arrived.

Outside, he locked the door and put on his shoes. The scent of pine and the cautious *er-ee, er-ee, er-ee* from a small choir of cicadas occupied the clearing. He crossed the gravel to the dark hunk of his car and opened the trunk. Just to be sure.

His hand plowed through a jungle of empty drink bottles, fast-food bags, newspapers, and newspaper-wrapped artifacts. He recognized by touch the old Sony voice recorder he had bought off eBay to conduct his first interviews. The mysterious glass elephant figurines from his twelfth article. The bloodstained ball cap from the woods of south Georgia, a possession of one of the University of Tampa hikers who had been mutilated there in 2010. Things he should have given to the police. Relics of a clumsy career.

At the bottom of the mess, his grip closed around the item he'd been looking for. Lifting it out, he examined the shovel in the distant light that drifted down from the study windows. This had been his first purchase after witnessing the old woman's burial. The barcode sticker still clung to the blade. He tore it off and tossed it in the trunk—just another useless bookmark, just another piece of detritus, like the rest of it. He examined the shovel again, feeling the weight. Then he put it in the trunk, too, and got in the car.

Briefly, he glanced at the house, at the bright study windows. What would happen if she came down the hall and found he was not in the study? Not in the house. As if he didn't care.

She knows I do.

He started the car and hurried it down the driveway, onto the nameless island road. The clay-stained bridge passed as a blur and a bump. The endless dark of the tree tunnel road swallowed him. His hands climbed unsteadily up and down the wheel, body still thirsty for the sedative.

She knows I need her. I know she needs me.

The headlights lit up the greens and browns of the forest canopy like daytime seen through dark glasses, unfolding into his untired, unblinking eyes, pushing him down the tunnel of memory to the night when he was fourteen and decided to stop taking the stuff. The night he told his mom the gecko was dead.

She'd hauled him down to PetSmart a month after he started on the drugs because his lethargy hadn't lifted. He needed a spur.

A spark. Taking care of something would teach him to take care of himself. But the tiny pale green creature just sat in its ceramic cave and never came out. It jumped off Brad's unsteady hands when he tried to hold it.

So, he stopped holding it. He just dumped the bag of crickets his mom brought home each Friday into the tank and left it alone. The months passed, and its tail got thinner, and dead crickets carpeted the aquarium. And then it was dead.

She didn't say anything at first. She went into the garage and got a hand shovel and held it out. "This is what happens, Brad, when you stop caring."

It only took one scoop in the small backyard to make a grave. He hadn't expected to cry when the lizard's weightless form fell off his palm into the hole. But he did. Not because it was dead. Because he thought he was like the lizard, and she had stopped caring. She was feeding him pills and leaving him alone and waiting for him to die.

Brad's hands locked in place on the steering wheel.

He glanced briefly in the rearview mirror at the small patch of pavement visible, lit scarlet by the brake lights, leading back to the island.

She knows I care.

Adamah Road was dead. He turned left while glancing at the lights down toward Three Summers: a few orange points on an inky canvas.

A few minutes later, the car lurched across the railroad and then he was at the Simmons Pike intersection.

The solitary house on the hill, the one he'd spotted on that first drive to the cemetery, was invisible.

He turned right onto Simmons Pike and left the inhabited land behind. Fuzzy moonbeams like pale roots reached blindly down through the stuffy ceiling of clouds. Brad continued driving until he saw one brush the slender spire of Simmons Creek Baptist Church above the treetops.

He parked the Accord in the deep grass on the roadside. He retrieved the shovel from the trunk and left the car. His shoes were silent on the pavement.

Beside the road, the ground dipped in a small gully. The metallic chatter of flowing water drifted up. Simmons Creek, he guessed. He cut through the trees toward the churchyard. The air was tangy with walnuts.

In the clearing stood the kudzu-covered church. He walked swiftly toward the graves, turning his eyes away from the stern gaze of the dark windows.

The grass had not been cut since the last time he was here. The headstones were shorter than the waist-high blades; they reared up unexpectedly, forcing him to weave between them. But he had pre-meditated this walk so often that there was no difficulty in finding the plot.

Week-old daffodils ringed the mound. Shriveled by sun and rehydrated by the river mist, they flopped around his fingers like dead eels as he collected them. He would replace them later.

Soft shoots of grass covered the lumpy soil of the grave itself. Filling his lungs, he lifted the shovel. Disgust twisted his gut. Whoever she was, she deserved to lie in peace. But the thrall was too strong. This was why he'd come. He had to know.

She was dead. She was dead when you took all those pills and said you were a doctor. Dead in the garden. Dead in the car. Dead in the grave.

With a thud, the blade stabbed into the mound—inside his memory, the door to a visitation room in Angola Prison slammed shut.

Ten years ago. His first case. A haggard face on the other side of a bolted-down table.

Tender roots tore out gently as he pried up the first scoop. This grave had not been disturbed over the intervening week. Even if the woman had been somehow clinging to life when she went in the ground, chances were slim that she could have shifted her body into any sort of position to prove it. Just like the chances that a worn-out drug hustler was actually an unknown serial killer.

The clouds thickened as he worked, the moonbeams retreating and leaving frosty pools in the thin places across the sky. The dew point was high and the imbalance in his system wrung more sweat from his skin than was natural. It dripped off his chin. His hands rubbed raw as he worked the shovel.

What if he was desecrating this grave for nothing? What if he had spent the last of his money relocating them here, jeopardizing his fiancée's recovery, for nothing? Stranding them in an empty town in a dead region of the world?

Ten years, and how far had he progressed?

Earthworms glistened in the dirt clods he wrenched up.

As the lip of the excavation climbed past his knees, the earthworms petered out. As it reached his hips, Brad prepared himself for the swarming white ones that would take their place, feasting on the un-boxed corpse. Each time the blade tore away a fresh bite of dirt and the ground exhaled the trapped air, he wrinkled his nose against the anticipated scent of decay.

By the time he was shoulder deep, Brad knew the body must be close. He carved out niches for his feet in the walls of the grave, so the carcass would not have to support his concentrated weight. He dug facing one direction for a few minutes, then rotated and dug out the other end. Fire rioted through his shoulders as he bent and hoisted the scoops of earth. How had Sorrel managed to dig this grave out in fifteen minutes? He'd spent at least forty-five already.

He pulled his phone from his pocket and crouched down, turning on the flashlight. He ran his hand through the crumbled dirt. Her face should be here. But there were no worms. No putrid odor. Bracing himself, he dug his fingers deeper.

Nothing.

Blinking back sweat, he sat for a moment. Around him, loose streams of dirt trickled into the grave. Surely she hadn't been deeper than this? He clawed at the earth and found it growing denser once more, pressing back beneath his fingernails. This new dirt had not been broken by a previous shovel.

His tired heart kicked back into high gear. He knew he was at the bottom of the grave. He was crouching in the space she had occupied. His hand groped the spot where her head had lain. Where her eyes had opened.

But the old woman was no longer there.

9

All around me in the churchyard the dead lay coldly, their presence seeping through the crumbling grave walls.

—"The House of Dust"
Southern Gothic

I'M BURIED, MISSY THOUGHT. Then she was rushing up from sleep, and her eyelids jumped apart.

Darkness spilled into her pupils. The smell of dirt crowded her nose. The back of her skull lay against a hard edge. Her muscles were stiff, limbs locked in place, one knee raised, her arms fastened at her sides. A mealy slime thick as cake batter wrapped her body. Her jaws gaped apart. In the back of her mouth, a wet clod nestled in her throat.

She gagged, forcing her teeth wider as she coughed the lump onto her tongue. From there, she maneuvered it over the brink of her lips. It rolled off her chin and landed with a strange *plop* on her collarbone. She coughed again and the sound echoed oddly.

I've been buried.

Deliberately, she felt every finger and toe and probed her body. The tendons and muscles were as tight as cold cables. It took a long moment of obstinance before each responded. Until she reached the big toe on her right foot. Despite all her concentration, it remained motionless. She rubbed it with the next toe over. Her big toe was bent down and lodged in something. Numbness had permeated it.

And then she felt something climbing up her leg. Hard and cold, it inched across her skin. It passed over her knee and climbed her thigh.

Missy hauled in a breath and thrashed her foot, tugging on the lodged toe. Her other toes pressed down around it, and she felt the rusty edge of the drain.

The drain!

Of course. She was in the house, lying in the tub. That had been gum in her mouth.

The immobilizing tension drained from her limbs. The thing wandering up her body was a circular knob of rubber: the drain stop. She gripped the sides of the tub and pulled herself into a sitting position. It was hard to believe she had fallen asleep in here, much less slept for hours.

She looked across the gloomy bathroom. The door was open. The bedroom beyond was black. He must be asleep out there. Why hadn't he awakened her? Groaning again, she leaned down and slipped her hands beneath her right foot. The rusty drain gripped her toe like a gorging serpent's mouth. The dirt smell built as she tugged at her foot and the water lapped more and more violently against the porcelain sides.

Her throat closed on a scream as she saw herself sucked into the drain, assailed by the same force that had held her in the creek mud. It was here again, inside the house, inside the rusty pipe, tiny hands clamped around her toe, trying to drag her down into the darkness beneath the island.

With a splash, her toe came free and her foot jerked out of the water. Rising, Missy climbed out of the tub. Her hand found the hanger beside the bathtub and locked around it. She held on while the blood flowed back into her trembling legs. Her breath steadied in the silence. She blinked hard, clearing the last fog of sleep from her brain.

And then she realized that the silence was wrong. The water rising through the pipes had whined in the same way it had at Grandmama's old house. The water draining away should cough and gurgle in the same way also. But the stillness was complete.

Bending toward the tub, she examined the dark water. The ripples had already stilled. Had the stopper somehow become lodged back in the drain?

Don't check, a piece of her whispered. *It doesn't matter. Leave it.*

But she wasn't about to have her actions dictated by fear in her own house, especially in such a straightforward situation. She dipped her hand into the tub. Gritty sediment swirled up as her fingers touched the bottom. The water churned sluggishly around her arm as she pushed her hand toward the drain. The corroded rim rasped against her nails.

The stopper wasn't there. Just the open mouth. And the water hanging in stasis above it. Her hand hovered over the opening for a moment, trying to detect a current. *There must be something lodged in the pipe.* She began to withdraw her hand.

It had moved only inches when a force clamped around her splayed fingers. Binding them together, it dragged her hand down toward the drain and sucked her fingers in up to the knuckles. Her cry bounced off the flat water as she dropped to her knees. Pushing back with her left hand on the edge of the tub, she jerked hard. Her hand came free.

Missy was on her feet in an instant. She took a step back. The gurgle she had been waiting for finally emanated from the tub. She flexed her fingers.

She looked back at the doorway, expecting to see his shadowy form standing there. Surely her cry would have awakened him?

He wasn't there, but the smell of dirt and flowers remained. That would be the open window. See? Everything had an explanation.

Missy waited for her breathing to settle, then wrapped herself in the white bathrobe. A metallic scent stung her nose as she arranged the collar on her neck. Her fingers smelled like gunk from the drain. No, like old blood.

She waded through the shadows to the sink and the mirror. Water coughed out of the pipes. She hesitated, then dipped her hands under the faucet. When she drew them away and sniffed again, the taint remained. All the pipes must be corroded.

Shutting off the water, she lifted her hands just in front of her eyes. They were surprisingly hard to see. The shape was there, but her skin was next to invisible. Behind her, the tub gulped down the water.

Frowning, Missy lowered her hands and leaned toward the mirror. In the dim glass, a bathrobe leaned toward her. Hair hung above it, and bits of a face. But not enough—

Not enough face.

She found the light switch on the wall and flipped it up. And then she stood perfectly still.

I am buried, she thought again.

Dirt covered her. It gleamed on her arms, a brown glaze.

It stained the exposed portion of her neck and smeared the bathrobe where she had touched it. It climbed up her neck, far past the line where the water had touched her skin, spreading across her cheeks and inside her nose, and up onto her forehead and into the roots of her hair.

This wasn't sludge vomited by the pipes and spread through the bathwater.

This had been rubbed into her skin. Hands had touched her.

Made her filthy.

And now her prints were on the sink and the wall and the light switch. Her mouth was too full and her lungs too empty to scream.

No stranger could have snuck in and done this. Not with the house locked up for the night and her fiancé sitting just down the hall. This wasn't the work of a stranger. *This was him. He placed the flower. He put the dirt in the tub. To try to break me.*

The tub coughed. She spun around and pressed back against the basin. She watched the black water drain out of sight, languidly, taking its time, mocking her in its exit. A smeary residue remained

behind, its reminder to her. That it could come back. That she'd
always be filthy.

Iron bands wrapped her lungs as she imagined how he had
entered the dark room, smiling down at her, pouring dirt into the
tub. The floor rose toward her. Her forehead and nose mashed
against the white tiles.

The bonds burst, and she dragged in air. Pushing onto her knees,
then her feet, she shuffled toward the bedroom. One nightstand
lamp was on. His body was not among the rumpled sheets. In fact,
his side of the covers had not even been drawn back. Could he still
be in the study *working*?

Going to the doorway, she peered down the corridor. Dusty
light yawned from the study.

Then she heard footsteps on the first floor, traveling at a strangely
rapid gait. Her eyes moved to the inky staircase.

No one came up.

The feet passed the stairs and moved toward the back of the
house.

She wanted to stomp down and scream at him and have him
reassure her—*lie* to her—and hug her. She wanted to be hugged.
Even the lies would feel better than this.

Retreating to the bed, she lay down. Her flesh was crusted with
grime. She shut her eyes against the light and picked at the stuff on
her hands. It came away in scales. She brushed it off the sheets.

After a while, she realized that her hands felt the same: the
roughness was not going away. Her silt-crusted eyelids opened to
examine her fingers. She sat up and rolled toward his side of the bed
and held her hands in the light.

It wasn't just a feeling; they were wrinkled. And not the water-
logged wrinkles from too long in the tub.

The skin was dry. Shriveling back from her nails. Cracking
around her knuckles. Scabby, like droughted soil. The hands of an
old woman.

Someone had taken her.

—"The House of Dust"
Southern Gothic

THE ROAD FLOWED from the darkness into the white bubble of the headlights.

Brad's eyes moved between the worn pavement and his dim phone screen. Pictures flicked past beneath his thumb. Each had been distorted by the flash, bright at the center and gloomy along the edges. They showed the grave.

First, he had photographed it from a few feet away, capturing the full length of the rectangular hole, with its fringe of drooping grass on one side and the edge of the dirt heap on the other. In the next he stood over the grave, taking in the crumbling lips of the maw, the uneven floor glowing down below like a wet tongue. In the third he lay on the ground and stretched his arm into the hole, showing the shovel marks riddling the floor. And in the fourth he had crouched in the bottom of the pit, taking a close-up of the place where her head had lain.

Just those four pictures. He flipped through them again and again. Faster and faster. But no white-shrouded body appeared in the grave. No staring face appeared in the dirt. The body was gone.

Someone had taken it. Or . . .

Brad brushed sweat from his forehead. The phone slipped from his knee and thumped onto the floorboard. He left it, staring out at the worn paint delineating the narrow lanes. Someone *had* taken her body. Who?

The townsfolk were obvious suspects—one, or perhaps a group of them. Surely the sheriff had not been involved. He had been the one insisting on a hasty burial. He had cut short their bizarre actions during the interment. But he had also known Brad was watching. And he knew what Brad was.

He was protective of her. Maybe he knew I would try something like this.

The moon had withdrawn to a backlight seeping through the dense curtain of cloud. Brad turned left at the intersection and followed Adamah Road toward Three Summers.

He would go to Sorrel first. If he was involved, it would show in his face. And if he wasn't, at least he would appreciate the tip and maybe even cooperate with his investigation.

The car bucked across the derelict railroad ties. Ahead, the town lights beamed through the murk.

He was going about forty-five when a sound came out of the gloom.

A droning hum wafting through the window, its volume rising with each passing second. He pressed the brakes and shifted his hands on the wheel to avoid the prickles that pushed through the vinyl. He knew that sound. It called back hot suburban days in Providence, wandering the sidewalks the summer after the funeral to escape the heaviness of the house. Without the sun in the sky, though, the hum was distinctly off.

The car slowed as the sweet, sharp, nostalgic scent washed across the road. It tasted wrong in the dead post-midnight air. The pale shape of Grammy's Grocery faded into view up ahead on the left.

He followed the humming to the last yard before the grocery store. There a row of spruce trees separated the residence from the parking lot. Something moved along that line of trees.

A lawn mower with weakly glowing headlights moved up the edge of the yard by the road, spewing grass clippings across the lawn. The rider was in his fifties and wore work boots, patched jeans, and a dirty T-shirt emblazoned with an orange *T* for the University of Tennessee. Sunglasses pushed back on his head restrained a curly thicket of gray hair. His eyes did not drift from his work as the car passed.

"He's cutting his grass," Brad said aloud. He looked at the clock. *1:37 a.m.*

Leaning out the window, he looked after the man. As the lawn mower faded from the backwash of the headlights, he saw it pass over a rough section of ground. The body atop it swayed, as if the man were stuck to the seat with superglue.

Probably drunk. Slowly, he lowered his foot onto the gas. *Find Sorrel.*

Passing the grocery store, he looked briefly out at the lot. Of the four lamp poles, only two emitted any light, a sallow green radiance that drizzled across a half dozen parked cars. It brushed up against the side of the neighboring warehouse and revealed something that he'd not noticed before.

An enormous mural was painted across the bricks. The characters bore the happy ruddy features of 1940s-era advertising. In the foreground, a woman wearing a strapless red dress smiled out at the desolate street. She held a long white cigarette in a two-fingered grip by her rouged cheek. Bold letters proclaimed: *She Smokes DeWitt's!*

Behind her, blandly handsome men in hats looked on with envy.

But time had worked its ravages. The woman's dress had faded. Her teeth were crumbling as the paint flaked away from the brick wall, and her eyes were becoming jagged holes. The admiring faces were almost obliterated.

A glimpse of movement drew his gaze across the street, where a woman with black and blond hair was fueling her red Chevy at the

Texaco station. She looked away from the pump as he passed, and a cigarette glowed between her lips.

The town was awake. Was it in fact day? Had he spent the whole night in the grave and this was 1:40 in the afternoon? He ran his fingers through his hair to banish the ridiculous notion.

Sure, it was a bit surprising to find such rural stores open twenty-four hours, but obviously they were catering to a peculiar clientele.

Things were more normal in the downtown area. The head-lights reflected in dark windows and the engine hummed past empty sidewalks.

Brad crossed Larkin Street at the center of town and followed Adamah Road toward the river. No sign of a police station.

Soon, the white specter of the Locust River Hotel loomed on his right, where the town ended at River Street.

As he turned right, following the curb, something flicked at the edge of the headlights.

Again, his mind short-circuited. He processed the image from memory. Someone was standing out on the bridge. A figure holding an umbrella, staring down at the water.

He hit the brakes, got out of the car, and walked back to the bridge's entrance. The putrid scent of the river rose around him as he stepped onto the pale concrete expanse. Stray gravel rattled away from his shoes.

The figure appeared abruptly, as if rising from muddy water. It was a tall person wearing denim overalls. A ragged umbrella was gripped by a frail hand, and the face was turned toward the river. Ash-colored hair floated down her back—it was a woman. Brad glanced over his shoulder. He'd left the car door open, and he could see the interior light from here. Just a hundred feet or so back to the road. He stuck his hands in his pockets and approached. "Good evening."

No response.

"Is it okay if I talk to you?"

The person rotated slowly, like a figurine on a music box. A small nose and colorless lips came into view. Impossibly wide eyes, unblinking, looked around the umbrella rod held a foot in front of her face.

Brad's feet caught on the pavement.

It wasn't a woman. It was a child. The wispy hair and undeveloped features placed her at no more than twelve. But her height . . . she was six feet at least; he was afraid if he approached any farther she would continue to grow, warping out of proportion like a reflection in a twisted mirror. The arm that did not hold the umbrella hung down limp and white, and bare toes peeped from beneath the towering legs of her overalls. Her voice was a high whisper. "I'm Harlow. I came out to watch the lightning."

Brad rearranged his stance. "Okay. It's going to storm?"

"Don't you see the clouds?" Her eyebrows inched up. "They're very thick tonight. And more are being shoveled on all the time."

"Okay. Do you know where the sheriff is?"

"Oh, yes." And then the briefest pause. "Mister Sorrel's in the mill. He thinks I can't see his lantern from here. Just a little glimmer."

"The mill. Where's the mill?"

"You were going the right way. Edge of town. Just cross the high grass."

Something wistful in her tone. His feet itched to retreat. "You all right? It's not a good idea to be out alone at night. Especially in the middle of the road." The words felt bland, required.

"I'm not alone," Harlow replied.

"Really?"

"See the doggy?"

The air blinked white-hot between them. In the flash he saw a large basset hound seated twenty feet farther down the bridge. Glassy eyes glittered. It sat as still as a taxidermized animal.

"I see that."

"The lightning's started." She rotated back toward the river.

"Well, thanks for the help."

"I'm Harlow. Don't forget it, now."

"I won't." He shot another glance at the stiff, motionless dog sitting off in the dark.

Brad's feet carried him quickly back to the car. Had the creature even been alive? And why was the girl allowed to wander the night like that? Nothing good happened when kids walked around alone for too long. Solitary thoughts became their companions. Rubbing his chin on his shirt collar, he drove over to the next street—DeWitt, it was called—and turned down it, away from the river.

On this flank of town, the buildings lined only the left edge of the street. Off to the right, a disintegrated sidewalk and a quiet procession of box elders bordered a field. The black-and-white police cruiser was parked there, an old Ford Galaxy straight out of Mayberry, complete with the bulbous single-cell emergency light on the roof. Flaky decals on the door read THREE SUMMERS SHERIFF'S DEPT. The back glass reflected brightly as he pulled up behind it.

He got out and closed the door gently. Walking to the cruiser, he examined the dark windows before turning toward the field.

The dark redbrick bulk of the old cotton mill rested across the sea of grass. As he crossed toward it, the lightning once again fizzed through the clouds and revealed the gaping eyes of row upon row of collapsing windows set three stories high. What was the sheriff doing in there?

By the mill, he followed a trampled path to a small doorway. He drew a breath and stepped inside. It was a narrow corridor, leading right. The heat and smell of yesterday afternoon were preserved in the old brick. He followed it for a short distance, then turned left. The vast interior of the silent mill opened before him.

The floor was dirt. About halfway across the building, the floors above seemed to have fallen in; he could see a jagged line where the ceiling ended, and grass grew inside the walls.

Just below the ceiling's edge, a figure labored in a corona of yellow lantern light. Sorrel, dressed in his same black suit, gripping a wide push broom. A collection of buckets stood around his feet. Brad watched as he leaned the broom against his shoulder, lifted one of the buckets, and poured water across the ground.

Brad felt ants in his shoes, biting his feet, crawling up his back, tingling on his neck. He pulled out his phone. He needed to have pictures of all of this.

Tossing the bucket aside with a clang, Sorrel repositioned the broom. With slow, even strokes he spread the water across the earth. The soft squelch of mud accompanied the strokes.

The instant the picture froze, Sorrel looked up. He straightened, as if Brad's entrance had sent a ripple through the floor that he felt through his boots and the shovel shaft. "Who's down there? Harlow?"

Brad restrained a curse: How clumsy had he become? For a moment he lingered in the shadow of the door, hoping his stillness would render him invisible.

The tired voice called again. "Bradley Ellison? So this is what your investigation's gonna be. Sneaking around at night in the dark."

Stowing the phone, Brad squeezed his hands in his pockets and walked into the open. The rain-starved floor scuffed like concrete beneath his shoes. "Actually, I came to get some clarification," he said.

Sorrel's face emerged from the gloom. He wasn't smiling. "You should be home in bed. With your wife."

Frustration was already twisted up inside of him. The mention of his fiancée wound it tighter. He pried a smile onto his teeth and looked at the mud puddle around the sheriff's shoes. "I could maybe say the same."

The sheriff scratched his forehead with the end of the broom handle. "It's cooler to work at night."

"Yeah, driving in, I noticed a lot of folks seem to agree with you on that."

"What can I do for you?"

Drawing out the phone again, he tapped on the photo gallery and held the screen toward Sorrel.

Sorrel squinted. As Brad scrolled through the pictures, the sheriff's grip on the broom handle became so tight it looked painful. He let it fall.

Then he lunged forward.

Brad recoiled, but the man only brushed him, knocking the phone from his hand. He was already halfway to the door by the time Brad retrieved it from the mud.

Stuffing it in his pocket, Brad sucked in his words and followed.

The lantern remained behind, illuminating the glistening mud bed.

Lightning flared again as he tracked the sheriff across the field. The man's giant strides carried him to his car a good ten seconds before Brad arrived. The police cruiser rumbled to life and heaved away from the curb. Scrambling into his Accord, Brad continued to pursue.

The sheriff drove without headlights. The white car swept along the curve at the end of DeWitt Street, running at the edge of his own lights.

They skirted the edge of the downtown district and approached an intersection with Adamah Road. The Texaco station appeared in the driver's-side window. By the light of its canopy, Brad saw a hunched figure pushing a buggy down the middle of the opposing road. She had almost reached the intersection.

Brad braked. The sheriff did not.

The woman trundled into the intersection, and the white car swerved to miss her. The woman drew up short, turning her head as it vanished down the gloomy road opposite.

Brad's fingers relaxed around the wheel. But as the woman passed through the channel of his headlights, they became taut again.

Hair, yellow as dying grass, sprouted and spilled from her scalp in all directions, leaving her face obscured. A blue jean jumper was her only garment. It cut off above bare feet, gray with dirt. Feet that never left the ground. Feet that rubbed across the rough pavement as easily as someone sliding on ice.

The rattle of the buggy drilled inside the car and into his ears until she had passed.

Blinking, he pressed the car forward again, turning his head as he passed through the intersection. The woman was heading into town. Heading home with her shopping. He looked at the clock.

1:59 a.m.

It was more than just a few folks. This town was alive at night. What was going on? Ramming the gas harder, he followed the curving road down toward the other side of town. Low brick buildings flickered outside the passenger window: 24hr Coin Laundry, Brotherton's Garage, Fillmore Deposit Bank. No police station.

But Sorrel had come this way. Out the other window, undeveloped fields stretched dimly to a chain-link fence, and beyond that to the forest line. Then the grass went from high to short, and a recently paved turnoff ran into the field, and out there just fifty feet away sat the white car, parked near a square building.

Brad slowed and twisted the wheel, leaving the road and following the drive. As it bent left toward the building, he squinted through the windshield. An older version of the drive continued straight on through a chain-link fence and down between an avenue of magnolia trees to a huge dark edifice lodged back in the throat of the cove.

For an instant, a brief scar of lightning revealed the building: sprawling, with a crenulated roofline, an arched portico, and arched windows along two stories. A structure to rival the old mill on the other side of town, though certainly one with a different function.

The lightning faded, replaced by the chill gleam of fluorescents as he entered the parking lot of the nearer building. Sorrel had left his door ajar and fled inside already. Pulling in behind him, Brad got out, observing the one other car in the lot, a beige Subaru.

If this place was what he guessed, who else would be here at two o'clock in the morning?

Kudzu writhed from the field and clung tightly to the single-story structure, transforming it into a building made of leaves.

Just like the church.

Here, though, there were signs of resistance. Gashes in the shroud let swaths of relatively recent brickwork show between the leaves. Wilted heaps of the vines lay on the pavement beside a rake and a pair of hedge trimmers. In a cleared patch above the door was an aluminum sign: THREE SUMMERS SHERIFF'S DEPARTMENT. He approached the metal door and went inside.

The smell of cleaner. Disinfectant.

A yellow slip warning sign stood atop polished white tile. A string of dirty footprints tracked past it down the well-lit taupe-colored hallway and turned into a room at its end. A hint of voices, murmuring in chorus, came up from that place.

He started toward them when a nearer voice came from a door on his left. The sheriff.

"Did you check? I want you to check. Do it quick."

The prints on the floor weren't shoe prints, but actual unshod footprints. He photographed them, then stepped toward the door with the voice. It was slightly ajar, as if it had rebounded after being slammed.

Inside, Sorrel sat turned away in a swivel chair, hunched over a peeling linoleum desk. A cord snaked beneath the arm that supported his forehead and ran to the phone cradle. An empty Mountain Dew bottle with the label peeled half off balanced atop a chunky computer monitor that was running one of those starfield screensavers. Brad remembered sitting before a screensaver like that in the Providence library, pretending he was flying into oblivion.

Pushing the door wider, Brad stepped inside.

The bright tile floors, the LED overhead lights, and freshly painted walls suggested this was a newly constructed building. Governor Haslam's photograph smiled from the wall behind Sorrel, and the state flag leaned in the corner beside a set of color-coordinated file cabinets.

The wall opposite held less formal furnishings. A collection of fishing poles sprouted from a stand in the corner behind the door; tackle boxes were stacked against the walls; sporting pictures and anatomical charts of various fish, primarily bass, were neatly tacked over the beige paint. Below them, a little glass case contained different types of hooks on three shelves, some shiny, some rusty, all razor sharp. And a picture. A black-and-white photograph in a round frame. A man with slick black hair and a wolfish smile.

THE HOUSE OF DUST

"Okay. Get it covered up before services tomorrow." A squeak from the swivel chair, and a clunk from the phone cradle.

"What's your favorite fishing spot?" Brad asked. When the silence dangled, he turned.

The sheriff was staring across the desk in his direction. His face was vacant. Eyes and lips slack. The visage of someone drowned.

Slowly, his face cleared. His hands scooted together and folded loosely on the desk. "There's a good spot just upstream, across from the mine. The river channels under the bank a bit, right by that graveyard." He looked up. "You know the graveyard."

Brad flexed his smile. "I want you to know that my deepest wish in all this is to refrain from misrepresenting anything I see."

"That's why you dug up the body of an elderly woman."

"I didn't dig her up, I—"

"Oh, come on." The man was on his feet, coming around the desk. "The day you arrive, that body goes missing. Wouldn't that be the perfect stone to throw into this pond and get some ripples going? I know that's what you're after."

He had come in close, close enough for Brad to pick out the roughed-up skin at the corners of his mouth from a recent shave.

Brad said, "Is there anything I can do to persuade you otherwise?"

"Sure. Come with me."

Sorrel led him out of the office and out of the building, into the restless night and to the back of Brad's Accord. He pointed at the trunk. "Open it."

Brad used the key and lifted the top.

Sorrel leaned inside and rummaged. Another silent jolt of lightning revealed the relics of his other cases. After a minute, the sheriff stood back and slammed the lid shut. He started back toward the station, then swerved over and ripped open the rear passenger door and examined the seats and the floorboard.

Then he slammed the door. "You could have dumped it."

Brad bit his tongue and followed the man back to his office. The lawman slumped into his chair, looking blankly at the glass cabinet with its tackle and picture, weighing the silence between them. Brad stood at one corner of the desk and asked, "Is there anyone else who might have an interest in that body?"

"To do what with, Mr. Ellison? I'd like to hear what you think's going on."

"I'm not thinking anything. I'm just here to learn what's going on."

"Don't give me that. You're a crime writer. You've got suspicions. I'd like to hear them."

"Okay." He put his arms behind his back: docile, giving a report to a superior. "I thought the woman who was buried last week wasn't dead. And I thought the behavior of those at her funeral was strange."

"That's all?" The man scooted his chair over to the file cabinets and shuffled through a lower drawer. Rolling back, he stuck out a wisp of pale blue paper. Brad took it and read the tight clusters of official text interspersed with blank spaces that were filled in.

It was a death record for a woman named Marilyn Britain, aged seventy-nine, signed by Michael McDowell, MD.

"I know," he said. "I stopped by Dr. McDowell's office down in Lexington last week. He didn't seem interested in talking, especially when I mentioned how less-than-thorough his examination had been."

"He'd been looking after her for a year. No one was surprised by her death."

"But you're surprised by her resurrection."

Sorrel jammed his arms together, and his chair creaked unwillingly as he rocked. "No, what I'm surprised by is your lack of respect for the law. Seems like a crime reporter should know better than to dig up a grave."

"Technically, it's not illegal in the state of Tennessee. And, technically, it wasn't even a grave when I dug it up since it wasn't occupied."

"Tryin' to be a smart aleck, huh? Well, *technically*, I don't have to let you stay in that house 'cause, *technically*, it's my house."

Brad nodded evenly. "So why are you letting me? If this isn't about uncovering things, then what's it about?"

Sorrel's chair stilled, and his eyes shifted, like the lenses on a telescope, allowing it to see into vastly deeper space.

Again, the amorphous sound of chorusing voices wafted from deeper in the building. Sorrel passed a hand across the fuzz on the back of his bald head. Reaching out, he jostled the mouse and rattled the keyboard in front of the fat monitor, and then opened a rickety desk drawer.

"Gum, Brad?" He held out a small carton with a few foil-wrapped sticks.

Holding back a bemused frown, Brad hesitantly accepted. "You don't have any cigarettes, I suppose? DeWitts', perhaps?"

The sheriff cracked something distantly resembling a grin. The effect was hideous on his tight-skinned face. "You notice stuff. Guess that comes in handy."

Keys clicked as he typed in a password.

"Do most folks have internet out here? I know it can be hard to get in rural places."

"I've been tryin' to up the access, but, to be honest, most don't care."

"Phone service?"

"Spotty, but it works. Most folks don't make phone calls."

"Really."

"No one to call." The mouse clicked, and the keys typed again. Was the man trying to act busy? Aloof?

"Huh." Brad unwrapped the gum and glanced up at the ceiling lights. "Where's the power substation?"

"Behind the grocery store."

"Trash service?"

"Local woman runs that."

Brad chewed. "I noticed a recurring name on several establishments; I wondered who it was: Adamah—"

"Here we are," Sorrel interrupted. "Come here and look at this." He scooted his chair and watched as Brad rounded the desk and bent down to look at the screen.

The gum squeezed between his molars.

Atop the webpage, the banner art depicted a silhouetted crane standing in a swamp of sharp marsh grass and bloodred water, looking backward. It was the *Southern Gothic* website. Sorrel had navigated to the contributors tab and scrolled to find one in particular. Now, the nine-year-old picture of a quietly defiant young man with thick black hair and black-rimmed glasses looked out of the screen.

Sorrel's hand came up to grip Brad's right shoulder while the other scrolled the mouse across the photo and accompanying author bio text.

"See, Brad, before I go spilling my guts to this guy here, I want to know if I can trust him. And from the picture, I can't tell. And from the words, I can't tell, either, because mostly it's links to articles he wrote that I have to pay to read. And I don't want to pay because I don't know if what the guy writes is true, either, or if he twists stuff."

He let the hand slide off. "I apologize for being short with you; I want this to go the right way. I'm sure you understand. Now, did I cut you off a minute ago? You were gonna say . . . ?"

Brad straightened up. He adjusted his glasses, looked away, and mechanically resumed chewing. The picture in the glass case looked across the room at him. "Did you go fishing with your dad a lot?"

Sorrel's voice dimmed. "Never knew him."

Brad glanced over.

The man was slumping again, gazing at the little shrine. "My mom said she was never meant to have kids. I wanted to, but never . . . Probably would have been a terrible dad, anyway. But for some reason, I always wanted to try and . . . guide someone."

"Yeah," Brad said quietly. "I understand." Immediately, he wished he could drag the words back. They were too naked. He cleared his throat, digging for something to follow with.

Sorrel hadn't noticed. He rubbed a finger on his temples. "I've got enough kids, anyway." Suddenly, his face brightened. "Now that's a great idea." He closed the magazine tab and stood up. "Kind of a guest lecture, eh?"

Bewildered, Brad followed him out of the office. With a muted roar, the rain finally assailed the roof. The blurred footprints passed beneath them as they closed in on the door with the chanting voices he'd heard upon initially entering.

"What's going on?" he asked.

"School," Sorrel said over his shoulder.

Brad slipped out his phone and glanced at the time.

It was 2:26 a.m.

The lights in the back half of the bleak room he led me to were burnt out. The walls were arrayed with posters of the state flag, state animal, state flower, and state motto; the floor was arrayed with school desks; the desks were arrayed with muddy-footed children.

—"The House of Dust"
Southern Gothic

THERE WERE TWELVE of them.

He guessed they were between the ages of eight and fifteen. The fifteen-year-old wore a full beard. The eight-year-old's head was sideways as she played with her topknot. All were dressed to varying degrees of shabbiness in worn denim and fraying cotton. And all twenty-four grimy feet were pressed solidly against the polished tile.

The twenty-four eyes stared at the newcomers in the doorway. Brad had interviewed a caretaker at a daycare once and had avoided the gazes that followed him across the playground. He knew if he stopped, if he looked, he would become lost in them. Children's eyes were too deep: wells that time had not yet filled with trash. He dared not touch and spoil.

Movement disturbed the bunch. The girl with the topknot shot from her chair and floundered through the desks toward Brad and Sorrel. The sheriff stepped inside quickly, motioning Brad to follow, and shut the door just as the girl reached them.

"Jackie!"

At the front of the room, a woman started up and came around a desk. She wore khaki pants and an untucked blue button-down and her hair was cut short with bangs. She rushed over, stopping short as Sorrel grabbed one of the girl's flailing arms.

"Hey now! Where are you going, young lady?"

"I want to drink the rain!" she cried, twisting in the sheriff's grasp.

Brad blinked and remembered the tall girl on the bridge. Harlow. Why wasn't she here? Trying to sound casual, he asked, "Why do you want to drink the rain?"

The girl stopped writhing and stared at him. "Because that's what *he* does."

Before Brad could ask who *he* was, Sorrel said, "Ms. Harper."

The woman moved closer and took the girl's other arm. "Come on, Jackie. We can't drink the rain right now."

As she tugged the girl back to her desk, Sorrel ushered Brad to the front of the room. Squeezing his shoulder once more, he said, "Kids, I want to introduce you to a man you might see around town for the next week or two, Brad Ellison. He's a writer for a big magazine, and he thinks we're interesting enough that he wants to write about us. Who knows, maybe they'll turn us into a documentary. The world, watching Three Summers, and each of you. Wouldn't that be fine?"

The fingers bit deeper. Brad barely concealed a wince.

"Now he's going to talk to us for a couple minutes and tell us about the stories he writes; that way, we can know what to talk about if he tries to interview us. You write about cults a lot, don't you, Mr. Ellison? Maybe start by defining for us what a cult is."

"I rarely write about cults."

Another pincer squeeze to his shoulder. "No, I've done my homework, and as I understand it, your first big article was pretty cultish. Tell us that story, Mr. Ellison."

Sorrel let go and stepped away. He walked into the gloomy rear of the room and motioned an irresolute Ms. Harper to join him in the empty desks at the back of the little huddle.

Brad's hands were humid in his pockets. He could feel his stomach folding together. *Just the soothers working out of my system.* He said, "I'm not sure that kind of story would be . . . "

The bearded boy gazed at him sleepily. Jackie played an imaginary piano on her desk and looked around restlessly. The faces of the other children were blank. Beneath each desk, their dirty feet were set close together. But several were moving now, methodically lifting one foot, then the other, as if pedaling an invisible bicycle.

"I'm not sure that story would be appropriate for this sort of setting."

What was this setting? What was going on? The dead lights at the back of the room made his position here by the teacher's desk seem almost stage-lit. He waited for the camera crew to shuffle in behind him, to capture the too-perfect setup for a Netflix doc: the rural kids in the chilly classroom in the dead of night. Being indoctrinated. Bound into the fold.

"Aw, we're rough around the edges ourselves, Brad," Sorrel assured him. "Tell us first what sort of stuff you write generally." Sorrel looked at the backs of the barefoot youth. "Don't you want to know what Mr. Ellison writes about, kids?"

Their feet moved and their eyes settled on him, drinking him in like rain. Twelve children.

Twelve victims of the explosion. The scent of raw oil in his nose. The flash of bright orange at the edges of his eyes. The heaviness. The burden that had to be lifted.

"Crime," he said.

"Crime," Sorrel repeated.

"That's my department. I write about crimes, both historic and modern."

"What sort of crimes?"

"Murders, mostly."

"They do tend to be the most interesting kind. Any we've heard of?"

"They tend to be obscure, which brings the challenge to my job. My most famous article—the one that launched my career, really—unearthed the Serene Flats murders. It was called 'The Futureless.'"

"That's the one. The cult one. Tell us about it. Tell us what a cult actually looks like."

The kids were quiet. Waiting. A bewildered moth wandered the yellowed ceiling tiles between the lights. A clock on the back wall stood at 2:30.

"We dismiss at three," Ms. Harper said, reading him.

"Serene Flats," Sorrel prompted. "Word was a guy named James Bell killed everyone."

The name brought back the weight of those early days. The dragging demand for the truth that pulled him down through layer after layer of false reports and bad evidence. James Bell's long-dead voice whispered in his mind. *Show them I'm innocent.*

Brad found the dry glow of the floor around his feet changing to the gleam of wet pavement. The rain sighed overhead. The taste of sodden air entered his mouth.

"Serene Flats was a housing project built in Jackson, Mississippi, in 1969. The clientele was predictably lower class: unwed couples, seniors struggling to maintain their independence, and a fair number of single folks. The place had a steady turnover rate but still ran smoothly for the first five years of its existence. The only illicit activity that took place was drug use, and, you know, considering the populace, that wasn't surprising or unexpected—certainly not to the management. When trouble came, though, it came in a big way."

He remembered Heather's enthusiasm when she first read the story, her call that came around this same time of night, her promise that he would be the hottest true-crime writer of the decade: book deals, film sales, TV specials. None of it panned out. He didn't want it to, really. With fame came exposure. Scrutiny. Questions about his own story.

"On the morning of July 3, 1974, water was reported leaking under the doorway of unit twenty. When the tenant, Sarah Murphy, did not respond, the maintenance men used a master key. The chain was also securing the door, so they had to cut it. Ms. Murphy was found dead in her bathtub."

He paused. The children's eyes seemed not just deep, but dry. Faucets cut off from their water source. He could drop coins into those eyes and they would rattle down through their legs, into an underground labyrinth. A shared reservoir that could be poisoned. They didn't need to know these things. Life would teach them soon enough. But not him, not here, not yet.

Tell them I'm innocent, came the imagined voice.

"Mr. Ellison?" Sorrel's voice cut through his thoughts.

Tell them about their world.

"Tell them," he persisted.

Tell them my story, came the voice he had created for James Bell.

"Tell them, Brad."

Sorrel's voice had merged with the plea in his mind, bearing down on him in dark harmony.

"Her wrists were slit," he said. "Apparent suicide. The police were ready to accept the obvious. That is, until the next morning, when Jimmy Olympus, who lived in unit twenty-one, appeared to have suffered the same fate."

"More water under the door?" Sorrel said.

"Same in all respects. Naturally, this put the residents of the building in a rather paranoid state of mind. They seemed to be part of an Agatha Christie novel, where each night the next highest unit number would experience death. The management advised everyone to lock their doors and even hired a security detail to watch that side of the building. Next morning, the same phenomenon was found in unit twenty-eight, this time striking down Al Jeffries and Nancy Cillian."

"My, my," the sheriff murmured.

"By that time, some people had had enough. There was a total of fourteen units on that side of the building. The residents of units twenty-five, twenty-nine, and thirty-three chose to evacuate."

"Surprised they didn't do so sooner."

"And that more people didn't choose to evacuate," Brad added.

The details tasted bittersweet as he spoke them, remembering the days of investigation that had resulted in each one: the cheap hotels, swampy prisons, forgotten records, and reluctant witnesses. "We must now introduce the person who, in my opinion, is the real victim of the whole ordeal. His name was James Bell, and he was an aspiring author. He lived on the other side of the building. The string of supposed murders fascinated him. It turns out he had been plotting a book with a similar concept in mind—unexplainable deaths in an apartment complex. According to witnesses in the building across from him, he would sit daily before his window and watch the other residents' comings and goings, smiling weirdly on occasion."

The children remained expressionless.

Tell them . . .

Brad's words came more slowly as he unloaded the story.

"The twist, of course, was the hardest part of the man's novel. He decided it would be worth his while to make a small investigation into what was truly going on behind his walls. On the fourth night, this would have been July 7, he went out and sat in his car, which was parked at the far end of the building in question. He watched, and the police watched, but all was quiet that night."

"No one died this time?"

"No one." He frowned. "Bell sat in his apartment that next day and wrote out scenarios from the killer's point of view, detailing how each murder was committed. He drew sketches of the place. He then spent the next night, from three to almost seven, sneaking around, trying to catch a glimpse of the killer and attempting to establish in his mind the look of the place at night.

"It rained that night. James Bell went up on the roof anyway. He thought that was the answer—he had heard people walking around on the roof before, though it had only been the maintenance men.

The ceiling had always seemed thin, to him, and the footsteps so heavy they might step right through into his apartment. It seemed the only possibility left. He stayed up there all night, crawling back and forth, waiting for someone to appear."

"No one did," Sorrel said softly.

Brad blinked. "In the morning, around seven, with the rain still falling, he came down as the police were forcing entry into one last unit—a tenant named Phillipa Meynes had not responded. With the patios and steps drenched from the rain, it was difficult to find the telltale sign of nefarious activity, but she hadn't been seen for days, so they made a check. And she was there, two weeks dead in her tub. First victim, last found."

He leaned back, mentally projecting the crime-scene pictures onto the fiberglass ceiling tiles. Broken vases, busted lava lamps, scattered beds, shredded books, blood- and alcohol-stained furniture, and dark soggy carpet. And the bathrooms, of course, where bodies, some clothed, some not, lay in the water and blood. "Five in all."

"It seems so obvious," Sorrel said. "They did it themselves."

"Not obvious in the heat of bad press," he replied. "The police were naturally furious. Though James Bell tried to avoid them, he was spotted coming down from the roof. They arrested him on the spot, both for his skin, and for the cuts the night on the roof had inflicted on his skin. They raided his apartment and found the sketches and written scenarios. They also found large amounts of various drugs—as an aspiring author, he had to have some source of income. He still had plenty of connections from his childhood in Birmingham, and the occupation allowed him to work a couple of hours each night and have the days to himself. The police questioned his neighbors and learned about his days staring out his window. They learned about his nocturnal habits, and they learned from one man that his car was wet every night when he returned. Since he had no family, no positive witnesses on his side, and a suddenly hostile management team at Serene Flats that had been destroyed by the affairs, he was quickly convicted of all the murders. He was sentenced to life in prison."

"He there now?"

Brad shook his head slowly. "No. Died there in 1992."

"And I'm guessing from the way you told it that you believe he was innocent."

"He was. He acted stupidly, but he was no killer. The opposite, in fact. He wanted justice for the killer and for the world—thus his little investigation and his desire to write crime novels where the bad guys go to jail."

"But how do you know?"

The kids were watching now. Their shuffling had slowed. Their gazes had livened. He had broken through into the backwater where their minds floated, and hooked them.

Tell them . . .

"Cults are terrible things. I know because I looked behind all the anomalies and all the faces and found the real killer. He called himself Jeremiah Johnson. Everyone else, all the dealers and mules, called him Disney. The man with the fairy dust. He ran a drug den outside Jackson. It was a nineteenth-century hotel on the outskirts, shrouded by sycamores outside and satin inside. Every night there was like something out of the Bible that needed fire and brimstone poured down on it."

Sorrel smiled.

"Ironically enough, some of the drugs that passed through James Bell's hands probably ended up at the Disney Castle. The people he was trying to save may even have used them. The connection was never made because the personal lives of these people were never delved into. They were just bad stats. Friendless victims whose lives held no importance. I looked at each of these people to make the connection to Disney and his Castle."

"Where did you meet him?"

"Disney eventually went to jail as well, though not until '79, after he was convicted of four blood-eagle-style killings in Louisiana. He was sentenced to thirty years and shipped off to Angola. I arranged an interview back in 2009, right before he got out. He was ravaged by cancer, and stared at the ceiling for most of the interview, but when I mentioned Serene Flats, he smiled and said, 'Such a curious name. I had to make it true. A place of peace.'"

Sorrel's smile had departed; Ms. Harper was popping her fingers with tiny snaps.

"He was a smooth, intellectual, spiritual sort of person. He would quote every philosopher and religious leader who ever existed as well as a few who haven't. He preyed upon the loneliness that cratered so many of his clients. He heard the pain knocking in their voices and answered the door. He sat with them and reminisced about their broken lives. He didn't promise to fix anything. He said they were broken. Futureless. But he told them their stories were beautiful. He promised to remember them. Each detail of each life, he would remember. It gave them fulfilment. He turned them from empty shells into evangelists. Willing, eager martyrs. And so, he chose a group from a housing project called Serene Flats."

Brad cleared his throat. "I . . . when I met him . . . when I sat across from him in that bare meeting room in Angola, I asked him why. *Why* he told them to kill themselves. Word for word, he said: 'Have you ever been loved? Really? In a way they'd die for you? Even from one person, it's quite a thing. But dozens? Hundreds? It's the light of a hundred suns, but instead of burning, you bask. And they're in love, too, with their own devotion.'" A clunky chuckle. "They had to place him in solitary confinement because of his influence on the other inmates. They even limited my time with him. I could see why. He asked if he could hold my hands. When I said no, he held them anyway. And then he said—" Brad stopped. Inside his head, Disney's voice—high, gentle, flavored by a childhood in Bayou La Batre—went on. *I know your pain. There's a past on your face. You carry it on your shoulders like it's your child. It's okay. You can share it with me. That's why I was born: to share people's pain.*

He trembled at the memory of those hands, those eyes. Those gentle lies, promising that if he just believed, all his burdens would be relieved. The call that had captured so many.

"Only one of his followers came forward with the truth. When the Castle was busted in '77, everyone was arrested. Disney wasn't there, but his disciples were. I was able to track down a fair number of them using police records, but only one would talk: a woman named Hilary Wegner. She remembered the group from Serene Flats and said she had no doubt what had happened—Disney convinced them."

Brad lowered his eyes. The pressure was gone. The voice was silent. The children were arrayed before him, utterly still.

In the back, Sorrel rose. He came into the light and stood where all the students could see him. "Cults." He lifted his hand and bunched the fingers together. "Like a fist inside your brain."

Turning back to Brad, he said, "Quite a story. Now, I'm sure we've taken up enough of your time."

Brad pushed himself off the desk. "If I could just ask you all some—"

"You're not from around here, are you?" Sorrel said.

"I live in Nashville—"

"I mean originally."

"No. I'm from Rhode Island."

"Rhode Island." Sorrel took his shoulder again. "I've never met a single person from Rhode Island. Do you kids know Rhode Island? Has Ms. Harper taught you about that state? Well, now you can say you've met someone from Rhode Island."

A smile, and the spell had been successfully dissipated along with his chance to question them. Warn them. Heads slightly cocked, they watched Sorrel usher Brad out.

Brad returned their stare for as long as he could. Then they were in the hall. Sorrel closed the door before beckoning him toward the entrance.

"So, what am I missing here?" Brad said.

"What do you mean?"

"All of that. At three in the morning, a room full of barefoot children learning second-grade material."

"We're making up for lost time." Sorrel walked down the hall, forcing him to follow. "The school was only recently reestablished."

"Recently? I think it's the law that kids have to—" He caught himself. Anger would lead to lockdown on Sorrel's part. "How about everyone else? What's everyone doing out there at night?" They were almost to the front door. Brad continued, "And how about yourself? Saw you working in that—"

"You have no idea how hot it is in there during the day. I spend a couple nights a week leveling the floor, fixing it up to get it on the state list of historic places. Maybe more fine folks like yourself would come visit us." The sheriff reached for the door handle.

He was throwing him out. Brad didn't have much time. "They'd have questions, too. Like about the woman I saw get buried, Marilyn Britain. She was special to the community. Why?"

Sorrel's fist hesitated on the handle. "Look, Brad, before I answer questions, I've got to find out what's going on myself. That's why I'd appreciate it if you'd lay off for a couple days while I work through this. Stay out of town, huh? Don't stir things up."

"That's why I'm here. To find out."

"No. You're here so maybe this community can get going again. But first, I need to get it back on the tracks." He tried to look placating. "Explore the house, the island. Maybe go down to the county seat again and look us up in the library."

Brad fought the bitterness in his mouth. "I did, same day I looked up the woman's doctor. You barely exist on the map, let alone in books."

"Maybe you'll help change that." He pulled open the door and a warm gust entered with the sound of rain. "Good night."

"One more thing. A name I've seen around. At the house, too: Adamah."

The way the door wavered beneath the man's grip made him think Sorrel was leaning all his weight on the handle. "That goes way back. The guy who built the house, DeWitt, came up with it. Kind of a founding family legend. Like a patron saint."

DeWitt. Founder's name was DeWitt. "A saint," he repeated. "And DeWitt *invented* it?"

"Well, do you believe in angels, Brad?" Another smile. "You have a good night. I'll get in touch in a couple days."

The door pushed him out. He walked through the downpour to his car.

Pausing by the door, he stood amid the drops, each one flashing as it passed through the LED glow of the building's mounted lights. Raising his chin a little, he parted his lips and let the warm drops splash across his tongue. The taste was like any rainwater: soft and vaguely earthy.

I had no doubt the body was still out there, in some bedroom or basement or back-porch freezer.

—"The House of Dust"
Southern Gothic

THE RAIN CAME down deep.

It gushed off the windshield beneath each swipe of the wipers. Even on the road headed back to the island, beneath the canopy of trees, the pavement danced with impacting drops. Lightning struggled to pierce the dense clouds.

By the wavering sliver of the headlights, Brad followed the craggy road until the turnoff to the house. Moss slapped the windows like sodden hair as he followed the drive. In the clearing, he turned sharply to pull up as close as possible to the porch, and the lights glared on a truck parked just before the steps.

His weariness evaporated.

Jerking the keys from the ignition, he threw the door open and ran up onto the porch. His heart slowed when he found the front door locked.

Turning, dripping, he examined the truck by the light from the upstairs study.

It was a nineties model Ford. A cage had been built up from the bed and bulging black trash bags ballooned between the bars. A worn white decal on the door read: IRONS' WASTE SOLUTIONS.

A clank came through the sound of the rain. He looked left. A cloaked figure moved past the far edge of the porch, dragging something along the ground.

The pistol. It was in the Accord, in the glove box.

Brad stepped back into the downpour but stopped on the second step.

It was too late. The cloaked figure was approaching, striding, dragging two trash cans. It stopped a dozen feet off. Water streamed off the hood of its shrouding green poncho as the figure studied him. A searing cicada chorus droned behind the sound of the rain.

Brad's lips parted to speak when the person moved. They removed the lids from the trash cans, lifting out two swollen bags. The person resumed walking toward him then, carrying the heavy bags. Brad retreated back onto the porch, rain prickling his skin. Then he caught sight of the face as the person reached the truck at the bottom of the steps.

It was the silver-haired woman who had approached his car last week, who had asked if he was the doctor, who had brought a shovel to Marilyn Britain's funeral. She flailed the bags into the back of the truck.

"Hello?" He started forward again.

Dashing the rain from her face, the woman glanced up and waved. "Good night, sir."

She disappeared around the truck. A moment later, the engine groaned to life and the twin fingers of her headlight beams found their way down the drive.

Brad stared. Diesel exhaust mixed with the humid air, churning his stomach, tightening his fingers.

Brad walked quickly back to the front door. He unlocked it and pushed inside.

All was still. And dark. As he'd left it.

The heavy oak door clunked shut behind him.

No, the air was different. That damp-earth smell was stronger.

Brad relocked the door. Going to the foot of the stairs, he felt around for the switch and flipped it. Overhead, the dusty fixtures flared to life.

His blood scurried back to panic speed.

Wet shoe prints had trampled the floor at the bottom of the staircase. His eyes fled upward, but the stairs themselves were free of marks. So far, no sign of intrusion toward the second floor.

He stepped around the end of the stairwell. The wet prints tracked up the hall to the back door. He followed them, conscious of the squeak of his own shoes on the boards. When he tested the knob, it did not turn. But when he tugged on it, the door opened. Broken lock.

That was how she had gotten in. And she must have known about it prior to coming. Perhaps the whole community did. Perhaps they all were planning to pay visits and prowl around the house, confident the new residents were asleep above.

Why?

The silver-haired woman would have used garbage collection as her excuse. But why had she entered, careless of her messy tracks? What had she sought?

Closing the door, he bore down on the knob a bit longer than was necessary, long enough to feel the metal rod inside start to bend. The silver-haired woman's middle-of-the-night visit must have some connection to the previous resident, Marilyn Britain. Either out of respect or revenge, her body had been exhumed, and now her house had been covertly entered.

Or—

His lips split as wild fancy galloped across his mind.

Or she dug herself up and came back here.

The unquiet dead, haunting her former home.

No. She was dead. You're grasping. That was just the trash lady.

Still, he was glad of the lights as he turned back into the hall and retraced his steps.

There had to be some sign. An indication of why the silver-haired woman wanted in: a missing item, a defacing mark . . .

He stopped. The intruder's tracks turned off and terminated before the basement door. A sheen of moisture clung to the rusty knob.

Brad stepped into the nook beneath the stairs.

With a squeaking hiccup, the door opened. The hallway radiance drained around him into the stairwell. The grimy footprints led down the stairs.

He got out his phone and turned on the flashlight. Far above, the rain on the roof sounded like someone exhaling without ever pausing to breathe in.

He went down.

The air in the tight corridor became colder as he went deeper.

Something fetid emerged as he turned right onto the last few stairs. A rotten smell. A stain laced into the dank atmosphere.

Stepping onto the hard-packed earth, he pushed back his wet hair and surveyed the heaps of refuse. There was no way he would notice if an item had been taken or moved. Still, he panned the light across the reliquary and then up to the vines, pale and twisted against the rafters.

Why did the intruder come down here? *And why did the vines?* Had she hoped to find something in all this?

As he turned, the floor gave just slightly beneath his heel. He shifted the light to his feet.

It wasn't easy to spot, but as he crouched down, thin faults in the dirt came into focus. His fingers traced them as his mind worked.

A sharp spade had been driven into the packed earth, and an almost perfect square foot removed. Once replaced, some liquid had been used to bond the seams in the floor; the displaced material had been pulverized and sprinkled across the floor.

Something had been buried.

Laying the phone aside, he braced his hands and clawed into the floor.

It came apart easily. He piled the dirt beside the hole. He uncovered the item eight inches down.

It was wrapped in wax paper and tube shaped.

His stomach was already tight as he turned it over. When he broke the tape and lifted the first fold of wax paper, the smell of rotten meat oozed forth. His teeth clenched against the rising bile as he continued unwrapping the package.

The dark, shriveled stump came first. A core of yellowish bone. Then came the rest of the hand. Limp fingers, oddly smooth. Shrunken to an almost childish size. Fingernails made prominent as the flesh shriveled and pulled away. Dirt thick beneath them.

Dirt from where she had dug into the flower bed out back.

It was the old woman's hand. Her body had been dug up, her hand severed and brought and buried.

Why?

Fresh sweat mixed with the rain on his scalp. A curse. A hex of some kind. Aimed at him, or his investigation, or—

Laughter broke into his consciousness. Wild laughter coming from high up in a throat that was high up in the house.

His fiancée.

He dropped the rotted flesh and his phone and ran for the stairs. At the top, he tore down the hallway and sprinted up the next flight. By the time he reached the top, the laughter had died down. It was gentle now, floating through the doorway of the main bedroom to meet him.

Of course he'd suggested they sleep in a different room. One of the smaller ones, the cleaner ones. She'd frowned as if he were joking and stretched their linens across the mattress in the master suite, ignoring the stains from the removed dirt. Now she was lying atop those stains.

Brad entered the room. Fading lightning stabbed through the drapes and leapt across the bed. She was stretched amid the fresh sheets.

Her hair spread around her shoulders, and her skin was gray. Her eyes were wide and roving in their sockets. And her hands lay at her sides, palms up.

An icicle slid down his back; it was the position of the old woman in her grave.

Her eyes rolled toward him and her jaws parted. Laughter gushed out.

Brad rushed to her. Clambering onto the bed, he pulled her up and shook her, slowly, then harder, and called her name. As she jostled, the blissful smile on her face caved in. Her eyes locked and her jaw clenched. Then she blinked once and was awake.

Drawing a rapid breath, she sneezed. When she saw him, she sat up abruptly. Then she began to shake silently. He reached for her face, but she looked away.

"My hands were . . . "

"Your hands are fine," he hushed.

"They were dirty," she rasped. "Filthy. And I was touching her in her casket. Smearing her with . . . and then she . . . got up! She climbed out of her casket!" The shaking grew more violent. "It was beautiful. I fixed her. And I knew I could fix all of them. Go back to Jasper and fix them so they never got hooked. I gave them . . . I brought them back—"

She broke off, then whispered, "Lie in my arms, Brad."

In his grimy clothes, he lay down beside her. She pulled him against her and rocked him while lightning from the dying storm brightened the curtains.

It had been the same, her third night in his Nashville apartment: the storm, the screaming, the dreaming of things she couldn't fix. Departed family. The hook that had nearly snagged her.

And now dreams of the girl every night since late April. The one whose funeral made her tear off the engagement ring.

The ring. Still lying out in the car, beside the gun.

Fear of using that gun had brought him here. To the town. To this house. It had brought both of them.

"Please, Brad," she breathed. "If I ever become addicted, please kill me."

Something lay behind my simple dichotomy of whether the old woman had been loved or hated. Something that ran far deeper.

—"The House of Dust"
Southern Gothic

"I HAD THE strangest dream last night," Missy said. "Well, a couple, but there was one . . . "

In the silence of the bedroom, she could hear the soft rasp of his razor in the bathroom. Everything around her was as musty as it had been the night before, but the sunlight pooling on the floor brought out all its potential. The fine oak alone made it a room fit for a queen.

A queen . . .

As the pieces of the dream coalesced, she drew the covers closer despite the warmth of the air.

"Tell me," he finally called back.

"You don't care about my silly dream."

"Tell me anyway."

She slid her fingers back and forth across the edge of the sheet. "It started with someone knocking. I got out of bed, thinking it was the front door, and went downstairs. But there was no one at the front door. The sound was behind me, so I went up the hall. You remember how the basement door was stuck yesterday? Well, there was knocking on the other side of that door. When I turned the knob, it swung open and people started coming up out of the basement—hundreds of them. They went out on the front porch, where you were sitting in a rocking chair. They picked you up and took you to a big tree in front of the house and—and there was a noose in the tree, and they hanged you. And then they lowered you into the ground, into a hole. Then they all lay down on the ground and went to sleep. I sat in a rocking chair and watched them sleep."

He stood in the doorway. "You didn't try to save me?"

"There wasn't time. The hole collapsed. You were dead."

"Well," he said, starting to turn away.

"They had a name for me in the dream," she said.

He paused. "Uh-huh?"

"Yes. They called me Queen of Hearts. What do you think it means?"

"I couldn't say." He went back into the bathroom.

Missy looked down. The sheets were clutched in her hands. Her dry, ugly hands still covered with dirt from the night before. Throwing back the covers, she got out of bed and looked down at the dirty bathrobe hanging from her body. She tightened the belt and straightened the collar, swearing to herself that she wouldn't cry when he insisted that the rest of her night had been a dream as well.

Mustering a smile, she entered the bathroom and came up behind him at the sink. Propping her chin on his shoulder, she said, "And how do I look this morning?"

His chin was jutting into the air, the razor on his throat. It paused as his eyes moved to her. "I told you to take a bath last night."

"And I did."

"Didn't do much good."

"I just *exude* dirt, don't I? That's why you wash your hands after we make love."

"You want to play?" He dropped the razor into the sink and turned around. His face became red and excited as he untied her robe. They always looked the same up this close.

"Sure," she said. "Truth or dare?"

He stopped. The redness deepened a bit. "Just say what you're accusing me of this time."

"This time? This time it's not verbal or physical abuse. It's *psychological*." She backed toward the tub. "Surprised I know about that? Yes, I read it in the encyclopedia."

He rubbed the remaining shaving cream off his face. "And I did this how?"

"Oh, simple stuff. Dumping dirt in my bathtub. Sticking daffodils in the floor."

"The pipes are bad. I'd expect some impurities in the water—there were when I bathed last night. There are right now in this sink. Come look."

"Impurities," she repeated. Bending down, she ran a finger across the tub floor. It came up caked with dirt. "And the flowers?"

He shifted. "I haven't seen any flowers."

"Of course, of course. That's what I meant by psychological abuse. So maybe I'll just oblige you, then, and go crazy." Using her finger like a tube of lipstick, she smeared the dirt across her mouth.

"Stop it!" He unfolded his arms and looked away. "Okay, I didn't want to tell you because I didn't want to unsettle you, but clearly that's already happened."

"Oh? What is it, baby?"

"We had a visitor last night. Someone skulking around the house. I was up late, you know, and I heard them moving around. They were inside. Came in through the back door."

She lowered her hand. "Who was it?"

"Someone from town." He stepped back to the sink and turned on the faucet, dashing water across his face. "Someone spying. That's the last thing we came here for. That's why I'm going to town." He left the tap on and moved away from the sink. "Now leave that running. It'll be clear in a minute and you can clean yourself up." As he entered the bedroom he added, "I'll be back in a couple hours."

Missy stood quietly for a bit. Frustration was a common feature in his voice. Anger, too. Both had been present just now. He wasn't lying about the intruder. A little of the relief she had felt last night at the idea he was innocent returned. *He's still hooked on me. Still needs me.*

But for how much longer?

She jammed the thought away. There'd been an intruder. And now she was alone.

The sink choked. Her eyes moved. The water was flowing clear now. She went over and gingerly lowered her hands into the basin. No unnatural force dragged them toward the drain. She cleaned her skin and wiped her lips. When she shut off the tap, the house was silent.

Uncertainty clamored inside her head, though. Her hands buzzed and her ears rang, just as they had after the gunshot in that closed-up room when she was ten.

She steadied herself on the sink until all the chaos calmed.

In the bedroom, she opened her suitcase and selected a pair of denim pants and a green short-sleeved button-down. She opened a fresh pack of gum and put two pieces in her mouth. Standing before the dresser, she ran a brush through her thick hair, then pulled it back, stretching the tie across her fingers until it almost snapped. It would be another day of sweat on her face and neck. Another day alone.

She opened the closet doors and examined the leftovers from the past resident. Shirts, dresses, shoes—all musty, many covered in horrible floral print. She pulled the old clothing out and put her own things in their place. He'd never skimped on buying her clothes. Not that she'd particularly wanted them. He had. *Clothes for his mannequin.*

But at least someone had cared to make her happy.

Missy squeezed her lips closed over a sigh and looked at the mess on the floor. Just leaving it wasn't an option; she'd have to find a place for all this stuff. Her eyes strayed to the rumpled bed, and a thought surfaced that made her smile.

Stripping the mildewed sheets from the bed, she bundled the clothes and shoes inside, then grabbed his cigarette lighter from his nightstand. She dragged the unwieldy sack into the hall and down the stairs. The weight almost bowled her over.

The sheets clawed at the porch, peeling up splinters, as she dragged them into the hot morning. In the clearing out front, she found a patch consisting mostly of gravel. Dropping the bundle, she crouched down with the lighter.

The thick cloth was loath to catch, and once it did the flames burned low and smoldering, and thick smoke billowed up. Missy stood back several feet and watched it, vaguely disappointed. Eventually, she shrugged and drew a breath, looking up at the trees and listening to the chirping bugs.

And suddenly she realized she had seen these trees just a few hours ago in the dream. But of course she had. She had dreamed of this place. Even so, it felt weird to stand where something so alien had happened.

It didn't happen.

Still, the ground seemed to ripple, beckoning.

She found herself walking toward the woods, in the footsteps of the people who had carried her fiancé to the hanging tree. Pushing through the thicket and the first tree trunks at the clearing's edge, she moved into the withered world of weeds and stunted bushes beneath the canopy. It was easy to see how this might once have been a parkland, with short grass between stately oaks. But skinny trees had shot up between the centuries-old ones, obstructing the view of the house from the road. She would have the place cleared out again, and—

Missy stopped. The dream tree loomed ahead. It was a huge thing, with ascending branches like a crown. Except for one. It jutted horizontally out fifteen feet above the ground. A noose dangled from that branch.

Something did happen here. At some point.

Unease wriggled through her stomach. She imagined the noose on her neck, closing off her air, drawing her toward the tree. Then she remembered the next part of her dream, the strangest part. Her gaze fled to the ground beneath the noose. As she stepped forward, the dirt thumped with a hollow sound beneath her tread.

The mouth of a crevasse appeared, a dark stab wound between the knuckles of two huge roots. It was wide enough to accommodate a bound body. A few spindly shoots of grass grew limply above the gap.

Shuffling as near as she dared to the hole, she stopped and surveyed the noose again. The rope was black with age. Vestiges of its final victim clung to the inside edge—the decayed material that had stuck and hardened when the neck and body finally separated and fell away.

Or were lowered down and left to rot.

Palms slick, she edged closer to the pit. Crouching, she braced herself on the root and leaned gradually out. The weary forest light revealed several feet of smooth sides unbroken by roots, but penetrated no farther into the darkness. How far down did it go?

Cool, mossy air, laced with the bitter scent of deep earth, stroked her face and twined around her straining neck. No matter the angle, nothing further revealed itself. A ridiculous idea skipped across the surface of her mind, and she called "Hello?" into the hole.

The slack air stirred against her face. The weeds around the hole trembled. An image of herself, as if seen by someone staring up from below, struck her vividly: her head and shoulders against the dim light, her features invisible. Missy through different eyes. Eyes that began climbing up the wall toward a silhouetted Missy. Toward *her.*

Missy's arms stiffened, pulling her away from the gap. She blinked hard, looking around at the woods, erasing the foggy image. Still, for a moment, things were fuzzy. She wondered if she had not actually awakened from the dream, if it was still going on.

But she was awake. She could feel the hard root against her knees, and the grime on her dry hands. It must have been something noxious coming out of the ground.

Cautiously, she sat forward and stuck her right hand over the hole.

The cool air from below collided with the warm air of the woods and created a mirage around her hand, smoothing the wrinkles away, softening the skin. Her lips parted. She started to withdraw her hand when the current of air pulsed. Then slowed. Then drained to almost nothing.

Then, renewed, it came rushing up from the deep. Again it petered out. And again it gushed. Becoming steady.

Missy pulled her hand back. Still withered. Standing slowly, she stared at the hole.

The few shoots of grass near the edge shivered as the air throbbed up from below. She had disturbed something. And now the ground was breathing. Or something underground was breathing.

She backed away as paranoia boiled up from the swishing weeds. The earth trembled with her every footfall, quaking like thin ice. The tree's great roots must have opened hollow pockets in the soil. She would break through. She would fall into the pit. She would join whatever else was lurking down there in the darkness. The conviction gripped her: It was following her from beneath the crust of earth, mirroring her movements, rootlike hands ready to burst through and snatch her.

Wheeling around, she fled, pushing through the foliage and vines and twiggy branches, raising her arms to shield her face as she burst through the shrubs along the tree line. She didn't stop. She walked through drifting smoke and climbed the porch. Leaving the front door wide, she went down the hall to the basement door beneath the steps.

She stopped in front of the door. This was where the dream began. The knob rattled as she laid her palm against it. It squeaked in its socket as it turned. The door groaned open.

Muddy air came out, flavored with decay. Nothing else.

Reaching into the darkness, she ran a hand along the left wall, then the right, until she found a switch. A bulb, mounted crookedly in the stairwell's sloping ceiling, came to life. In the yellow light, she looked down the stairs. They were surfaced by red peel-and-stick tiles, like the ones in the bathroom at the Club that always bubbled up when it rained.

A little way down, the passage turned right.

There's nothing down there. Nothing waiting. Nothing hunting you, Missy.

And it would be a good idea to find out how much storage space they had. Seeing the abandoned space would also reassure her that no lurkers were living down there, coming and going by night, playing cruel pranks.

Missy went down. For a second, the fear of falling into the darkness gripped her, but each foot landed solidly on the next step.

Not much of the light followed her around the bend. At the bottom, a long void stretched before her: a whole room beneath the dance hall. She shuffled across the dirt, clicking her tongue and judging the sounds that came back. All of them stayed close, so she decided the place was almost full. This was confirmed when she bumped against a bristling array of chair legs stacked on a table.

She stood still for a bit to rein in her panting, listening for movement amid the darkness. Satisfied that she was alone down there, she turned, heading back to the stairs and the light.

Something snagged her feet as she reached the stairs. She leapt onto the first step and whirled around. An overturned box was visible in the dimness.

Muttering a laugh, she reached out with her toe and teased open the flaps. She prodded inside the box and lifted something out. Small and pink. A tiny sock.

She snatched it off her foot and put it carefully back in the box.

She carried the box up to the little landing at the turn of the staircase and crouched down to examine the rest of its contents in the light. Baby clothes, many still marked with price tags. Shoes, and a few colorful rings with sliding beads. And at the bottom, a cheap notebook.

Lifting it out, she flipped through the pages. Mostly blank, entries written sparsely throughout, with a page torn out near the middle. But there was a name at the top of the first page: *Ellen King.*

Below, a few uncertain lines were scratched:

You told me to write what I see, Pastor, like St. John wrote what he saw on the Island of Patmos. I don't see the LORD. I see something that stands in the bedroom doorway at night. It comes toward me when I close my eyes. It must be a dream, because John doesn't see it. But then, he doesn't sleep much anyway.

Missy swallowed. "It must be a dream, huh?" In her crouch, her knees burned against the edge of the steps, but she didn't move. She remembered St. John and the Book of Revelation. In it, things happened in messed-up order. Just as they were now.

The knocking started as she reached for the next page.

Her eyes shot up the stairwell. The door at the top was still open. The sound came from beyond. From down the hall. Knuckles on wood, steady as dripping water. The front door was still open, too.

She stood up, shutting the notebook and gripping it tightly in both hands. The knocking bounced down around her as she climbed the stairs. *Tunk-tunk-tunk.*

At the top, she turned into the hall.

The sheriff stood in the front doorway. Dressed in a black suit, he carried a leather satchel over one shoulder and a brown box under one arm. Beneath his thick hair, dark sunglasses hid half of his slick face. His right hand knocked steadily on the doorframe.

He continued knocking, even as she approached. Smoke came in around him from the bedding fire in the clearing.

Missy wadded the notebook into a tube and stopped directly in front of him. "I guess that's the encyclopedia I'm expecting?"

A grin strained Ezra's too-smooth flesh. "I have a delivery here for a Ms. Missy Holiday."

"So, now you're a postman."

"Only for this special delivery."

She was careful to avoid touching his fingers as he handed the package over. Had it been him after all, with the daffodil, with the dirt in the bathtub?

Holding the box close against her chest, she reached up to shut the door.

But his foot moved to block it. "Little place like this, I don't have too much of a schedule to keep. I'd like to speak to you for a minute. Could I come in?"

"No."

Behind those sunglasses, she was sure he wasn't blinking.

She waited until he backed away before stepping outside and pulling the door shut. She stood against it, still clutching the box. "What do you want?"

"To talk."

"About what?"

"What're you burning out there?"

"Just some trash."

Unslinging the satchel from his shoulder, he grabbed the nearest rocker and dragged it closer. "Would you like to sit?"

"No. What do you want to say?"

"I want to make sure you're all right. Seemed a bit upset last night."

"I'm doing well, thank you."

"You still seem . . . "

She smiled at him pleasantly.

"What happened to your tooth?" he asked.

"What?" She let go of the smile.

"The corner of your front tooth is chipped. The right one."

"Oh." Her tongue darted, feeling the place. "It's been that way since I was eight."

"How did it happen?"

She worked her gum forward and began chewing again. "I don't know you."

He shrugged—*fair enough*—and stepped back to look along the front windows. "Well, have you ever lived in a place like this before?"

"Why?"

"I'd like to know your plans for the place. Sometimes people model their homes on the places they grew up in."

"Well, I know I'd like a couple more locks on the back door."

"Were there a lot of locks on the doors of your childhood home?"

She switched her gaze to the police cruiser sitting out by the steps. Its two-tone paint was spotless, the silver siren on the roof gleaming beside the fat red flashing light. "If you're asking if I like to be left alone, the answer is yes. You've delivered the package. I have things to do."

"Okay," he said softly. "But I didn't deliver everything." He lifted a stack of envelopes from the satchel and approached, holding them toward her.

"Just leave them there." She motioned vaguely.

He paused, face inscrutable. Then he retreated a few feet and left the stack beside the rocking chair.

"Good afternoon," he said, and went down the steps.

As the car left the clearing, she advanced to the pillar at the top of the stairs and watched him drive away. She listened until the engine had diminished up the tired road. Then she went back to the rocking chair and sank slowly into it.

She hadn't sat in any of the chairs until now; they were actually quite comfortable. The wadded notebook and the box flopped down in her lap as she relaxed her arms.

Bending over, she gingerly retrieved the stack of letters. The top one was simply addressed, *The House, Angel's Landing*.

The rest were the same.

Her fingers went stiff. With such vagueness, they could only have come from the town. And by the sheriff's manner, they could only have been written to her.

Brittle skin split as she cut herself while opening the first letter. The thick paper inside wicked away the blood.

She unfolded it and read the simple lines. Then the last part of her dream came true. Printed in pen were the words: *Welcome, Queen of Hearts*.

That name—from her dream.

There were eighteen more letters.

Her heartbeat pulsed through her fingertips. The folded papers fell around her chair like wounded birds as she ripped into each one.

They were all written the same, and said the same.

Welcome, Queen of Hearts.

Missy gathered the letters and carried them to the burn pile. They wilted and caught fire. But as she folded her arms, an odd flavor of excitement bled into the fear quickening her heartbeat.

She looked back to the porch. A smile pulled at the sides of her mouth as she watched the chairs rocking in the breeze.

Although I had taped wax paper back in place around the hand, I had to stop halfway to town and wrap it in a Walgreens bag and put it in the trunk because of the smell.

—"The House of Dust"
Southern Gothic

THREE SUMMERS WAS empty that Sunday morning.

At the Texaco, a man with blue cataract eyes recognized the description of the garbage truck and said it belonged to Jezebel Irons. This time of day, she would be across the river at the waste facility. He gave directions and then frowned when asked where everyone else was.

"They had to go to church."

After crossing the Locust River Bridge out of Three Summers, the way to the facility was an inconspicuous little turnoff from the main road, perhaps a quarter mile into the woods. Weeds sprouted from the faulted pavement and formed a thick fringe along the road. Lichen-covered tree trunks hunched together and blocked the river from view. The sallow smell of rot thickened the air, growing stronger as he drove. Brad's lips pinched together and his eyes, dry and tired after his sleepless night, searched the curves of the road. Staying clean would make rest impossible for a while, but a lack of Prozac wasn't the only thing keeping him awake. It was the thing in the trunk. And his fiancée's dreams.

She just needs time to adjust. Heal.

After two miles, a chain-link gate—open just enough to allow a car entrance—jutted out of the woods to obstruct the road. Brad edged through, leaving the wooded gloom and entering a vast gravel lot that lay along the riverbank. To his right, the lot stretched to the base of the nearby ridge. A few thousand feet off, the derelict tower he had seen that first day from the graveyard rose beside the ridge. Faint words were visible across its oxidized side: ADAMAH MINING CO.

Below the tower, the mouths of dead mine shafts pockmarked the hillside, vestiges of a past industry. Large newer buildings constructed of white corrugated metal occupied much of the level ground between the ridge and the river. Block letters on the nearest building tagged it as part of Irons' Waste Solutions.

Rows of fans were mounted beneath the eaves of these buildings, sucking the hot, sour air from the interiors and blowing it across the gravel lot. A parking lot along the inside of the chain-link fence held a fleet of trucks similar to the one that had visited their house the night before.

Smoke rose from a point farther in the complex.

The roads between the processing buildings were marked deeply by truck tires. Brad steered through them, heading toward the smoke. He emerged in an open area near the base of the ridge, where he stopped the car.

A smoldering mountain of trash occupied the center of the clearing. Blackened debris made up the base of the mound, and shredded pinkish-white heaps were piled on top. Bitter smoke billowed from simmering crevasses, bearing ash into the sky. The flakes drifted down again and settled across the windshield.

Taking out his phone, he rested it on the steering wheel and snapped a picture. He spotted activity on the ridge and raised the lens.

A hundred yards off, a yellow CAT wheel loader, its scoop trailing clumpy gray powder, was descending a dirt track from one of the mine shafts. The rumble of its engine faded through the silence. A gouge in a charred section of the cremation heap showed where it had taken its last bite.

Climbing from the car, Brad walked back to the trunk and took out the Walgreen's bag. He placed it on the hood and stood beside it.

The wheel loader came off the track and drove into the clearing. It powered down. The door opened, and the woman from last night climbed down. The same woman who'd rapped on his car window when he'd first arrived in Three Summers. She pulled a dust mask off her nose and mouth and glanced at him, running a hand through her short silver hair.

Abruptly, she approached. "Good morning, Doc. Something I can do for you?" It was a dull, thin table knife of a voice, but the glimmer of a smile twisted her lips, remembering his lie.

Brad tried to look contrite. "It's Bradley Ellison. I'm sorry for misleading you that day."

She stopped a dozen feet away from him and tugged off a pair of gloves, eyeing him in a way that said she knew that, too, was a lie. "Misleading, yeah. Medicine is an area that you might not want to pretend about. But we were all a little crazy that day. I should have recognized right away you weren't the doctor, but so few folks drive through here, and the timing was right, so I thought you must have come for a reason." Mud clung to her fingertips, and a gleam lurked in her pewter eyes.

"Well, today I just came to return this." He held out the bag.

"What have you got there?"

"Take a look."

"That's okay."

"No, really. It shouldn't startle you. You're obviously comfortable with rotting things."

Jezebel studied the ground for a minute, pushing the gloves into her back pocket, then stepped past him.

He blinked, then set the bag in the shade below the car and followed her. "Can I at least ask why you brought it?"

She was moving down a gravel avenue between the corrugated metal structures that led toward the river. Humidity seeped from the grimy ground and bled off potholes brimming with brown water from the previous night's rain. "Why'd you say you were the doctor?" A quick laugh, as if the answer were obvious. "No, that's okay. Ask anything you want."

Brad swallowed. "I know you dug Marilyn Britain's body up. Why bring a piece to the house?"

"Look, I'm sorry I scared you. I was hoping it might ease things up for you and your wife."

"That"—he had caught up to Jezebel, but he paused to point back toward the Walgreens bag—"was meant to help us?"

Jezebel didn't stop. "Again, didn't mean to scare you. Or her."

Brad pulled out his phone, turned on the mic, dropped it into his breast pocket, and caught up again. "Do you think you could explain that?"

She shrugged. "Local superstition. Burial appeases the one below."

"The *one* being?"

"The angel of the earth."

He hesitated, then ventured a guess. "Adamah."

"The angel Adamah, yes."

"Adamah has been a part of this community since the beginning."

"That's right."

"And Adamah lives in the ground."

"Uh-huh."

"And I'm assuming you buy into this superstition, at least partially?"

"I do."

Gravel crunched. "So explain why you would dig up the old woman and chop her into pieces. That doesn't sound like a good way to appease anyone."

The woman tugged at the mask hanging around her neck. "I'm going to ignore the way you phrased that because I think it's clear you have no idea what you're talking about."

He grimaced. "How'd you come by the hand? Did you act alone or were other townsfolk involved?"

"Since I doubt you'll report in good faith," she replied, "I don't think I'll divulge specifics."

"You know I could take all this to Sorrel."

"Do it. I haven't admitted anything."

She was right. Too hasty, too desperate.

Lead into it. "Tell me about your establishment," he said. "Seems sizable."

"That's right. We collect ninety percent of the waste in Henderson county, as well as some collection in surrounding counties—Carroll, Decatur, Madison. We bring it all back here: sort through it, burn some, contract with recyclers for some, bury the rest."

"Bury it in the mine."

"That's right. Dump the ashes, too."

"Adamah doesn't mind that? Dumping trash down where he lives?"

Jezebel didn't smile. "I actually take it seriously. I try to be respectful. If you saw how waste is handled in most places, you'd understand what I mean: trash just thrown in random holes. But here we've got an exhausted mine that runs deep. We're refilling those tunnels. Healing . . . healing wounds, almost." She seemed uncomfortable with the analogy and hunched her shoulders beneath her denim jumper.

"The mine bore his name, though, from what I can see." Brad paused and glanced back at the rusted tower and the faded name. "It's like a monument."

"Well, all of them end. A new one will come."

"New one? New monument?" He remembered the Adamah Theater in town. And Adamah Road. There were other places, too. Different structures, but all named the same. Variations on the same theme. As if nothing were enough.

His eyes moved to the dark column of smoke. "What year did the mine close?"

"2000."

2000.

A pebble leapt away from his toe—*tap, tap, tap*—and the echo of distant heat flared across his skin. For an instant, he saw a figure standing beside the smoldering cremation fire. No, standing *in* the fire. A figure dressed in orange. Its claw of a hand reached toward him.

Brad turned away, running his knuckles across his forehead. He and Jezebel resumed walking. He said, "You must employ a lot of people to keep an operation like this running."

"Right around eighty. All from town."

"Looks like you're the last real business left."

"That's true enough. When the mine shut down, I got permission to use the land and set up operations."

"You say you got permission. Didn't you have to pay?"

She shrugged. "Owner let me have it. Nothing else it could be used for. The ground was tired. And empty."

"Did local folks own it?"

A vague nod. "Local folks. They sold it off in the fifties, but the company that took over was shut down by the state prosecutor because of unsafe working conditions. So, the locals took over again and ran it until it was exhausted in 2000."

"What were the owners' names?"

"Originally, it was the Larkins."

"And after the company got kicked out?"

"It got muddled after that."

"I like muddle."

She was silent.

"Who got the money? A mine like this had to rake in millions. But when I look around the town, I don't see much sign of affluence. Same goes for the old house."

Jezebel shook her head. "A whole lot went into legal battles. The company that got kicked out wasn't happy with the way things went. They fought it for a long time, and she—"

"She?"

Jezebel Irons rubbed her nose with the back of her hand, then waved the hand. "Yeah."

"Marilyn Britain."

"Yeah."

"The woman who occupied the house before we came. She seemed to have some strong connection to the community. And to you."

They were at the river now. The odor of mud and decomposing plants cloaked them.

After years of construction on the lot, gravel had spilled and collected down the bank and stuck in the mud, lying now in mossy mounds just beneath the surface, interrupting the current and dimpling the surface of the thick green water.

"What did she do to get dug up and cut up and reburied in her own basement?"

Jezebel was staring fixedly across the river. Music came from the direction of her stare, and Brad followed her gaze to the white church on the opposite shore. The windows must be open, for he could faintly hear the organ playing. He recognized the tune. They had played it at the funeral of his fiancée's patient. "The Old Rugged Cross." The singing had died as they advanced up the aisle that day. The eyes had turned. Then the screaming started.

"Queen of Hearts," she said, turning toward him to answer his question.

He blinked. "Queen of Hearts?"

"They have a special connection to Adamah. This place, this bit of the world, has always suffered from a festering unknown. A heaviness. A burden." She tapped her chest and looked at him. "You ever felt that?"

The music wafted. Like the hymn he'd heard despite his headphones at that funeral much longer ago. Meaningless condolence that could not lift the pressing weight. "Sometimes," he said.

"The Queen soothes that. But Sorrel . . . " She motioned across the water. "He wants things different. He always resented her. So he took her and threw her in that grave. Wasted the . . . " She did not finish.

"Why did he resent her?"

"I don't know. She didn't really want to have him. But she didn't want a procedure, either. So he was just sort of there, growing up in that house."

"Marilyn Britain was his mother?" He had vaguely suspected something like this, but it still came with a jolt. It made their drive to the cemetery with her body seem even more bizarre.

"Yeah. I think he identified her with her role. And he resented the role."

"The role as Queen of Hearts. Is there another Queen of Hearts?"

"Not yet. But there will be. There always will be."

"And how is the connection with Adamah formed?"

Jezebel's arm twitched; she checked her watch. "If you'd like to stop by my house someday, I'd be happy to talk more. I'm usually there midafternoon."

Brad withheld a sigh. "That'd be great. Where do you live?"

"The house up on the hill at the end of Adamah Road."

"I know the place."

She paused, then added, "If you're going over to the church, you can keep driving up the riverbank a bit and you'll come to Hanging Elephant Bridge. Used to be railroad, but we modified it to accommodate cars."

He resisted questioning her about the odd name. "Thanks. I'll check it out."

"Tell your fiancée I said hello."

At Hanging Elephant Bridge, thick boards had been laid across the rails and buttressed by beams from below. The boards creaked as his tires passed over them. There was little clearance to either side, and no barrier protected the edge. Squeezing the residual unsteadiness from his fingers, Brad edged the car across. Sixty feet below, the river crawled along its course.

On the far bank, Brad followed the gravel-covered tracks until the road abandoned them and bent down through the woods to Simmons Pike.

There, to his right, the road dipped to pass through a tunnel beneath the tracks on its way west. Brad turned left, the way toward the church. The woods thinned out as he drove, allowing pockets of meadow and glimpses of the river. Soon, the spire appeared above the treetops.

In the churchyard, cars clustered around the vine-wrapped building. Sorrel's old police cruiser crouched by the doors.

Brad pulled in beside it and stepped out. The smell of smoke was blessedly absent on this side of the water. As he approached the door, he glanced out at the graveyard. A mound of orange dirt marked the refilled grave, doubtless Sorrel's hasty work.

Closer by, a great heap of boards lay beside the building's southwest corner, not far from the entrance. Torn-up flooring, by the look of it. A few tenuous fingers of kudzu reached from the building to claim the mound. He took a picture.

Phone in hand, he found one of the church doors partially ajar and slipped through.

Inside, there was no floor. Bare earth, hard and dusty from years without rain, stretched smoothly beneath unbolted pews and rows of unshod feet.

There was only one light on in the building, a very small one up front, mounted on the pulpit. The pastor stood behind the pulpit, but the light was angled so only his weathered hands and the Bible they held were visible. White curtains crumbled the noontime sunbeams coming through the windows. As his eyes adjusted to the gloom, Brad realized he had never seen curtains across church windows before.

Hesitantly, he walked to the unoccupied backmost pew and slipped into it.

The pastor was reading a familiar passage from Ezekiel Chapter 37. "So I prophesied as I was commanded: and as I prophesied, there was a noise, and behold a shaking, and the bones came together, bone to his bone. And when I beheld, lo, the sinews and the flesh came up upon them, and the skin covered them above. But there was no breath in them."

His voice spilled down from the pulpit and flowed across the congregants as slow and steady as the river outside. Brad searched for Sorrel among the people. Most were quite oddly positioned. Shoulders were slumped. Heads tilted, most down, chins against their chests; a few lolling back, throats drawn tight, faces turned toward the sluggishly swirling ceiling fans.

All the eyes were closed. The lips slack. But they were not asleep. The cadence of their breath was too rapid, their eyes briefly and sporadically flickering open.

They were pretending. The people of Three Summers were sitting in this little church on this sunny afternoon, listening to the pastor and feigning slumber.

Brad raised his phone. He tapped off the flash and the shutter sound and positioned the view.

As the image froze on the screen, a hand fell like a brick on his shoulder.

He dropped the phone. It thumped to the dirt floor. A few eyes opened and heads turned. He just had time to snatch the device up before a fist was at the back of his collar, dragging him to his feet and into the aisle. He knocked the arm away and spun around.

Sorrel was standing in the gloom. He pointed to the door.

Heat prickled on Brad's forehead.

Drawing a deliberate breath, he rubbed the phone on his shirtfront.

The sheriff was on him again in an instant. Grabbing the front of his shirt, he hauled him toward the door, shouldered it open, and shoved him into the sun. He came out after him.

"I told you not to come around here! I told you that *last night!*"

Brad pushed his glasses up on his nose. His hands were shaking. He hid it by folding them behind his back, still gripping the phone. "I found something. As sheriff, I thought you should know."

Sorrel's hand became a fist, closing the door. "What's that?"

"Come see."

Sorrel's shoes crunched behind him as they crossed through the gravel. At the car, he opened the trunk again and took out the Walgreen's bag. "Open it."

Sorrel snatched the bag and pulled the handles apart. His head turned as the smell hit his face.

"That's one piece of your puzzle," Brad said. "I know where the rest is." The words tasted bitter immediately after he said them. *That was his mother.*

Sorrel considered for a while, holding the bag open, eyes moving between it and his opponent. Finally, he closed the handles and folded them carefully around the bundle. "I apologize. You opened the curtains quicker than I was prepared for. Pardon me for flinching." He nodded back toward the church. "Let me invite you back inside."

"No, thank you."

"Aw, come on, Brad. After services I can take you on a tour of Three Summers. Point out all the old buildings, give you what little history I know. Maybe even introduce you to a few folks."

"Feed me the soft version." He switched his hands to his pockets. "No, thanks."

"I'm trying to be helpful."

"You're trying to get your version told: a backwater town with a few quirks coming into the modern age, or something like that. But why do you think people read this stuff? Why do you think I get paid to do it again, and again, and again, and. . . You think they care about the names of a hundred-year-old family, or the date a building was put up, or what percent of the kids are below-average readers? They want blood. And I know there's blood in this soil."

"Well, where's there not?" Sorrel's voice became dangerously gentle. "Where's there not? Huh? What town? What square foot of earth? Have you checked your own backyard, Mr. Ellison?"

The step Brad took away from him was involuntary. He caught himself before he took another. "Yeah. I have."

Sorrel rearranged his hold on the bag. "This. . . this is the kind of stuff that lost me my brother. This is what I'm trying to get rid of. And it's not easy. Because it's *old*. Its roots go way down. But I want you on my side. Your fiancée, too. I want you two to look after each other while you're in that house."

"So tell me what Adamah is."

The man kept looking at the bag. "It's this. It's angel worship that got out of hand."

"Do you believe in it?"

"Who cares what I believe?" He nodded between earth and sky. "Who cares if I believe in what's down there or what's up there?"

"Because that changes what happens right here."

"Things happen everywhere. Either way."

"Here," Brad said. "What happens here?"

Sorrel folded his arms. "And do the lives of the people you report on get better after you've shredded their reputations?"

"This can't be contingent."

"This has to be contingent."

"I don't work that way." Brad shrugged and backed slowly away, hoping the man would relent. "I just don't. I'm sorry. I need the truth. Unvarnished."

Sorrel did not budge. "I'm sorry, too."

"I'm gonna keep looking."

"Fine. While you're doing that, don't forget to look after *her*."

Brad squinted, raising his arms silently: *What does that mean?*

The man shook his head and turned away. Brad got in the car, slamming the door. From behind the hazy windshield, he watched the sheriff walk into the cemetery with the bag containing his mother's hand. He kicked the floorboard and started the engine.

As Brad turned off Simmons Pike onto Adamah Road, his phone rang. No caller ID.

"Brad Ellison," he answered.

"Mr. Ellison?" A breathless voice. "This is Brooke Carney. From the Henderson Public Library? You came in to see us last week."

He slowed the vehicle. "Yes. Thank you for getting back in touch."

"I know it's Sunday, but . . . we have some new items. I think you should see them. Can you drive down this afternoon?"

"I can be there in half an hour."

"Good." She hesitated. "Yes, I think you really should see this."

"Be there soon." He tossed the phone into the passenger seat and pressed on the gas.

As he passed the turnoff to the island, he considered stopping by to check in on his fiancée, but decided against it.

It seemed to me then that if I understood what Adamah was, I would understand everything that sprung from this being. And so, initially, I paid little attention to the "Queen of Hearts" mythology. That was a mistake.

—"The House of Dust"
Southern Gothic

MISSY TOOK THE journal into the dance hall.

The room was still a mess, of course. Shrouded furniture rung the outer wall and dust crusted everything, the floor especially. Motionless years had stuck the stuff down good, like hard-water residue left behind on glass. Her feet left no marks as she moved toward the fireplace. Dust on the mirror above the mantel turned her reflection to a blur. She sat down at the piano, closed the lid across the keys, and placed the notebook atop it.

So much work to do, but first this. First to find out how a previous resident had dealt with the mansion. "How did the house treat you, Ellen King?" she murmured.

A yellowed price tag was fossilized to the back of the notebook. She ran her dry fingers across it, then let the book flop open to a random entry.

They are coming out of the floor now—and the walls. They're coming for me. I love you, dearest John. Our baby loves you, too. I say this because I'm not sure either of us will be able to say anything when you return.

Missy flipped back page after page, until she found another entry. *"The king shall come when morning dawns."* *I love that old hymn, Pastor. It has sustained me through these endless nights. John can't sleep, so I stay up with him. I see the dark thing moving in the hall, mocking my faith by covering its head and its feet and still reaching for me, like a perversion of Isaiah 6.*

"What's Isaiah 6?" she asked aloud. Grandmama had probably read it at some point. There might be a Bible upstairs in his desk, but she didn't feel like looking right now.

The pages of the book turned loudly, dryly beneath her fingers, until she came to one without words. Her hand paused.

Here was a drawing, skillfully rendered, of a faceless six-armed figure inside a circle. She knew that symbol. Her eyes rose to the murky mirror.

There was the piano. There she was, seated behind it. And there was something standing just behind her. Arms, many arms, extended. Narrow fingers touching the back of her head.

Air rushed from Missy's lungs. The bench screamed back as she stood. The notebook flapped off the piano as she spun around.

Nothing.

Only sunlight occupied the front of the room. She sank back onto the bench. She turned toward the mirror.

Nothing. A trick of the distorted glass, swelled up as it was to form the same symbol that was drawn in the book. And there was her scared little face.

Wagging her finger at the face, she picked up the book and scooted back to the piano. Her brittle skin ached as she worked her fists to steady herself. She turned more pages.

An early entry said: *The island seemed so perfect when we first came. The daffodils perfumed the air, and the locusts sang all night, and soft rains turned the field and the forest bright green. I imagined it like*

Beulah in Pilgrim's Progress, *the land where angels walk. DeWitt, the man who built it, even named it "Angel's Landing." But did he mean to evoke those who fell?*

Hunkering down, Missy turned to the middle pages, scanning the poor woman's jumbled thoughts. They made the same amount of sense read in any order: *not much.* She read the entry just prior to the torn-out page.

John says it is time for us to leave. I'm loath to think he triumphed over us, but I cannot continue in this miserable state, especially with the baby coming. It must have gained purchase here long ago.

It. What was "it"? The final entry came only halfway through the book. She turned through the rest of the pages, expecting to find them blank. And most of them were. But near the end, something strange began to happen.

She sat up.

A plant stem, drawn as two parallel lines and shaded just slightly for dimension, sprang up suddenly on one of the pages, climbing to the top of the paper. The page whispered as Missy turned it. The stem curved down the following page and threaded along the bottom onto the next sheet. And then the next. And on and on, up and down, twining, pulling Missy's fingers through the remainder of the book until there was just one page left. She slipped her finger beneath it and turned.

A daffodil exploded across the paper, drawn in exacting detail. Just beneath it, Ellen King had written, *She breathes for me now.*

Missy shut the book.

From far away, a howl rose.

And was cut short.

No. She shook her head. It was part of the slow nightmare the journal had painted in her head. She stood up, arms at her sides. She wouldn't participate.

The howl came again. The direction was discernible this time. The backyard.

Leaving the notebook on the piano, she walked up the hall. The sharpness of her senses dazed her. She winced at every shift in the floorboards.

Again, the wail rose, ending in a shriek.

Something was in pain. Something real. Her footsteps quickened.

Passing through the dining room, she stopped at the back door. Her breath fogged the glass. There was nothing on the porch. Beyond, the screen door was latched. She squinted.

A small figure crouched in one of the old flower beds. The wail came again, and the figure drew back a hand and struck at something in the weeds. Missy opened the door and stepped out cautiously. She crossed the abandoned porch and opened the screen door. She squinted again. A person.

The high grass obscured the stranger's actions. But judging from the dirt flying in the air, Missy guessed the person was digging. She descended the steps and the shrieks continued.

Her walk became a sprint. As she approached the crouching figure, a raspy little voice became audible between the wails from the grass: "Shut up, now, shut up! Only way, kitty, only way. Sorry, but it's the only way. Queen of Hearts and all, you know? Queen of—"

"What are you doing?" Missy barked.

A little boy looked back at her. Black hair hung in his eyes. "Oh, you must be *herrrr!*" He threw the shovel aside and dragged a writhing cat across the ground. A small metal bucket stood beside him. "Be done in a second!"

He stuffed the shrieking creature into a messy hole. Pressing one hand onto the cat's back, he used the other to rake dirt clods on top of the animal.

It was surprisingly quick work. In just a few seconds, only the writhing head and tail remained above the surface.

It took that long for Missy to assure herself she was seeing correctly. Ignoring the daffodils that poked up through the weeds, she forged into the flower bed. Pinning the half-buried cat with one hand, the boy dumped the bucket of water over it.

"You horrible little bastard!" She smacked him so hard her hand ached. "What are you doing?"

The boy sprawled backward in the dirt, clutching his head. "I did it for you!"

As she lunged toward him, he picked himself up and leapt away. "This is all for you!" he shrieked.

"Get out of here!"

The boy turned and fled.

Immediately, she crouched down and scraped the mud off the cat. The dirt stuck to her fingers, easing the ache in her withered skin.

The poor creature didn't struggle as she lifted it from the muddy hole. It hung limply in her hands, eyes wide, as she examined it. Shock. It must be in shock.

"You poor thing," she whispered. "Why would he bury you alive?"

A different figure occupied my thoughts, one that was gradually emerging from the gloom. One that I could now give the name Adamah.

—"The House of Dust"
Southern Gothic

BRAD PARKED HIS car in front of the library. It was a single-story dark-brick structure, just off Church Street, the sunbaked central avenue through the Henderson county seat. He cleaned his glasses in the car and jammed his shirttails into his pants before crossing the empty parking lot to the entrance.

A woman in her mid-forties paced just inside the library's entrance. Black-rimmed glasses rested atop a prominent nose, and thick brown hair was combed down in two apostrophes around her face. She unlocked the door when she saw him. "Thanks for driving down, Mr. Ellison."

"What's changed?" he asked.

Rubbing her palms together, the woman led him into the unlit library. Gray carpet scuffed beneath his shoes. The air was papery and pleasantly cool after the shut-up car. It was the same hazy atmosphere he had retreated to on autumn days after school when he was twelve.

Headphones playing static, he would log on to a computer and click through images that drew the looks of others: fire, collapsing buildings, billowing smoke.

His reminiscing had been especially acute since last Sunday, since trying to down the pills. He blinked as the woman ducked behind the circulation desk.

"Ms. Carney?"

"Please, just Brooke." She came around the desk holding two pairs of white silk gloves.

"You've acquired some new items since last Monday?"

"We . . . yes. In fact, we received them just a few hours after you were here."

Brad inclined his head.

"Yeah, it's weird," she said. "The whole thing is weird. I think . . . I think you should know who this man is." She laid the gloves on the desk and pulled out her phone. It lit her pensive face as she scrolled and tapped for a few seconds before holding it out. "This is Richard Hettinga."

On the screen, two people stood where Brad and Brooke were standing now, leaning against the circulation desk, smiling. One was Brooke Carney. The other was a short man with a high reddish forehead and a white goatee. He was dressed in plaids and denim and his teeth were bad. His cheeks were thin. His eyes were bottomless.

"Richard is a great patron of ours," Brooke continued. "We have the Tennessee Room here that chronicles a great deal of local history, and he has helped us track down and acquire a huge number of documents. But his prime interest is the place you're investigating: Three Summers."

She lowered the phone. "I didn't tell you about him last week because he's . . . I'll just say it, he's a paranoid person. He regularly thinks someone is standing behind him when there's no one there. And he fears that people are hunting for the same information he is. He thinks if they reach it first, they'll destroy it. Almost like a cover-up. But it all pertains to hundred-year-old records, so I've never understood why he's worried."

Brad frowned. "And he suddenly decided to surrender these items?"

She retrieved the gloves, twisting them together. "Seems so. Just before closing on Monday. He gave me the box and told me to keep it safe. He seemed flustered, so I asked what was going on. He said he'd been hearing a voice for a long time. He said he heard it through his feet. I'm not sure what that means. Anyway, he said that the day before, the voice had gotten louder and changed direction, so he was going to Atlanta."

"Why Atlanta?" Brad asked.

She shrugged. "He'd be livid with me for telling you this, but I'm honestly not sure what else to do. He's been a friend for years and he wasn't well when he left here. He may have suffered a stroke, and that was contributing to his behavior. And now he isn't answering his phone, which he always did before."

He came in the day after the old woman died. "Did he say where in Atlanta he was going?"

Brooke shook her head.

"If you can give me his contact, I'll try to get in touch."

She nodded and handed her phone back. He took down Richard Hettinga's number, then said, "Let's see the stuff he left."

Brooke relaxed her hold on the gloves and handed him a pair. Slipping them on, he followed her across the main floor toward the children's corner. Sunlight, turned watery by its passage through glass, came in behind a bank of picture books. It slanted across an area hemmed in by low shelves, across a low table, which sat atop a blue rug bordered by the letters of the alphabet. There was a small box atop the table.

The librarian motioned and they sat in the child-size chairs. The box was no taller than Brad's thumb. He could feel his pulse in his fingertips. At last something definite. Citable. *Real.* "You can open it," Brooke said.

Brad pulled the box toward him. Dust motes rose through the sunlight as he delicately lifted the lid. Inside lay a stack of four orange ten-by-thirteen envelopes. Drawing them out, he found names written on each: *DeWitt, McCloud, Larkin,* and *Recent.*

"When I put everything back, I tried to remember the order he had things in," Brooke mentioned. "I might have confused DeWitt and McCloud."

Pushing the box aside, he laid the envelopes out.

"DeWitt founded everything, so he's first. And obviously 'Recent' comes last." He pushed the other two around. "We should be able to date them by the material."

He picked up the envelope labeled "DeWitt" and uncinched the clasps. His gloved fingers drew out the contents: a newspaper clipping, a loose photograph, and a small stack of photographs bundled together with a hand-drawn map.

The map depicted the island, Angel's Landing. The house and the road—dividing the forested southern half from the fields in the north along the river—were marked. Seemingly random places in the field were numbered 1, 2, 3, 4, and 5.

He turned to the bundled photos. Five of them. Likewise marked. They displayed ragged, shapeless garments, laid out on what might have been a basement floor to be photographed. Once white, all were heavily stained with red soil. Holes marred the coarse fabric of several. One was so disintegrated that the shreds had been arranged to represent the shape of the original outfit.

A brief inscription marked the back of the first picture: *Slave burial shrouds. Eight feet down. Dozens more suspected.*

Puckering his lips, he scanned the map again. Why bury them aimlessly throughout the field? Apart, unmarked, and at such depth. A form of humiliation? Given their lives, a denial of dignity in death was not to be unexpected. Even so, it seemed peculiar.

The newspaper clipping was a headline and story fragment from *The Nashville Daily Union* dated April 10, 1862. "Rebel Holdout Destroyed on Shiloh Return." The fragment read:

A company of men returning from battle near Pittsburg Landing destroyed a plantation called Angel's Landing, which is situated about ten miles north of Lexington, on the Locust River. This particular house and its inhabiters had been succoring enemy causes and were thought to likely continue so, so the house was put to fire and the resistors slain. The founder of the house, Darrin DeWitt, is popularly believed to have been slain by his slaves shortly after the completion of a cotton mill in the neighboring settlement of Three Summers more than a decade ago. His wife, Martha, has since— The ink blurred and the story concluded on the next line.

The final fate of Martha DeWitt and her house is unknown, for shortly after the fighting and flames commenced, a dense fog rose, smothering the surrounding area for about four hours.

Laying the fragile paper aside, Brad examined the loose photograph. It was grainy, but he could make out a small figure in a white cloak and hood, noosed, hanging from the jutting limb of a massive oak. Peering, he realized the body was not actually small, but regular size. The illusion came because the body had been partially lowered into a hole beneath the tree. Around the dead man, a few grim-faced soldiers lounged with rifles.

Frowning, he turned the picture over: *The hanging glen. 1866?*

"But the DeWitts were gone by then," he murmured.

"What?" Brooke was sitting crouched, elbows on the table.

He checked inside the envelope again. "I'm just wondering why this is in the DeWitt folder if it's after their time. Which it is, according to the clipping."

"Honestly, I think it's just to have something to pad the folder. Richard would often lament how little documentary evidence there was—" She stopped. "And here I am talking like he's dead."

Brad replaced the items in the envelope. "If his research was as exhaustive as you say, then I'm reconstructing a dinosaur from a few teeth."

"He knew more than is here," Brooke said. "Much more. I can't say for sure, but I think he grew up in that town. I think he had its history ingrained."

"Then why all this? If he already knew."

"I think so people would believe him."

A smile drew up the corner of Brad's mouth, and he lifted the next envelope with a little added reverence. "With that I can empathize."

The McCloud file was more bountiful: a stack of photographs accompanied by a small collection of documents. He decided on the photos first, flicking through the stiff cards.

The first one was a picture of the house. It was taken from a distance, and the façade was blackened by fire. But the mansion was not abandoned. The chairs on the front porch were visible, and all were occupied by slumping, bent-necked people in gray clothes.

Dead? Sleeping?

On the back, the words were stark: *Sleeping sickness.*

The next photo was taken behind the house. The garden was in bloom in black and white. The trees around the edge of the garden were much sparser back then; the creek was visible through the trunks like a long black snake. Among the garden beds themselves, people lay sprawled, hands flung out.

Brooke stirred. "You said you're living there? I don't know how you can do it."

"Ah, just do my job for long enough."

"But living there all alone . . . "

"No, my—"

An odd sort of terror crystallized across his heart as, for an instant, he imagined his fiancée sitting back there right now, perhaps idly pulling weeds in the exact spot where these bodies had once lain. Perhaps disturbing bones beneath the garden soil.

"My wife is there." He shuffled faster.

The remainder depicted the town throughout the 1870s. There was no bridge spanning the river then, and only a single row of brick buildings lay along a dirt road, looking across at a huge structure with a high chimney. The cotton mill, and what was now DeWitt Street on the eastern edge of town. But as the pictures progressed, they showed the construction of a second huge building, this one half a mile opposite the first. A white structure with a crenulated roof and an abundance of windows.

He had seen this building, too, by storm light, when driving up to the sheriff's office. It lay now behind high grass and a chain-link fence. The building's name was written on the back of the photos: *Angel Adamah Hospital.*

He lingered over that for a moment, before examining the next picture. A panorama of a vast field, striped by trenches. Each trench was filled with shirtless young men, working to deepen and broaden their ditch. The field beneath the lonely hill house, he realized, the one he'd spotted on the way to the funeral. On the back was written, *Preparing for war, 1917.*

And then, abrupt among the landscapes, the last picture: a portrait. A woman standing just before the porch steps of the house. Long black hair rippled across each shoulder, reaching to the hands clasped at her waist. Her face was narrow, her lips so slim they blended with the rest of her pale face; she almost appeared to have no mouth.

On the back was written simply, *Magdalene.*

An itch crawled just below his skull. Something about the photo was familiar. If he reached for it too quickly, the similarity would recede, so he resolved to brood on it. He stacked the photographs and set them aside, reaching for the documents.

All besides one were contemporaneous newspaper clippings that seemed to match the photographs in the folder: "Curious Malady Leads to Congregation at Ruin," "Yankee Dr. Sets Up Practice at Former Plantation," "Construction Begins on Rural Hospital," and "Army Establishes Camp Near Three Summers."

The distinctive item among the group was a letter. Paper whispered dryly as he unfolded the single sheet. A clog of words occupied an ancient page dated September 12, 1877.

> *Clement,*
>
> *I am not sure if word has traveled beyond the immediate vicinity, but I can decidedly say that a recent event has convinced me to get out of Adamah Hospital as soon as possible: the utterly shocking demise*

of the chief physician, Dr. Jerimiah McCloud. I was unfortunate enough to witness his final moments, and will not hold you in contempt if you resent me later for relating those moments to you.

The truth is, Saturday was hot and my fever was running high. Even with all the windows open, the ward was unbearable. There is a grove of walnut trees near the southwest corner of the building, and I went to sit among them about 3:00. Mostly concealed, I there observed, after a while, Dr. McCloud come out of the facility and go to a pump that stands in the backyard and begin washing his arms from what appeared to be a bloody operation; his clothes were all stained.

He had nearly concluded when two creatures rushed from the very door he had exited. I say creatures, for though they were human, they seemed possessed by something unnatural, beyond madness attributable to illness. They were cloaked in some sort of thick ooze, as if coated with plaster, and they traveled with great speed.

A refuse heap of materials left over from the building's construction lay near the pump, and each assailant snatched up a stone block and were upon the doctor before I could call a warning.

They battered him with the stones until he fell, and then, one at his head and one at his foot, they beat upon him until I suppose every bone in his body became soft. I shall not describe his cries, for I cannot remember them. I do recall how his right arm remained sticking up behind him for some time during the assault, gripping the pump handle, and how water ran down from the spout, turning the earth to mud. Though it seemed long, it could not have been much over two minutes later when his attackers flung aside the rocks and folded his body more times than should have been possible, until he was a small lump on the ground.

They retrieved their stones and began to hammer him into the ground. It was then that the hospital guard appeared. Forthrightly, he drew his pistol, approached them in their madness, and shot them both.

I stayed where I was for a while, until evening came and his remains were carried away, and the others. Then I saw the silent woman who was his wife appear and sit beside the residue of her husband and stroke the earth where he had been, even, I thought, smiling as she did it.

Forgive me for writing—I had hoped to gain strength from the sharing of this horror.

Julian

Brad laid the letter aside.

His back and legs were cramped from hunching in the tiny chair. He wet his lips. "I found something similar in the plantation house. A record book of patient's words. *Utterances of Adamah*, I think it was called."

A disquieted sigh from across the table. "I'm sure Richard would love to see that."

After packing away the material, Brad reached for the third envelope. "Larkin," he muttered.

First was a twine-bound stack of photographs with a card placed atop them: *Party Field Massacre, June 21, 1923. Photos Taken June 23.*

The pictures were slick between his gloved fingers. The first showed a gray field stretching down to a gray river, beyond which rose a gray ridge. Pale gray objects speckled the darker gray field. Gray and white remnants of carnival-like tents also lay sprawled on the grass, as if blown by wind.

He tapped the photo. "I know that place. It's the field in front of the house. The field's all grown up now, and there are a few trees, but that's it. This picture must have been taken from the road."

He lifted the next picture. A young woman in a gray dress, lying in the grass. One arm was beside her body, the other thrown above her head in almost a swimming posture. Her face was turned toward the camera, mouth open, eyes closed. "She's dead."

"They're all dead," Brooke said.

He chuckled mirthlessly. "Massacre. Makes sense."

In the next photo, a man with a pistol and a large mustache sat in the field, leaned up against a barrel. Behind him lay the ruins of one of the tents. A tangle of wire and blackened canvas was all that remained. "It burned," he said. "But it rained. The tent wasn't completely consumed. And look at the man's hair, plastered down around his head and then dried stiff."

Feeling for the next, he found it was the last picture. As he retied the twine, he said, "So why did they kill each other?"

"Richard mentioned that event. An ownership dispute after the First World War."

"What happened to the last family, the McClouds? And who won the dispute? And . . . "

His words dried up at the next loose photograph. In sepia yellow, it depicted a swath of river. The span of a bridge crossed the top of the picture, connecting two forested banks. Atop the bridge, a rail-mounted crane had swung its boom over the water. A cable extended down from the boom and looped around the neck of an elephant. The beast's trunk was jutted in a stiff curve down from its face. Its limbs dangled limp from its bulky body. The soles of its lower feet hung twenty feet above the river.

Flipping the photograph, Brad nodded, then shook his head. "Hanging Elephant Bridge. I drove across it this morning."

"That's something of a local legend," Brooke said. "The poor thing broke its hip while performing in downtown Three Summers back in the twenties. Its trainer tried to bury it without actually putting it down. They dug a huge pit and led it in, but once they started putting the dirt in, it became frightened. The trainer was standing near the hole. It grabbed him and pulled him in and flung him against the wall. While he was lying unconscious, before they could retrieve him, it stepped on his head. So they got the beast out, attached it to that rail-mounted crane, dragged it out to the bridge, and hung it. When it was dead, they just let it fall in."

Brad had gone through the accompanying newspapers while she spoke. "It says here the trainer's name was Rex Emil, a carnival owner. Says he was the husband of Miriam Larkin. And it says the event where the elephant was injured was the opening of the Adamah Theater."

The little chair groaned as he leaned it back from the table.

"What?" Brooke asked.

"A pattern." Dust motes frolicked between them. "Does that name ring any bells? Adamah? Anything aside from what's here?"

She shook her head. "Why?"

"Because it connects all of this. People driven by devotion to this *Adamah* put up a building in town, named it in its honor. And then something happens to knock them off. And that pattern repeats over, what, eighty years? Antebellum to Roaring Twenties."

"That's amazing."

"That's not a coincidence."

"What is Adamah, exactly?"

"I don't know." Idly, he flipped through shots of the town growing, the new theater glowing, the Locust River Bridge being built. "A supernatural being. They call it an angel. And this pattern . . . an order of worship?"

He paused at another portrait. A woman with short blond hair, dark lips smoothly smiling, and too-large eyes staring, standing before the house. Again, the itch darted across his cranium. He flipped the picture. *Miriam Larkin, circa 1930.*

"I don't know what to make of those last ones," Brooke said.

Reluctantly, he laid the portrait aside and examined the final four photographs. They were all shot from the same angle: looking through a doorway into a room with curtained windows and a long table. In profile, a body lay upon the table. A woman in a white dress, arms at her sides, palms open. Her eyes were closed, but her jaws were parted slightly. The hair, though whitish, was styled the same as in the portrait he had just seen.

"This must be Miriam Larkin," he said.

Weary light came through the windows, touching Miriam's body and the figure of a little boy. He stood behind the table, staring over the body. His face was hidden because he was looking with the light.

"That's the dining room," Brad said. "They laid her on the table for a visitation."

The four pictures were duplicates. Except they weren't.

As he went through them again, he found that the light diminished. And so did the body.

It collapsed. The form beneath the clothes shriveled. In the final one, a withered corpse was lying where a whole one had been just before.

"The thing is," Brooke said, "it looked to me like it was all the same day. Like extremely rapid decay."

He nodded slowly. She was right. The wrinkle in the boy's cravat remained the same in all four pictures. And the position of the curtains behind him. And the progression of light was right. Each had been taken perhaps two hours apart.

"What do you make of it?"

Again he said, "I don't know. I think there's a personality cult that surrounds the person who lives in the house, but that doesn't explain why her body would break down so quickly. She can't have been very old, either, dead before 1946, when the next couple moved in, John and Ellen King."

"I don't see anything about them."

"They were the last registered owners on the house's deed. At least, they were when I checked last week." Brad opened the final envelope—"Recent."

His weak grin faded as he examined the materials. As with the first file, this one was sparse, two items only. A newspaper clipping from the *Lexington Progress* dated the week of July 9, 1963. "One Year

Later, Fate of State Prosecutor in Locust River Mine Case Remains Mystery."

The story briefly detailed an investigation into unsafe working conditions at the Locust River Mine the previous summer. It then stated that a few weeks after the investigation's conclusion, a key player, Walter Lloyd Collins, left his Nashville office on a Tuesday evening and was never seen again.

The other item was a map from the county surveyor's office dated 1978. It depicted the streets and structures of Three Summers, as nearly as he could tell identical to how they were today.

"I found an item belonging to Walter Collins in the house," he noted. "His Book of Common Prayer. Marilyn Britain kept it—that's the woman who died recently. She must have come to the house with him." He sat up straighter, running his thumbs along the bunched-up shirt inside his pants. "Nothing about the Kings, though. And nothing about the court battle for the mine."

"You could try the courthouse."

He nodded. "And nothing about old Walt Collins building any-thing. Nor the Kings."

"Pattern kind of runs aground, huh?"

"Kind of." His hands were sweaty inside the gloves. He slipped the items into their sleeve, then drew the map back out. "Is there any way I could get a copy of this?"

"Absolutely." Brooke stood up and carried the map toward the desk.

Brad looked around at the shelves of brightly colored plastic-covered book spines. The daylight had nearly withdrawn from the windows. How long had they been sitting here? Slipping off his glasses, he rubbed bleary eyes. But he could feel excitement buzzing below his weariness.

The photocopier hummed. Brooke returned and handed him a warm printout.

"Thanks."

"I forgot, there's this also." She held out a small color photo. "I took it to my office to clean off some residue. It's from the 'Recent' folder."

Replacing his glasses, Brad took the picture. Another portrait. Another woman standing before the house. Another itch in his brain.

This time it clicked.

The dress. All the women had worn the same dress. It was the white gauzy thing the old woman had been clothed in when he found her in the garden. The dress she had worn into her grave. He recognized it now because this *was* the old woman, at least fifty years younger.

Loose brown hair, glossy in long ago sunlight, was pulled over one shoulder. The camera had caught her mid-laugh, full lips pulled away from white teeth. One of those teeth, the front right one, was chipped at the corner.

"She's beautiful," he said lingeringly. He flipped the picture over.

Missy, 1962.

THEY THAT SLEEP

In the early sixties, a couple named Missy Holiday and Walter
Collins came. Walter, a state prosecutor, was investigating the
recently constructed Adamah Mine for safety concerns. Missy,
called Marilyn by some, was the one I found that day, the one I
drove to her grave.

The man who had delivered these artifacts to the library was
named Richard Hettinga, a regular patron of the library. He had left
for Atlanta during the previous week, but Brooke Carney was kind
enough to give me his number, despite the fact that he hadn't been
answering her calls. In the car, I tried Richard Hettinga's phone. It
went to voicemail, so I left him one. Then I drove back.

—"The House of Dust"
Southern Gothic

FOR A WEEK, the cat did not blink.

It did not eat or drink, either. It lay as it was laid and sat as it
was set and never moved. It was slumped at the foot of their bed on
Wednesday night when Walt snapped shut his little praying book,
tossed it on the nightstand along with his glasses, and rolled on top
of her.

"Not tonight," Missy said.

He scowled toward the cat, then nudged it with his toe beneath the covers. "That thing's ready to go in the ground."

"We can't just throw it out," she said. "Look at its eyes. Its eyes are alive."

The cat's eyes sent a pining feeling through her as she remembered Mutt's eyes. She'd adopted Mutt out of an alley behind their Piggly Wiggly in Atlanta. Because she was still recovering from breaking her tooth, Grandmama had decided to let her keep him for a little while.

Missy cleaned his fur and eyes, but his fur always matted and his eyes refilled with goo.

Still, she loved those eyes. Old and hazy, they were the only ones that looked at her with real adoration. The only ones that *needed* her. The only ones that mourned as she was hauled off to HUG, the Home for Underprivileged Girls. *What ever happened to Mutt?*

The next morning, Thursday, Missy force-fed the cat. Between futile sessions of scrubbing the dance hall floor and tearing up the molded carpet in the parlor and tearing down the wallpaper in the main hall, she went out on the porch where she had made a bed for the creature with a bowl of warm milk.

It was a struggle at first to get its mouth open. Once the jaws were wide, though, the muscles seemed to disconnect from the brain. Just the slightest touch and its chin would drop down and it would gape at her like a piece of roadkill. She then took an eyedropper and trickled milk across its tongue. Invariably, though, after a couple minutes, the liquid began to build up in the back of its throat.

It wasn't swallowing. Rubbing its throat with her thumb only made bubbles well up through the milk. She turned the cat over and the milk splattered onto the porch.

For two more days, she kept trying. Nothing changed. The cat became stiffer, and Missy stopped sleeping. At night, she lay and watched the motionless lump in the dark. She thought she could hear tiny howls coming through its teeth, like cries far down in a well.

A week after she had dug the cat out of the ground, Missy set the unused bowl of milk on the wire table beside her chair and cradled the cat's limp form. She sat and looked around at the mats of leaves and sticks that still covered the porch and the cushions decaying in the chairs. Then she stood up, putting the cat back on its bed.

She walked down the hall and entered the study. The air was stagnant despite the open door. Her fiancé hunched in his chair, his hands plastered atop the pages of a binder, reading text between his fingers. Stacks of yellowing papers cascaded around on the desk. He hadn't shaved all week, and a mangy beard had gathered around his mustache, making his face seem heavier. Gently, she approached and touched his greasy dark hair.

Walt jerked, and his fingers closed across the page. Collecting himself, he sat up and blinked at her.

"The cat's dying."

"Okay."

"I'm gonna try to find a vet in town."

"Okay."

Missy's fingers withdrew. No condolences? No protestations? No *I don't want you around those people*? No *I want you here where I know you're safe*? Back in Nashville, he had discouraged her from going out without his company. Glancing down, she caught a title at the top the page he was reading. *MTMC Safety Commission Report on Locust River Facility.* Surely, that couldn't be holding him enraptured.

Working too hard, she thought, and softened a bit. "We need groceries, too. And some varnish for that floor. And paint. I'm thinking of a nice creamy yellow in the main hall, instead of that yucky floral print. Wouldn't that look nice?" She reached toward the nearest desk drawer. "So, if I can borrow the car—"

"Yeah. Okay." Brushing her hand aside, he opened the drawer just a few inches, snaked his fingers inside, and drew out the keys to the Pontiac. She reached for them, but he hesitated, then placed them slowly in her palm and folded her fingers shut. He didn't let go.

"You know, I never taught you how to drive."

Looking up, she found a vague focus had coalesced behind his glasses.

"It's okay," she said. "It's just into town."

"Never got you a license or anything," he continued, studying her dry, cracked knuckles. "You know, I was just thinking, if something were to happen to you . . . if you were to end up in a bad spot, folks wouldn't have a way to identify you, wouldn't know who to contact. They'd check your purse and find, what, a little cash? Some gum? They wouldn't even know your name, Missy."

Something about the words made her throat dry. "It's just to town, baby."

"Yeah." He raised her hand to his bristly cheek for a moment, then let go. "Just watch out."

Missy put the cat in a covered basket and put the basket on the passenger seat.

Potholes were abundant on the green tunnel road, so she drove slowly, one hand on the basket to keep it steady. Each time she glanced over, an excruciating awareness swept her of the skin flaking off her knuckles. She'd tried to conceal it, but had he finally noticed? Was that the reason he seemed so oddly detached? The enamel wearing thin on his doll? Because the dryness wasn't going away. In fact, it was getting—

I'll add lotion to my list. She buried the thought.

It was the middle of the day, one o'clock in the afternoon, but the town was comatose. Along Adamah Road, vines twined across white wicker gates, and rows of trees shot out of the forest behind the houses and separated the unkempt lawns. Since no one was on those lawns, she continued driving until she came to the grocery store. Cars moderately populated the parking lot, so she pulled in.

As Missy stepped from the vehicle, the crumbly smell of cigarette smoke caught in her nose. Turning, her gaze was drawn to the side of the neighboring warehouse. A beauty in a red gown grinned from an ad on the worn bricks. Behind her, a small group congregated. Even through the flaking paint, it was easy to see the expression in the eyes turned toward the woman: adoration.

She closed the door carefully. "Just a silly old cigarette ad."

Inside, the day's heat was pooling atop the dirty tile, and roaring fans propped in doors at the back of the store tried to make ripples in it. Hornets wandered among the rafters and the half-dead lights, and people wandered about with wire baskets. Some smiled, some chewed their lips, all watched her from the other end of the aisles. How many had written her those cryptic letters?

Quickly, she went through the store, conscious of the temperature in the car where the cat was still motionless in the basket. Dumping boxes of dry pasta and two cases of tomato paste at the register, she wiped hair, sticky with perspiration, from her face. "Do y'all have a vet in town? I've got a sick animal outside."

A blond-haired woman with short bangs and no eyebrows stared at her as she wrote out a receipt. "You're . . . "

"Yes, we just moved here."

"Her. From the house."

"My name's Missy."

"Mmmmmmmm-issy . . . " The woman's body began to jolt. Her throat clenched, as if she were about to vomit. Then her lips split, revealing teeth that stabbed through her gums like broken-off fingernails.

Leaning forward, her eyes darted left and right. Fetid breath washed across Missy's face as the woman whispered, "You're very welcome here."

Missy kept her lips together and turned them into a smile. Paying, she gathered up her things and shouldered out into the simmering parking lot. She was within ten feet of the car when a raspy little voice called, "Hey! It's the fake queen!"

Missy rotated on her heel. The horrible little boy who had buried the cat was crouched before the advertisement mural. He couldn't be more than ten years old, but he had a smoke clamped between his teeth. "The fake queen has come to town, well, well. Tryin' to win us over, fake queen?"

"Are you tryin' to get smacked, little brat?" Missy called back. "Have you already tortured an animal for the day?"

"Aw, gettin' mad, fake queen? I'll show you what happens to people like you in that house!" Reaching into his pocket, he pulled out a worm. He tossed it on the pavement and dug a loose brick from the wall behind him and pounded the wriggling creature to pulp. "See? See?"

Her stomach churned. Dragging her purse off her shoulder, she tossed it onto the hood of the car. "Stay right there, and I'll come show you what happens to little boys like you." She walked briskly toward him.

"Gonna try and hit me again?" the boy shouted. "I don't think so!" He hefted the brick and flung it at her.

It didn't hit her, but it hit the car. Missy jolted to a stop. And she was driving *his* car. "Do that again, and I'll get the police on you."

"Tell 'em!" the boy responded. "They'll tell you what happened to the last fake queen!" He was pulling another brick from the crumbling wall.

"Don't you—"

He threw, and again the missile impacted on the car. There was now a definite bent to his throw, and a definite dent in the passenger door. Steel gray showed through the Pontiac's red paint. The window was rolled down, and the cat's basket was just inside.

"Fine!" Missy said. "If that's the way you want it."

She controlled her pace most of the way back to the car, but when a third brick clanged against it, she ran. The boy bellowed a laugh. She grabbed her purse off the hood and scrambled inside. Starting up, she drove blindly out onto the street and turned deeper into town. With her foot firmly on the gas pedal, she relaxed her shoulders and blew out a burning breath.

In the side mirror, she saw the boy chasing after her on the sidewalk, chanting his stupid "fake queen" moniker.

"I know what he said about not getting involved in anything," she explained to the cat. "But I'm not going to let that little bastard get away with this."

She pressed the accelerator even harder.

Three Summers jutted up around her.

At the intersection in the town center, she slowed and examined the vehicles parked along the curbs. The police cruiser stood before a quiet redbrick building with curtained upper windows. An OPEN sign was displayed on the first floor, along with a placard out front: THEATER GRILL. Missy drove across and pulled in behind the police car.

When she stepped out, the echo of the boy's voice was distant down the road. Distant, but approaching. Pushing more sweaty strands into her ponytail, she put her purse on her shoulder and crossed the sidewalk to the diner.

Fresh cigarette smoke assailed her as she opened the door. There weren't many people in the place, eight on quick count, but every hand was clutching a cigarette. And the skin of nearly every hand was wrinkled. Not old, but weathered, like a sailor after years in brilliant sun. Except the opposite seemed to have occurred; instead of too much light, it was too much darkness that had sunk into their pores, until they were as withered as a winter garden. She looked away as a gawky man with a rooster crest of red hair stared at her. They all stared at her.

Why were they *all*—

No, there was someone. A ninth.

Someone with his back to her and a full head of greased black hair, sitting at the counter in the rear of the room. He turned slowly on his stool as the door creaked shut, and a smile spilt his very smooth skin, drawing it tightly across his checks, spreading tiny wrinkles around his eyes.

"Ms. Holiday." There were those perfect black lines between each of his perfect white teeth. *Ezra.*

Gradually, she approached. "I just had a run-in with a dreadful person, and I wondered if the sheriff might . . . " Arrest him? Lock him up? *Punish him.*

"Can you describe the person?" the sheriff asked.

"Yes. A bratty little boy with black hair. He's following me here now."

"Roy. Perhaps he's been a nuisance for long enough." His chin rose. "Abe? Would you and the men *see to him*?"

Missy turned away, a smirk tickling. The way he spoke those last words was delicious.

The lithe fellow with red hair and the weary men stood up, and she acknowledged them gratefully before walking aimlessly toward the nearest wall, her purse strap twisting between her hands.

Dozens of black-and-white photos hung on the walls, most stuck in place with thumbtacks. She strolled along the wall, examining the pictures, feeling the sheriff's eyes. The photos showed the Theater Grill and various other parts of the town. They also showed people. Many groups of young people spread randomly through the array of location shots. She stopped.

People stood before the theater across the street, and behind them the poster boxes were lit, and the border lights were dancing.

People sat inside the theater, only their faces visible in the light of a giant screen.

People stood on the bridge over the river, holding lanterns that glowed in their hands like shapeless orbs.

People stood in a great field while behind them fireworks shot up from a lonely house on a lonely little hill and glittered across the sky.

All were happy. All were beautiful. And all their eyes were closed.

The pictures were taken at night, she thought. *The camera flash was bright.*

But it was impossible: All of them happened to blink at the same moment in every single photograph? The camera had not captured even a sliver of an eye. They must have closed their eyes on purpose, she thought. But why? Why such a strange photo? She swallowed, and the sound was loud in the diner. Awareness returned.

Everyone had left. Except the sheriff.

She turned. He was standing there, arms crossed.

"Roy is being dealt with. I'm sure he won't bother you again."

"I'm grateful."

"How else can I serve you?"

There was an echo of the little boy's mocking tone in his words. She pulled the purse strap back onto her shoulder. "I have a very sick cat in the car. Does Three Summers have a vet?"

Ezra considered for a moment. "One that should serve. I'll drive you there."

"Oh, I'd rather not leave the car here."

His grin twisted free again. "We're not all so bad." A pause. "Let me drive your car, then. You'll need to be shown the way."

"Thank you, Sheriff."

"It's Ezra, you remember. Ezra Larkin."

"I remember."

"And you're Missy."

"I'm Missy."

"Ezra and Missy." He tasted it and nodded. "All right then."

Together, they went to the door.

For the next two days, I stayed in the study, patching together the scraps I had collected in a document titled, "The House of Dust." On the third day, Wednesday, I rolled out a photocopy of the town map, took a pen, and drew a line across Three Summers, connecting the old mill at the eastern edge, the theater in the center of town, and the old hospital at its western edge.

If I wanted to learn about Adamah, the obvious way was to explore the shrines dedicated to it.

—"The House of Dust"
Southern Gothic

WHEN BRAD LEFT, she was in the backyard, sitting near one of the flower beds amid the thickening noontime heat. From the porch steps, he could see her head was down and one hand was moving rhythmically at the edge of the bed. Digging.

"Jennifer?"

She looked up quickly at his approach and spoke with the hazy focus of someone skirting sleep. "I guess you're heading out."

Her right hand was heavy with dirt. She'd dug a small trench out of the weeds and daffodils. Her ponytail was loose, her bangs greasy on her forehead. She wore her pale blue pajamas, the ones that reminded him of medical scrubs.

"Jen." Brad pushed down the questions crowding his throat. "What are you doing?"

"You remember the night it rained?"

"Saturday." The night he went to Three Summers. The night she woke up laughing.

"That's when it must have happened."

"What, Jen?"

She pointed with her clean hand. A couple feet away, two squirrels lay in the shaggy grass. Bodies muddy. Eyes glazed. Dead.

"I found them this morning. They were in that mud slick by the back steps. Got stuck, I guess. Had their heads all jammed down in the . . . must have suffocated."

Brad crouched. He put his hand beside her in the grass. "How's it going with you?"

It was what she'd said to him on that day four years ago, when he'd left Jasper after completing the investigation that resulted in his "Scarlet Seven Miles" story. He'd gone to the diner each morning for a week, camped in the corner booth, writing the story of a monster who'd kidnapped an Alabama family and dragged them behind his pickup along the nearby stretch of Interstate 24.

Halfway through the week, she'd ventured over and asked if she could share the space. Her break coincided with the late lunch rush and the other tables were full. He'd rewritten the same sentence eighty different ways just to keep the keys clicking, to show he was working, that her presence didn't faze him. And when she'd caught him frowning at her reading a textbook on the brain, she said, "Got something against psychology?" He just shrugged.

On the last day in the diner, after the keys stopped clicking, the article finished, she looked up and said, "How's it going with you?"

And Brad realized she was the first person in years to ask him that besides his editor, Heather, and when she asked it, it meant *How much of your next article is written?*

Jennifer hadn't smiled when she said it. She hadn't raised her eyebrows. She'd just looked at him, and all his tension receded as he realized what a relief it was to be with someone who placed no obligation on him to be cheerful or bright.

In the grass, her hand touched his. "I'm fine, Brad."

"You haven't been sleeping. I've heard you. You've been mourning."

"Well." She examined her caked fingers. "You never really stop mourning, do you? You go through the day and you're fine. You're fine. And then at night you split wide open."

This is what happens when you stop caring. His mom's words.

"I need you to recover, Jen. People who don't recover get hooked on things. You're stronger than that."

"I'm sloppy. I should have noticed. I could have pulled them out of it." She was staring at the dead squirrels.

Brad folded his fingers around hers. They were so limp. And dry. "It was an accident."

With a tug, her hand withdrew. "I'm glad I came here, Brad. I belong in a place like this." She squinted up at the silent trees. "Where I can't cause any more accidents."

"Jen—"

Abruptly, she looked at him. "Go on. You've got work to do."

On the drive into Three Summers, in the flickering green along the tree tunnel road, he decided to spend time with her that evening, instead of his computer in the study.

At least make her smile.

She had smiled so much their first week together in Nashville. Not big smiles, just crooks at the corners of her lips. Smiles in the grocery store, smiles in the elevator up to the eighteenth floor, smiles in the little kitchen while they cooked. Even after their third night together, when she cried her way out of a dream of her departed family, all of them stuck full of needles, she'd mustered a smile as he held her close and rocked her in the sheets. And at the week's end, in

Riverfront Park, as they sat in the grass and looked across the water at LP Field, she'd leaned her head against him and said, "I've been awfully happy these last couple days."

Now nothing. No smiles since her patient's funeral, since the screaming drove them from the church and she tore off her engagement ring. No smiles in the house.

Half a month. Grief had its time. Regret, eventually, had to relent.

DeWitt Street was sunken in silent heat. The row of box elders stood in stasis along its broken sidewalk beside the field. No cars hid beneath their shade, and none lined up before the buildings on the far side of the street. He got out and looked across the heat-laden lot at the mill.

In the afternoon glare, the bricks were the color of old scabs. No sound came from within, and no movement disturbed its eye socket windows. The mill lay amid the high grass, bulky and collapsing, a whale carcass of a building.

And I'm the maggot, burrowing in, Brad thought. He checked his phone. 1:37. A dead time in this town if any existed. Sorrel had said he avoided the heat of the day. He would go in, snoop for half an hour, then leave. And he would keep his ears attentive for any tires or footfalls. In this stillness, that should be manageable.

It was not fear of the man, but if interaction between them could be minimized it would benefit them both. For now, at least.

Retrieving his shovel from the trunk, Brad waded out into the grass. The brilliance of the sun brought tears. When he reached the sliver of shade beneath the front wall, he pulled his shirt collar up and wiped the sweat from his nose so his glasses would not slip down. The little door to the interior was there, but he decided to first walk the perimeter.

Nothing unusual presented itself during his hike down the long southern wall. At the corner, he paused to snap a photo of the decaying roofline against the bleached-out sky.

As he passed along the rear wall, however, an oddity appeared near the center of the façade. The outline of a doorway, much larger than the one on the far side of the building, had been filled in with a paler shade of brick. What was now the back of the building, he realized, had in a distant decade been its front. Carts mounded high with cotton would have passed through this door, coming in from the fields up Angel's Landing way.

Now, graffiti filled the space as if it were a canvas; writhing, twisting shapes that sprouted from ground level. No words, just tangled, slashing lines and spray-painted circles. Dropping the shovel, Brad raised the phone and backed into the weeds a little way to snap a picture.

He frowned at the wall through the viewfinder.

It was strange that the tag artists had limited themselves to that one section of the building. The paint wove its way back and forth up the doorway. There was only one unpainted area, a spot on the right side of the doorway, just visible above the high grass. It wasn't brick. It was a slab of stone.

Lowering the phone, he moved back to the wall, crouching, tracing his fingers over the weatherworn stone. Markings etched its surface. Letters. But the contours were eaten away. The inscription was illegible.

Huffing, he sat back and dropped his phone. Roots popped as he ripped up a large grass clump. Digging earth from the clod, he smeared it across the stone's face. His fingertips burned as he rubbed dirt into the crevices of the lettering. Gradually, words emerged.

Adamah Cotton Mill
Est. 1842
D. DeWitt

"Darrin," he muttered. "Darrin DeWitt." So all this went back at least 175 years.

The Lenoir Cotton Mill had been built around the same time in another part of the state. Destroyed by fire in the 1990s, its remnant was now a museum to old industry. This place out in the silence, far from any traveled road, forgotten, was remarkably preserved. Sorrel's plans for it must run along similar lines. Salvage it from the waves of weeds; bring back the people.

He tried to rub the dirt from his fingers, but he found it reluctant to leave. He took the shovel and proceeded around the building, detouring the collapsed remains of the old chimney. On the town side once more, he proceeded along the wall to the crouched little entrance and ducked inside.

Lethargic heat occupied the close corridor. A memory flashed of moving down the silent hallway in the mildewed house near Interstate 24 where the "Scarlet Seven Miles" family was held during their final days, where the sound of weeping seemed to have stained the walls.

Quickly, Brad pushed away the memory and proceeded to the main room.

The space was just as chasmal as it had been in the dark. The dirt floor stretched out long and dim before suddenly brightening halfway across the room where the upper levels had fallen in.

No trace of the old floor remained. Perhaps there had never been a floor. Perhaps the plodding workers' feet and the clattering cacophony of the machines had thrummed uninterrupted deep into the earth.

Brad stopped at the center of the room, in the twilit space where sunlight blasted down ahead and shade hung thick behind. This was where Sorrel had stood.

Crouching again, he touched the floor, gently, like it was the hide of a slumbering beast. The sheriff had watered and swept the floor to make it match the rest. Which meant the floor had been disturbed.

Dug up.

Raising his eyes, he squinted at the grassy sunlit yard that made up the second half of the mill. There were naked oval patches of dirt in the grass, each about five feet long, the size of a bathtub. There were dozens of them, spreading all the way back to the wall.

Brad snapped a picture of the array. The grass had been culti-
vated or worn that way for a purpose. He picked up the shovel. It was
time to uncover the cause.

The edge of the blade bit into the shaded ground. He placed one
foot on the shovel's neck and prepared to hoist his weight onto the
blade when a dull clank skipped around him off the walls.

Startled, he stumbled off the shovel.

The sound came again, from behind him.

Rotating around the shovel, he examined the recesses of the mill.

A figure in the doorway. A woman watching.

Not a woman, a girl, unnaturally tall. The one from the bridge
in the dark. Harlow.

She wore jeans, a tie-dyed T-shirt, and green flip-flops. Yellow-
white hair was held back by a dirty sweatband. She held a two-gallon
bucket in her right hand. It clanked against the wall as she stepped
through the doorway. A soft splash followed.

She was bringing water.

Brad stared at her. She stared back. Then she took her left hand
from the wall and stretched it toward him. Her fingers twitched.

As he watched her next movements, his lips parted.

Her hand returned to the wall. She pushed it across the brick,
following it along the wall into the corner of the room. In the corner,
the hand slipped onto the next wall. Again, she followed it, walking
steadily, bucket locked in her right hand. Occasionally, water sloshed
over its edge.

When she reached sunlight, she stopped. She was directly parallel to Brad. A ninety-degree turn brought them facing. Harlow
walked directly toward him, deliberately placing one foot before the
other, her mouth opening and closing like a drowning fish.

Brad's toes clenched inside his shoes. Those eyes were impossibly
large and white. But they looked through him, past him, at nothing.

Her gasping mouth was forming numbers, *thirteen, fourteen,
fifteen.*

Gripping the shovel, Brad held himself in place. *She's blind. And
she's counting toward this exact spot.*

Abruptly, Harlow stopped ten feet away. Her mouth stilled. She sank to her knees. The bucket clanked down beside her. Her head remained up. Those too-large eyes stared at him as both hands reached for the ground. Something was wrong with those eyes besides their blindness.

A smile spread across her face as she leaned forward and drilled her fingers into the ground. Dragging her fingers back toward her body, she raked deep furrows in the dirt. She repeated the action. And then again, her hands widening, clawing at a larger swath of ground, like a huge, flightless bird preparing her nest.

Once the ground had been sufficiently wounded, her dirty hands fumbled for the bucket. She slowly poured the water across the ground. It pooled on the hard surface and flowed in dark tentacles into the gashes.

Dropping the empty bucket, the girl plunged her hands back into the mess, smearing the dampness into a wet lather, until the ground wrinkled around her fingers. Her head lolled back as she worked, her face slightly contorted, the skin around her blank eyes twitching.

The air left Brad as he realized what was wrong with her eyes. The eyelids were missing. Cut away. Only ragged fringes remained to hold the opaque pebbles in place.

Very gently, he lay down the shovel and drew his phone from his breast pocket. Tapping the red camera button, he filmed even as loathing gripped him.

She was hurt. She needed help. She was a child.

He froze as her hands stilled and the squelching sound of mud ceased. She sat, legs tucked beneath her, head down. But not entirely still; she trembled.

Then she lifted her hands, each dripping mud, and pressed them into her eyes. Dark water snaked down her arms and stained her shirt. Breath hissed through her teeth as she pushed the mud into her sockets. Her roving eyeballs were now smeared dark.

Bile rose in Brad's throat. His teeth gnawed the knuckles of his free hand even as he held the camera toward her. The killer in

"Scarlett, Seven Miles" had photographed the kidnapped family's faces before hauling them, bound, onto the interstate. *Southern Gothic* had rushed to publish them. His nausea hadn't abated for months. Why was he recording this?

After half a minute, she stopped. She dropped her hands. They lay in the mud puddle, palms up. Her head drifted. Slow, black tears oozed down her cheeks.

Brad dropped the phone. It smacked the earth.

The girl looked up. Then she reared away from the ground. "Who's there?"

Brad stumbled to his feet. "It's Bradley Ellison. The guy from the house."

"What are you doing?"

"Just came to have a look at the place. I'm . . . I'm sorry if I disturbed you."

She wavered in the mud. "You came with *her*, didn't you?"

"Who?"

"*Her.* Is she here now?" Her arms extended toward him once more.

Jennifer? "No . . . "

"I dreamed of you." The mud was streaking away, leaving her eyes yellow. Her voice calmed to a lilt, spiraling like a falling leaf. "Both of you. I dreamed that you came out of the forest and crossed the bridge to Three Summers. She led the way in a white dress, and you followed, wearing glasses without lenses. Do you really wear glasses?"

"I do."

"I'm glad you're here." The corners of Harlow's mouth lifted, the dirty tear marks on her cheeks bending out of shape. "I hope soon more will come."

"Is there a reason they would?" He glanced at the phone. If it was still recording, he would at least have audio. Again, disgust punched him. How often had he swooped in, scooped up testimony, and left the victims to rot without another thought?

She's just a kid. A child.

"They'll come because of you," Harlow said. Seeming to read his bewilderment, she added, "You don't understand it yet? I don't really either. But soon, maybe. Soon."

He hesitated. "I want to understand. That's why I'm here. Why are you here?"

"For my old man."

"Your father?"

"Yeah."

"Did he—"

"He went to rest here. Yeah." Her muddy hands wadded her shirtfront. "He went to rest here. And I hope maybe he'll share a bit of it with me."

"He's dead?"

"Resting."

"When did he . . . go to rest?"

"Couple weeks ago. I don't count."

"And why here? Why in this place? The mill?"

"A lot do. This is a good spot. A shallow place. Everyone goes to a shallow place."

The desire to jump on those last words surged, but he caught himself. Grabbing too hard might cause a break, especially with someone so fragile. He kept his voice low. "Did your dad have a full life?"

"Oh, he was real old. And my mama was, too, when she went. Real old."

"I'm sure you got to spend many happy years with them."

A sagging nod. "What about your daddy? Has he gone to rest?"

Somewhere up in the guts of the building, a bit of debris fell.

Tap.

"Yeah. He's gone."

"It's a chopped-off feeling when someone goes, isn't it?"

"I know." Then he said, "Have you got someone to take care of you? I remember it's not nice being alone."

Her hands refolded. "That's why I come here. Then I'm not alone."

"They must have really loved you. Were they old when you were born?"

"Yeah, I was born from old parents."

"Do you remember the mine across the river? Do you remember when it closed down?"

"They had me right after that happened. That was right at the end, when everything started dryin' up."

Either she had eased to his presence, or weariness had asserted itself, for she sank back down to sit in the mud puddle. Maintaining his distance, Brad crouched so their voices would stay on the same level. "You said this was a shallow place. Are there other shallow places?"

"A couple."

"Where are they?"

Her smile broadened. "One of them's the house. Where you live is a real shallow place. That's why I can't wait for you to invite us over. It'll be so nice, then, like it used to be."

"You remember how it used to be?"

"No. Like I said, things were dryin' up when I was born. But my momma and daddy told me about when they were small. And before them, and before them . . . "

"You think it will be that way again?"

"That's why you're here."

He paused. "I don't think the sheriff would appreciate that."

Recognizing his tone, she lowered her own voice. "You'll just have to go careful for a bit. But you wouldn't be here if it hadn't pulled you down here."

Had he missed something? "What is . . . what is *it*?"

Her grin became conspiratorial. "My daddy used to say no one knows why you yawn, but *it's* why. 'Cause you want rest. And that's what it is. God threw us out of Eden, made us work, but it . . . " She chuckled. "Momma'd say, if you look deep inside your mouth when you yawn, you'll see it looking out."

"Adamah," Brad whispered.

She drew up a bit. "Not respectful to say its name."

"Other folks around here say it."

"Other folks drive out to that church on Sundays 'cause Sorrel makes them. They're fraying. That's what Momma would say, fraying their bond. But you'll bring it back. And *she* will. And bring more folks, too."

He thought of Jennifer sitting alone in the house, in that dim bedroom.

Softly, he said, "Why did you cut off your eyelids, Harlow?"

"They got too heavy." She chuckled again, bending her head toward her kneeling knees until blackened hair pooled in the mud.

"Did *it* tell you to?"

"No."

"Why did you?"

"I told you, they got too heavy. I wanted to be able to see better. So now . . . " Scraping up more mud, she rubbed it into her helpless eyes.

He chewed back an objection, an urge to grab her arm, to stop her. "I don't like prying people, either. When I was young, I would go to a library and look at pictures of disasters on the computer. The people who worked there called my mom and she took me to a psychiatrist, a mind doctor, because she thought I was going to hurt people. I didn't like her because of that, and never went back to the library. I hated how they didn't trust me. But still . . . it's important to be safe, to not hurt yourself, especially when you're young, and—" He stopped as he saw her objection rising.

But when it came, Harlow's voice was gentle. "It's okay."

He barely kept back frustration. "What about infection?"

Although she remained hunched over, her head came up, like a sheltering animal surveying the underbelly of a forest. "This heals." She lifted hands filled with seeping earth.

Brad rose as revulsion boiled through him.

Matted hair swaying, Harlow tracked his movement. Blind eyes pinpointed him, as if a vestige of sight remained. Her whole face widened in a babyish smile of dawning excitement. "I know you need rest. Why don't you come down and try it?"

Always the same lies. The same promises of healing if he just believed the proper thing, performed the proper ritual. "I can't do that," he said. "Can't rest right now."

As he left, her laughter followed him across the floor. "Soon you will."

This Adamah was depicted the same in all the artwork I came across: a human form with two legs and six arms spread-eagled. Masculine language was used in reference, but the figure had no sexually defining characteristics. And no face.

—"The House of Dust"
Southern Gothic

HOW ODD THE sun is today, Missy thought. *Hard. And not a shred of cloud to blunt it.*

The car lurched as Ezra turned it off the road onto an unpaved drive that stretched across dull green lawn and up a low hill to a solitary house. Where they were exactly she wasn't sure—somewhere south of Three Summers, after crossing some tracks and curving through some woods and making a turn at one intersection. She could probably remember the way home if she needed to.

An ache formed behind her eyes as the car jostled and dust seeped up outside her window, forming a tail behind the car. She gripped the door with one hand, steadying the cat's basket with the other. Inside, the creature was motionless. Almost there.

"Just here in the grass is good," Ezra murmured, nudging the car up the incline before steering off into the front yard.

Her blood churned in her temples as the car stopped sideways on the slant. A headache was coming on. Lack of sleep, probably. She hadn't drank enough water this morning, and she had no gum to salivate her mouth. And her hands were still dry as—

"Would you like me to carry the animal?" The sheriff was studying her from his seat.

"No, thank you." Hoisting the cat's basket from the floorboard at her feet, she popped the door and slid out on the hill. She heaved the door shut and met Ezra at the rear of the car, where she squinted through the saltwater light at the driftwood-colored house atop the lawn. Its twin peaking roofs were arched eyebrows. A central section that connected the two wings was a high forehead of faded shingles that stopped just above a broad porch.

"So, there's a vet here?"

"His name is Irons. I can't vouch for his credentials, but I can for his character."

Shrugging, Missy hefted the basket. Ezra fell into place on her left as she climbed the hill. How was he not melting in that suit?

"At least take my arm. So you don't fall."

"I won't fall."

"You're still afraid of me, aren't ya? No need for that."

She shook her head, looking west toward the tracts of land at the bottom of the hill. "Just cautious. But I do appreciate you driving me out here."

The claws of a huge burrowing beast had broken through the green skin of the field, tearing up grass from the base of the hill to the fringe of the woods a half mile distant. The claws had then withdrawn, but the scars remained: deep trenches, five of them, sunken in the face of the ground.

"Then tell me about your tooth."

Her tongue flicked, feeling the jagged place.

The trenches had not been left to heal. They were planted as vegetable gardens. Cornstalks and okra stalks occupied the ground between them, and vines tapestried the walls within.

"I bit someone the wrong way."

Within the trenches, people were moving about, their big straw hats just below the lip of the troughs. They were tending the plants from battered wheelbarrows and harvesting them into tattered baskets. The air coming off the hill rippled and obscured them, like looking into the bottom of a lake.

"You can't just leave it at that," Ezra said with a chuckle.

"It happened when I was nine," she said, face still turned away. "A man hit my grandmama. So I bit his ankle."

"You were living with your grandmother?"

"Yes."

"Your parents?"

"They . . . Because of me, my daddy didn't want my momma. And so my momma didn't want me. And so my grandmama had to want me."

"An orphan who wasn't really an orphan," Ezra said reflectively. "You seem like a very interesting person, Missy."

That made a smile break through. She looked at the ground to hide it. The grass bending beneath her shoes and the swath of the field stood limp and pale, a doldrum sea exhausted by days of relentless sun. She repeated his words in her mind: *A very interesting person.*

"Hungry for some fruits of the earth?" he asked with the same softness.

Shaking her head, she shifted the basket's weight and looked ahead. Nearly to the house.

"It's community run, so feel free to take some. If you're hungry."

"Thank you."

A paved path snaked from the drive to the porch steps. Hanging pots dangled along the porch eaves and dead vines spilled from each, the thick strands reaching down, brown and rigid, toward the railing like stiff hair from trophy heads.

As Missy proceeded down the path, she heard an undulating creak from the porch, gentle as a wrinkle on a pond. *Creak . . . cak.*

Stepping into the shade after the brilliance of the sun, the porch was a fuzzy daguerreotype. She turned right, following the sound, and something coalesced from the gloom.

A man, sitting in the only chair on the barren porch. Above the chair, a fan rotated. Missy peered at him as the sun haze cleared from her eyes.

Bony legs in cuffless khaki pants propelled the squeaking chair. Waxy hands with bulging blue veins gripped the chair's arms. The man wore a red sweater and a pair of sunglasses with small round lenses that perched on a gently crumpled face.

"Joash!" Ezra approached the chair, hands on his sides. "Time to get up. I've found some work for you."

"Joash?" The man's voice was the coo of a mourning dove. "Now who gave you permission to call me by my front name?" Chuckling, he added, "I saw your guys from town. Is it noon yet?" Pulling up his left sleeve, he examined a shattered watch face. "We'll be gathering in the meeting room at noon."

Ezra stopped short of the chair and his voice flattened. "They came here? They were supposed to wait."

Mr. Irons looked up. "It's been almost three weeks, Ezra, practically a drought for— Ah!" He shot from the chair with jack-in-the-box abruptness. Missy jerked. She resisted the urge to retreat as those tiny round sunglass lenses closed in on her. "So, this is our newest neighbor? At last. So good to meet you, Miss . . . ?"

"Oh. Holiday. Missy Holiday." She clawed back her hair and then offered her hand when he demanded it. In spite of his frail appearance, the man's grip was as hard as his name.

"Holiday? Now, I thought your husband was named Collins: Walter Collins."

"We're not—well, we're about to be, but we aren't yet." She coughed out a laugh and glanced at Ezra. He still faced the empty chair.

"I see," Irons replied. He clutched her hand. "And I understand. You're a very beautiful lady. With a dozen disappointed suitors."

Missy finally got her smile on. "Well, that's what I came through this dusty day to hear!"

Irons grinned. "What is this task you have for me?"

She shifted the basket on her arm. "It's . . . it's not eating."

Irons let go of her hand and reached into the basket. He drew the cat out and turned it before the dark disks of his glasses. Slowly, he massaged the bony frame. "What happened?"

"He—that little boy who attacked me? Roy, he's called?"

Ezra turned around. His brows had slid so far down they obscured his eyes.

"Well, he was trying to bury this poor thing outside my house. The way he was hittin' at it, I guess he must have damaged its brain."

"I don't think that's far from wrong," Irons said. "And if that's the case, well . . . " He shook his head. "But for you? I'll try. Come inside."

"Thank you."

Missy followed them off the porch into the slightly cooler cavern of the main hall.

The air was dry and sweet, like hay. No lights were on, and doors lined the left wall, letting into dim rooms. The right wall was almost unbroken, except for doors at the front and back of the house, as if between them was concealed a much grander space. As she followed the men toward the back of the house, her gaze caught a huge, delirious sort of painting hanging on the right-hand wall. Her head turned to study it as she passed.

The elements were arranged in strata: a night sky, a dark canopy of trees, and a road beneath the trees. A horde of people holding crimson lanterns struggled with empty eyes along the road toward some unidentifiable destination. But she knew those eyes; she knew those smiles of communal frenzy. And she knew that road and where it led.

The island. Our house.

The brief rustle of a whisper drew Missy's eyes to the two men. They were almost to the back of the house. Abruptly, Irons turned. "It might be best for you to wait out here, Ms. Holiday."

She shook her head. "It's okay. I've seen things. I'll be fine."

"You haven't seen this," Irons said. "This is not your regular case of—"

"Irons has a process," Ezra interrupted. "It'll just take a minute. You should wait out here."

She blinked and let the basket handle slide down into her fingers. "Okay, then."

"Why not step into the kitchen?" Irons suggested. "There's lemonade in the fridge and some cream by the sink."

"Thank you." She hesitated. "Cream?"

Irons hefted the slumping animal and stroked its head. "Hand cream. I noticed when we shook hands . . . "

The dryness split on her knuckles like a mask of baked mud. "Oh. Yeah. They aren't normally this way."

Ezra nudged Irons and they continued down the hall, whispers passing between them. They went through a door in the back corner of the hall. It clunked shut.

Missy set down the basket.

Were they putting the cat down? Probably. She'd held off coming too long. And if anyone deserved to be put down, it was that horrible little boy.

She blanched at the thought, then shrugged. It was true.

She turned and walked back down the hall. Near the front door, a grandfather clock counted out seconds in the noiseless house. Ten till twelve.

She looked at the long, unbroken wall with the painting. Her eyes wandered to the nearby door. What was back there? The kitchen, maybe. Where she'd been invited to go. And she did need a drink. And her hands were so dry.

She crossed to the door. Against her fingertips, it swung inward.

On the other side lay emptiness: a large bare room with white walls.

Holes honeycombed the floor. Oval-shaped gaps, dozens of them, spreading to the corners of the room. Each just large enough for a person to lie inside. Blue smoke drifted from their mouths, crumbling the sunlight entering from the windows, filling her nostrils with ashy sweetness.

Cautiously, Missy stepped between the two nearest holes and moved in among the bazaar lattice. The gaps were so closely spaced that the floor seemed in danger of fracturing beneath her feet. They must drop down to the foundation of the house.

Or somewhere deeper.

She advanced still farther into the room, treading carefully between the holes. They breathed their smoky sweetness around her, and the throbbing in her temples built. What was this place? Then she saw the painting on the wall.

It was a life-sized six-armed figure painted in red, bounded by a circle. The circle was not complete, however, and the figure stood truncated, the portion of its legs below the knees lost beneath the floor.

Because it's rising out of the floor.

Missy's fingers flinched together as an asphalt voice said, "Here early?"

She turned.

"Or is it time already?" A face was looking up at her from one of the ponds of darkness by her feet.

Missy retreated as a woman in a green jumper with long steel-gray hair stood up in the hole. The woman's eyes drew together, squinting. Her mouth widened. She beamed at Missy as somewhere deep in the house, a howl broke out.

A sound like wet wood being torn apart.

Missy stumbled backward.

"Don't go!" the woman rasped. "It's time to start!"

The scream from far away stretched out as Missy turned and staggered between the holes. Behind her, the woman called out: "It's time to *start!*"

Reaching the front of the room, Missy bolted through the door. She nearly collided with a tall ruddy man with red hair. His face jumped to mind at once. He had been there earlier at the Theater Grill when she reported the brat boy.

She backed up the hall, trying to remember his name.

People stood motionless behind the man, forming a line to the front door. Men and women, tanned and tired. The people from the garden. Coming to the smoky room. All paused to stare at her.

She turned and hurried up the hall. The door Ezra and Irons had entered wasn't locked. Heat blared in her face as she pushed through.

It was a bright room. A sunroom with glass walls and a concrete floor. In the middle of the floor stood a metal table. In the center of the table lay the body of the cat.

"Shut the door," Ezra said. His face was gleaming. Irons leaned on the table.

Missy shut the door and approached. Her eyes watered in the glare, but she didn't blink. Her gaze clung to the corpse. Something had roused it in its dying moments. It had abandoned its slumping posture and lay like a starkly cast shadow, legs stretched out, back arched. Bloodstained claws were extended.

She looked first at Ezra, then Irons. Thin scratches burned down the side of the old man's face and the backs of his hands.

"I'm sorry," she said. "I didn't know it could . . . it seemed so—"

Ezra pushed his coat back. "Is anyone out there?"

"People are coming in from the garden."

Irons picked up one of the dirty rags and wiped his face. "Then I guess it's noon."

Ezra said, "I'm sorry, Missy. Regrettable how this turned out."

The entire week of care. *Regrettable.*

For a second, her lower lip felt quivery, the same way it had when the vet in Atlanta turned her and Mutt away after his leg got run over.

"I'll take the body." She started to reach for the cat.

"No need," said Irons. "I'll take care of it."

Looking at the twisted corpse, she was surprised by her rush of relief. "Thank you. I'll go now."

"Won't you stay?" Ezra hesitated. "I'd like you to meet the folks."

That line of sweaty, staring faces? "No. I should go."

"This way, then." He pushed open a dirty glass door at the side. Through it, she saw the hillside that sloped down toward the garden trenches. "Just go around the house and you'll find your car. I'll make sure no one else bothers you."

As she stepped into the sharp sunlight, Irons said, "We pride ourselves in being a hospitable community."

Then the door closed.

The woman at the mine, Jezebel Irons, had said Adamah was an angel. Outside of this Southern backwater, though, I had never heard the name, and my acquaintance with the major religious texts was sufficient to know that they contained no record of such a being.

—"The House of Dust"
Southern Gothic

OUTSIDE THE IRONS house, Missy stopped in the watery shade of a slouching sycamore.

Behind the tree was the row of windows that let light into that smoky room. They were gathering in there, meeting beneath that six-armed symbol on the wall, around the holes in the floor, with the woman who had come out of a hole. And the way the cat screamed . . .

She growled to remove a knot in her throat. Muck was bound to surface when you dredged around in backwater like this. And the Club had taught her all about muck. You had to wash it off or else it sank in.

The cat hadn't been the only reason she'd come to town. They were running low on food; hadn't had fresh vegetables for a week.

And the gardens were right there, now empty of people because of the meeting. And Ezra had invited her to make use of them.

Brassy sunlight scorched her scalp as she left the shade and hiked down the slope. Shallow roots from the tree reaching down toward the garden clawed at her sandals.

At the bottom of the hill, cornstalks ran out between the trenches. Vines and leaves squeezed up from below and braided between the top of the trench walls, scar tissue sealing wounds. She fished a basket from a tangled heap by the mouth of what was apparently the main trench. A rubber water trough stood beside the footpath leading in. "Shoes" was painted on the side.

"As if this were a religious site," she muttered. Still, it might not be a bad idea to take her sandals off. She had selected them for paying calls, not shuffling around in the dirt. Tugging them loose, she dropped them into the trough. There were no other shoes in the trough.

What were they meeting about anyway?

The ground sloped down beneath her feet and rose up on either side as Missy entered the trench. The sweaty soles of other feet had packed down the path and polished it smooth. She reached out to steady herself as she went down, and a bit of the earth broke off and clung beneath her fingernails. Light diminished as the thatching plants closed in overhead, forming a long, green, twilit corridor.

At the bottom, it was wide enough that if she stretched her arms, only her fingertips would touch the walls. Specks of sunlight filtered through the netted leaves. The air was dead as ditchwater.

Clutching the basket, she moved along the trench. The shade deepened. The air cooled.

Cucumber vines hung around her thick as coats in a closet. She needed tomatoes.

The soft slap of her feet followed her along the level track. Down here, the sound seemed condensed. Heavier. The wind of her passing reflected off the leaves and they rustled feebly, creating a quiet chorus in her wake. The whisper of her breath sank into the walls and came murmuring back changed; prolonged. She was a bug crawling down the throat of something sleeping.

Missy stopped after about two hundred feet. Tomato vines drooped heavily from either wall. How had they grown so lush, shaded from the sun? What were they connected to that gave them nourishment? Her fingers slipped around a large red fruit. Lush, but firm. Skin flawlessly tight and smooth. So different from the cracked skin on the hand that grasped it.

The stem popped loudly. She looked up and down the trench as she lowered the tomato into her basket. The leaves lay limp. The gloom stood still.

She worked quickly, plucking half a dozen before spotting even plumper fruits deeper among the foliage. The hairy vines itched around her wrist as she reached in and pulled them free. Counting nine, she decided on one more. Her roving fingers burrowed through the leaves. They brushed the trench wall.

Something like a physical shimmer wriggled into her skin from the cool ground.

The tingle was so odd that she almost withdrew her hand. The next instant, however, her fingers encountered a heavy bulbous fruit. She tugged it from the vine.

That would be ten. Ten would be just—

All the muscles in her right arm contracted as her hand emerged. The tomato burst apart. Juice splattered across her face and the front of her shirt. It ran down her wrist as she raised her hand before her face and spread the fingers.

Impossible, she thought.

Beneath the juice, her skin had changed. It looked *new*. Smooth, lush, ruddy, as if it had just been vigorously washed. The splits around her knuckles had vanished. The skin pulled and relaxed around the peaks of bone without tearing. The flakes of dying skin on her fingers were gone. All was whole, just like that.

The basket thumped to the ground as she raised her left hand. It was still dry, splits around the joints and blood on the knuckles.

Her gaze inched toward the wall. She had touched the dirt for no more than ten seconds and this had happened. *The dirt.* There was something in it.

Hesitantly, she dipped her left hand into the leaves, pressing it flat against the wall of cool earth, and waited.

Something squirmed under her left foot. A tiny tingle sprouted from the ground and pushed into her heel. It traveled up her body as a worm of static, then sizzled through her arm into her hand. It happened in the space of a blink.

Missy withdrew her arm. The tomato leaves parted a fraction of an inch above her skin, lifted by the minuscule hairs on her wrist. Her breath hissed as her hand came into the gray light.

Beneath a slight layer of dirt, the skin was whole.

From in front of her and beneath her and behind her, the sound of her sharp breath came back. The same hiss, but gentler, came from behind the vines. The sound floated in the air for a second, then evaporated.

Missy turned gradually, closing her hands into fists.

There was no one else in the trench. Up above the canopy of leaves, the rows of corn stood silent. Even higher, the chinks of visible sky were vacant. But down here . . . it was the ground breathing.

The pit beneath the tree with the noose back at the house jolted to the front of her thoughts, the place where she had imagined something following her beneath the ground. But that had been her imagination. And this must be an echo. Something about the shape of the ditch drew the sound out. Or the density of the walls reflected it back.

Calm down. Calm down. Calm—

Something caught at her foot.

She barked and thrashed her leg.

The tomato basket bounced down the path. It tumbled to a stop, pitched on its side, and three of the tomatoes rolled out. The things she had taken.

Missy huffed. This was too much. She was letting the shadows lead her imagination—

The sound of her breath returned again. It was deeper this time. It did not match the sound she had made. It was a long, murmuring sigh that enveloped her like slow water.

She lowered her fists and felt her fingers pressing slickly together, suddenly so wonderfully, horribly smooth.

The sound droned on for a few more seconds and then ceased gradually: dry lips drawn together. The sleeping thing was waking up.

Something is down here.

She drank an unsteady gulp of air. Yes. Something just an arm's length away, inside the dirt, mimicking her sound. But it had healed her skin, so maybe it was—

Get out. Now.

She faced the end of the trench. Had she really come this far in, or had it stretched? There, far away, was the house atop the silent hill.

Walk. Just walk.

Her feet sprung from one step to the next, but she managed to control her pace. Then her breathing came more rapidly. Her heartbeat became loud behind her eardrums. A horrible idea entered her head again, that the soles of her feet were touching the feet of another person who was walking upside down beneath the path.

And then the ground breathed again. A rattling gasp, just behind her head.

Missy ran.

Her breath burst free and her exhalation became a scream.

Just ahead, a small gray hand unfolded through the vines on the left wall and reached for her. Dirt crumbled from splaying fingers. Nails, black and ragged, reached for her hair.

Missy staggered rightward. The trench was too narrow. She tried to duck, but the fingers caught in the hair bound on top of her head. Her head jerked back. Pain budded from the roots of her hair. She reeled around, body doubling over, grappling with the fingers.

The breaths still emanated from the earth, but they were now high, raspy wails.

Missy gripped the wrist that thrashed in tandem with her head. It was clammy, and the skin was tender. Squeezing, she turned her hands in opposite directions and felt the flesh straining across thin bones.

The rapid breaths changed to a baying cry. The tiny hand released her hair. Missy jerked her head loose, and backed away. She stared through her mop of hair at the hand protruding from the leafy wall. It trembled for a moment. Then it went limp. The breathing stopped, too. Everything stopped.

She slumped against the opposite wall. Looking down, she turned her hands over. The friction had rubbed the dirt from her palms. The skin was still whole.

It had really happened. There was something here. It had healed her. And attacked her.

Just get out.

She raised her head.

The hand still drooped from the earthen wall of the trench.

So small. Streaked with mud. The nails clumsily bitten off, leaving scabs around the cuticles. Almost like a child's hand.

A child.

Panic galloped through her chest. Biting into her cheeks, Missy straightened up. She forced her feet to move. She forced herself to approach the little hand. The fingers were curled together, like the legs of a dead spider. Grabbing the vines on either side of the arm, she peeled the sinewy curtain apart.

Half-light seeped across the wall. The earth around the protruding hand was moving. Faint movement, but perceptible. And repetitive. The sound of breathing.

Missy's fingers crept trembling across the wall. Warmth emanated from swelling cracks. Holding the vines back with her left arm, she clawed at the cracks. Chunks fell away. The dirt had been recently dug out and replaced. The hand began to wriggle as more clods fell. A large piece collapsed, and a bloodless face gazed out from the dirt tomb.

Its eyes were open and red. The features were undeveloped. Black hair hung in damp spikes across a waxy forehead. Ashen lips were pulled taut across craggy teeth. Behind the teeth, the tongue writhed, black with filth.

It was a child. It was *the* child. The little boy—Roy.

She almost fell. Bile squeezed up her throat

Roy is being dealt with. I'm sure he won't bother you again. Just an hour ago Ezra had said that. Just a little over an hour ago, the boy had been bounding after her car, screaming abuse.

Me. They did this for me. He's here because of me.

Missy tore into the dirt. The rest of the soil fell away from the makeshift crypt. The boy's body hung suspended in the womb of earth. One arm was trapped behind his back while the other—the one that had grabbed her—flopped down at his side. He pitched forward and Missy caught his shoulders as he slumped to the trench floor.

He was unconscious. Crouching in the gloom, she turned Roy on his back and pumped his chest until his breathing returned.

The townspeople had done this; they were gathered up in the house right now because of it, doing God knew what.

And she?

She had wished him dead.

She'd be as responsible for the death of this horrible brat as he had been for the death of the cat. Because he was the cat now. He was a corpse in her arms.

The corpse stiffened.

He sat up.

She reached out, but her hands slackened when he looked back at her. The bloodshot red had left his eyes. Now they were pit black. His jaw dropped down from his face. Words spilled out like gravel. "It's not finished. It's *not* finished. *It's* not finished! It's not *finished*!"

Missy covered his mouth as the last word broke into a grating wail. Wrapping her other arm around his chest, she said in his ear, "Shh! Shh! They'll hear. We have to be quiet. I'm going to take you away from here."

Where? Where would she take him? Not the island, not the house, not when they'd done this. Where? The boy twisted in her hold, and his muffled scream heated her hand.

"I know, baby, I know." She crammed the words around a dry wad in her throat. "I'm sorry. I won't hurt you. Gotta come with me if you want to be safe. Gotta hush now."

Tensing her back, Missy stood and held the boy close to her body. The sun had slipped past its noontime apex, cloaking the trench in deeper shadow.

She had to get the boy to the car. But what if he broke loose halfway there and started screaming again?

They'll bury us both! But they're still in the meeting. It's only been a few minutes. If we just hurry—

She started back toward the hill. Rapid inhalations dried her lips. Her heels thumped hard on the path. He was *heavy*.

Faster!

The ground rose beneath her feet. Brightness flooded in from all directions as she climbed out of the ditch.

At any moment someone would appear from the house. They would all appear. They would rush down on them.

Barefoot, she labored up the slope. Her sandals were lying in the bin. No time to go back. She angled away from the house and tried to hold in the grating sound of her lungs. He was so heavy.

Pale grasshoppers leapt away from her unsteady feet.

"Just a little farther," she wheezed to the boy. "Almost."

And then, there was the car.

She turned a quick circle. No one was watching.

Hauling the boy to the passenger side, she tugged the door open and heaved him inside.

Missy rounded the car, praying the sheriff had left the keys in the ignition.

He had. The air inside the vehicle was oven-thick with heat. The boy's forehead lay against the searing passenger window. She started the engine and backed into the drive. Her gaze jumped to the rear-view mirror.

Still no one. Only the house staring back. But not for long. Their flat faces would fill those dark windowpanes.

Her bare toes pressed gently on the gas pedal. The car descended the hill at a leisurely pace. The boy's head slid off the window and bumped against the dash. His eyelids did not flicker.

At the bottom of the hill, she increased the speed. A white dust tail rose behind the car as they crossed the field to the road. At the road, she turned left and pressed down on the pedal.

Gently. No panic.

The boy was panting. Low, steady, relentless.

The weary green field scrolled by outside her window.

Missy squeezed the wheel. Sweat tickled down her face. "It's okay, Roy. Your name's Roy?" Her voice quavered.

The child didn't answer. Saliva slipped between his lips.

The sign for Adamah Road appeared on the right. Her arms jerked by reflex to turn the wheel. But that was the way to the house and Three Summers. They would follow. She had to leave. She could drive until she came to another town and then call Walt.

Yes.

A plan.

Dropping all pretense, she sped up. The Adamah Road turnoff flashed by. Soon, forest pressed in on both sides of the road.

For half a minute, the tires hummed. Then a humming sound began in the passenger seat.

She looked at the boy. He was staring straight into the vinyl dashboard. Saliva flowed down his chin and formed a dangling cord. A mounting moan issued from his parted jaws.

"It's okay. We're going far away." She looked away to guide the car around a bend, then back. No change. Fixed eyes and jaws. Cry transforming to a gurgling wail.

He's becoming like the cat.

Outside, a slouching steeple jutted above the treetops. A moment later, a white church flashed by, sitting in a clearing out toward the river.

God's house, Grandmama would say. Maybe it had a phone. She could call Walt now. But they'd already driven past. Too late. She couldn't go back. Couldn't waver.

The moaning broke off. The boy sat up, spine straight. He peered out the windshield. But he did it very oddly, head back, looking down his nose. Then his lower lip jutted forward. The panting returned.

With each breath, though, it became shallower. With each breath, she could hear more saliva building up in his windpipe, pooling, could see his throat straining as if he were drowning. Or being strangled. As if a noose were stretched between his neck and an anchor back in Three Summers. Each passing foot was pulling it tighter. *Killing him.*

"What is it, Roy? Hey." One hand left the wheel and reached for him. "Take it easy. Take it—"

His head pivoted.

His arched body twisted toward her even as his left hand reached back. His eyelids retracted into his sockets, and his eyes were goldfish bowls of black water. His throat clenched, sucking in a desperate breath as his hand fumbled behind, reaching for the door handle.

Her voice was dead. She tried to say, "Don't touch that," but it withered.

His lips rolled away from his teeth and his mouth opened, cavernous. The air inflow stopped for a split second. Then he screamed.

The sound knifed through her eardrums.

Her foot found the brakes. She reached for him, trying to make him stop, but he recoiled, and his hand tightened on the door handle. The door opened. Engine noise came in and mixed with his scream and filled the car.

The vehicle lurched.

The forest was a hot green blur. Except for just ahead. There the ground dipped, and a black hole opened up, and the road rushed into it.

Missy swerved. The tires bucked. She looked ahead for a split second and when she looked back the boy was sliding over the edge of the seat, out the open door. A cry broke through her teeth as the body vanished.

Missy threw herself forward, bearing all her weight on the brakes. She felt the land grow rough and rise beneath the tires. Her head bent toward the wheel, her body bracing as the car slid to a stop. The passenger door quivered like a broken wing. Gravel dust floated in.

Flinging her own door open, Missy spilled out. The car had diverted onto an unpaved track. The road lay two dozen feet back. Stumblingly, she descended toward it.

She hadn't felt him under the tires. And she hadn't been going that fast. *He's fine.* But where was he?

A mourning dove cooed in the trees. Mounds of honeysuckle grew around the mouth of a tunnel. No sound of cars. No cries or snapping sticks in the forest.

"Roy?" Her voice was mangled.

No response. She scanned the road a second time in both directions.

There. Movement in the tunnel.

She approached the entrance. Broken cement abraded her bare feet. The underground passage breathed on her with gritty coolness as she stepped into its shadow.

Yes. There he was, visible against the light from the other end. Standing up at least. Hadn't gotten far at all. Strangely, he was facing her direction. He was looking at her. His face was scrunched up, on the brink of tears. She approached carefully.

"Roy!" Then more softly, "Hey." Bits of old busted glass strewn across the pavement bit her soles. She ignored it, raising her arms. "Hey."

His head began to shake as she approached.

"I won't hurt you." Blood was soaking through the right knee of his jeans. His palms were shredded from the fall. "Let's go back to the car, huh?"

With each step, the headshaking grew faster. The saliva pendulumed from his chin.

"What is it?" She was a dozen feet from him.

Roy raised a crooked finger and pointed at her.

"What?"

In an echoed whisper, he said, "There's something behind you."

Missy stopped. He wasn't pointing at her. He was pointing just past her, to something over her left shoulder. But there had been no one on the road, and she had heard no one come out of the woods. "There's nothing there, Roy." She continued forward. "Don't be scared. We're alone."

"Don't! Don't come closer. It's following you. It's right behind you."

She knelt down just a couple feet from him. "Roy, we need to get back in the car."

His chin jerked. "It was in the car. Sitting behind you."

"There wasn't anyone in the car."

"It was reaching around your seat, trying to get me." His arm shuddered. "Like it is now. It's leaning down. Its head is right next to yours."

A chill stroked her neck.

"No! There's nothing—"

Glass crunched behind her.

Missy shot to her feet and turned. Something dressed in black was approaching. Something small, walking with a slight crouch. Her spine hardened and her fists closed. It was a man, she saw now, with a shaved head and wide ears. A tightlipped smile spread across his thin face as he crept closer through the gloom.

"Hello, there," the man said.

"Hello."

"What are you running from?"

"Nothing." Missy moved to shelter Roy as the man edged to look around her.

He caught a glimpse anyway. "Boy's hurt, isn't he?"

"I'll take care of him."

"You're hurt, too."

"I'm fine."

The man had stopped ten feet off.

"You can go on," she told him. "We don't need your help."

The man tilted his head. Then he fell to one knee and began untying his shoes. The laces hissed in the silence. Missy reached back for Roy's hand. The boy did not flinch at her touch.

"What are you doing?" she said.

"At least take my shoes, since you have none."

She glanced down. Her filthy feet against the concrete, her clothes smeared with dirt, sweat stains beneath her armpits, and hair hanging around her face. He must know what was happening here. He was trying to stall her. So *they* could come.

"We have to go," she said.

She drew Roy forward quickly, giving the stranger a wide berth.

The man paused and watched them pass. "Do you know where you're going?"

Walt, she thought, but didn't reply. Instead, she murmured to Roy, "Let's go to the car. We'll get help. We'll be fine."

"The thing went away," he whispered. "But it will come back."

"No, no," she hushed.

When they reached daylight, she looked back. The man wasn't following. He was standing in the middle of the tunnel, one shoe off, watching them go.

Anger smoldered inside me over the girl who had blinded herself. It was one thing to travel the underside of the South and see abused adults: Hilary Wegner from Serene Flats with her broken mind, the Tampa University hiking party's severed ears, even the burnt survivors of the New Horizon oil rig. But it was another thing to see a child in such condition. How had she been allowed to wander alone, to harm herself? I needed answers.

—"The House of Dust"
Southern Gothic

ROUGH PAVEMENT CHANGED to gravel as Brad turned off Simmons Pike and followed the drive up to the doors of Simmons Creek Baptist Church.

Slamming the car door, he squinted toward the vine-strangled structure. The leaves looked especially lush in the afternoon sun. Through the quiet, a melodious singing hooked his ear. He followed it toward the building and then around the heap of torn-up flooring that he had noticed last time, at the southwest corner. The kudzu had progressed from that initial tendril on Sunday; now dozens of fingers wrapped around the pile of boards.

A frail, balding man in black dress pants and a white undershirt stood atop a ladder positioned between two windows. He was tearing down ragged kudzu vines, dropping them in a pile on the ground.

The window nearby was open, and fuzzy voices were coming from within, frail remnants of a radio transmission: *Visions of rapture now burst on my sight; angels, descending, bring from above echoes of mercy, whispers of love.*

Brad approached the base of the ladder, dragging his feet through the grass to try to attract the man's attention. Gaining no notice, he cleared his throat and called up, "Good afternoon, sir."

The man jerked and the ladder trembled. His head strained over a hunched shoulder and deep-set eyes focused on Brad, then narrowed. Totteringly, he descended the ladder. His frown became a smile and he stuck out a green-stained hand. Then, thinking better of it, he clasped both behind his back. "I'm sorry. Been waging war against this kudzu since 1963. I tell you, it grows a mile a minute." His voice was parched.

Brad mustered a smile. "It looks like you're putting up a valiant effort."

"It only wants the structure, not the lawn. Which I suppose I should be thankful for, because you can see how well I've been doing on that count." The man leaned back a bit, the small talk seemingly an excuse to scrutinize Brad.

Brad pretended not to notice, nodding wry sympathy at the man's words and glancing up at the building. "Some of your congregants should be out helping you. The kids could probably use a summertime job."

The older man's gaze broke off. He rotated and retrieved a cloth from one of the ladder's rungs and mopped his face. With his back turned, Brad studied the way his neck jutted forward and his shoulders sloped precipitously beneath his sweaty T-shirt. He noticed his hand grip the ladder as he replaced the rag, as if fortifying himself.

Then the man turned back around and they both resumed smiles.

"You're the pastor? Pastor Burger?"

"And you're the writer, Bradley Ellison. I've been expecting you."

"Speaking of kids, there's one I wanted to ask you about. I'm . . . very concerned about her. Named Harlow? I don't know her last name."

"Harlow *is* her last name. Her mother, Susan, is buried out there." The man waved a slender arm toward the northern edge of the graveyard, near the riverbank. "All the recent arrivals are out there."

Brad looked across the high grass toward the plots. "That's interesting. Her father, from what I was able to gather, is buried beneath the floor of the old Adamah Cotton Mill."

The man's arm fell. His voice did, too. "Yes. I imagine he is."

"How recently did her mother die?"

"I'm ashamed to say I can't recall exactly. My mind is not what it once was. But we can look."

He beckoned, and they left the mowed grass around the church, wading through weeds toward the graves.

"I bring it up because she seems to be taking the losses very hard. She's harming herself. I've also found her out alone at night, standing in the road. As far as I've been able to tell, there's no one to take care of her." He remembered his drive through Three Summers on Saturday night, the strange activity of its people. "I was hoping you might have some insight on her condition."

"It's the cult," Burger said.

Something about the man's bluntness set him at ease. He felt free to be blunt in return. "Do you mind if I record?"

A moment's hesitation, eyes frozen, considering. Then a quick jerk of his head. "Not at all."

Brad folded his arms, phone unobtrusive in the crook of his elbow. "You mean the cult of Adamah?"

"The cult of the Queen of Hearts."

Jezebel Irons had mentioned that name on Sunday, as they stood on the far side of the river at the waste plant. It was a title for Marilyn Britain, or Missy, as her true name was. Someone with a special connection to Adamah.

"Adamah may be its root," the pastor continued, "but the Queen of Hearts is its flower. And the suffering of the Harlow child is part of its bitter fruit."

They had reached the new graves. There were five of them, each already crowded with weeds, rough headstones sunken in the soft reddish soil.

Burger's wavering hand moved across them. "2017. Susan the last, in November. Beau the first, in March. None before."

Brad frowned. "What do you mean?"

"I mean before that, no bodies had been laid to rest here since 1971. And even then, it was not a town native." Turning, he nodded toward the far side of the simmering cemetery, near the road. "A man was driving drunk down the pike and wrecked going through the tunnel under the railroad."

Brad looked between the distant spot and the new graves and considered Burger's claim about the Queen of Hearts cult. It did not mesh. As if the pastor had rehearsed this presentation but was delivering the pieces in jumbled order.

Slowly, Brad asked, "The people buried here . . . how many of them have you actually witnessed being put in the ground?"

"Seventeen. Not counting Missy Holiday. Or Marilyn, as she introduced herself to me."

"And how many of those were exhumed?"

A sideways glance. "You were the one who discovered her absence, yes? None besides her were taken. She was the Queen, though, so I should have been more cautious of her body."

As if by silent agreement, they moved toward the center of the yard, toward her grave. Brad walked gradually to keep pace with the man. The grass whispered around their knees.

"You say that, besides 2017, no one has been buried here since 1971. Do you have an explanation for that?"

"The cult," Burger repeated. His lips disappeared between his teeth. "It follows a pattern. A cycle. Haven't you asked yourself why there are no graves in Three Summers?"

Brad hesitated. "I assumed this was the site."

"It was for some. For those who died between the cycles and were less bound by Adamah's influence. Or for those who were placed here as cover. Or for those like the man in the wreck, who happened to die near here, unclaimed. But look around: there isn't enough room here for two centuries of death."

Peering at the passing headstones, Brad remembered the slave shroud photos from the library, and the rough map charting the unmarked graves they had been condemned to. Given their status in life, mistreatment in death seemed almost a given. But had the practice extended past the antebellum years, and to other groups?

"So Harlow's father being buried in the mill is not the exception," Brad surmised.

"Not outside of a cycle. Outside of a cycle, they will go to certain sites that they consider sacred, places dedicated to Adamah. But inside the cycles, when there is a Queen to give permission, they all wish to be buried on the island, because that is her home."

"But those five back there died in 2017, when Marilyn Britain was still alive."

"In the waning years of a cycle, a Queen is often not herself." Burger hesitated. Sweat beads had reformed on his brow. "Despite my years here, I have not been able to learn the exact history. I know that before Missy, there was a woman named Miriam Larkin whose death was rather strange."

Again he remembered the photos from the library: the body disintegrating on the table. "What are these cycles exactly?"

"Periods of waxing and waning influence by the woman who occupies the house on Angel's Landing."

Once more, something about the answer struck him as rehearsed. How long had this man waited to have this conversation?

"And what happens when there is no Queen? No influence?"

Burger shook his head. "Fractured influence, weakened, sprouting from many places. People feel great weariness. They feel untethered. Perhaps you noticed a certain friction in Three Summers since arriving."

"And how was it when you arrived?"

"Even greater strife. That was 1960. It had been twenty years since the last Queen died. A couple had briefly lived in the house sometime in the forties and died suddenly. Destroyed by Satan for resisting the pull to become part of the cycle. Then when I came, men were perishing in the mine at a rapid rate. Their bodies surround us now."

They stopped to examine the hunched little stones rising around their feet. "Were they buried like her?" Brad asked. "No casket?"

"No. They kept a supply of pinewood caskets down at the hospital. When a poor soul died over there, they'd load them in a box. If there was no family that wanted them back—and most times there was not—then they would be laid to rest here. This one, for instance. Paul Arterburn."

"1935 to 1962," Brad read.

"He'd be my age, were he still alive," Burger mused. Shaking his head, he looked up, then motioned to the walnut trees shouldering the yard. "The first sleepers are in the woods. A few Union soldiers, I believe, although the markers are so worn it's hard to say."

They continued walking, and Brad studied the names of the stones they passed, trying to piece together what the pastor had told him. Jacob Wiersbe, crusted in lichen; Oswald Burns, fallen down; Floyd Stringfield, wrapped in Johnsongrass.

For a second, he thought he saw another name: *Martin Parker Ellison.* His brow clinched. That name, cut in stone, was long ago and far away. He'd returned to the cemetery where it stood just once, a month after the funeral. Headphones on, he'd stood shivering in the February cold, examining the marble slab his mom would never have paid for, even though the dead had willed her all his money. The company had paid for it. To show how sorry they were for the accident.

In later years, he'd visit the other headstones. Some fixed with flowers, some forgotten to moss, scattered all across the South. Twelve of them. Twelve names. Twelve victims of the accident.

Brad wet his lips. They had stopped. A patch of churned dirt lay before them. No daffodils. No marker. Just weeds taking root, stitching the wounded earth shut. Missy's grave. "Did you know her?"

The pastor exhaled. The energy that had carried him through his rambling tale of cycles was gone. His voice, which had started out hoarse, was a rasping whisper. "She came once to visit me. Once long ago. She was very earnest but very guarded. She called herself Marilyn. I could see in her stance she had been . . . stung many times by Satan's darts. She stayed only a few minutes."

"And you never saw her again?"

"I did at times, by accident on her part. I tried to visit, but she would never answer the door. Then one morning, it might have been 1982, as I drove to the grocery store, she was standing at the end of that long road that leads to the old plantation house—just standing there. I rolled down my window to speak. She was friendly, I'd say. Plenty of energy, and her wits"—he tapped his temple—"very sharp. She'd say things that were off, sometimes, but even so . . . "

"Even so . . . "

"It was a façade she put up for me. After I left, it wouldn't surprise me at all if she became a different person. She was like a single coat of white paint over a dark wall. It was pronounced the last time I saw her. It was the last summer I could walk my old route along the old railroad tracks. I came down the gravel track in the woods and saw her returning through that tunnel beneath the ridge, as if she had been out somewhere beyond Three Summers. I tried to speak, but it was like meeting a shadow cast by someone standing a long way off. She passed me, wordless." A second sighed by. "Now she is here."

"Is she?"

"Sorrel regained her body Monday morning."

Had Sorrel forced Jezebel Irons to return it? Or were her purposes with the corpse fulfilled? Had it lost its potency with the being below?

"The people . . . " Brad started hesitantly. "Are they religious? Do they worship the Queen?"

"They worship Adamah. The Queen is their medium."

"Your church was packed last time I stopped by."

It seemed impossible, but the man's slumping shoulders bowed still farther. "Sorrel compels them, not the Spirit of God."

Brad watched him carefully. "Why?"

"He brings them here to try to sever the ties that bind them to the endless cycles. To this cult of the Queen of Hearts."

"He considers it dangerous?"

"Stifling. And the rituals, satanic."

He gripped the phone and dared to hold the microphone a little closer. "Rituals."

"Dark, very dark. From the pit of—" Pastor Burger stopped. His lips were dry. The sweat had dried from his forehead. He was trembling. Shock smoothed his face. "I can see . . . " His voice dropped to nothing. He crouched down, lips moving, eyes boring the ground. His faint eyebrows arched, as if the surface were splitting between his feet. "I can see you," he whispered.

Brad looked at the ground. Below the bent grass of one of their footsteps was the mashed mouth of a crawdad hole. Slightly odd this far from the water, but nothing to provoke such a reaction. He stepped closer.

"Pastor? You okay? We can stop." He touched his back.

The man went rigid. He tried to straighten. Brad jammed his phone in his pocket and helped him up.

"It's okay, we can stop," he repeated.

"No! I mean—" A breath. "I think I've been in the sun too long. But I don't want you to stop. I want you to continue your investigation!" A concerning note of panic elevated his voice.

"Sure. Definitely. We'll stop for today, though."

Brad helped him back through the heat to the shade of the church. "I can come back another day."

"You need a better witness than I. The only soul I ever saved out here, Richard Hettinga—you need to talk with him. He knows the history, the cycles. He knows the danger of the Queen of Hearts. I'll give you his phone number."

"I already have it. But thank you."

Pastor Burger took another breath and mustered a straighter posture. "I'm sorry about that." He nodded at the graveyard, features drawn. "Like I say, the sun . . . I don't know how you manage in that black shirt."

"Yeah." Brad forced a smile. "I'll stop by in a couple days."

As he left, he found himself treading lightly across the ground toward the car.

Later, sitting at my desk in the house, I played the eyeless girl's words back. Out of everything she'd said, one phrase burrowed into my mind and lodged there: shallow place. Shallowness conjured something subterranean; from shallow places you could reach into the depths. And the depths could reach back. The house, she'd said, was one of these places.

—"The House of Dust"
Southern Gothic

"YOU KIDNAPPED A CHILD," Walt said.

He still hadn't shaved, and the stubble darkened his face. Behind him the windows were black, the curtains open, letting out the light. Letting in the night.

Missy set down the spoon of tomato soup she had been attempting to fit between the boy's tight teeth and got up. She rounded the table, gripped the drapes, and pulled them closed. Even then, the house did not feel secure. It was the central cave in a labyrinth, eager to carry their voices to a prowler.

Resuming her seat, she picked up the spoon. Her hands were still smooth, revived. And trembling. "I wish you'd been here earlier. Some explaining needs to be done."

"Understatement."

"By you."

Walt looked right through her, spooning up his soup in even increments. "About what?"

"About a lot of things. About this place."

"I thought you decided you liked it here."

"I said if being here meant more of you. But it hasn't. Just a *lot* of other things."

The spoon pointed. "I have to work. It's my responsibility. And it's yours not to make that harder by abducting children."

"They were *killing* him!" she burst out. "They had buried him alive in a field! And if you're not surprised and *horrified* by that, then there's a lot you need to tell me."

He blanched. "No. Of course. But could you see a motive? Why were they doing it?"

"I don't care *why*! He's a child! He doesn't deserve to be treated the way—"

Walt's spoon had shifted to point at the boy.

"He's saying something."

Twisting, she looked at Roy. He had straightened a bit from his slump. He was looking earnestly at Walt. His lips had formed a tight oval that opened and closed.

Leaning nearer, she listened. "He's saying *him*." Then the boy's voice was loud in her ear, and she pulled away as he spoke clearly.

"They were giving me to *him*."

Walt lowered his spoon and swirled it in his bowl. "Who is *him*?"

The boy rocked and then flickered, as if the electricity in his body had shorted out for a second.

Missy stood and gripped the boy's shoulders. She shot a gaze at Walt and opened her mouth to speak.

Three short knocks at the front door bounded up the hall.

"The sheriff!" Her guts cinched. "Is the door locked?"

Walt blinked. Rising, he went into the hall and looked toward the front door.

"Don't let him in," she said.

"If he's looking for the child, I have to—"

"No. He doesn't know Roy's here. But he'll ask. You have to tell him he's not here; tell him to go away."

He put his hands in his pockets. "If the sheriff wants that boy, there's a reason."

The knocking again, three quick hammer blows. From the chair beside her, a low moan began, burrowing through the boy's ratcheted jaws, just like in the field. He'd be wailing soon.

Plastering her hand across his lips, she pulled him from the chair and hauled him into the hall. "I'll take him upstairs and keep him quiet."

Walt was already walking.

"Wait!" She stumbled after him.

"I have to answer it."

"Wait until we hide."

He didn't wait. She was halfway down the hall when he reached the door. They were exposed. Those deep eyes would look into the bright hall from the dark and see them, and those gapped teeth would smile.

Lurching to one side, she dragged the boy into the nook beneath the stairwell. The pressure of his groans built behind her fingers. The sheriff would hear. Using the fading creak of the front door opening to mask her sound, she squeaked open the basement door. With the boy, she shrunk through the gap onto the upper steps and pulled the door shut.

In the cool earthen dark, she listened. Past the boy's dull moan, greetings were exchanged. Affable. And taking place inside the threshold. Just a few dozen feet off. It sounded, though, as if the distance were greater. As if the voices were far above and she at the bottom of some chasm. As if a great fall were deforming the voices.

She leaned down toward the crack of light beneath the door, trying to hear the words. The movement disturbed her lock on the boy's mouth. His whimper spiked to a cry. Clamping her fingers tighter, she pulled him against her chest and down a few more steps.

"Quiet! We need to be quiet. Nothing's gonna happen, but we need to be quiet."

Hair hissed against fabric as he jerked his head. Static built on her skin.

"I'll let go if you promise to be quiet."

The bucking head changed directions. Nodding.

Gradually, she relaxed her hold. Lifting the hand from his face, she whispered, "Shh. That's right." It was what Grandmama had always said when they heard people yelling at night.

Down the hall, the voices were humming conversation. The hum moved away from the front door, deeper into the hall. Nearer to the stairs.

This is our house. Don't let him search.

Her gaze paced the crack of light below the door.

"It's not finished," the boy whispered.

Missy's hand leapt to his lips but paused. It had come out in only the tiniest whisper.

"He'll always come until it's finished."

"This is my house," she assured him softly. "If he comes again, I won't let him in."

Again, his head moved. Shaking this time. "Not from town. From down there."

"Down where?"

"Deep down." His voice dwindled still further. "He's coming up."

She sank down on the step and gathered him close. "No one's coming."

Outside, the voices went on, humming, humming.

Then his mouth was beside her ear. It was an eek, a breath of air through a rusty pipe. "He's coming out of the ground."

An itch broke out on her feet: sweat and dirt mixing. "Shh."

"I can hear *him* down in the basement."

"Be quiet." It was louder than it should have been. She had to stop this.

"He's at the bottom of the stairs."

She shook him slightly, hissing, "Be quiet."

He hunched against her. "He's coming up."

In the hall, the humming was faint. Very faint. Or had it gone? Was her fiancé watching helplessly while the sheriff prowled around, looking through doors? Or had he sent him away?

The static seemed to have concentrated in her feet. But the tingle was building through her limbs. It was sliding up her neck, too, moving across her scalp. It burned like the fuzzy fire in a bloodless limb. She was getting dizzy just sitting here.

Not enough air. The boy was holding on too tight. She needed to breathe.

Wait. Now he must be standing up, because she couldn't see the line of light under the door anymore. And he was playing with her hair. She could feel it lifting away from her head and tugging gently at the roots, twisting between fingers.

Missy tried to smooth down her hair, but it wouldn't go. "Roy, stop it."

The point of his chin slid on her chest as he looked up. In an airless whisper, he said, "He's got your hair."

Her heartbeat sped to a driving clamor and she clambered up the steps. The line of light came back, but she didn't stop. The atmosphere was thick and prickling around her, like a wool blanket. Slamming against it, she scrambled for the handle, threw the door back, and spilled into the brilliance of the hall.

It was empty.

"Walt!"

The front door was closed.

"Walt!" She rushed down the hall and hauled the door open.

Beyond the porch, beneath the fringe of moss at the edge of the clearing, two sets of taillights vanished down the drive.

"Walt."

Gone. Like he'd go off for days at a time when he was bored with her, leaving her alone in the grungy apartment. *Walt.*

Missy turned back into the hall. Bright. And still empty. Roy hadn't come out of the stairs. Unsteadily, she walked back down the corridor. At the door, she turned and stopped.

Roy stood just inside. Only his face and hands were visible. The rest was lost in gloom, like a body drowning in dark oil. The hands were reaching toward her. The mouth was moving, calling. Calling without sound.

"Get out here," Missy growled.

His hands splayed. His mouth gaped wider, screaming at her noiselessly.

Steadying herself, Missy leaned over the threshold, jamming a hand into the stairwell. Grabbing his fingers, she leaned back, towing him out and letting him flop onto the floor. She slammed the basement door and rounded on him.

"Stop this!" *Stop acting like you don't hear me. Stop pretending you can't talk. Now he's gone and left me 'cause of you!*

The wretched little creature looked up, tears etching his greasy face. "They wanted him to go."

"Walt? Who wanted him to go?"

"The hands." Despite his quaking, the boy straightened. His neck craned back, and his own hands matched his words as he reached for the ceiling lights. "The hands reach from the ground. They direct the things that happen. They move your feet." Head dropping, he pointed. "See? They've got your feet."

Missy looked down. Her feet were gray. Too smooth, as if a file had rubbed away every detail. As she backed away from him, dusty outlines of her soles followed.

She stopped. Her chin jutted. Stalking forward, she dragged him up.

Upstairs, in the bedroom, she shut the door. After lugging him onto the bed, she went into the bathroom and shut that door, too. In the brightness, she went to the sink and turned on the hot faucet. Raising one leg, she rested her heel on the lip of the basin. She splashed scalding water across the skin. Heat-numbed fingers worked her feet, nails scrubbing at the dust. Minutes passed, the water ran, and the dust remained, plastered in place, gripping her.

Wanting her.

Steam blurred her vision. Perspiration gathered on her face. It couldn't have her. She wouldn't let it have her. Wouldn't let it strangle Roy. Wouldn't let it drag Walt away from her. She'd fight it.

Her fingers hardened. Her nails gouged deeper. Soon, the water splattering the basin was pink.

Around midnight, Jennifer came into the study and asked if we could go for a walk. She hadn't slept since Saturday night, when she dreamed about the girl coming out of her casket. It showed in her eyes and translucent skin and slouching gait. She was fighting slumber and losing. I wanted her to lose. Even so, I agreed.

We went outside and down to the road. The cicada choruses rasped our ears as we walked up and down the island in the moonless night. I tried to speak about us. She cut me off: "Don't, Brad. Things are fine until we try to talk about them."

Sometime around dawn, we returned to the house. I waited up with her through the morning, until around ten, when she sat down in a dining room chair and didn't get up again. I carried her upstairs and put her in bed. Then I left. It was time to visit the second shrine.

—"The House of Dust"
Southern Gothic

THE THREE SUMMERS power substation stood behind Grammy's Grocery store. Brad parked there.

Drowsy woods along the west edge of town shrouded his walk to the hospital. The more direct approach—the driveway from McCloud Street—ran past the sheriff's station. It wasn't that he was sneaking, but his exploration might go more smoothly without Sorrel's scrutiny.

A chain-link fence greeted him at the edge of the hospital yard, and a lichen-crusted metal sign dangled by a single zip tie, warning him to keep out. Barbed wire looped irregularly along the top of the barrier. He scaled the fence, maneuvered his hands around the wire, and dropped nimbly down on the other side.

As he crossed the lot, a memory phased through his mind of traversing the barren parking lot before the Martlet Mall, an abandoned shopping center bordering the small town of Drayton, Louisiana. The sheriff had been hostile there, too. And the locals all shrugs and nervous laughs and mumbled warnings. That had been 2012, his sixth investigation. Or was it seventh? Or did it matter?

He looked up at the approaching building. Large windows on two floors, interspersed along the marble façade by ornamental columns. He knew it had once been white, from the library photos. Now, it was the color of fog. A procession of magnolias led to a covered portico jutting from the front of the structure, sheltering a portion of the drive. In its shade, brass letters corroded green hung above the double doors: ANGEL ADAMAH HOSPITAL.

"Adamah," he muttered. "Here you are again." He snapped a picture.

The doors were also plated with green brass, the large rectangular glass panes they had once contained replaced by plexiglass held with screws. Brad placed his hand against the right-side door. Heavily, it scraped open. No lock? No wire or chains? Did people still visit the place? He hung back for a moment, then slipped into the moldy dimness and waited near the threshold for his eyes to adjust.

They did, slowly, and the hospital's foyer became visible.

It was a curious setup. Metal staircases to the right and left, and three walls in front that reached only halfway to the bare rafter ceiling. Beyond this little box, he guessed, was the hospital's main holding room. A door stood in the wall directly opposite, wide enough to admit a stretcher. Buttressing the door were two metal-topped desks, and in the corners behind these desks were clusters of file cabinets.

He crossed the room and crouched down, finding that the cabinets, like the building, were unlocked. He drew open the bottom drawer of the first one with a dry rasp. White-gray light from the outer ward drained over the foyer walls, highlighting dust that rose as he brushed his fingers across the bank of entombed documents.

He began digging.

Most of the papers were patient profiles. They gave a date, a name, body characteristics, and a brief summary of the medical condition upon admittance. Stapled to each profile sheet were various receipts detailing drugs administered along with dosage, and procedures performed along with time to complete. The most recent of these sheets was in the very back of the drawer: an almost untouched paper dated March 23, 1997. A woman named Mary Lasney had been admitted with a broken wrist. But an X had been drawn across the page with a black pen.

Brad frowned and logged the sheet with his camera. Moving up to the next drawer, he found that, in jumbled fashion, the records were traveling back in time. The back of the drawer reached 1979. Men were being admitted regularly during this period. Broken appendages and head trauma were common; lung problems were most common. He nodded as he realized why.

The mine across the river. The Adamah Mine, up and running and under the ownership of the woman called Marilyn Britain. He tipped his head back for a moment, trying to recall the convoluted path of ownership. The original company had been thrown out by a state prosecutor for unsafe work conditions in . . . 1962? His fingers trembled as he moved to the top drawer. Similar records as in the other drawers, ending in 1965.

Sliding the drawer shut, he moved to the next cabinet. He squatted and reached for the handle, but just an inch short of it, his fingers froze.

A heavy sound like a metal rod striking wood, slow and laborious, broke out on the floor above. It echoed through the rafters from a stationary point. Not footsteps. Perhaps a window, stirred by late-morning wind? After ten seconds, it stopped.

Brad held his breath and counted back the same amount of time, then wrapped his fingers around the handle and pulled out the drawer.

Even in this light, the sudden change was immediately discernible. Instead of bundles of limp white papers crammed into place, this drawer contained a block of crisp yellow pages about an inch thick.

Drawing the stack out, he laid it on the floor. Radiance spilled across neat lines of text as he turned on the phone's flashlight. A typewriter had been used to draw up the forms. Once again, names and body features were listed, but so were birthplaces. Cities and towns passed beneath his fingertips: Knoxville, Cookeville, Nashville, Maryville, Newport, Bristol, Jefferson City. Places outside of Tennessee, too, in Alabama and Georgia and North Carolina. None of the men were Three Summers natives.

Again, he remembered the Martlet investigation, the time spent piecing together the list of names, prostitutes from across Louisiana and Alabama and Mississippi who had suddenly gone missing, no trace. Few details available on any of them, occasionally a sallow photograph.

Faceless victims. As here, where birth dates were given—and death dates.

These were death certificates.

Causes of death were listed, each eerily identical: suffocation. In one instance, the secretary had added a colorful addendum: "Quenched by earth's unremitting thirst."

The bang of the metal rod returned. Louder.

The flashlight jarred in Brad's hand. He shut it off. The sound clattered on above, lasting much longer this time. Using it as cover, he gathered up the rustling papers. He held them close and stood up. Stepping around the desk, he went to the doorway of the foyer and looked out into the deepness of the hospital's main hall.

No windows graced the back wall, and only the frontal ones gathered any of the light from the aging afternoon. Both right and left, rows and rows of bed frames, only half of them clothed with mattresses, extended across a floor of fractured gray tiles.

His gaze walked the ceiling, trying to pen the source of the clunking sound.

The noise stilled.

If it was a person, why hadn't they come down to confront him? He adjusted his grip on the papers and rotated, walking back toward the entrance. He chose the right-hand set of steps and pushed his glasses into place before ascending.

The metal steps were blessedly quiet beneath his feet. The same could not be said of the wooden floor at the top. At the first shrill creak beneath his weight, he jolted back and retreated down a step, turning his head while sweat traveled from his palm onto the papers.

No rapidly approaching figures appeared, though. No one in sight at all. No sound, even, except for a very faint buzz, traceable to the sagging ceiling fans running down the middle of the hall, grudgingly churning the dead air. Someone had left them running.

Feathery light came in through the front windows and touched more beds, seventy-five at least. All with mattresses and ash-colored sheets. All made up and waiting. Brad drew out his phone and aimed it down the hall from where he was standing on the step, lining up a nice shot of pale cots beneath milky windows.

He didn't take the picture. In the far background of the shot, something disturbed the smooth surface of one of the beds. As he lowered the phone, several other beds at the southern end of the room—two dozen, perhaps—drew his focus. They were rumpled. Something lay beneath their top sheets.

Shrouded forms. The unmistakable outline of two peaks, nose and toes, separated by a long gently sloping valley. Bodies.

Brad's pupils itched as he refused to blink. He left the stairs. Memories of the Martlet Mall circled in his mind: the wide, dim hall and the lost women leaning in shop windows, well dressed and dead.

The aisle between the cots was suddenly a thousand feet long. Were they sick? Sleeping? Each was totally covered. And none of the covers stirred. His nostrils flared: no smell of decay. Just dust.

The click of each step ricocheted off the walls as Brad advanced toward the occupied beds. Thin-armed radiance reached around him, blinding as he passed each window, folding across the veiled shape of the nearest body as he closed in on the beds. Should he leave? He wasn't a doctor; he had no business disturbing a patient in bed.

If this is still a patient. How could it be? This hospital had clearly been abandoned long ago.

Keeping his phone raised, he pressed record on the camera app and stepped out of the aisle. He stopped beside the first bed. Through the lens, his hand looked very scrawny. For a heartbeat, he filmed it hovering above that splotchy, mildewed sheet. Then he pulled it back.

A bald head. Cavernous eyes. Gasping jaws set with grimy pebble teeth. Inch after inch of a dusty, crumbling reddish body revealed as he drew the coverlet back. In places, the stuff stuck to the sheet and broke off from the body in clumps; what remained lost its fragile cohesion and disintegrated to reveal yellow bone.

At the foot of the bed, Brad let the coverlet fall.

The thing lay alone in the fresh light. A corpse, a naked man, coated long ago in wet clay. His hair was withered. His straining mouth was clogged with dirt, quelling any thought he might still be alive.

The phone shook as he moved to the next bed and the next bed, pulling back the covers from each faceless form. He should stop. He should leave. He should report this. He'd waited until he had all the info he needed on the mall's deceased owner to report the embalmed bodies he'd found inside the Martlet, and so he'd faced legal consequences; he should remember that.

Instead, the book in the basement came rushing back, *The Utterances: A record of the things spoken by those anointed with Adamah.* The words came, too, as if from the withered mouths around him, returned.

It's so dark.

The air just trickles down here.

How long is its arm?
It's coming through the cracks in the boards.
The floor is standing up.

All that, dated from the hot months of 1877. And then the September letter that detailed the death of Dr. McCloud at the hands of people smeared in dark paint.

Clay. Wet, sucking earth.

All the bodies in front of him were gaping, drowned by dirt. Some retained thin vestiges of hair. Could these be the people from that distant summer, preserved somehow? Or had the practice continued into recent years? Seen as beneficial, or medicinal, or—

He reached the final bed and tugged back the sheet and the body lunged at him. A scream like tearing paper scorched his ears. Grasping hands seized his right sleeve.

Pounding metal shook the borders.

One of the bed's legs was shorter than the others. It banged against the floor as the writhing creature wrestled with his arm. The cell phone slipped from his captured hand. It landed amid the sheets. The thing released him and scooped it up.

Not thing.

It was a white-haired girl. Pale arms and legs, unnaturally long, whipping about. The billowing reek of excrement searing his nose as he wrenched the phone free from the weaker hands.

"Not come to finish it?" the girl roared as Brad backed away. "I can't wait forever! They'll come through the floor! Even up here they'll come through the floooorrrrrr!"

The last part tumbled abruptly into a gentle purr. The flapping form stilled; the stretched face relaxed. Shriveled, lidless eyes stared at him. Brad stopped ten feet from the bed. Air rushed through his slack lips. "Harlow," he said. The girl from the bridge, from the mill. "Harlow."

She was just a kid, a little girl. Tied up. Left alone. What had happened to her since the mill? What had this place done to her? He started to approach.

Again rage contorted her face and she coughed out words: "Come to gloat?" Tilting her head back, she pushed out a high, thin scream and gyrated in the moldy sheets.

Bile ravaged his throat as he backed away. The papers stuffed under his arm absorbed sweat. The phone grew hot in his hand as he squeezed. Sorrel had done this. And so had he, by not confronting Sorrel about her condition.

Turning, he stalked up the aisle between the beds. As the screams followed him, he broke into a run. He tried to pound them from his ears on the stairs. He tried to scatter them in the gravel as he fled down the drive between the magnolias.

The gate at the end was unlocked. He heaved it open and strode through the high grass to the vine-wrapped sheriff's office. The parking lot was empty. He tried the door anyway and rammed his shoulder against it when it refused to open. Turning away, he jabbed through his phone contacts, searching for the sheriff. At that moment, the phone vibrated. Jennifer was calling.

Briskly, he tapped answer. "Jen, I—"

"You should get back here, Brad." A parched voice. Sorrel's voice.

His tone leapt. "Why do you have my fiancée's phone?"

"I'm at the house. I had to contact you. It's her—you better come."

Jennifer.

He started walking.

Through a closing throat, he said, "I'm coming." Jamming the phone into his pocket, he gripped the death records from the hospital and ran up the western edge of town toward the grocery store and the power substation where he'd left his car. The muggy afternoon air burned cold in his lungs.

2 4

The cicadas were blaring when I leapt from my car in the house's clearing, and in that instant a question and realization collided in my mind and shook me. Dr. McDowell on that first day had said he never heard the insects sing out here. They had started the night we moved in.

—"The House of Dust"
Southern Gothic

THE SHERIFF'S CAR stood parked in the center of the clearing. Brad threw the Accord door shut and strode toward it. A shout broke through the brushy wall of the woods. "Brad? Are you there?" It was Sorrel's voice, rough, but elevated to something approaching panic.

He ran. Twigs popped as he dashed into the woods. Holly branches dragged at his shirt. Sunlight particlized in the canopy, drifting hazy between the tree trunks. Sticks hooked his pant legs. Then the foliage parted and he pounded into a clearing centered by a vast, rising oak.

Sorrel stood beneath the tree, coat off, sleeves rolled back, gripping a rope that looped over a jutting branch. A noose dangled at the end, four feet above the ground.

Brad stumbled to a stop, taking it in and then making a quick turn to survey the rest of the area. He looked at the sheriff. "Jennifer?"

Before the man could reply, a trill of birdsong penetrated the clearing. It landed in his ears as human laughter. Very rapid, as if released from behind a cork. Something rare, but something he recognized. Something he had heard last Saturday night as Jennifer struggled from sleep.

Again, his head jerked around. But it wasn't coming from the trees. It was coming out of the ground.

"Where is she!"

Sorrel glared at the noose. "She used the old rope to go down the hole."

Brad stepped forward. *Hole?*

Then he saw it, just below the place where the noose dangled. A narrow chasm opening between two of the oak's huge roots. Charging forward, he slammed onto his knees and looked into the pit.

Pale light drained down the sheer sides and landed on Jennifer's body twenty feet below. She was still in her pajamas. Her hair lay loose on the pit floor. And she was quivering.

No. Laughing.

A second peal rose up, bubbly, intoxicated.

He felt his face constricting as he looked at Sorrel, but there was no hint of triumph or gloating in the man's eyes. Instead, he nodded at the noose.

Brad looked, too, then understood.

Pulling the noose larger, he stepped into it. He cinched it tight below his hips and stepped to the edge. For a second, he flailed as the feeling of depth opened below him. *There's nothing down there except Jen.* He eased off the edge.

Sorrel staggered and braced himself as he let out the rope, lowering Brad into the pit.

The cool, dampish musk of earth closed around him. The light diminished. His feet kicked the walls, releasing small dirt cataracts. The keening sound of the cicadas faded, replaced by the solemn silence of the deep ground.

A third laugh rattled up around him before his feet touched bottom. Dropping to his knees, he gripped Jennifer's shoulders. The muscles below her shirt knotted up. Her flesh was cold. Her hands flapped gently as he pulled her up against him. The fingernails were black with dirt.

His eyes jumped to the floor where she had lain. It was scarred with furrows. She had been digging. Like in the garden. Only now there was nothing dead in sight. She was digging for herself. Digging toward something.

Cold leached through his pants and spread through his legs. *There's nothing down here.*

His heart kicked harder as he leaned over her. "You're getting out of here, honey."

A lilting murmur escaped her lips: "I have to get closer." She spoke with happy hopelessness. But her eyes were closed.

Sleeping. Locked inside a dream.

And if she came out of it here, it would only add to her instability.

"Hush now." Trembling, he folded her close and stood to give some slack to the rope before jerking on it. To yell would risk waking her. But nothing happened.

The cold climbed his legs. What if Sorrel left them here? What if he had thrown Jennifer down here and tricked him into going in after her?

Again, he jerked the rope.

This time, it responded, tightening against his legs. Brad held her tight to keep from brushing the narrow walls. She groaned slightly but did not cry out as they were lifted. At the top, he grabbed the nearest root and dragged them both onto solid ground. Standing, he kicked off the rope.

Sorrel stood a little way off, hands raw, chest heaving.

"Is she all right?" he called.

Brad kept his lips tight. Swiftly, he carried her through the branches and green dimness to the light of the clearing and the house. Climbing the stairs, he crossed the porch and jammed the door open and lurched through. He closed it behind them and leaned against it, hugging her.

Jennifer stirred as he moved toward the stairs. Her head shifted and her eyes flickered.

"Shhh," Brad soothed.

"No. It's okay. I can stand." She was awake.

He let her down by the foot of the staircase. She looked at her clothes.

"I guess I should clean up."

"You were—"

"I know."

"You were asleep, Jen."

"I know. Finally, right?" She shrugged uncertainly. "And I feel fine. Good, actually. Rested. Maybe . . . maybe things will start to be fine again."

Turning, she carefully climbed the stairs.

This was wrong. He'd longed for those words, but hearing them was wrong. Something had changed in her. *Maybe* the grief was at last relenting, but what had brought the change while she was sleeping? What had driven her out of the house and into the woods? Into a pit?

"Jennifer."

"Yes, Brad?"

"You didn't—" He bit off the end.

Jennifer stopped halfway up the stairs and turned. She said softly, "How dare you."

His jaw tightened. He gripped the scarred railing and climbed toward her.

"Please, roll up your sleeves."

She didn't blink. She waited for him to reach the step below her, then jerked back her sleeves and stuck out her thin arms. Unblemished.

"Here, check my feet, too. Or do you want me to undress? 'Cause there's a thousand places I could stick a needle. Or maybe you want to shine your flashlight in my eyes, or go upstairs and go through my stuff, or check my phone 'cause maybe I'm texting a dealer!"

"Stop it, Jen." He turned away.

"I *slept*. I didn't dream about dead people for once. And if it takes lying in a hole to do that, fine. I feel good, Brad. No thanks to you. I thought we were supposed to support each other."

Heaviness wound around Brad's feet as he went down the stairs. He waited for voice and footfalls to retreat, then drew a breath and walked to the front door.

Outside, Sorrel stood at the bottom of the porch steps, facing away. Crossing the whining boards, Brad looked down at him.

The man didn't turn. His voice was soft. "Is she all right?"

"Why did you come out here?"

"To check on you both. What happened to her?"

"What happened to *your* people? I went to the old hospital. Didn't expect to find the living among the dead."

The sheriff's fingertips kneaded his lean biceps. "Harlow is confined for her own safety. She went in the old mine one time. Tried to swim down to the bottom of the river another. Looking for *rest* in the wrong places. That night at the mill? I was waiting for her. To try for the hundredth time to talk her out of all that."

"She needs someone to take *care* of her!" He was jittery with adrenaline.

"That's what I'm doing! And that's what you should be doing with your fiancée. In a state like that, she could end up in Deep Creek, or in the river."

"Jennifer's fine."

"I'm glad." Rotating, Sorrel looked up at him. "I really am. And I hope you are, too, Brad. I hope you do everything you can to keep her that way." He backed away a couple steps before turning and walking to his car.

After he was gone, Brad sat in one of the rockers. He swayed slowly and watched the dust settle.

I stayed with her for ten days.

We went places in that time: down to Lexington, to the library, to eat at a little place called Dan's Café, to visit Pinoak Lake. About the middle of the following week, the seventeenth, I think, we drove west for about seventy miles, following the course of the Locust River. While we were out and the signal was strong, I tried again to call Richard Hettinga, but he didn't answer.

Jennifer took everything in stride. She was very quiet, and would smile occasionally, but always seemed slightly anxious to return to the house. When I tried to speak of the past, though, I detected ripples. She had not completely healed. Deeper currents flowed beneath her placid face. And deeper currents flowed beneath the things I had discovered—a connection I could feel but not yet express.

—"The House of Dust"
Southern Gothic

DURING THE NIGHT, Missy imagined that the bathroom floor softened, molding to fit her body. She imagined the dust on her feet closed the wounds she had inflicted while trying to remove it.

The illusion of comfort almost lulled her to sleep. Almost. She heard Walt come in around seven o'clock in the morning. She watched the dawn light pool on the tile and waited for him to come find her. Kiss her. Undress her. Comfort her.

He didn't bother.

Around eight, she came out into the bedroom and found the boy huddled beside her nightstand, staring trance-like at the eyes painted above the hallway door. When she took him to the kitchen and offered him toast, he wouldn't eat. She took him to the front porch, and they sat in the rocking chairs and listened to the ticking sounds of the morning bugs.

"So who are your parents?" she asked. "Where do you belong?"

He gazed at the trees, mouth slightly agape, shaking his head.

Missy rolled her lips together and looked at the trees, too. "I know what you mean."

The boy couldn't stay. Eventually, the sheriff would come back. Maybe today. But she couldn't take him away, either; she couldn't risk triggering a fit like the one he'd had in the car yesterday. The farther they went, the worse he'd become. There had to be a closer place of safety. Someone in this town who could help.

Leaning her head back, she stared at the underside of the upper porch. *Walt. Would he help?*

At noon, she stood outside the closed study door and listened to the stillness inside. She eased it open. The doors leading to the porch were wide. Walt sat in his chair, sprawled forward on his desk, asleep in the rising heat. Same way he'd spent weekends at the apartment, when they weren't making love. Leaning down, she said gently, "Walt?"

He twitched. His eyes slitted. They were leaden. "I'm really tired, Missy."

The stubble on his face was verging toward a beard. It wasn't like him to be so unkempt. "Can you tell me where you went last night? With the sheriff?"

"Missy . . . " He said it like a chore. His eyelids resealed.

Missy remained bent down, studying him. He didn't seem tired. He seemed dazed. Hunching closer, she sniffed his breath. No alcohol. No sign of injury, either. Just sweat and the musk of dry mud. Still, he had been out all night with that sheriff. Maybe with others. Together in that awful town.

Her eyes stayed on him as she slid open the lower left desk drawer, took the Pontiac keys, and shut it again. She backed out of the study and closed the door.

Downstairs, they passed all the hideous wallpaper that needed ripping down and crossed the floorboards that needed shining. They went out to the car. The boy struggled a bit, but she forced him in. They had to try for help.

After crossing the clay-stained bridge, she buckled her seat belt. It immediately felt too constricting against her chest, so she unclipped it and flung it away. Her hands climbed up and down the wheel. In the passenger seat, the boy sat inert. As the speeding tires brought them closer to town, though, he grew restless. His left hand stiffened and began to thump against the center console. "I'm not taking you back to them," she said.

At Adamah Road, she told him to lie down on the floorboard. He slithered beneath his seat belt and lay on the dirty carpet and drummed his hand. As they approached Simmons Pike, he began keening. Could he feel the presence of those trenches thrumming up from the ground? "We're not going back," she repeated.

Taking the turn hard, she drove west. They passed the lonely gray house and the field of trenches where she had found the boy. Soon the woods came back and hid the property. The road wiggled on into the wilderness. Then, just as it had yesterday, a gray-shingled steeple broke through the trees up ahead on the left.

The sight of it did not bring the cathartic flood she had hoped for. A smattering of the shingles on the spire's peaked sides were missing; torn off, perhaps, by high wind, leaving the tar paper and, in places, the pale wood.

As she turned into the drive, the high grass of the churchyard crowded in around the car, coming right up to the edge of the gravel.

Beyond, in a paint-peeling state of dejection, the holy house looked out at her arrival from windows with crooked-shutter eyelids.

No cars occupied the rounded gravel patch by the front steps, but tire tracks went off through the grass to a place behind the building. Missy stopped the car in the middle of the parking area and looked out her window at the cemetery. Trampling feet had cut paths between the forgotten headstones to a more recent smear of red dirt. Had the person laid to rest been dead? Or bound, screaming until the dirt crowded into their mouth?

She blinked and remembered the boy. "Come on," she said. "We're here."

Power lines drooping across the yard from the road buzzed softly as she helped him from the car. She brushed off his clothes and then looked down at herself and realized she was wearing slacks and an oversized T-shirt. Hardly church clothes. Taking his hand, she repeated, "Come on."

The right side of the double doors was open, though the way it slumped on its hinges made it look more like an accident than an invitation. An acrid smell drifted out to meet them. It coated the insides of her nose and caused her to hesitate on the threshold. She glanced at Roy. He was not looking at the doorway, but over his shoulder at the graveyard.

Tightening her nostrils, she pulled him forward.

The church had no lobby or antechamber. When she stepped through the doors she was in the sanctuary. A portable radio sat behind the back pew, its antennas extended. The fuzzy voices of a 1940s choir rode in on waves of static. Their song accompanied her as she surveyed the room.

Are you washed? (are you washed?) In the blood? (in the blood?) In the soul-cleansing blood of the Lamb?

None of the lantern-like lights were on, but the windows allowed in a syrupy sort of light to highlight the cracked plaster walls. The pews were dusty. The air tasted oily.

Are your garments spotless? Are they white as snow? Are you washed in the blood of the Lamb?

At the front, in the right corner, a side door was propped open with a floor fan. The machine hummed loudly. The air carried a sharp smell, almost like varnish. The floorboards up there were darker than the ones toward the rear, and gleaming. Someone was at work here, sanding and finishing.

Unease corkscrewed through her intestines. She looked down at the boy again. His chin still clutched his shoulder. This time, she looked back, too.

A figure in black was rising up in the doorway. A short man was climbing the steps, one thin arm clutching the railing, propelling him up. His head was sunk between vulture-like shoulders. His eyes, deep-set, were fixed on her. It was the man from yesterday. The stranger in the tunnel who offered her his shoes.

She had nowhere to go, so she retreated into the church. As he strode in, she backed up the aisle.

"Good afternoon," the man thundered. A little smile twisted the corners of his mouth as he pursued. "I'm Mark Burger. I'm the pastor here at Simmons Creek. I'm glad you're both safe."

"We're leaving," Missy said. "We were just passing and saw the door opened so—but we're leaving."

"What were you looking for?"

"Oh, nothing."

"Would you like to talk about it?"

She was at the head of the aisle now. The fresh varnish off the boards burned her throat, but she stopped and took a big gulp of it. This little man wasn't what a minister should look like. A minister was the giant who had served the church Grandmama had made her go to. He had bent down, down to her, and looked at her through his thick yellowed glasses. He had smiled and remembered her name. "I hope to see you next week, Miss Missy. Remember you're God's special creation." And that made her smile a little bit, because she imagined maybe it was true.

This man was too small. And he was wearing tattered work clothes. And his fingers were scuttling busily along the tops of his pockets as he stopped a few feet from her. But he was all there was.

"I . . . " She took a breath. "Yes. Thank you."

She followed him over the freshly varnished floor, up onto a dais and past the pulpit. Again, she noticed his shaved head and wondered if he might have been in the military. He led them to a row of chairs against the front wall. A big wooden cross hung from the wall, flanked on either side by a framed picture: one showed a pair of stone slabs marked with numbers; the other was of Jesus.

The pastor arranged two chairs opposite one for himself and sat down. The fan in the open doorway droned a dozen feet behind him.

Missy sat slowly. Roy stood behind his chair. When she tried to pull him around in front of it, he whined and she dropped her hand.

"This is where the choir sits," she blurted.

Pastor Burger raised his pale eyebrows. "If we had one, yes, that'd be right."

"My grandmama took me to church." She added uselessly, "Well, sometimes."

"But that was a while back?"

"Yes."

He folded his busy hands. "What are your names?"

A breath. "I'm Marilyn. This is Roy."

"And what has the Devil been doing for you today?"

"Oh. I'm not really here for me, to be honest. It's him." She motioned to Roy. "He needs . . . something. I don't know any doctors close by, so I came here." Jesus was frowning from the corner of her eye. "I mean—" But she couldn't lie to him *again*, so she folded her hands in her baggy shirt.

"The child," Burger said, ignoring her wording. "Is he yours?"

"No! He's . . . " Didn't he know this community at all? "I think he's an outcast or something."

She looked at Roy. He was clutching the back of his chair, examining his knuckles.

"How did he come to your care?"

"I found him in trouble, sort of took him in."

"*Trouble*."

"Yes." The shirt fabric strained against her fingers.

Ask him. Ask him. It clawed at her. Then, hot Atlanta Sundays with Grandmama again. Packed in the shuffling departure line. The giant bending down. *Trust in the Lord, my dear.*

Ask. Trust.

"Pastor, what I really wanted to talk to you about—and I guess you won't think this is silly because you said it a minute ago—is . . . "

Ask. Trust.

". . . devils."

Pastor Burger sat forward, his hands struggling with the bonds of his folded fingers.

"You're new to Three Summers?" he asked.

"We moved here a couple weeks ago."

"To the old plantation on the island?"

"Angel's Landing." The protective way she spoke the title felt odd.

Burger didn't notice. "You heard of me from your husband?"

"My—no. Just passin' by one day I noticed your building."

"Your husband did come by. He seemed troubled when I met him. And something similar, I take it, is afflicting you."

Missy nodded. "And Roy. And everyone, I think. The whole town. They don't all show it, and they try to cover over it, but there's something inside dragging them down." Her feet shifted. "I know I'm not the only one. Others must have come to you with this? You said my fiancé did?"

"Your . . . *fiancé* was interested mainly in the graveyard's occupants; he's working on the Locust River Mine case, I understand. But I could see it in him. And yes, I can see it in others. In the sheriff. In the few townsfolk who speak to me. A great weariness. A sense that each is a traveler crossing an endless field, searching for a shade tree."

She said quietly, "Are they possessed?"

Burger tilted his head back for a moment and closed his eyes. Missy clutched the inside of her shirt and looked between him and the picture of Jesus.

In a higher and softer voice, eyes still closed, the pastor intoned, "In the field of this world, the Lord's enemies creep through the wheat, planting tares to diminish the harvest. Both are permitted to grow together until Christ shall come with his sharp sickle. But until that mighty day? Yes, I find myself assigned to a portion of the field filled with tares, where the footprints of the enemy abound in the rocky soil." His eyes opened and fixed on Roy. "And this child has witnessed the handiwork of the enemy, has he not?"

She didn't know what any of it meant, but she knew the answer: "Yes."

The pastor reared up from his chair. Roy sank down behind his chair and watched the man through the slats.

"Roy," Pastor Burger said. "Tell me what happened to you."

Missy tried to steady her voice. "Stand up, Roy. Don't be scared. The pastor won't hurt you."

His voice came back in a small quaver. "But *he* will."

"No, he—" Her heart locked up. She stood. "It's here?"

"Here," he repeated.

Pastor Burger's eyes darted. "In this room?"

Roy was looking past him. "Behind you," he whispered. "It's crawling out of the fan."

Pastor Burger wheeled around. Missy pressed her heels together. "Is it coming closer?" the pastor demanded.

"Just standing there. It's motioning with all its left hands."

The pastor's hand stiffened, and his chair screamed across the floor to crash against the others. Something ravenous leapt into his eyes. Forcing his neck up and his shoulders down, he straightened and raised his right hand. The fingers trembled, rigid. He strode toward the open door and the fan and his yell made her jolt.

"Unclean spirit! In the name of Christ, I command you to depart from this place!"

The fan went on blowing. The light in the doorway did not flicker. He stood there for a long time. Slowly, he reverted to his sunken stance. When he finally came back, Missy was holding Roy's hand while he cowered behind the chair.

"It'll keep coming back," she said. "It came yesterday, and last night, and now . . . How do I make it stop?"

"I will pray for you," the pastor said. "But you need to get out."

"You mean leave the house?"

"That house." He sighed. "I'm not from here, so I don't know the history, but I know it is one of blood. There are places even the Lord will abandon so they rot away. Evil resides in that ground, like nuclear radiation, poisoning everyone who makes their home there."

She was already shaking her head before he finished. "There's got to be another way. My fiancé bought that place for me. We lived in a two-room in Nashville and he'd go sit on the fire escape and smoke all evening because he got so tired of listening to me beg for a nicer place and . . . I'm sorry. Look. I know it's got problems, but there's always salvation, right? Jesus is stronger than the demons, right?" She faltered at the end, as Ellen King's desperate journal entries needled her mind.

They are coming out of the floor now—and the walls. They're coming for me.

"Yes," Burger said. He glanced wearily at the dusty pews. His voice was quiet. "Christ is stronger. But Christ lives in hearts, not places. And only the heart armored with his Word can withstand the full attack of Satan in those evil places."

"I know evil places!" Missy felt a *sickness* smoldering in her guts, and she felt herself failing and the heat rising. "I know what it's like to lie in a bed one night and lie on a metal table the next and have the life scraped out of me. All my life, I've—"

For a moment, the pastor averted his eyes.

"Didn't he tell you what I was?"

"Who?"

"My fiancé. No? Well, I will: I used to be a hooker. And so maybe you think this is all happening because I used to live in sin. Maybe you think that's all I still am. But that's just wrong, because plenty of great people did bad things and turned their lives around. You know St. Augustine? He did plenty of bad things when he was young. But they still call him a Church Father. That's big. That means there must be some leftovers for me." She felt her chin sticking out the way it had when she fought with Grandmama.

Letting go of Roy's hand, she stood up to be at Burger's height.

He was nodding, and deep furrows had filled his high forehead. "Yes, Marilyn. Where there is sin, there is much more Grace. I *will* pray for you. And I will pray for Roy. But if you stay in that house, Satan will sift you like wheat. Leave now, and God will provide you another dwelling place. Go down to Lexington. Let the lease expire. Your fiancé can finish his work from—"

"Lease? There's no lease. We bought the house."

The pastor blinked. "Not from my understanding. The sheriff would never allow that house to be sold. The lease probably expires at the end of—"

"There's no lease! The house is ours. He told me that."

Burger simply shrugged.

Missy felt the floor fracturing beneath her shifting feet. "It's time for us to go."

Peeling Roy's hands off the chair, she hauled him down from the pulpit platform and into the aisle.

"Is there nothing I can do to help you, Marilyn?" Burger called.

She started to shake her head but the smell of varnish infiltrated her sinuses afresh. Bending, she picked up three of the canisters waiting by the front pew and turned toward him. "Let me borrow these?"

He appeared confused but motioned his unsteady hands.

"Thank you." Her tongue felt leaden. "Here, Roy, you carry one."

They left the church and walked down the steps in the hot, humming power line silence. When they reached the car, she threw the canisters in the back seat. The wire handles of the two she had carried were bent out of shape.

I stood in the dance hall several times during those days, looking at the shape on the mirror above the fireplace, at its many out-stretched arms. What drove this cult? What happened to those who entered that embrace?

Jennifer slept at night, deeply, eerily. I did not. I sat in the study, computer open. Each time the chasm of sleep approached, a top-pling, plummeting sensation jolted me awake and my eyes would land on the Newton's cradle at the edge of my desk. Silent. Urging action. One muggy morning, I jerked up in my chair to find her kneeling beside the desk. She hardly noticed me. She was going through the death notes retrieved from the hospital, nodding to herself, smiling softly.

—"The House of Dust"
Southern Gothic

BRAD HELPED HER make peanut butter and jelly sandwiches for lunch. She wore her blond hair loose. She used to wear it in a pony-tail all the time, except when sleeping. Even that first uncontrolled week in Nashville. As time went by, and he wrote worsening articles, and she worked through school, the ponytail became more severe, the hair tighter across her scalp. Even the night they got engaged, as she sat beside him on the couch, she had twined it over her shoulder.

Now it hung limp.

They vacuumed curtains until early afternoon, and he coughed explosively the entire time. The dust seemed attracted to his lungs. She, on the other hand, only occasionally rubbed her nose. When they set about window-washing, he kept on coughing.

As her cloth squeaked across the glass, Jennifer finally said, "Really, you look like hell. Shouldn't you be out working on your story?"

He sniffed heavily. "We need to stay together." The line he'd used when he gave her the ring. The ring that was right out there in the car, in the glove box.

"Brad . . . " Jennifer shook her head at her reflection. "Brad, I'm fine. You're the one who's . . . "

"Who's what?" His hand with the rag pressed too hard. With a sharp crack, a smooth, arcing line appeared in the glass.

"Careful!" She gazed at him while tenderly wiping her pane. "Can't you feel how old these windows are?"

Minutes later, from the car, he could see her standing behind the same window, face obscured by her loose hair and the frail glass.

He thought to drive just to the bridge, but the heat compelled him into the tree tunnel, and then he drove all the way up the dead green road to the bright brink of Adamah Road. There he paused, panting.

Jennifer was not *healing*. She was changing. Something she had encountered in her sleep or in the pit had stuck. Sunk in. Altered her. *Was* altering. Every moment a little more.

No. There's nothing down there. Whatever's wrong with her, you brought here with you.

Turning right, he drove out of town. The swarm of questions he had collected over those quiet days coalesced around the image of Jen's calm, ungrieving face. At the end of Adamah Road, he sat for a minute and looked at the wide field and the sudden hill and the gray house atop it.

Jezebel Irons had invited him over almost two weeks ago to talk more about the Queen of Hearts and Adamah. But no car was out front. Instead, he turned right and drove down Simmons Pike.

Queen of Hearts. Adamah. He pinched the wheel.

Simmons Creek Baptist Church sat hunched and abandoned as usual on the riverbank, but something had changed. Brad scanned the leafy exterior as he stepped from the car. His eyes landed on the ripped-out flooring. It was now completely smothered by kudzu.

As he approached, though, significant tears in the foliage became evident. Someone had reclaimed a substantial number of the boards from the green fist. Stepping around the corner, he glanced down the west side of the building.

The ladder the pastor had been using more than a week ago leaned in the same spot. The grass surrounding the church had grown higher to match the graveyard. Dread lanced him—he suppressed it. He walked to the doors and knocked.

No answer.

He tried a second time, then tested the latch. The door groaned open, exhaling stale hot air.

It was dim inside. Curtains still cloaked the closed windows. The pews sat dull and empty and the needling smell of the dry earth beneath them pricked his nostrils. But not all the floor was bare. A slew of loose boards had been arranged down the center aisle like a bridge toward the pulpit.

A hunched figure in black pastoral garb sat on the steps beneath the pulpit, hands folded, head bowed.

"Pastor Burger?" The unsecured boards clunked beneath Brad's feet. "How are you? I realize it's been a little while." Closing in, he slowed when the man still did not look up. "Sir?"

"Have a seat, Mr. Ellison." The pastor's voice was low and steady, but his folded hands trembled. "And what has the Devil been doing for you today?"

Brad eased down onto the step beside him. For a while, he said nothing, deciding whether there was anything to say, whether his fears would sound foolish when put into words.

"I'm concerned about my fiancée. She had an . . . episode since we last spoke. She'll probably be fine."

"You don't believe in Adamah."

"You do?"

"I believe in what's up there." His eyes nodded to the rafters. "Which compels that I also believe in what's down there."

Brad looked at the half-restored flooring. "What is down there?"

"Satan, who imagined he could be like God. Who warred against God. Who was thrown down from Heaven with the angels that rebelled with him. Who tempted our first parents to sin and was condemned to crawl in the dust."

The pastor's tired eyes studied the barren stretches of earth beneath the pews. "One of those fallen angels is here, Mr. Ellison. In this land. In this ground. This church is an embattled outpost. Beulah is the name of Heaven's border region, and this land is the back door to Hell."

Brad thought about his phone, about recording, but decided against it. This went beyond names and dates. "Why did you come here?"

"I was called," the man said hollowly. "I was a boy with my mother in Arkansas in 1942 when a letter came from my father. He had been brought to Camp Simmons, just south of here, for army training. He described an uneasy malaise across the nearby town of Three Summers and said he wished there were a pastor in an abandoned church by the river. He never returned from war, but I tried to follow. Broke my back without ever being deployed. A cripple is of little use in the military, so I joined the ministry. Still, I was not expecting such a battlefield."

"I assume not many converted."

"One. One soul. Perhaps I went about it all wrong. Instead of seeking God, I was pursuing Satan. Is there a difference? I should know."

"That one soul was your friend?"

"Richard Hettinga. He grew up in this town. I rebuked an evil spirit that was plaguing him. He did not return for many years after, but God's word bore fruit. He collected artifacts that chronicled the dark history of the region, drawing the ire of the Queen. She cast him out, and he willingly departed. It's phone conversations with him that have kept my spirit buoyed over the years."

Brad didn't mention the difficulty he'd had trying to contact the man in recent days. Instead he said, "Sorrel once mentioned something about a brother."

"It was Hettinga. Sorrel was a young man when he left. He felt bitterness toward his mother, and toward me, I think. But it was necessary. The darkness must be lifted. He sees that now. You and he and Hettinga will do what I have only been able to pray for: bring an end to these cycles of slavery.

"The cycles began with the evil of human bondage, and have continued for two centuries, holding this town in place. No freedom. You are the agent God has sent to end it. A man of words where a man of the gospel failed."

A touch of the manic quality he remembered from the end of their last conversation had returned to the pastor's voice. A latent energy moved in his eyes, a pent-up zeal from the sermons he never preached. Brad watched the man consciously quell it.

"I'm sorry. Last week I turned eighty-two. Just now it struck me that I'll only see you for a couple more minutes in my life. Believe me when I say you are an agent of God."

"I don't think I'd be a very good agent," Brad said.

"But you'll write your article, won't you?"

"I'm more concerned about my fiancée at the moment."

Burger sighed and wiped his hand across his brow.

"Then take her and leave. Now. This afternoon. Richard Hettinga will help you finish the article."

"You think it's that urgent?"

"The Evil One reaches up for all who enter this land. He is reaching for your fiancée right now, to transform her into his vessel."

Brad looked away. He'd been with her there for over a week. Nothing had happened.

There's nothing down there. No Devil.

"You don't believe?" Burger said.

Brad examined the dusty church. The air and the light were constricting. The warmth drew sweat from his scalp. He shook his head.

"It's dangerous not to believe."

And there's nothing above, either. Biting back the words, Brad rose.

"I really appreciate your time. It's been insightful."

As he walked back down the unsteady aisle of boards, he heard the pastor clamber to his feet. The effort must have drained him, for he only weakly called, "I will pray for you."

There's only what's inside people.

Brad glanced back from the door. "I appreciate it," he said again.

In the car, he checked to make sure Richard Hettinga hadn't returned his calls. Then he started the engine. He saw movement reflected in the rearview mirror. His pulse quickened.

The church door was open. Burger was standing, but barely, clutching the door for support with one fist. His other hand jutted straight out, finger rigid, pointing at the back of the car. His cavernous eyes sunk deeper into his skull. The mottled flesh across his face stretched painfully as his jaws twisted apart. Even across the yard and through the glass, his bellowing voice was audible.

"Ad-am-ah! Leave him!"

I called Jennifer from the road. She sighed flatly when I asked if she was okay: "Brad. I'm fine." Still, I decided it was time to conclude the investigation. In Three Summers, I parked by the Theater Grill and went in and had chicken fingers and tater tots for lunch. I looked across the street at the arched cut-glass window above the marquee sign in the theater's limestone façade. The diner was empty besides a Stan Lee look-alike behind the counter. I asked him when the theater was last open, and he said, "I'm not giving any quotes," and went into the back. Before leaving, I took pictures of some photos hanging on the wall that showed people gathered around town, all with their eyes shut.

—"The House of Dust"
Southern Gothic

LIQUID, RIPPLING HEAT filled the alley behind the theater. Beneath a faded canvas awning stood a single metal door, corroded brown. The knob was gone and the hole was plugged up with plastic grocery bags. Tugging the knot free, Brad threaded his finger through and pried the door open.

A bubble of investigative excitement broke through the membrane of anxiety constricting his brain. Perhaps, since this place was more recently built, it would contain a greater number of clues. Clues to the people's interactions with the Adamah being. Seances or something. Fumbling out his phone, he tapped on the flashlight.

The air was marginally cooler inside. The door thumped shut and the darkness grew dense. A staircase cloaked in ragged carpet slanted down to the right.

He eased down the stairs, gripping an old brass railing. On the last step, it became clear that he was not entering a basement. Nor a service hallway, either. It was a wide hallway that stretched before him and bent left at the edge of his light. The carpet under his feet was a rich cobalt, vivid despite a frosting of dust. The zipper-like bodies of centipedes fled his roving light.

Brad moved up the hall. Blue drapes hung against the gold-painted walls, which were adorned with decoratively framed posters. Names he remembered from the house's basement stuck out—*The Thin Land, Angel's Island*—as well as some new ones: *The Quiet Visitor, Shade Tree Kingdom*. Every poster featured the pale-haired woman whose portrait he had studied in the library, Miriam Larkin. Her name painted in scrolly letters. Her face, with oddly long eyes, looking from below green trees and staring out blue windows and holes in the ground.

Just gazing out. Like she *was when I left*. He dismissed the thought as he stepped around the bend in the hall. A doorway in the left wall caught his eye.

A doorway framed by drapes. It must lead somewhere special. As he stepped into the doorless threshold and felt a vast openness pressing against his face, he realized just where he was headed.

The theater. He wasn't beneath it. He was in the access hall just outside of it. Holding his phone flashlight high, he saw row after row of blue velvet seats emerging from the gloom like relics in a sunken ocean liner. They sloped past him, from the main entrance off to his right down toward the stage and the huge screen on his left.

As he moved into the vastness, a recollection touched him: rushing through stale buttery darkness behind his dad, popcorn bucket in hand, searching for a seat as *The Matrix* began. They ended up at the very front and missing the first couple of minutes of the movie, but his dad had already seen it four times and filled him in on everything they'd missed, explaining things before they happened, excitedly ruining the experience. As they walked out of the theater, his dad tapped his skull and said with curious levity, *See, Brad? We have to see through it all and make hard choices sometimes.*

Reaching the main aisle, he turned left and descended toward the stage. At the bottom, he rotated and shone the light up across the auditorium. All of it lay underground, below street level. The façade, the walls, all of it was just a superstructure to shield this crater. Up at the top of the main aisle, light bled down the stairs from the foyer above.

They wanted to be closer to Adamah. But what had they actually done here? Did this place have a function beyond a movie house? Proceeding along the edge of the stage, he found a small set of steps at the end that led up to the dais. Cautiously, he advanced onto the stage. The searing sound of complete quiet tunneled into his ears, and he suddenly felt the presence of all those empty seats.

Sorrel—what if he was back there, sitting somewhere out in the cheap section, arms folded, watching him?

Well, what if? He kept moving, swiping the light across the narrow platform. The screen rose beside him, a silver wall, an empty canvas waiting for life.

Brad stopped. Near the middle of the stage, a lone rocking chair faced the auditorium. He put his hand on the armrest and set the chair rocking. The old woman phased through his mind: Missy had been her name. Had she sat here? Held community meetings here? But what did that entail? No clues lay around it on the gritty floor, and no doors led off behind the stage. This had not been a performance hall.

On the far side of the stage, more steps went down to the audience. The brittle odor of old cigarettes rose from the worn carpet as he climbed the aisle to the main entrance stairs. At the top, double doors with porthole windows let out into a foyer.

The carpet ended here. Masked daylight penetrated the cloudy façade window and seeped across amber tile. Turning off the flashlight, he approached the row of doors and raised one slat of the shielding blinds and drank in the sun and the desolate intersection.

He must have tried to suck in the outdoor air, because another cough swelled in his throat. Letting the slat fall, he bent into his sleeve and cleared his lungs.

When he straightened, a man standing twenty feet to his left did the same. And another to his right.

An endless line of men with crooked glasses, untucked dress shirts, and week-old beards occupied the mirrors paneling the walls. When he scowled, they all scowled back, like a clown in a funhouse mirror. Still, Heather, his editor, might like the shot, so he snapped a picture. He photographed the rest of the foyer, trying his best in the auditorium gloom, when he noticed a door partially obscured by an untethered drape.

The door was surmounted by a brass casting of Darrin DeWitt's Adamah symbol. The knob turned inside his hand. Rekindling his cell phone, he prepared to step inside when a thin creaking drifted up the stairs from the theater. Faint. Unnoticeable. Like a feather brushing his eardrum.

He considered calling out but decided it must be the rocking chair out on the stage, still drifting from his touch. *Must be.*

Stepping through the door, he turned left and found himself in a narrow undecorated corridor. Heaps of discarded drapes clogged the floor. He left the door open and stepped forward, nearly tripping over a dry mop bucket and a stack of paint cans. After a few dozen feet, the corridor bent left and climbed a short staircase.

He scaled the stairs and turned right, nudging through a door at the top. It clicked shut behind him.

His lips involuntarily puckered in a low whistle.

Just across the little room, beside a wooden table, a huge film projector crouched before a small square window, peering out at the auditorium. The words PEERLESS MAGNARC were stamped across the rear of the machine. A metal tag on its side said RCA.

Now here was something.

Metal racks crowded against the walls, all mostly empty, all dusty. Except for the bottom shelf of the rack nearest the projector. There lay round metal dishes, covered in dust, but marked by fingerprints. Streaks in the dust showed that they had been reorganized.

The phone flashlight swept to the table next to the projector. Above the table, a viewing window looked into the auditorium. Behind the table sat a metal chair, scooted back. An empty Mountain Dew bottle stood on the table with the label peeled half off.

Sorrel. The sheriff had been here. Recently.

Crossing quickly, he squatted down and lifted one of the dishes from the shelf. A piece of masking tape was calcified to the top, marked in pen with the word *Sleepwalkers.* That name had also branded one of the posters in the house's basement. Lifting the lid off, he examined the metal reel and coiled film inside.

Yes, here was something.

Brad took the film reel to the table. There was a switch by the door. When flipped, it dredged a greenish light from a fluorescent bulb on the ceiling. Turning the Dew bottle over, he propped the phone against it and set it to *record.* Then he opened the magazine on the projector and loaded the reel inside. Threading it down into the chamber beneath, he navigated the end of the filmstrip through the rollers and sprockets.

Minutes slipped past and the phone lens watched his back, witnessing his ineptitude.

Didn't matter. He just needed stills. Fuzzy photographs to nestle amid the text on *Southern Gothic*'s pulp pages. Something to win a smile from Heather, show her that he'd tried this time.

Finally, the film's course seemed correct and he attached it to the lower reel. Now if it would just play. A lever at the front of the projector sparked the arc lamp, and a second later, with a murmuring clatter, the film began its journey through the machine.

He turned out the fluorescent light and sat at the table, rubbing the grime from the projector's innards off his fingers. The screen in the theater brightened. He rotated the phone toward the rectangular viewing window. For a moment, only formless light shafted above the empty seats. He could see the rocking chair on stage motionless. He imagined the quiet town outside and braced himself for a blast of old-time orchestral music.

But the credits came silently.

Sleepwalkers.

Starring Miriam Larkin.

Darkness.

Then the front of the house was filling the screen. Its paint was bright. Its columns were twined by streamers instead of vines. The amount of light hitting the façade meant the trees were younger. What year? Sometime in the 1930s, perhaps, given the quality of the film. His speculation was cut short as the camera closed on the porch.

Miriam Larkin sat in a rocking chair just above the steps. Her eyes were closed. The camera climbed the steps and approached. She wore a thin white dress. *The* dress. The one the old woman had been buried in; the one he had unearthed before the house; the one that was now, presumably, back in the Simmons Creek Cemetery.

The camera closed in on her face. Her short hair sloped down the right side of her forehead in white finger waves. Her lips were dark. Her eyelashes even darker. Her eyelids opened.

Long dark eyes looked through the screen and began to glow.

They became headlights that bore down on and then swept past the screen. A black Oldsmobile Coupe was crossing the Locust River Bridge toward Three Summers. The sky was deep gray with evening.

In almost Hitchcockian style, the camera watched from the top of a building as the car approached the main intersection. It must be the top of the theater, he realized, not far above where he sat now. All of the buildings visible on-screen were still out there now.

The car parked by the Theater Grill, and a figure in a gray flannel suit got out. A cut to street level and his face became plain. A Laurence Olivier type, with blond hair and a pencil-thin mustache. He smiled at the town, and the camera swept around him to reveal neons in every storefront and marquee lights dancing around every sign. The man turned and went into the diner.

As he ate, a fan swirled above him. The shadows from its blades stretched across the ceiling, longer and longer. Then they slowed to a jerky rotation. The man's chewing slowed, too.

Brad glanced at the projector. Its sound had not changed. This was an intentional effect.

Yes, now a door in the diner was opening at regular speed. Miriam Larkin came inside wearing a long overcoat. She approached the startled man, smiled at him, and touched his forehead. Other people in the diner exchanged looks as Miriam took the man's hand and led him toward the door. The lights went out as they left.

Out on the street, the same strange viscosity was affecting the town. The marquee lights blinked slowly—on, off. The people on the sidewalks seemed to be wading through wet sand. The man smiled confusedly at them. Miriam smiled at him, the sluggish radiance reflecting in her pupils. She tugged the man down the street, and as they passed each building its lights were quenched.

An abrupt cut, and the camera was pointing down into the town from a low passing airplane, capturing an unsteady shot of people gushing out of buildings and alleyways to follow the couple, moving as a dark mass, like oil seeping from the bones of the old town.

Oil.

Brad rubbed his fingers across the tabletop. The old dirt from the projector was still ingrained in his skin, burning harsh and cool, sweetly foul, like petroleum.

Refocus. He was back on the road, walking with Miriam and the nameless man away from Three Summers. The town was dark behind them. Among the crowd, lanterns appeared and lit dozens of faces. Bright-eyed men in fedoras and dark-lipped women in drooping bonnets. All with wide smiles. All with shut eyes.

He shifted in his chair.

The projector whirred.

At the forest road, the party turned left and began the long walk toward Angel's Landing. The camera seemed to jump ahead a mile or so and looked back at the group as a far-off collage of lights.

Back with the crowd again. On and on through the trees. With each minute of film, their movements became more and more drawn out. Spoken words twisted faces out of shape. Newcomer man's uncertain grin became a grimace. Miriam's steady smile seemed maniacal.

The ebony surface of Deep Creek reflected their passage over the clay-stained bridge. Then the camera pushed in around their feet as they walked up the road and spilled into the fields blanketing the northern half of the island. The whir of the projector became the whisper of grass blades across clothing.

The man's feet grew unsteady. A pronounced limp developed in his right leg. He stumbled on the pavement. He looked to Miriam. Her hand, now on his back, compelling him forward.

And then another abrupt cut: the bright face of the house seen from the dim parkland of trees across the front drive. The focus was on the porch, on the line of rocking chairs, but something closer was obscuring the central one. Slowly, focus shifted. A noose was dangling in front of the lens.

Another cut. Looking down the rope to a tear in the ground below. A gash between two huge tree roots. The pit that Jennifer had gone down. The place she had started changing.

Brad's spine tightened against the back of the chair.

Then a steady pastoral shot. Crowd on the right edge of the frame, lanterns lifted. The house on the left, a quarter of a mile off, windows bright through a sparse assemblage of trees. Journeying up the road.

Then darkness.

Brad's hand was on his throat, massaging its way up toward his chin.

A slow fade-in. A great tree silhouetted against the house, all limbs rising except for one that jutted straight out. The one that held the noose.

The next instant, the light was dizzying and the camera was circling a heaving assembly gathered around the tree. The man in the gray flannel suit was being borne up on their lifted hands. His clothes strained as dozens of fists gripped the borders of his pants and coat, and reaching arms spread away, like petals from the heart of a flower. Like the spokes of a web holding writhing prey.

Miriam appeared in the crowd. She had shed her coat and wore the white dress beneath. She lifted her arms, and the man was lifted. His jolting head was pushed through the noose. His legs were pulled to tighten the loop. As the man was lowered down, she leaned out from the top edge of the hole to clutch his head. To squeeze his cheeks.

The man thrashed in slow motion and bellowed silently as she guided his body into the ground.

Miriam took her hands away, and with a snap, all the others let go.

Again, the shot switched to straight above. The rope slackened, and the man plummeted into the ground. Everyone else retreated from view. For a moment, it was just him in the spotlight, sprawled far down in the grave. Slowly, he stood up. Then he reached up. Then he jumped. But the grave was deep. Then he tried to free himself from the rope, but it was too taut. Then he tried to climb it. He was too weak.

As he scrabbled at the sheer sides, the party people reappeared. They advanced from all corners of the frame, arms laden with dark earth. They came in ranks. Reaching the edge of the hole, they lowered their arms and the dirt gushed down; then they turned away so the next row could advance.

Amid the cascade, the man leapt and threw his arms against the walls and yelled, the rope jostling, his frenzy almost mistakable for that of a frolicking child. The people came and came and the dirt poured down. Then bucket carriers advanced and poured silver streams of water down atop the man until the sides of the grave were gleaming and the ground was oozing around his frantic feet and climbing up his knees. And then more dirt came on huge shovels and the thing in the pit became dark with mud.

Soon it was waist-deep and stuck. Then it was chest-deep. The soupy earth writhed around it. Then it was shoulder-deep, and the chin was pried back and pointed at the sky in a final gasp. And then it was just the hands, filthy, clawing at the lights and the camera.

The film skipped and the grave was full. Hundreds of hands flooded in to smooth it flat. The light faded.

Brad's fingers were sunk into his cheeks, locking his palm across his mouth.

The view returned. Low to the ground. Camera moving. Wandering over the grass like the nose of a prowling animal. The outer edges of the picture were in shadow, while the center was a quivering orb of light. The operator must be holding the camera at waist height with a light mounted to the top, moving through the park. Roots appeared starkly on the massive screen and were passed over. The fat white bodies of crickets leapt away from the intruding lens.

Suddenly, the camera was moving over the body of a woman. She was curled up on the ground. It paused for just a moment on her peaceful face. Sleeping.

The camera veered away and lurched through the trees until it found another face and paused above it. A man, also sleeping.

And then another man. And then another woman. And then the view rose and looked toward the house. The lights were softer. The rocking chairs on the porch were full. Miriam sat in the middle, eyes closed, face placid. They were all asleep.

The End.

The screen went out.

Brad didn't turn on the lights. He sank forward until his forehead pressed against the table. He finally *knew*. He knew the old woman he had driven to her grave—she hadn't been dead. Not quite. And dozens like her across decades. Hundreds. Folded into the land around this town, smothered by damp earth. Forgotten.

He breathed in the dark and whispered, "I'm sorry, Missy."

I left the place reeling. Jennifer and I would leave today. There was
just one last call to pay.

—"The House of Dust"
Southern Gothic

THE DUST WAS coming away now.

Missy didn't really notice. Wringing the wet rag into the bucket,
she felt the water bubble between her fingers, falling droplets breaking the murky surface and sending ripples across a sweaty face with
tied-up hair. A pointless sort of face, when not dolled-up. Forgettable.
Like a mannequin's in a shop front.

She looked back at the glistening dance hall floor where she had
spent the four hours since returning from the church. It would be
ready for varnish when it dried. But what was the point if it wasn't
even hers?

But it is.

She squeezed the rag until it was stiff and warm inside her fists,
then she got up.

Roy was standing before one of the open windows in the dining
room, crushing fossilized fly carcasses on the sill with gentle taps of
a hammer.

"Did you get those nails out of the wall in the kitchen?"

He nodded.

Coming around the table, she held out the rag. "Let's trade. You can clean that."

Glancing over, he blinked and took the rag.

"If you want water, there's some in the bucket in the other room. Okay? I'm going upstairs for a minute. You be sure and tell me if you see anyone coming."

He began scrubbing the windowsill with jerky movements.

Missy rubbed wet knuckles across her forehead and wiped her hands on the baggy front of her shirt and left him. Armed with the hammer, she climbed to the second floor and went down the hall to the study. Working the stiffness from her shoulders, she reached casually for the handle. A spike of disappointment struck as the door opened. No lock, no excuse. He had gone somewhere on foot while she was away in the car. She had waited, expecting his return. But he hadn't returned, and probably wouldn't until late in the evening. Which left time. And no reason not to try to find out.

None of the hallway air followed as she stepped inside. The study's atmosphere was marshy. Clogged by cigarettes and rebreathed to the point of sourness, it had curdled against the ceiling.

She approached the desk, and memories of the Boss's office at the Club leapt behind her eyelids each time she blinked: sour breath, the *National Geographic* magazines on his couch, the turtles in their tanks across the room, blinking at her sleepily beneath their heat lights.

Walt's desk was the aftermath of a hurricane, awash with loose sheets of paper and jumbled pens and empty water glasses and the edges of plates containing stale lunches eaten thoughtlessly and alone.

She knew where the truth lay. Not among the mess; in the drawer below.

Still, she glanced at the newspapers and documents, more to stall than anything else. Shifting the hammer between hands, she glimpsed headlines and the first few lines of stories. Most concerned industrial accidents where people died by burning or suffocation, or they were crushed. The grainy pictures showed billows of black smoke and heaps of rubble.

An uneasy admiration twisted in her belly when she thought of Walt, an inhabitant of this realm. Her own situation had enthralled him in a similar way. A mutual cocktail of revulsion and respect that they'd gotten drunk on together.

And now he's sobering up.

Her gaze dropped to the drawer that he'd opened so cautiously the day she asked for the car keys to drive the cat to town. The drawer she herself had opened so quietly this morning while he sat there sleeping, taking the keys to drive to the church. Moving to the chair, she leaned down and tried the handle.

Sure enough, locked.

She steadied herself on the desk and raised the hammer. The handle and lock face tarnished and deformed as she rained blows. The shocks vibrated up her arm like springs jumping together. The wood flecked white and began to split.

Missy's lips drew together. There was no reversing this.

A last blow, and the drawer recoiled and drifted open.

A gun lay inside. A little snub-nosed revolver. A .38, like Grandmama's. Her arm quivered as she laid the hammer aside. *Hush now, honey,* Grandmama had said. *They're not comin' around here. I'll have to put that somewhere you can't reach it, though.*

Missy swallowed. Just a gun.

Still, it took her gaze a few seconds to penetrate past the weapon to the manila folder it lay atop. She pinched the edge of the folder, dragged it out, and shut the drawer. When she laid it on the desk, her fingertips were tingling.

Sinking into his chair, she opened the folder.

A letter. Legal allegations. She almost laid it aside, but her gaze snagged on a cluster of letters: HUG. She scanned down the page.

Dear Mr. Collins,

Concerning your allegations of sex abuse against staff at the Atlanta Home for Underprivileged Girls (HUG) last spring, I wanted to follow up briefly with some questions about your own connections with the place and also with the Back Creek Club, a bar and brothel in northern DeKalb County—

"Huh." It was like a bag of cement hitting the floor. "Well, what do you want to know, Missy?"

She slammed the paper down. Her splayed hand propelled her from the chair and pushed aside the letter to reveal the next document. But there was no time to read it.

Walt stood in the doorway. He'd finally shaved. His mustache was sharp again, and pink patches of irritated skin stood out on his sweaty cheeks. His combed hair slumped.

He approached, hands thrust deep in his pockets. She didn't try to smile. She didn't back away, either. She found the edge of the desk and held on to it.

"Well?" he said.

"Just tryin' to find out if you still care for me." Scanning the next document, she shrugged. "By the looks of things, you don't." *A lease for the house and property at Angel's Landing, expiring the first day of—*

Crisp cologne wafted over her as he came around the desk and stood close beside her. Withdrawing his glasses from his breast pocket, he placed them on his nose and leaned past her to read the document. That scent had enchanted her when they first met. Most of the men were so sour.

When he straightened, he was breathing through his nose. "I don't care? Because I waited to see if you liked it before dumping in tens of thousands of dollars?"

"You didn't have to spend anything. I just wanted us together more."

"You didn't seem to want me much in that apartment."

"Of course I did. That's why I hated that place. It was tiny, it was nothing, it was temporary. *I* was temporary. I wanted a home. And that's what you said this was. But this"—she looked at the paper—"says it stops being ours on September first. Four months. You tell me to do all this work for four months. You distract me for four months. Is that how long it takes to decide what to do with me? To have your fill?"

The red patches were becoming scarlet on his shaking head. "Don't care?" he repeated, as if he hadn't heard anything else. As if it were just registering.

She edged away.

"I understand. People are getting nosy. You can't be hooked to a whore. Not permanently. You just came to the Club to see what sort of people you were sending to jail. And there was somethin' fascinating about that dirty prostitute Missy. But in the end she was still just dirt. To be washed off. And this house? Just something to make her behave."

"I don't care?" Walt said. He looked at her. Deathly calm, like the instant before an avalanche. If she withdrew, would it trigger the quake? She backed off anyway.

"I don't *care*?" He lunged.

Missy tried to scramble away from the desk, but his fingers were on her shirt, gathering fistfuls of loose fabric. Her feet fought. She shoved her hands against his shoulders, but he was too strong. He drove her against the wall. The lips of the bookshelves slammed against her spine.

"You were *nothing*!" he shouted. "I took you from that place, and I shared *everything* with you. I tried everything to keep you. You think it was *easy*? And when I brought you here, it was because I wanted to keep you longer, and maybe make you happy, just a bit. But it can't work, hiding out here with you. It can't work, Missy. You can't be in my life. 'Cause I'm a coward. *I'm* nothing."

He was kissing her frantically then, and his hands left her shirt and clawed into her hair, pulling it from its tie and dragging it around her face, straining it in its roots until she sobbed.

Eventually he weakened enough that she could shove him back. He stumbled all the way to the desk and knocked the stack of yellow papers from its corner. They cascaded down as he slid to the floor.

Missy staggered. She pressed the back of her hand against her sore lips and teeth and lurched toward the porch doors. She rested against them, eyes bleary, the heel of her palm on the glass.

No. Not Walt. Not *her* Walt. She let her hand drop. She rasped, "Not nothing."

He stirred. In the glass, she watched him stand up. "I am nothing."

His hands went back into his pockets. "I am."

His shoes clopped across the silent floor. "I am."

His reflection loomed around her shoulders.

A yell gushed up her throat as she spun around and dove away from him. He caught her on the floor, pinning her with his knee, cramming the handkerchiefs from his pocket into her mouth. Her hands came up, and he caught those, too, and tied them behind her back with a sinewy cord, falling over her as she thrashed.

She gagged. The porch doors rattled as she kicked, until he tied her ankles, too. The lump of cloth had sucked all the moisture from her mouth, but still she managed to expel it halfway through her jaws before he jammed it back in and tied a last loop of cloth around her skull.

Then he stood up, and she heard him turn a confused circle. She writhed on the boards, knees and forehead burning as she tried to flip onto her back. Again he knelt down, and one unsteady hand stroked her hair as he might have stroked a dying horse.

"I am Marilyn."

His arms came around her and picked her up, and the smell of his cologne came through the dust that had smeared onto her nose from the floor. Now the sweat was palpable. Holding her tight as she flopped, he carried her down the hallway and down the stairs. The front door was open and a rusted pickup sat in the clearing in the bluing evening.

Someone's feet came around the vehicle, but she couldn't see who it was from that angle. The pickup bed squeaked open, followed by a rasp and a huff and a crunch as something weighty was set in the gravel. He moved forward again. Then she was being lowered.

Placed. Pale wood walls came around her, crushing her shoulders closer. Her body pressed down heavily on her bound hands as his arms withdrew. A fresh, sticky smell crowded away all the other smells.

Pine.

She was in a coffin.

Two men stood above her. Walt and Sheriff Ezra. Above them, a swath of sky and sighing trees, sharp in the surrendering daylight.

Then darkness came down and fitted in place. The lid. She heaved. The lid jostled and then was held in place while banging started all around her ears. *Hammering.*

They were hammering it on. Hammering her in. Hammering the light and air away.

Missy roared in the darkness.

I drove back up Adamah Road and looked across the field at the house. Jezebel was home.

—"The House of Dust"
Southern Gothic

THE GRAY HOUSE stood gaunt and sharp against the late-afternoon sky.

Brad crossed the porch to the front door. He smoothed back the hair on each side of his head and used two fingers on his cheeks to lift his expression from the ditch it had fallen into. A solid minute of knocking yielded no results. So, he tried the handle.

Inside, a large dim hallway stretched as empty as the loft of a summer barn to a branching staircase at the back of the house. A smell like lilac ashes radiated from a room to his right. He stepped toward the doorway.

The room was empty except for a mild, almost-odorless smoke. A few slow flies cut trails through the fog. No sign of Jezebel Irons.

As he stepped deeper into the room, the gloom and smoke cleared, revealing something extraordinary. Huge holes cut into the floorboards.

Oval gaps about five feet long. They pitted the room's entire floor.

Immediately, the hive of bare patches inside the Adamah Cotton Mill reprinted on his mind. Here, a twisted network of jigsawed wood laced between the openings. The blue smoke wafted from the gaps like fetid breath from sleeping mouths.

The skeleton of floor whined as he moved farther among the archipelago of holes.

Suspicion slid gently up his back. A static electric wave of dizziness washed through him. He imagined pale arms sprouting from the holes, reaching for his feet. The smoke must be making him dizzy. He focused on placing his feet.

Then a pewter-colored voice rose with the smoke. "I can feel you up there."

He stopped.

"Come on down."

Jezebel Irons's voice. Below the floor. Crouching, he peered into one of the murky holes. "Ms. Irons? It's Bradley Ellison." He hesitated. "Are you all right, ma'am?"

A cough, followed by a dry chuckle. "Come on down, Mr. Ellison. I'm just about to start." The dull monotony of her tone from their first conversation had taken on the careless cadence of someone awake too long.

He hesitated only a moment. Bracing his hands on the floor, he lowered his feet into the darkness. A good portion of his body slid in before his straining toes touched ground. Letting himself down onto his heels, Brad found the floor level with his shoulders. He did a quick turn, like a swimmer gathering oxygen and checking for landmarks, and noticed a messy rendition of the Adamah symbol painted in red across the room's inner wall.

Then he ducked down.

It was like plunging into a scummy lake. The smoke was thicker, and light from above did not shaft through it. It smelled of rot. Squinting, he turned on the balls of his feet.

About twenty feet off, the woman sat in a bubble of light, leaning against the foundation wall. Her legs stuck out before her, and her hands pressed the earthen floor. She looked toward him with drawn-down eyelids.

"I'd like to be more hospitable, but it's on days like these . . . "

"No problem," he breathed. Still crouching, he hobbled toward her.

Extension cords coiled around support beams to feed a crescent of workshop lights set on the floor before her. The light flowed toward a small hole, perhaps a foot deep and a foot wide, dug between Jezebel's heels.

"You've been crying," she said.

Brad sat back on his haunches. "It's the smoke."

"It's incense. Stuff just smokes and smokes. Cuts down on the smell. Flies, too."

"Why are there flies?"

A sleepy smile pulled her face apart. "You didn't come here today by accident. You're shaken, I can see. You've come from another shallow place?"

"I didn't know this was a shallow place."

"It became one. When the mine was dug and the town had more traffic and we needed a private gathering place. But these later years . . . not much activity. Just me sittin' down here most afternoons."

Their voices were close in the low space.

"I was at the theater," Brad said. "I watched one of the films in the projector room. I'd like to ask you about it and record our conversation."

"Memories must be fragile things for you."

He tapped the mic. "Maybe."

"Go ahead anyway."

"How long have people been buried alive in Three Summers?"

Jezebel's eyes closed softly. "Since the beginning. Since before the beginning. Since the foundations of the house were laid. Or maybe it happened before that—thousands of years before. Maybe this was

Eden, and Adamah was the first burial, forced onto his belly in the dust by God?"

Brad swallowed the smoke. "I don't understand. Who is killed? And how many? And why?"

The eyelids parted. In the brightness, the blood vessels in her sclera were starkly apparent. "Why? Haven't you read any scripture, Mr. Ellison?" Gathering her feet away from the hole, she sat up and rubbed calloused hands up her face and back through her short hair. "Take off your shoes."

He did not move. Was she serious?

Jezebel sat forward. Her face was fully alert now. The blend of darkness and yellow light had smoothed the wrinkles around her eyes and mouth, masking her with an odd youthfulness. She beckoned to his feet. "This is a shallow place. You want to know? I'll show you."

Dropping the phone into his breast pocket, Brad unlaced his shoes. His fingers jerked stiffly. What was he doing?

The woman watched as he slipped off each shoe. "Socks, too."

"Good thing about the incense," he said clumsily. She didn't smile. The next minute, hard, dry dirt kissed his bare feet. He squatted across from her, the hole between them.

Jezebel met his gaze and held it. Then her jaw split.

Slowly and loudly, she breathed into the air. It washed across his face, warm and faintly bitter. He did not flinch. He waited for her to speak. After a while, she did.

"You asked why. Because Adamah is in the dust. He is smothered by it. He was cursed by God to crawl in it. But we were cursed, too. Cursed to toil and regret. Surely you can see this is a tired land. Full of tired people who get up every morning feeling the ache of broken history, broken families, broken dreams. Tired because we were cursed to be tired. To live by the sweat of our brows until we return to the dust. Adamah is in the dust. Adamah knows our tiredness. So we share with him breath, and he shares with us rest."

"*Share breath* . . . the live burials."

"Yes. When we do not share breath, we feel fatigue, anger, the burden of our past mistakes. And so we must share breath to gain his peace. It is a high price. But it must be paid regularly. Unless we have someone here who can breathe for Adamah."

"Like a medium."

Her eyes were bright now. Slumping to the right, she crawled to the edge of the light and reached into the darkness. Carefully, she lifted something. It came into the radiance swaying from a wire handle. A cast-iron pot. The lid rattled as she set it down. Brad's grip tightened on his knees as a waft of green odor reached his nose.

Jezebel's palm hovered above the pot as she spoke. "Once, this contained the crumbled remains of Miriam Larkin, retrieved from the house."

The image from the library, a woman disintegrating on the dining room table at the house, jumped into his memory.

"Through the years, her dust was sprinkled on these floors. But here is something better." Her grip closed around the pot lid and lifted it away. The stomach-squeezing smell of rot boiled up and a few flies escaped as she reached inside.

What came out looked like a fat brown dead spider, legs drawn together. In the light, it was more clear: a clawed-up little hand. Skin peeling, nails long, joints blackened. Cupping the thing, the woman held it toward him.

Brad shook his head. For the microphone, he said, "To be clear, what you're showing me is a severed hand, several weeks decayed."

"*Her* hand." An element of rapture had entered the vanilla voice. "A medium's hand. You're observant, so I'm sure you've noticed how for us the feet are important; they connect us to the earth, to Adamah. Many go without shoes. But for her—for the Queen—it is also the hands. Beautiful hands. Adamah's hands. She breathes for him, and he fills her and spills from her like a broken vessel. He uses her to reach and touch. Give peace."

He hardly heard. "You cut off Marilyn Britain's hands and returned the body to Sorrel."

"Sorrel." Her voice wrinkled. "He wants to escape Adamah, destroy the order of the Queen of Hearts. But you can't live without peace." She lowered the claw into the hole. "Adamah brings peace."

As she raked dirt over the hand, Jezebel beckoned, and after a moment of hesitation, Brad rubbed a bit of dirt over the brink of the hole. Withdrawing quickly, he asked, "How is peace given?"

"By returning us to the past—the real source of our tiredness. When we set things right there, we are refreshed."

"I don't understand."

"No? Don't you feel the tiredness the past causes? Mistakes, regrets, everything that left you where you are today? Don't you feel tired, Mr. Ellison?" The words slid out as a heavy sigh. His focus faltered as memories moved.

"I . . . suppose that sometimes, like anyone, I . . . "

"That's what I saw when you came in. Not tears. Tiredness." She moved away from the hole. "Lie down."

A lurch in his heartbeat. Harlow, sitting on the floor of the old mill, had invited him to do the same thing. Perspiration formed between his feet and the floor as a gentle burning gripped them. Like the blood being drawn away. Something sucking him down. His toes stuck briefly as he shifted.

It's not real. There's nothing down there. It's just rituals. Just dirt.

"You need to know. If you don't, you'll never understand. Lie down. Feel Adamah's peace for yourself."

It's just dirt.

He stared at her, then pushed a chuckle through his teeth and shrugged. Bending forward, he rested on his hands on the ground while stretching his legs out behind. Then he lowered his body onto the dirt. Its coolness sank through his clothes. His neck remained stiff, holding his face away from the earthen surface.

Jezebel's hand gently pressed his head down. "I'll help you. Tell me what's been hanging on to you? What hasn't been right?"

Brad's nose rubbed against the dirt. He sucked in air and smelled the moldy ground. Its petrified dullness ached against his eyes. Blank, empty earth. He felt the stupidity of the situation. He started to get up, but her hand remained steady.

"It's okay. I know what you think. I'm an idiot old woman who burns trash and lives in a broken-down town. But where's the town that's not broken? Where's the place not trying to hide its trash? You don't have to tell me your tiredness. Just think it—Adamah will know."

The ground was getting thinner. The old weight was melting through him. He would fall through into—

No. There's nothing down there.

"You don't have to fight, Brad. No one will know. Only me, and you, and him."

Her hand lightened on his head, but he stayed put, held by her dwindling voice. "What has been following you? What *is* following you? Don't say it—Adamah knows. Just turn in your mind and look . . . look . . . "

No.

But he was already there, lost in the bleary years in Providence after the funeral, drowning in the quiet of the house and the indifference of his mother, wandering through psychiatry sessions and Prozac bouts, surviving high school with headphones. Then he was south, at school, at Poynter, paid for by benefits awarded after the "accident." And then he was on the road, in the muck, digging through trash, bottling tears, living off blood. *The Futureless, The Devil's Camp, Night Gallery, The Glass Elephant, Scarlet Seven Miles.* Carefully crafted reports sent off to Atlanta to be printed and distributed and read and forgotten.

Ten years of hiding from the true crime. Ten years of dragging the original sin.

He was tired. And now it wasn't just the blood in his feet that was shivering, but all over his body. Inches from his eyes, the earth was rippling. Softening. Seeping up around him.

Embracing.

He shut his eyes.

The accident wasn't your fault.

Orange gouts of fire exploded in the darkness behind his eyelids. He jerked as the smell changed from incense and dry dirt to salt water and sulfurous burning. He opened his eyes, but the flames continued, blossoming through crumbly smoke, hot, thick, dark, getting hotter and thicker and darker, binding to him, weighting him.

Brad tried to stand up. Jezebel's hand still pressed into his hair, holding him down. She was speaking again. Her words were different this time, however. They were soft and high.

"Hello. I see you there. Come on closer."

She was speaking over him to someone out in the gloom beyond the lights.

"You honor us with your presence. Please, come closer." Her voice dropped. "He's coming, Mr. Ellison. For you."

The smoke was in his throat. He choked. "Who's coming?" His lips picked up earth.

The woman's voice dwindled with each sentence. "He's dressed in orange, in industrial-looking coveralls. His hair is black and greasy like yours, but it's real grease that's covering it. It's all over his face . . . and his hands. Oh, he's awful burned."

The words were lost amid the flash flood of blood inside his brain. No one knew that. No one knew his dreams. Even Jennifer did not know them. It was impossible that this person who he barely knew could describe the demon that had stalked the perimeter of his mind since adolescence.

"No!" Pushing up from the pressure of her hand, he sat back. Her fingers, striving to hold him down, dragged his glasses off. He snatched them and crammed them back on. He turned, peering through the hazy lenses.

Empty dark. Nothing coming through the avenue of floor supports.

Of course.

"He's there, Mr. Ellison. Just in front of you, past the lights. Why not say hello?"

Twisting back to face her, he fought off the heat of smoke and the icy imagination of eyes tracing his spine. "I came here for answers, ma'am, not rituals."

"This is the answer."

"*Nothing is there!* There is nothing in this ground!"

"There is. Let your eyes adjust."

"No, there's—"

The woman sprang from her crouch and came at him, catching his cheeks in her hands. In something that echoed maternal pleading, she said, "Let yourself have peace, Brad. You've done so well. You've come to a shallow place and broken through. For a moment, you felt the peace of Adamah. Now you'll start to see."

His lips puckered as he dragged himself free of her grip. Standing up as much as he could, he wiped his face with an arm, then grabbed his shoes.

"He's behind you, Brad. He's reaching out to shake hands. Who is he?"

"I'm leaving. If you really want to be helpful, you'll tell me how you knew that."

Jezebel's chin jerked. "I didn't. You've broken through. You'll start to see."

"I'm leaving." His gaze skipped to the hole for a minute, where the severed hand of the house's last resident lay. *Buried alive.* "We're both leaving."

Rotating, he stepped out of the light, right through the place where she said the burned man stood. Tingles rippled through his body.

"It's too late for that," the woman called. "You've broken through. Adamah will always be with you now."

Taking advantage of the first opening he came to, he placed his shoes on the floor above, then braced his hands and glanced back at her one more time.

The woman was gone. Something much closer blocked her from view. Something dressed in orange and smeared with black, back hunched to avoid the ceiling. As he watched, it bent even lower so it could raise its head. Light came around a blistered face, a melancholy grin. Welts broke open on its cheeks, leaking fluid as it mouthed two words.

Hello, Brad.

His knees buckled. The weight was everywhere, crippling him. As he slammed into the floor, the figure leaned toward him, eyes shriveled, nose raw, hair burned away.

It wasn't an accident, Brad.

The instant of paralysis departed.

Heaving to his feet, Brad floundered out onto the floor above. Clutching his shoes, he ran. The woman's laughter warbled through the gaps as he navigated across the broken floor. The sound only faded as he slammed the house door shut behind him

Beyond the shadow of the porch, late-afternoon sun lanced his eyes. The residual smoke pooled in his belly as he stalked to the car. Seated in its heat, his stomach contracted. He bent and pressed his face into his fingertips, battling the urge to vomit.

It had been a hallucination. Just a hallucination, like so many he'd had before.

But what if it wasn't a hallucination? He was depressive, but he wasn't deranged. Yet over fifteen years he'd had the same vision. What if it wasn't a vision? What if it was real? Living. Crawling after him out of Hell.

No. It was the nature of regrets to hang on, clenching even tighter each time they were disturbed. This place had split open his core. They had to leave. Jennifer couldn't stay in that house a moment longer than it would take to pack. If she found out any of this, or somehow became entangled in it, or had a hallucination of her own, everything would shatter.

She's already entangled. He fought the thought away, but it lunged to the surface again and again. Tugging on his shoes, blinking through sweat, he reviewed the previous week. Her apparent recovery, her deep slumber, her seeming calmness, her uncharacteristic carelessness.

Adamah brings peace.

He turned the key in the ignition.

The car tore down the drive. He pulled hard at the end, skidding onto Simmons Pike.

Adamah brings peace.

Chewing the steering wheel with his fingernails, he tried to think of how to explain it to her. That the retreat was over. That they would return to some urban scape less drowned in malaise, less prone to inspire delirium.

It didn't matter what he said. It just had to be done. They had to leave.

Braking hard, he turned on Adamah Road and bore down on the accelerator.

The emergency lights only entered his consciousness when they were close. Refocusing, he discovered a black car with a domed strobe coming up the road, throttled siren wailing.

Sorrel. Didn't matter.

The vehicles converged toward the railroad tracks that cut the road halfway to town. Brad's foot remained steady.

Without warning, the sheriff's car slung itself across both lanes and stopped broadside on the far edge of the tracks. Gulping air, Brad stomped on the brakes. The car lurched as it coasted across the rails, grinding to a halt fifteen feet short of the opposing vehicle.

What now? Using the backs of his fingers, he brushed dirt from the front of his shirt. He threw open the car door and climbed out.

The sheriff did, too. Their doors slammed simultaneously.

The tracks spread away on either side. Insects ticked in the weeds growing from the gravel pilings. Brad approached the man, and the man approached, running a thumb over each sparse eyebrow.

"I drove out to the house again."

Brad studied him through his dirty glasses. "What's the obsession with my fiancée?"

"Same as yours about my . . . mom, I expect—the story of this town." He stumbled on "mom," then flinched a shrug. "Yeah, no point in me hidin' stuff that'd just make you want to stick around. 'Cause you can't anymore. Let this conversation serve as a notice that you're to be out of that house by midnight."

Brad spread his hands. "Sorry to spoil your fun, but that's just what I was planning till you pulled in front of me."

The man frowned at him, then looked past him up the road. "Where you been?"

His hands dropped. "Went down to the old theater and watched a movie. You have a favorite?"

Sorrel came in closer. "Stop bein' a smart aleck, Brad. I *needed* you. I let you in here to write your piece because I thought it might clear away the clouds. This town needs sunlight. Needs to see a way out of these cycles. But I see you're just bringing back the dark. And I shoulda seen it from the start."

"Seen what?"

"That you'd get caught up in the whole thing. The Queen of Hearts, the rituals, the . . . " He turned away like he might spit. "You know, for a while I didn't know about any of it. But she'd pick out someone twice a year, summer and winter, and invite them over. Usually someone on the edge, less-liked, loners. Someone from out of town. So in '73, some kids came poking around town one night in June on a rumor the old place was haunted. Two guys and a girl.

"Momma—" He chewed the word. "She drove down, picked them up, and sat on the porch with them, until dawn. I sat upstairs and listened. You could tell they were scared: the girl was crying, and guys were repeating themselves a lot. She just kept talking. Told them she knew all about being lost and knew what it was like to finally come home. At dawn, they walked out in the field, she and the kids. The town folks had dug three holes, and the kids just . . . stepped in. Richard Gilbert. Alec Mullen. Teresa Samson. I read their names later in a newspaper. Missing, it said. Never found." He shook his head. "Any idea what that does to a kid's mind?"

Brad moved a little to stand beside the man. They both looked east down the dead, desiccated miles of metal. "Why didn't you ever do anything? Leave?"

"You know, there's days that I come out to these tracks and I walk. Day after my brother left, I walked forty-seven miles. Farthest I ever been from here. Every step was the one I thought would break my feet. Finally a train showed up on the tracks ahead. And you know what I did? I hopped on and rode all the way back to this very crossing. Every couple years I try it again. But I always turn back around after a couple miles 'cause my feet stop working. Because what *am* I outside of this place? I mean, look at me. Started balding when I was eighteen. Fallow scalp in my youth."

He rubbed his head and kicked gravel at the pointless comment. "You are where you come from, huh? Well, my dad was Ezra Larkin, sheriff of this hellhole town and son of a Queen of Hearts. And me from the womb of another Queen. Place is in my blood and bones. I *am* Three Summers. And Three Summers is everything it's been. So when it goes down . . . "

The desolation in the sheriff's face made Brad take a step backward.

"You're not like that, Brad. You can quit all this. So do it. Go. Now."

Brad's lips thinned. "Can't quit. I'll go, but I can't quit. My dad left me an inheritance, too. That's what's in my blood that keeps me stuck. I'll have to write everything."

Sorrel surveyed him. "Got any proof? Besides creepy old photos and stories?"

Brad tapped his breast pocket. "Couple interviews: testaments to a cult that's buried people alive for two hundred years. People will want to believe."

Sorrel eyed the phone as if his gaze could crush it. Then his mouth twitched. "I don't care what you write. But I'm not gonna let you stay around. I won't let *her* drag us deeper into the pit."

"Leave my fiancée out of this."

"What happened to her, Brad? It must've been something real bad." The sheriff's tone sent a chill up his back.

"Why? What's she done?"

"I went out there. You need to go home to her, Brad. You need to get her and leave now."

That was Tuesday, May 22. My last day in Three Summers.

—"The House of Dust"
Southern Gothic

HEAT FILLED UP the coffin. Heat from her squirming body. Heat from itching blisters on her arms as the pickup lurched across rough pavement, running splinters into her skin. Heat from the breath burning through her nose, reflecting back in her face thick and sappy from the pine lid.

Missy tasted grit on the rag in her mouth and remembered the lurching cars that would drive a half mile off the main highway to the pine-shaded parking lot in front of the Club. She remembered the exhaust and cigarette smoke that mixed with the smell of those pines as the patrons came and went.

Mostly, she remembered *his* car, creeping down the drive and wandering around the lot in an uncommitted hunt for a parking spot. She had stepped out for a fresh breath after a long day in the dank interior. She rubbed the clammy chill of the new air conditioner off her skin and watched the dust stick to the bright red paint of his car as he drove around. She remembered his head turning as he passed her.

Missy had lifted her head and stared at the cool evening sky. She stayed like that as shoes came crunching across the lot. Trailing blades of the decorative pampas grass shivered across his silver suit legs as he came up the side of the building. When he stopped, she looked down and he adjusted the knot of his tie. They had both been so young not so long ago.

"Hello," he said, smelling like cologne. "I see your sign every evening as I drive by."

Her tired cheeks smiled. "Hello, sir. Come right on in."

Then he did something weird: he held out his hand. Missy felt a switch in her blood.

He wants to hold my hand?

When the pickup stopped, both doors slammed. "Wait for the car to pass," she heard Ezra say.

Immediately, she started thrashing again. The box rocked, scooting across the truck bed. She screamed into the gag. Trembling and snorting, she maintained the cries until the car, oblivious, whisked past.

The tailgate banged down. Hands grabbed the coffin and dragged it out. Arching her body, she slammed her hands against the lid. She was carried a few dozen feet and then the box was roughly set down. Rusty door hinges squeaked. Then she was lifted again.

Even inside the coffin, she heard the sounds change. Scuffing footsteps, huffing breaths—everything became louder. A clunking echo as again she was set down.

"Okay," Ezra said.

Walt, speaking low, hoping she wouldn't hear: "The lid won't come off?"

"No. But we can put that on top of it if you want."

Feet scuffed again. A heavy item clunked down on the lid.

"Feel better?"

No reply. Walt must have nodded. Timid. Just as he had been that evening at the Club.

They had sat at the bar, and Missy watched him drink. The comfortable way he wore that tight collar told her he was the kind who ate Sunday dinner in a jacket and tie. She smiled at the way he sucked air through his nose and blinked rapidly every time he sipped his cocktail, cheeks ballooning to cough.

"Need a handkerchief?" she'd asked.

"No," he said. "No, no."

"And the highballs here aren't even real drinks, just ice cubes with alcohol rubes."

There was a latent sense of angst in those watering eyes that flashed at the people around the Club. They returned to her as he drained the glass. "Where's your cigarette machine?"

"I'll get them. Give me some money."

"I can get them."

"You wouldn't know how." She smiled and opened her palm. "Sorry. I don't mean to be snarky. I hate snarky people."

Reluctantly, he reached into his coat and found some change. Missy slid off her stool and wove through the tables to the machines by the door. Theresa was cursing at the hostess stand.

"What's wrong?" She put the change in the machine.

"Sound system's down," Theresa said. "Boss just came in and went in the back, but I'm the one by the door, so I'm the one who gets chewed-out."

Missy smiled and fished out the new pack of smokes. "You're new, darling—you don't know chewed out."

"Yeah, really? How long have you been here?"

Missy ignored her and returned to the bar, climbing up beside the silver-suited man. He held out his hands for the pack, but she kept them close.

He looked confused. "What?"

"Let me."

She opened the pack, drew one out, placed it between her lips, and grabbed a nearby lighter. The flame glistened in his staring eyes as she lit the cigarette. A quick breath in, then she gently blew out. He did not blink.

"Like that." She handed it to him and put her elbow on the bar. She watched from the cushion of her palm as he studied the filter where her lips had just been. Then he put it to his own.

Inhaling, he motioned weakly with the cigarette. "Seems like a popular place. Lot of guys here."

"A lot of guys," she agreed. "Not many men."

A door to the back burst open and the Boss, a toddler of a man with a treble voice to match, pushed blond-haired Meg into the common room. She clutched her violin and stared around at the heads that rose.

"Gentlemen!" the Boss announced. "I do sincerely apologize for the lack of music. I cannot help the foolishness of my maintenance man."

A few granted him a chuckle.

"Here, however, we have a lady who can play this violin. She has big dreams! Big dreams! So, give her a hand, and enjoy a few Bohemian melodies until such time as we can effect repairs." He turned away and loudly hissed, "Play!" then vanished into the back. Trembling, Meg raised her violin.

People started talking again before her music began. She played something thin and slow, and Missy looked away.

"What's your name anyway?"

The silver-suit cleared his throat. "Walter. Yours?"

"I'm Marilyn. How'd you end up in a place like this, Walt?"

"Like what?"

"Meg there—she wants to be a concert violinist. She practices every morning. But she's been here longer than any of us. She'll never leave. And I won't leave, and none of these others here will. And you won't leave. Because from now on when you drive by, you'll have to come back."

He shook his head. "I'm from out of state. Strictly here for professional reasons."

"Really."

"Yes. I want to get a psychological read on . . . these sorts of people. See what's behind their courtroom behavior."

"First time away from home?"

"How'd you end up here?" he asked instead.

Missy shifted her chin. "Oh, by the regular routes, I suppose. No gravity as a child, and then way, way too much of it when I got older. Enough to bring me crashing down . . . "

"To here." The sorrow and sympathy coalesced behind his eyes in a way that made her seethe inside. It said, *I understand, you poor, pretty, lost child; I will pity you. And then forget you.*

"It's funny," she said, scraping Coke residue off the bar with her thumbnail. "A professor from Emory used to come see me. He was the nicest man. He'd bring me volumes of the *Encyclopedia Britannica* to read while he wasn't here. I think he thought it was cute, like giving a tiny dog a giant bone. But I read them. And when he was here, both before and afterward, he'd sit in bed and talk and waste time so I wouldn't have to come back to work. He always talked about the Civil War. I asked him, 'Don't you read anything besides the Civil War? Are you lookin' for a different ending?' And you know what he said?" She looked up from her nail and found Walt's gaze steady. "He said the South won by losing. That all those years of getting walked on actually turned it into somethin' beautiful. Maybe even somethin' people could love."

She held his gaze until he blinked. Then she shrugged. "I think about that sometimes."

It was night now.

The light in the box hadn't changed, but she knew what midnight felt like. She lay on her dying hands and breathed through raw nostrils, recovering her lungs for another attempt.

A couple times an hour, the rattle of shopping cart wheels was distantly audible. They must have stowed her inside the empty warehouse beside the grocery store. On the other side of the near wall was the painted cigarette ad, the woman in the red gown grinning at the parking lot, watching the people pass.

Could she somehow gain the attention of one of them? Would any of them care, let alone help? Did anyone in this wretched town care? Or in the world? If her own fiancé didn't . . . if Walt didn't want her . . .

No. No time to cry. Her lungs had recovered. Time to scream.

"It's just right over here," Missy said.

Walt's shirt was open and they were both still sweaty as she led him through the twilit forest. They traversed a little path through the land behind the Club. It was the end of April, too early for lightning bugs, but the sun was blushing and lingering, staining the sky the color of melted peach ice cream.

"Where are we going?" he laughed. An hour ago he had been so sure of himself that he had let her lead him right up to the edge. Then it was nothing to make him trip. One week of visits and he had fallen. And he was enjoying it.

They reached the edge of her little clearing and she stopped and flung an arm and breathlessly proclaimed, "There we are!"

The grass was cut raggedly short—best she could do with the rusty shears from the maintenance shed. The weathered wooden chair sat in its accustomed spot by the rusty lawn table. And the mason jar of Southern fleabane sat atop the table, right where she had left it this morning.

He released her hand and stepped past her into the clearing. Looking at it with him made her realize how dingy the whole setup was. The fleabane was already drooping in the jar. And he noticed. He went right over and pulled the weeds from the water.

"Ma'am, allow me to collect you some new flowers."

She grinned regardless, watching him go to the edge of the little glen to forage for something fresh. The grin was harder to keep when he straightened up with a fistful of yellow daffodils. He carried them to the table and arranged them in the water while thoughtfully looking around.

"So, this is your dream."

Missy's arms went behind her back, fingers tying in knots as she followed him into the open. "What's that mean?"

"Somewhere quiet to yourself. That's what you get in a garden."

"I wouldn't really call this a garden."

"Who trimmed the grass? Who arranged these flowers? Who lugged this chair here?" He sat down in it and opened his arms.

"I don't think it could support us both."

Walt cocked his head. "That wariness, that morose little smile—it's why I'm so interested in your upbringing, Marilyn. You know you never really told me."

"You'd love me on the witness stand, eh? A piece in one of your plots."

"No." He patted his knees. "Right here."

Sighing, she sat down gently and leaned back so their heads were together. The chair groaned but held. A feathery breeze passed through the clearing. The scent of the daffodils wafted from the table.

"Well?" he said.

"I'm not really Marilyn. A guy named Warren Dawson called me that. Said I looked like the actress, though I don't see it. The 'Britain' part came from those encyclopedias I read. Really my name's Missy. Missy Holiday. It's kinda stupid."

"No, it suits you." He combed hair behind her ear so her face was more visible. "What about this Dawson fellow?"

"He . . . " One hand struggled from the crook of her arm and batted the air in front of them. "He was a slippery man. Head warden at HUG. That's where I lived since I was ten, after my grandmama died. The Atlanta Home for Underprivileged Girls. They thought it was cute to call it HUG. And Dawson always said, 'Call me Dawes.' He had eyes on me from the first day I came into that place. But he took his time. So when it came around to when I was fifteen, it almost seemed . . . " She refolded her arms, and he held her, too.

"And of course he gave me all sorts of little favors and promised to get me set up with a family and I was confused at first, thinking he liked me just because. Early on, when people came to see me, I was glum and sulky and didn't try to make a good impression, and all the people would say, 'She looks like she's got an attitude. The last thing I need is an attitude.'" And so I never got picked, even when I broke down crying and begging, and even when I tried to be my best self. By the time I was fourteen, I knew no one wanted me. Except Dawes. Me and him spent a lot of time together. He said he'd have a job lined up for me when I was eighteen and had to leave. He did—right here at this filthy little club. And then I knew even he didn't care."

Noticing Walt's expression, she quickly brightened her face. "Sorry. I don't mean this to sound like the memoirs of a fallen angel."

"That's not right." He got up to pace, leaving her in her rotting wooden throne. "An orphanage warden grooming girls for sex work? And you know he's not just sending them here. Probably got deals all over the state. Is he still at the girls' home? How long have you been here?"

"Couple years. I'm pretty sure I'm twenty-two."

"That bastard needs out of there. And you need out of here. Ever considered running away?"

A beetle had climbed up to smell the daffodils on the table and fallen into the jar. It lay on its back among the chopped-off stems at the bottom, legs carefully folded.

He nudged her.

"Run away?" She sucked in a mouthful of the warm breeze that again ruffled the glade. "Everyone does run away, don't they?"

"You should."

The daffodil trumpets, already shriveling, caught the wind and rotated around the edge of the jar. The beetle rolled in his grave. "I might, if I could get some guarantee that what comes after would last longer than these flowers do."

By morning she was mute.

Besides flopping about in the box, she couldn't make much fuss as they carried her outside. They must have acquired an enclosed vehicle to transport her in because there was no wind and less rattling. Did Three Summers have a hearse?

The tires hummed below. Cemetery soon. She wished she could be buried in something nicer than the shorts she had scrubbed the floor in, now damp with urine, a sweaty T-shirt, and grimy unshod feet.

They were white sandals—a present from him in the mail. Her toenails were painted red. She walked the tightrope of a crack in the new parking lot pavement and watched him approach from the corner of her eye.

"Hello there." This time he wore no suit, just shorts and a polo shirt.

She glanced at him, then at the red car he'd climbed out of. "Better not leave your car there, mister. It'll fill up with pine straw from outta these trees."

"Missy Holiday, don't even pretend."

She let her arms drop, ending the high-wire walk on the concrete fault, and turned toward him. "Hear that violin?"

Someone had left one of the Club's few windows open by mistake. Meg's music fled the smoky interior, soaring across the parking lot and up into the June evening. "She's turned into a big hit."

He folded his arms. "Well, since you want to know, our business wrapped up a little early and we had to go back to Nashville. But I've since had the opportunity to plant a few seeds. Maybe soon your violin friend will be able to fulfill her dream."

"What kind of seeds?"

"Who knows until they bloom?" He came closer. "You look nice."

"Aw, thank you." She dabbed her pinky on the fever blister that had developed at the corner of her mouth. This was her night to stand out front, dressed so eyes could easily undress her, and greet people.

Walt held out his hand.

"Why do you want to hold my hand?"

"Because I'll have no peace without you."

She examined the blood on her pinky, then wiped it away and slowly held out her other hand. He grabbed it and pulled her close and they kissed until he said, "Let's get you out of here, Missy."

They ran to his car and piled in, he reached for the ignition, then pounced, tickling her until she screamed. With peals of laughter, they drove out the long drive toward the highway. Since the Club hadn't paved the drive, and since it hadn't rained yet that month, it took a while for the very pale, very powdery dust from their passing to drift back to earth.

Nearby in the hot darkness, a man was speaking with tidal ebb and flow.

The pastor. It was the pastor speaking; reading aloud.

She could feel sun warming the coffin lid. Morning. In the churchyard.

"The waters closed in over me, the deep was round about me; weeds were wrapped around my head at the roots of the mountains. I went down to the land whose bars closed upon me forever; yet thou didst bring up my life from the pit, O Lord my God." A moment of silence. Then: "It is in. . . hope of the resurrection, that we commit her body to the ground. For all are earth. We are all ashes; we are all dust. And to dust we shall all return."

Sweat wormed across Missy's scalp. Her lips squirmed and cracked against the gag. Her tongue was wax. Air whistled through sore nostrils.

Another sound from nearby: soft rustling. Feet in grass. Then the man's voice again. "I will pray for you, Mr. Collins."

Mr. Collins.

His voice replied, starched and constricted behind a tight collar. "Thank you, Pastor. Please do."

Walt.

"Walt!" It was a tiny cry that thumped uselessly against the wad between her jaws.

The darkness pitched. Straps hissed against the outside of the box. The fluid in her ears told her she was descending.

Beneath her body, her hands flinched. Last chance to get the lid off!

With a lurch, the rocking descent halted. The straps snaked away. Quiet.

Then a cluster of taps punctuated the darkness above her face. She shut her eyes. From somewhere, her body rallied enough moisture to send hot tears welling between her lashes. Inadvertently, her jaws stretched apart, wide enough to create an opening around the clot of cloth, wide enough that gurgling sobs filled the coffin.

The taps came again. And again. Thicker. Heavier.

Dirt, coming down like rain.

Premature evening fell as I drove back to the house.

—"The House of Dust"
Southern Gothic

THE FRONT DOOR was bolted from the inside.

Weeds tore around Brad's legs as he ran around to the back of the house. A mud-smeared tarp was spread across the porch, anchored by a stained metal bucket. Muddy tracks led to the door.

It, too, was locked, but he remembered the loose knob and jogged it until the door whined softly open. The footprints continued down the hall, off into the gloom. They were closely spaced at first, shuffling, then became longer, as if the originator had started running. Closer at hand, they came out of the dining room and crossed into the kitchen.

"Jennifer?" He entered and closed the door behind him. No noise in the hall. Moving ahead, his vision clung to the kitchen doorway until he was standing there looking in.

Dark footprints on the kitchen floor. Muddy handprints on the cabinets and refrigerator. A dirt-caked knife lay on the counter by the sink. The footprints looped and came back to the door and passed beneath his shoes.

Toward the dining room. *Dinnertime.*

A soft clink behind him; a cup jarring a plate. Then an excited whisper: "Brad? Is that you?"

He turned. Dried mud crunched under his feet as he crossed to the dining room. The great table stretched out black and long. Fading radiance from the windows masked the dim far end.

"It is you. I locked up when that creepy sheriff came around. Come here, honey!"

Someone sat in the darkness at the far end of the table. Someone melded with the dark.

"Jennifer," he said again.

"It's fine, Brad. Don't get worked up. I'm fine. In fact, I feel wonderful. Didn't realize how little I'd been eating!"

Brad advanced down the left side of the table, gripping the back of each chair he passed. The thing at the head of the table wasn't Jennifer.

The figure in the chair was charcoal. Scaly. Skin cracking at the elbows and finger joints, revealing paler flesh beneath. Its crumbly fingers plucked a half sandwich from a plate and lifted it to an ebony face. Teeth flashed white and the tongue that sucked in the food glistened pink. Stringy, glistening hair fell across the forehead and around the face, framing bright eyes.

It wasn't Jennifer. But those eyes, pale gray, were hers.

"Jen," he whispered.

The thing swallowed and sat back. It wore her tank top and lounging pants. "So, I took a look at some of those records on your desk. Turns out they treated all sorts of stuff by just applying mud to a patient. I didn't think it would work, of course, but anything's worth a try. So I did, and it does! All that stuff about Lila Simmons—it doesn't hurt anymore! I feel like I've been able to go back and talk with her and make her understand it was an accident—"

"Jennifer—"

"No, I'm saying this for you, Brad. Because I know you've got hurts, too. Deep ones."

"Jennifer. We have to go. I can finish the article somewhere else. I'm going to go upstairs now and get some things together, and you can sit right here. When I come back down, we're leaving." Turning sharply, he walked out of the room.

Upstairs, he breathed out hard through his nose, flushing the humid, rotting creek smell of her from his sinuses. In the bedroom, he stuffed clothes into suitcases. In the study, he jammed his computer into its case along with a couple of wads of paper from the desk.

Only the Newton's cradle gave him pause. The Christmas present from his dad, fuzzy now with dust.

Leave it. For once in your life.

He grabbed it and crammed it rattling into his backpack.

Clattering down the stairs with the bags, he unlocked the heavy front door and dragged them out to his car. He threw them in the trunk and walked quickly back to the house. They'd have to leave her truck. She couldn't drive in her current condition.

"Jen!" He walked back in the house, down the hall to the dining room. "We're ready, honey."

The table was empty.

Traces of dried mud led into the dance hall. "Jen?" He followed. The floor was bare, ready for a cleaning that would never occur. He felt something then, even amid his charging blood, that made him slow. He was leaving, but he didn't really *know* the house, even after all these weeks.

He looked at his reflection in the mirror above the fireplace.

"Jennifer!" He left the hall and paused in the front foyer. The front door was still open. The dirty feet had gone through it. A soft creaking came in from the porch.

He went out. She sat in the nearest rocking chair, swaying lazily in the diminishing light.

"It's time to go," he said again.

Her eyes were shut. "You go."

Everything in him plummeted. *No, no, no.* Instead, he said carefully, "You have to come, too, honey. Sorrel wants us out. It's his house."

"No, you go ahead. You go finish your article. But I'm not leaving this newfound . . . dream." She stretched her arms with a contented sigh. "And you shouldn't leave, either, Brad."

"Honey, we don't have a choice. He'll throw us out. He said he'd come by at midnight to make sure we're gone. Now we're getting in the car to—"

"I'm staying."

"We'll find another place to stay, and you'll still have time to recover."

Her head rolled toward him. "I am recovered, silly. That's why I'm not going anywhere."

"No, Jen, you aren't."

"If I went with you, we both know what you'd have to do. Where you'd have to put me. Because what if I went crawling around in my sleep in a place where other people were? What if I doused in dirt in the city park? Where would I go? I'm broken, Brad. But here, I'm just fine." The dirt around her mouth crumbled as her lips moved. And it was a real smile. Sad and resolved. "Thank you for bringing me here."

Brad turned and looked away. He shoved his shivering fingers in his pockets. "You know I can't leave you."

"Good."

The chair squeaked, and he looked back.

She held up her arms to embrace him. "Come here, honey."

He moved back to her and slipped his arms around her. She was warm and grimy and he held her tight. Slowly, he began to lift her.

"You're broken, too, Brad," she whispered.

A humid presence welled against his cheek. He jerked up, releasing her and stepping away.

In her hand was an oozing lump of mud. She had brought the bucket from the back porch and set it beside her chair.

Picking it up, she rose to follow him. "Something's got you, Brad. You've never told me what, but I've watched you struggle. And I haven't been able to help you before, or give you anything to take away the pain." She scooped fingers into the sludge and lifted them, dripping. "Now I can."

He stepped backward. "Stop it, Jennifer." His voice cracked. "I don't want any part of this, and neither do you. This place is caught in some very bad traditions. We need to get away before we get trapped by them."

He teetered at the edge of the stairs.

Jennifer stopped smiling. Even beneath the dirt, he saw her expression change to sad determination. Maternal. Like Jezebel Irons. Her fingers approached his face, caked tips reaching for his eyes. "Let me help you see."

Just in time, his eyelids flinched closed. For a fleeting moment of darkness, he believed she wouldn't do it. She would hesitate. She would look at her hands, at herself. She would realize she had changed.

Then she smeared mud across his forehead and down over his eyes, down his nose, and across his lips. The wet stink filled his lungs. Tingling broke across his skin.

Brad toppled off the steps. Recovering his footing at the bottom, clawing his face clean, he strode to the car. He ripped the driver's-side door open and threw himself into the seat, locking himself in. He gripped the wheel, twisting, until the bones in his fingers burned.

Yelling wordlessly in the stale air, he slammed his forehead against the steering wheel and basked in the reverberating pain. It made him imagine he was in a dream. Back in that comfortable alcohol blur last October when he proposed to Jen.

It was a Tuesday. It was cold and raining. Jennifer was swamped in schoolwork and didn't want to go out. He dragged her. They ended up at Black Rabbit in Printers Alley, sitting on the couch in front of the fireplace, eating brisket and rolls and drinking one Devil's Temptation cocktail after another until the bill was past two hundred dollars.

"Must be quite an occasion," Jennifer had said.

"That's true," Brad replied. "Heather turned down the article I've spent the last five months on. Never had that happen before."

Jennifer didn't try to comfort him. She just looked at him and twined her ponytail until he said, "Those eyes are why I love you. 'Cause they show me you're just as lonely and pathetic as I am."

She drained her glass and set it on the coffee table. "What a team."

Brad tried to set his own glass down, but only placed it halfway on the table. It fell off and shattered. He waved it good riddance and plunged his hand into his pocket and pulled out a small faux leather box. Cracking it open, he held it out. "We need to stay together."

The ring. He lifted his bruised forehead and looked at the glove box. Maybe if he offered her the ring again she would—

Something thumped against the car.

Brad turned.

A hand pressed against the window. Slow grime seeped from the palm and fingers down the glass.

Jennifer stood just outside in the algae-colored evening. She looked in at him wistfully. He stared back. The beautiful desolation had left her face. Her gaze, once so lonely, was now content with companionship. She was no longer alone behind those eyes.

Brad started the car and drove away.

BRING ME UP SAMUEL ▶

I should have been more aware of her; aware of how we were slipping. But it happened during those ephemeral midweek days when I was unearthing the intergenerational connections between house and town. Before I realized we'd become a part of it.

—"The House of Dust"
Southern Gothic

HEAT SILENCE BLANKETED the land.

The sun had risen scorching that morning, and the air hung across the fields and between the trees like bogged-up creek water. The cicadas keened away until shortly after noon, when a southwest wind pushed a herd of clouds up from the Alabama line. Rain torrented down for the better half of the afternoon, turning the clay basin of Simmons Creek into a pulsing orange vein and flattening the high grass in the cemetery. By four o'clock, the storms had cleared out. Sun glared through the crumbling vapor, slanting across the graveyard, warming headstones, and drawing steam from the grass around a red mound of earth.

A fresh burial.

Five feet down, the coffin was damp. Rainwater filtered through the broken earth and seeped across the pinewood lid. Inside the box, in the dark, lay the body.

The body had twisted itself onto one side and drawn its legs up as far as the narrow confines of the walls would allow; the right shoulder was pressed against the lid. Sweat had formed and dried multiple times across the tepid flesh, but the process had ended hours ago, leaving the skin waxy. All the limbs were locked in stasis. The only movement in the coffin was up by the head, where the faintest trickle of air passed between the shriveled lips.

Missy didn't know if her eyes were open or shut. Eyes were worthless in the ground. That's why moles barely had them. And worms didn't have them at all. And she was with them now. She listened for them moving outside her box, for their soft passage through the ground.

It didn't come.

The earth was empty. Except for her.

The weight of all that unrelenting soil. The idea of being folded into the land. The unyielding wood against her flesh. And dirt outside the walls. And the lid, inches above her head.

That she couldn't sit up.

That she couldn't stretch her arms from behind her back.

Couldn't breathe fully.

Pressed flat here in the dark, drowning in a morass of air, feeling it ooze unbidden into her lungs like warm water.

It made her want to scream. But she couldn't scream. Couldn't thrash. She was buried in a churchyard. Just meters of earth to the surface, where there was sun and grass and movement. But it might as well be miles.

Down in the world of roots and rot and black, a realm of boundless quiet.

She lay still. She waited to die.

Waited with the silence.

Close now.

Heavy . . . so heavy and close it felt like a person stretched across her.

A person . . . a being.

A loose lock of hair moved across her cheek.

The trickle of breath halted.

Missy turned her face up toward the lid. She heard the soft liquid sound of her eyes rolling in their sockets. The gentle *plap* of her eyelids batting.

Nothing else. The twitch of dying nerves. Frail-fingers of silence, stroking her. Gentle ripples of her flattening consciousness. The oxygen had left. She was ready to go also.

Thunk!

Something powerful struck the top of the coffin. Residual instinct made her twitch.

Thunk!

The force vibrated her body.

Before she could decide what it was, or if she cared, the sound changed. Sliding, scouring, scraping, it raced up the length of the box from her feet to her head. It paused a moment, then crawled back down to her feet. Then it came back up. Then it went back down. Then it stopped.

Thump. Thump. Thump. The blows moved along the top of the box like fists.

Missy's head jerked as a clumsy rattling fumbled down the sides of the coffin. Something metallic. *Claws.*

They slid into the gap between the box and the lid. Wood groaned, squealed, then splintered. Heavy panting. Planks squirmed and whined. Moist earthy air flooded in. The lid blew upward and the light blinded her.

Tears squeezed between her eyelids. A dark figure was silhouetted against a steaming purple sky. Strong fingers slid under her neck. Her head banged the edge of the coffin as another hand grabbed her numb right arm. Her head rocked, grazing the cold wet wall of earth.

"Breathe, Missy." Hands slid under her armpits, lifting her out of the darkness. A voice, low and gentle, spoke in her ear. "No, don't struggle. You're safe now, Missy. Just breathe."

She did, and the fresh air was so potent that her brain went dark as her hitching chest tried to draw it in. A sensation of sand tunneled through her veins.

When the light came back, she was lying in wet grass. Someone had untied her numb arms. They burned as the blood rushed back in. A man squatted beside her with a silver thermos, saying again and again, "You're all right, Missy. You're all right now."

Finally, her eyes focused.

Muddy dress shirt; thick black hair; tight, sweaty skin. White teeth with a perfect line between each that grinned when he saw she was awake.

"You're fine, just dehydrated." He helped her sit up and held the thermos to her mouth. She drank ravenously and tried to grab it back when he pulled away.

"Not so quickly. You might—"

She pitched sideways and vomited. When she looked up, saliva dripped from her quivering lips. The man held out his hands.

"It's me, Missy. It's Ezra."

Missy tried to shout a word—*bastard*—but mucus clogged her throat. Soon fresh tears completed her wretchedness.

Beneath his gaze, she hunched on the ground, screwing her fingers into the grass. She continued the process, tightening each muscle until her blood was retuned and coursing through her limbs.

Then she stood up. She swayed.

"All right," Ezra said, unfolding his arms. "Let's get you home."

Home.

That house. That dark, dusty box where she was kept for the whims of others. That lie.

Never.

The Three Summers police cruiser stood in the drive. It faced the road. Missy bolted.

Behind, Ezra released a flat sigh. He floundered after her, calling, "Might not be a good idea to get behind a wheel in your condition."

Skirting headstones in the high grass, she came out on the drive and pounded toward the car. Mud and gravel burrowing between her toes. On the brink of passing out, she toppled against the passenger door.

"That's right, slow down and we'll—"

Missy jerked at the handle. The door came open. She dove into the passenger seat and slammed the door shut. After jamming the lock down, she clambered across the center console and locked the door on the driver's side.

The keys were in the ignition.

The sheriff's hand slammed against the passenger door's window. She started the car. His palm thumped the glass. She shifted into gear.

"Don't try and run," he barked. "For your own sake."

She squashed the gas pedal.

The squad car lunged forward. Ezra was dragged along a couple of feet before he let go, reeling. The drive ended in a few bouncing seconds and Simmons Pike lay before her. She hauled the wheel right and floored it.

She didn't know what lay in that direction, but she knew it led away—away from the house, the town, and its horrible people. The boy, Roy, was probably hiding somewhere; he'd get by. He'd have to. She was leaving. Going away from it all as fast and far as the car would carry her.

Rubber burned as the lumbering car sped westward. Her shoulders pressed into the seat, straining the pedal all the way to the floor. Steering the car was like steering a ship. As the road bent, the vehicle veered across the yellow line. It took all her strength to get back on course.

Speed was all that mattered. The road was dead. No one came this way. They knew to avoid it. To flee from it.

The road dipped and passed through the tunnel where she'd met the pastor. He'd betrayed her, too. Buried her! Hadn't even opened the coffin to check the body. *Her* body. If he had, he would have seen her tied up, delirious, and alive.

Missy shuddered. She was very much *alive*.

She drove fast through woods for at least two rain-slicked miles. No other cars. Vapor rose off the pavement. She pressed the car harder, the needle edging toward seventy-five. Dying daylight the color of peach ice cream melted through the blurry windshield. The pulse of the wobbling tires worked up her spine into her hands. Minutes passed without much progress along the stretch of road. As if the road had become a treadmill. As if the land itself were rolling beneath her on a loop.

The pool of bile in her stomach welled up again. Perhaps the things Roy had imagined in the house were following her, harrying her progress, reaching up to grab the wheels.

Then, blessedly, the road bent left.

A sign appeared up ahead. It was getting dark, so she fumbled for the headlights. Their glow faded across the sign, revealing weathered white lettering.

THREE SUMMERS—TWO MILES

Instantly, her muddy foot hit the brake pedal. The car slid to a halt beside the sign. It stood outside the passenger window, knee-deep in ditch weeds, letters blistered by the sun.

"Simmons Pike is a circle," she whispered. Her lips twitched into a smile because, of course, Simmons Pike wasn't a circle. Three Summers lay behind her. The road was running westward, toward Memphis. Someone must have put the sign up by mistake, or moved it, or altered the letters. Yes, probably altered. A prank. It often happened in rural places.

She eased her foot back on the gas and started forward again. More slowly. But turning around wasn't an option.

Once more, only the sound of the tires accompanied her as the forest canopy thickened overhead. The trees cut off the last of the daylight. Inside the car, the dark hugged her.

A minute passed. Up ahead, a break in the trees appeared where the twilight fell back onto the road. Eager to escape the confines of wood, she accelerated beyond a tentative twenty miles per hour. But just as abruptly, she braked. The nose of the car stopped short of the tree line.

Just ahead, the road continued across a bridge and the ground sloped precipitously down to the gliding green surface of a river. On the far bank, the dark brick structures of a town rose up through the dusk. And just outside her window, a second sign crouched in the fringes of the wood: LOCUST RIVER.

Missy's heart kicked her so hard she doubled over the wheel. The road had bent. The land had folded in on itself. The thing in the ground was trying to pull her back.

This time, she didn't hesitate. Throwing the car into reverse, she turned around on the narrow road and sped back into the forest. Back toward—she didn't know anymore. She would not return *there*.

The cement felt spongy beneath the tires as she steered down the wiggling forest road. With a jolt, she realized the road was different from when she had driven it just a minute before. Then it had been straight; now it was a maze. She longed for a pair of headlights to appear; anyone to lead her from this nightmare.

For no reason, she began thumping her fist against the car horn. She flipped dash switches until the car's siren came on, too, and red light painted the flying trees.

After a few torturous minutes, the woods stepped back. She was on the open portion of Simmons Pike once more. The evening dew was heavy, and still in places steam curtained off the pavement. The headlights pushed a wedge through the writhing haze. The road dipped again, passing through the tunnel.

And then the gray steeple of the church appeared, separated from the dark clouds by some spectral radiance. Below it, invisible, was the graveyard. And her grave. What if the sheriff was still there, waiting for her at the bend of the road?

Missy brought the car to a squealing halt.

Slamming the heel of her hand against the dash, she silenced the siren and cut the lights. She sat in the quiet deepness of the road for a moment. In the rearview mirror, her reflection, a deformed shadow, rocked in the seat.

This was where the boy had leapt from the car. Twisting, she inspected the tunnel and the forested ridge. There was the gravel track she had swerved onto, leading up through the trees. A spark of hope glowed to life. Maybe if she left the roads, she could escape. Perhaps the thing that was manipulating her would be thrown off. It felt futile, but what else was there?

Nothing. There was no one to help her.

Missy rolled down the windows. The humid night gushed across her sweaty wrists as she sat up straight and positioned herself behind the wheel.

Because nobody loves you, Missy. Not now, not ever in your whole life.

No. That's not true.

Turning the car around, she drove back toward the tunnel and steered onto the gravel path. The vehicle lurched. Keeping her spine stiff, she extended her leg against the accelerator. The engine's whine climbed as it propelled the vehicle up the hill. Trees blurred past in the headlights. Gravel dust masked her wake.

Suddenly, the road leveled out. It became a straight track leading her deeper into the woods. She bore down harder on the gas pedal. This had to be an escape route. At the end, she might come out in a different county, on a road uninfluenced by the devilry of this place. Until then she wouldn't blink, wouldn't deviate her eyes from that end point. But then something obscured her view.

Hair. Thick, tangled masses of it dropping from the trees. Swishing across the windshield.

Missy cringed as it lashed through the open windows. Not hair. Moss. Green curling strings dragging at the side mirrors.

Moss, where just before the way had been clear.

The feel of the road changed as well. It roughened, and the tires chewed through dips and roots.

No! She wouldn't fall for these wicked illusions. She pressed her foot down harder and shut her eyes and held the wheel straight and screamed through the roar of the car's engine and the flying gravel and the tearing moss.

Until the next instant when the sounds fell away. She was in the open. She had broken free. She switched her foot to the brake and let go of the wheel.

The car spun.

Momentum flung her into the steering wheel. The impact emptied her lungs. Through her eyelids, she saw the headlights spinning. A sound like churning water filled her ears.

Then everything stopped. The engine kept running. Instead of water, dust settled across her skin.

Missy opened her eyes. She stared through her spilling mane of hair.

Outside, in the steady glow of the headlight beams reaching across a roiled expanse of gravel, scabby white columns and tall dark windows loomed.

Missy shrank as her breath and strength and vitality were wrung from her body.

Despite everything, she had returned. The smears of earth from the graveyard tingled on her hands and feet. The boy had been right. The pastor had been right. There was something inside the house. And it had called her back.

Because it loved her.

The whole land seemed to hold its breath as I drove away.

—"The House of Dust"
Southern Gothic

IN LEXINGTON, IN the Dairy Queen, in the shabby men's bathroom, Brad stared into the sink drain.

Just a little black hole in the white ceramic. No grate. An entrance to an interconnected labyrinth buried beneath the town. Dirty water dripped from his chin. Pale brown, it streaked down, collected along the seam of the drain, trembled, then vanished into the void. Dirty water from the dirt she had smeared on his face.

Straightening, Brad rubbed a hand down his face, collecting the last moisture before grabbing a towel from the dispenser. The paper turned brown as he dried his hands. Tossing it into the overflowing trash can, he began to wash his hands again.

Again the water ran murky off his scrubbing palms. The stuff was deep in the pores. It was stuck to him, desperate to draw him down, make him return. Make him wallow like her.

In the warm gurgling stream, his wet skin flushed red as he scrubbed his palms together harder. Harder.

There's nothing I could have done. She wanted to stay. Sorrel won't hurt her. She'll be fine.

Standing straight again, he scraped his cheeks. Her fingers were still there, still smearing dirt on his face. When he shut his eyes, hers were there, occupied territory. And deep down, the hallucinations flickered, orange and burned, dripping. Ephemeral pieces of him that had become real in that place. Mined from his mind by something dwelling there. In the dirt.

Adamah.

He shut off the water and stood in the dripping silence. They were just hallucinations. And she was just sick. Very sick. Psychologically trapped in an ancient narrative loop. If he could just—

His phone buzzed in his pocket.

Drawing it out, he frowned at the caller ID.

Didn't ring a bell. Damp fingers wavered as he swiped to answer. "Hello?"

"Hello!" A raspy voice, broken by static. "Is this Bradley Ellison?"

"It is. Is this . . . is this Richard Hettinga?"

"Yeah. Good to speak with you."

Brad paced in a quick circle, but the static remained.

"Sorry, I just got your message," the man continued. "I know it's a week or two old. Still, I was wondering if you wanted to talk."

"Yes, I certainly do." Brad pushed out of the bathroom and walked out the side door of the restaurant and into the parking lot.

The other man's voice crackled. "Well, fine. I'm actually, uh, I didn't plan for this 'cause no one's showed much interest before. Still, we can meet up this evening, if you'd like."

"That would be amazing. Are you in Lexington?"

"I'm in Atlanta. Are you in Lexington?"

Brad stopped halfway to the car. "Yes. But I can leave right away. I can drive down tonight and maybe we could meet up tomorrow morning?"

"Or tonight. I'm really fine with either." A fuzzy chuckle. "Like I said, excited to share."

"I'm excited to hear it. I can be there in, say, five hours." He pulled away the phone to check the time. "That'll put it close to midnight."

"Fine."

"Where should I meet you?"

"You know the Gulch?"

"Yes."

"Okay. I'll see you there."

The line went dead. For a second, he frowned at the phone. Why the Gulch? No matter. It was a chance to piece everything together. To see through the clot of memories that had built up over decades in the quiet corner of the county. To perhaps learn how to extract her from them.

Rubbing the sandy feel of static from his ear, he walked quickly to the car.

The orange lights came out along the interstate, the clock climbed toward midnight, and Jennifer shadowed his every thought. What was she doing back in that dark land, far from the city lights?

—"The House of Dust"
Southern Gothic

EVERY ROOM IN the house was empty. In the dance hall, Missy sat in the center of the floor beneath the blazing chandelier. Her chin was on her knees. A Bible lay before her dirty toes. The boards spread around her, still bright from yesterday afternoon's scrubbing, still awaiting their coats of varnish.

Right now, she was glad they reflected nothing. If they did, they would reflect a monster. A corpse dug from the earth, not meant to live again. She hadn't changed her clothes; hadn't washed her hair or skin. She had gone through the entire house, turning on every light she could find, until, in the study, she had found the Bible, the only thing left in his desk.

She had opened it and pressed it to her nose, seeking the reassuring scent that Grandmama's Bible pages had once exuded. But as she stood there, eyes closed, an inexplicable conviction came over her that the walls were reaching for her. Quickly, she went out. She took the Bible downstairs to the dance hall, where the bright spread of boards separated her from everything; there she hunched.

She touched the black cowskin cover gingerly, as if it were the edge of a sword. An unbidden moan escaped her teeth. It vibrated across the bareness. It almost echoed in the interminable stillness of the house. And for a moment, a second sound seemed to answer it, disguised behind the echoes. A sound like the absence of sound. Like the breathing void inside a cave.

hsssssssssssssssssssssssSSSS

Before she could decide if it was imaginary, it faded into the native quiet of the house.

As she opened the Bible, the spine split and a small panic stabbed her. It was almost new. Not well read. Not heeded. Maybe not effective enough to drive away *evil.*

She began to flip through the book, looking for some red ink. Red ink meant Jesus was talking, she remembered that much. Her chest eased as she came across a block of scarlet. She read and reread the words, though she had no idea what they were about. Jesus was talking, that was all that mattered. Evil couldn't touch her. Even if she herself *was* evil deep down. Hadn't Jesus talked about walking in a valley of the shadow of death?

A second desolate hiss trickled into the room—

hsssssssssssssssssSSSSSSSSS

—and ebbed away.

Just the electrical wiring, unused to the burden of all the lights.

Where was that bit she remembered Grandmama reading to her? "The Lord is my shepherd . . . " Thinking about Grandmama made her think how disappointed she'd have been in how she turned out. About how stupid she'd been to think *he* cared more about her than his occupation. About how she stank of herself. Hot, pathetic tears brimmed and spilled.

She couldn't read anymore; things were too blurry. She was lost in the black text anyway, searching for that bit about the valley of the shadow. It might be a Psalm, but where were the Psalms? She put the Bible aside and rubbed her eyes.

hsssssssssssSSSSSSSSSSSSS

Jerking her hands down, she found the room was wrong.

It was shrinking. Perhaps it was just too much light, light from all directions, from every door, eliminating every shadow. The walls crept closer. The ceiling bowed. She stood, wavering as vertigo struck her. The floor sagged like the stretchy surface of a trampoline, caving toward her weight.

The house was folding in. Coiling. Embracing her.

And this time, the empty sigh would not cease.

hsssssSSSSSSSSSSSSSSSSSSS

Where was Roy? Why had he left the house? Had they carried him off? Or was he still here, hiding?

"Roy?" She turned a quick circle, then stepped over the Bible and wavered across the bending hall to the dining room. The lights were bright above the table. The outline of a shape hovered in dust on its surface. She averted her eyes to the window she had told him to clean. It was shut. He must have left, thinking she was dead.

Stepping through the doorway, she felt the dining room crouch down around her.

Maybe she *was* dead. Maybe she'd died in the coffin. The Devil had dug her up and pulled her back here. And that sound—that endless empty sound—was the sound of his gradual approach.

Stepping into the main hall, she looked right.

hSSSSSSSSSSSSSSSSSSSSSS

It came from beneath the stairwell, from the basement door.

Missy wrapped her arms around herself and rotated toward the door. The hissing diminished as she approached. Then all was still.

She stopped in front of the door. She grasped the knob. Cool and scaly with rust, it turned. Abruptly, she jerked the door wide.

Darkness. And the bitter scent of the basement below. The gloom within was so dense it could hide someone even on the upper steps. Someone who could grab her roving hand to pull her down.

Growling in disgust, she thrust her hand into the darkness, found the switch, and flipped it.

Nothing. The bulb was dead.

Fine. She shoved the door closed and turned away—but the squeak of rusty hinges didn't follow.

Missy hesitated, glanced back, then turned. The door hovered there, halfway between the wall and its frame. Edging closer again, she nudged it. The door swung closed slightly before rebounding, coasting even farther toward the wall.

"Roy?" she mumbled. Stepping closer, she placed her hand on the outside of the door and gave it a gentle push. It swung toward its frame again, then bumped into something within a foot of closure and swung back out. Even wider than before.

There wasn't a doorstop. Swelling, perhaps? She stepped even closer and ran her toe along the portion of the floor where the door had stopped. The boards were level.

Purposely not thinking, Missy placed her hand outside the door and gave it a good hard shove. It rushed closed, coming within an inch of the frame. Then it was knocked back. She stumbled away to avoid being struck. The door banged against the wall and stopped there, quivering.

Something's standing there. In the dark. Invisible.

"No," she said. "No, no, no." Forcing her fingers out, she grabbed the edge. The surface was cold. She pried the door away from the wall. It felt like it was being held open by a current of water. She pushed it inward.

It was easy at first. The door swung ponderously shut. The gap closed to almost nothing. Then, gently, pressure built until the door stopped, a gap of half an inch between the door and the frame. Not enough for a person. Plenty wide enough, though, for darkness to pour through.

Missy leaned against the door, pressing with all her weight. The door wobbled, pressure vibrating in the gap like the pulsing air through the lowered window of a fast car. With every extra ounce of strength she applied, the pressure built. The *thing* was leaning in on the other side, applying more and more weight, growing more and more insistent that she not close the door.

Her heart was a fist beating on a cell wall. Her bare feet pressed against the floor. Her legs trembled. Even as she hurled her body against the door, the gap remained. Her dry hands slipped on the dry wood. "No!"

The cry choked off as a new sound entered the house. Quick and sharp, knuckles rapping on wood. Someone knocking at the front door. Someone solid and human.

Flinging herself from beneath the stairwell, Missy ran. Behind, the basement door slammed back. The thing was coming out. Pursuing.

Reaching the front door, she tugged at the handle, then frantically found the lock and threw it back. Heaving the barrier open, she lunged across the threshold.

Hands caught her shoulders.

For a moment, she hoped it would be Walt, come back to her, saying his job was not more important than she was. If he had, she would have really loved him. But it wasn't him. It was Ezra.

"Tired of running yet?"

"Let go! There's something coming!" She attacked the hands holding her captive.

Ezra maintained his grip and looked into the house. "Nothing's chasing you."

"It's there! It's . . . " She stared into the bright hall. "It was coming out of the basement."

"Let us see." He drew her inside.

"No! It's behind the door."

Ezra maneuvered her up the hall. She struggled, feet dragging across the boards, but his grip was unbreakable. And she was still so weak.

"It will kill you," she hissed as the distance diminished. "It wants to kill me."

Together, they stopped. The door was wide open, resting against the wall. The space within the stairwell was empty and dark.

"There?" he said. "You see?"

Missy's gaze fastened on the back of the door. Her muscles went lax. She sank down.

A handprint stuck there. A bare spot on the wood where the dust had been rubbed away by the pressure of a steady hand. A long hand. Thin fingers splayed. Clear as a paper cutout, floating in the center of the door about halfway up.

"Nothing to be afraid of," he murmured. Pulling her up, he guided her to the door. "Touch it."

Missy shrank back, wordlessly jerking her chin.

"Come on." Tugging her closer, he gently but forcefully placed her hand over the imprint. Missy bucked in his hold as the skin on her palms and the pads of her fingers crawled, as if each cell were being shuffled, rearranged.

The same sensation she'd felt back in the garden trenches when she touched the wall.

"See? Just saying hello."

He released her. She sank down again and leaned against the wall. Sighing, he turned and pushed the door closed. Softly, solidly, it shut.

"You think everything's against you," he said.

She looked at him through her matted mane.

"You think something in this house wants to hurt you. You think the people in Three Summers want to hurt you. Mostly, you think I do. I can understand. But if I wanted you dead, I could have left you in that box. I don't want you dead, or hurting. None of us do. We need you, Missy."

"I'm nothing."

"I know." He crouched in front of her. "I know what it's like when someone leaves so abruptly. Abandons you. That collapsing-star feeling in your chest. Makes you want to gag your heart out because obviously no one else thinks it's worth a thing. The other Queens felt that. He feels that."

A finger snaked behind her ear, smoothing back a dirty lock of hair.

"Now, it's been a long day. Let's get you to bed. Got enough strength to walk upstairs?"

She nodded but did not move.

"Okay." Ezra's arms came around her, drawing her close; her arms folded limply around him. Standing, he carried her down the hall. An odd sort of intimacy sparked at the proximity of their bodies and their faces and mixing breath. She felt its charge in his shoulders, its current in his hands. It built as he climbed the stairs and carried her toward the bedroom, his hold becoming an embrace, both tighter and more tender, as if discovering she was a prize possession.

She knew where this led. She knew she should struggle against it, get down from his arms, stop him at the door.

But she was just so tired.

It was midnight when I arrived in Atlanta.

—"The House of Dust"
Southern Gothic

CENTENNIAL OLYMPIC PARK DRIVE lay empty amid the bright darkness of the southern metropolis.

Brad turned left at the public parking sign, driving down a ramp into the Gulch, a region of rough parking lots and scruffy trees and rusted train tracks beneath a tangle of downtown Atlanta's elevated highways.

He drove slowly through the shadows and pools of yawning orange light, passing billboarded pylons and chain-link fences, his gaze wandering across the empty acres of concrete. Had Richard Hettinga really agreed to meet in this place at this hour of the night? Why hadn't he insisted on a more precise meeting spot?

Passing beneath Martin Luther King Jr. Drive, he slowed as the end of the parking lot approached. Pulling into a random spot, he turned off the engine and leaned his head against the wheel for a moment. It still throbbed. Jennifer still burdened everything. But this was for her.

And the burning man.

He shoved open the door.

There was an emptiness to the air as he stepped out. No hum of cars coming down the streets above, no footsteps on the broken pavement, no audible shiver from the railroad tracks that lay just ahead beyond a stand of trees. There was something somewhere, though. A very low purr.

Leaving the car, he followed the sound across the parking lot toward the Bankruptcy Court tower, a pale block against the black sky.

There. A lone car crouched below a dead light pole. Its taillights glowed deep red. Idling.

Brad paused. He looked around the abandoned lot and into the shadowy corridors beneath the bridges, then advanced toward the vehicle.

It was a strange design, and unbranded: modernly sleek on the front, yet with the unusual fins of a Swept Wing '58 affixed to the back. The windows were tinted. He stepped up beside the driver's-side door and waited for something bad to happen. Anyone could be down here at this time of night. Hettinga could be anyone.

When nothing happened, he rapped on the glass.

There was no response. If someone was inside the car, they were asleep, or dead.

Brad moved away from the car, reanalyzing the lot. The city stirred in its sleep, restive breath rustling the unkempt trees on their barren little islands, setting them swaying like hooded figures. Suddenly he realized he didn't want to meet anyone in this place at this time of night.

Heather would chastise him. *Coward.* She'd be right: he'd devolved since his early days.

He was beside his own car, reaching for the door when a clicking sound penetrated the nearby wall of shrubbery. Something out on the tracks. Gravel kicked up by clumsy shoes.

He moved cautiously into the weeds. Crouching down, he pulled aside a few limp branches to peer through.

A person moved out among the rails. It was too dark to distinguish features, but he made out a rumpled suit borne on sunken shoulders. Dusty black shoes paced back and forth. One hand gripped the wrist of the other behind the stranger's back. A sudden cough raked the frail frame.

Brad looked back across the concrete sea to the idling car. Then at the man again, glimpsing him just as he turned. The clothes differed markedly from the blue jeans and plaid he remembered in the photo the librarian had shown him. But the high forehead was the same, and the white goatee. Rising, he pushed through the shrubs onto the railroad.

"Mr. Hettinga?"

The man looked over. His feet stilled.

"Mr. Hettinga? Good evening. Sorry I took so long to find you."

The man's eyes shimmered like mercury as he faced toward him.

"No trouble, Mr. Ellison." His voice was a musky rasp. He gazed at Brad unblinking for a moment, then passed a hand over his face. "I've been waiting. Was . . . was there something particular you were wondering about?"

Irresolute, Brad spread his hands. "Pretty much everything."

"Everything? That's a lot. More than I have to offer." The man's foot twitched, and a pebble rang against the nearest rail. The sound traveled as a diminishing clink down the iron miles. "So, you're a writer. *Southern Gothic* magazine. Fairly long career?"

"That's right. Brooke Carney up in Lexington referenced you."

He paused as the man coughed again.

"Are you all right, sir? Is that your car back there? You left it running."

"I know, I know. I just . . . " Hettinga waved his hand, then passed it across his face again. His cheeks were oddly hollow, as if he were biting them inside his mouth. "Things are becoming rather confused in my mind. I came down to this city because it held significance in the life of the house's last resident. I heard her voice calling and followed. I never shared any of this because I— No matter." He squared his shoulders. "I'll tell you the story. And when you tell it to others, people will listen to you. Have you got something to take notes with?"

Just like that? No probing questions about his intentions or motives? And right here? He could hardly recall a more ready witness. Drawing out his phone, Brad squatted down on one of the rails, feeling slightly surreal as he squinted at the man outlined against the haze of distant lights. He knew almost nothing about Hettinga, just the fragments the librarian had shared. He tapped the phone's microphone.

"You grew up in Three Summers, sir?"

"I was born there and left before I was twenty," Hettinga said. "But distance doesn't protect. You can't ever escape it after you've been there, I think. It follows your footsteps. It can hear us now, even from three hundred miles away. "

"*It?*"

"The demon that has lodged in that land since the beginning."

"What was that beginning?" he asked.

Hettinga stood rooted for a long moment, then slowly resumed his pacing. "I guess it all started on a dreary December day in 1830 when a wealthy inheritor named Darrin DeWitt went into the slum quarters of Charleston to seek advice from a fortune-teller after the untimely death of his father. Thrown suddenly from the golden meadows of his youth into the lockbox world of his father's shipping business, I guess it is understandable that he suffered a fair bit of anguish. Something happened, though, in that witch's den. He went in to consult with the spirit of his father, but the counsel he received was certainly nothing his father would have given."

"What did he see?" Brad asked.

"A vision of a different life. One that filled him with peace, reconciled him with his father, and appealed to his spring-day consciousness. To the chagrin of his family, he sold off the DeWitt firm and all its assets and went west, into the wilderness. And he took the beautiful young witch with him—her name was Martha."

Hettinga coughed again, then resumed, his tone melodic as he settled into the story. "Summer of 1831. Darrin DeWitt peaked a ridge in rural Tennessee and looked down on a river and an island and a green expanse of forest. His party had traveled specifically in search of a place removed from the world. The rumors about Martha, whom he always referred to as his 'angel,' had contaminated his reputation in the tidewater. So, when he looked down from that ridge and saw the island, like a green gem in the deep green river, he probably turned to his companions and said, 'There, friends, is my angel's landing.'

"Darrin could see even then what it would all become. He could see the forests becoming fields and the fields becoming white with cotton and lush with tobacco. He could see the boats coming and going along the river, being loaded with goods at the dock on the end of the island. He could see his fortune growing. And he could see the house sitting in a clearing among the trees, ruling the land for miles around. I don't know if he saw in that moment the others who would come. I don't know if he saw the town of Three Summers spring up a few miles down the water. Of course, it wasn't called Three Summers then.

"Whatever he saw, he made it his life mission to accomplish great things. And he did. He plowed those fields, and he grew that cotton and tobacco, and he acquired that money, and he built that house. All on the backs of slaves, of course. And, of course, the victims of rituals were always selected from their population. On the night of sacrifices, he would pick one at random, a mother, father, child, and order the whole community into the fields before the house. Each time they tried to resist, but Martha's terrible, soothing influence compelled them. For those who tried to flee, it was said the land itself bent beneath their feet and returned them to the house."

A car sighed by on one of the overhead bridges. Hettinga's voice seemed to wander free from his motionless frame.

"In 1834, the first child was born. They had a total of seven, I think, all sons. For the next twenty or so years, the house and plantation thrived and grew. Three Summers sprang up a few miles down the river and exports were shifted to that location. In the early forties, a cotton mill was constructed and consecrated in honor of a being called Adamah. Its rise, however, heralded the end of Darrin DeWitt. One August evening, after seeing off a shipment of goods from the new pier at Three Summers, he slipped near the end of the dock and fell into a sloughy patch of mud. Rage overcame him, and he berated the slaves who dragged him free. They, filthy as he was, succumbed to similar rage and soon all present, even the foremen, banded together and carried him to the mill and trampled him with their feet until he died. Martha, unafraid, came to collect the remains, burying them in her garden."

Brad nodded, recalling the vague fragments from the library.

"The killers were forgiven. Some said such leniency would breed further violence, but it was not so. Martha's voice, her touch, even her glance, seeded one with an elated sort of calm. Still, some changes led to unease. After DeWitt's death, an odd practice began at the plantation and in the town: Martha compelled the slaves to carry out their labors at night. She assured them that their vision would adjust and their attunement with the land they worked would be enhanced. Many were wary, but her influence was strong, and so they began to sleep by day and rise when the sun had set."

"A tradition that stuck," Brad murmured, remembering his night drive through Three Summers.

"Angel's Landing became a playground for the DeWitt boys," Hettinga continued. "Instead of wagons toting bailed goods, surreys carrying the silken elite of the surrounding county rattled across the bridge and up the road to the house. Every year, as the visitors arrived, they would look out of their coaches and see the seven young ones running to greet them, coming out of the forest and field, a little older, a little taller, a little more handsome.

"And so, the DeWitt house became a center of social excitement in western Tennessee as the antebellum years waned. Instead of sneaking out at night to play in the woods, the children would leave the house behind at twelve or one o'clock in the morning, arm in arm with a lover, the windows still full of yellow light behind them, and the wine and whiskey bottles mostly empty. They would wander out across the rustling fields and lie by the river and watch the stars sparkle and the lightning bugs blink high over the land. They would listen to the riverboats chugging by in the darkness and listen to the sleepy music that drifted from their smoky saloons. Then, when they were sure no elders would wander down to the water with lanterns and discover them, when the wind died down to nothing, when the land lay still and lost in slumber beneath them, then they would find some quiet spot by the water, or among the trees, or in the high grass, and make love to a person they had perhaps never met until that night and might never see again."

Hettinga's pacing outline seemed to float like vapor above the tracks. His gaunt cheeks stretched softly with each word.

"That's what the DeWitt children did before the war. At least, that's what I think. But when Lincoln was elected, Martha vowed that there would be trouble. No Republican scallywag would conquer her kingdom. So, Angel's Landing became a rallying point. All the boys went off to war, all save the youngest. And so, none save the youngest survived those bloody years.

"He was swimming in Deep Creek, with a girl whose family had taken refuge with the DeWitts, when a band of Union soldiers returning from Shiloh came upon the plantation. It was hot and dry and the river was low, so they swam their horses across and onto the island. It was hot and dry, so most everyone was asleep. Martha was smart. She didn't try to fight. The soles of foreign shoes on her soil woke her. She took her slaves, and fled down the hill to the creek, swam across, and disappeared into the desolate plantation fields on the mainland. They never came back out of those fields. Just seemed to sink into the ground. I've always wondered where they went. The soldiers set the house on fire, but it was saved by a sudden mist, like those that rose to water Eden."

Brad felt Hettinga's gaze touch him and glimmered a smile.

Drawing a long breath, the man continued. "The area was a hotbed of resistance and resentment during Reconstruction. The region picked up the pieces, but without the oversight of the house, it was a place of poverty and violence. It was rumors of a curious exhaustion malady that drew a northern doctor named Jerimiah McCloud to set up a philanthropic practice in the house around 1870. He was a man who had served in the war, felt his hands soaked in its carnage, and traveled later through the war-ravaged South, where pity took root in his heart.

"He was accompanied by the Southern woman he had fallen in love with, a girl named Magdalene. The only explanation he gave of their meeting was a tale of finding her in a burned-out church in a rural county, caring for a small band of orphans. Magdalene never contradicted this account. Perhaps she could not. People questioned whether she was mute, for she never spoke.

"Others, though, said she had a voice of a different kind. An inaudible one that reached into the heart. Her attentions became more valued by the sick than her husband's. A hospital, consecrated to a being called Adamah, was completed in January of 1877, and the coinciding construction of a railroad just south of the town caused the number of visiting patients to increase. Thanks to the special nature of Magdalene's influence, many of those who were cured never left Three Summers; and so, the town was revitalized from the destruction of the war.

"But again, devotion led to death, this time for Dr. McCloud. He began experimenting with applying the region's earth to wounds in hopes of healing."

Brad stiffened.

"This, in turn, led to experimentation in reaching beyond the patients to the source of their mysterious healing. The thing beneath. But in plumbing the depths, he broke the surface. Reports of patients succumbing to insanity plagued the hospital's first summer. And in September of that year, he was slain, beaten into the ground outside the building; his wife bore away his remains."

Hettinga's breathing was becoming labored. Carefully, he lowered himself onto the section of track opposite. Brad remembered what the librarian had said about his health, but he knew better than to change the subject. "What happened then?"

"Then came war, again," he said. "A training camp—Camp Simmons—was set up south of Three Summers and oversaw the soldiers who dug trenches in the nearby fields in preparation for the plains of Europe. Magdalene, though elderly and said to be of diminishing influence, managed to assure the local boys that the earthworks would protect them."

Hettinga shook his head. "Instead, they drank their blood. The town cast blame upon her. One night in the winter of 1918, they came to the island. They took the old woman and tied her beneath the arch of the concrete bridge between the island and the mainland as a December flood was rising. Days later, when they returned, her body had vanished from the bonds, and the bridge had attained the clayish red hue it has maintained ever since."

"I've seen it," Brad murmured.

"What happened to her I cannot say. As with her predecessor, her fate held some ambiguity. After the war, the few sad young men remaining came back to that humid land of summer night dreams, looking for their pasts. They made do with what they found and settled down and became the next generation of Three Summer's inhabitants. A bridge was built that spanned the river and brought traffic into the heart of the town. Industry stumbled along in that forgotten land while America became the shining capital of the world. But the house once again lay fallow.

"Then the land across the Locust River was found to be rich in coal. The value of the vast plantation rose as a mining company sought to acquire the land. After much contention over the true ownership of the century-old estate, people from Three Summers, as well as outsiders, met on the evening of June 21, 1923, to decide who owned what. The night of the Party Field Massacre."

"Describe it."

"At around seven in the evening, through the huge tents that had been set up on the field before the house, a fight broke out. The thousands of acres would bring tens, hundreds of thousands of dollars. Who would get those thousands? The lightning bugs rose through screams and flying bodies and blood-mist that evening as the negotiations degenerated into slaughter. Everyone must have foreseen this course, for everyone came armed.

"Miriam Larkin, the only unarmed person among them, survived that night by taking refuge amid the flower beds behind the house. She lay there through the night while the ground imbibed blood. In the morning, she was found among the bodies. She was the only daughter of a Nashville dressmaker who had worked at the Adamah Cotton Mill in his younger years. Her sad story attracted the attention of Rex Emil, the king of a gypsy circus touring the region. He brought his band to Three Summers and within a week they were married, though he was significantly her senior. Animosity had developed between him and the leaders of the many towns he had toured, though for what reason I never discovered. He seemed to view Three Summers as a haven.

"With his funds, Miriam won the property ownership battle. Instead of selling the land, though, she advertised the whole place as a great fun park for the South to come to in their new automobiles. The bridge saw increased traffic from the state highway, and Three Summers became a party town. Fireworks filled the summer air, and bars flourished along the streets, and the woodlands filled with shouts of pleasure, and the fields with frolicking figures under the canopy of stars. A theater was constructed in 1927, dedicated to the same being, the one they called Adamah. At its inauguration, Rex Emil met his end under the feet of his own elephants, leaving Miriam pregnant with their only child. She did not, however, consider herself destitute. Rather, she thought of herself as a fairy queen, spreading her influence greatly to build up the house and the town. As a consequence, it was remarked how quickly she aged. She died in 1939."

"Just like that?" Brad asked.

Hettinga nodded. "Some said she spread herself too far, drawing too deeply from a dangerous well. She aged like a flower in bright sun. When she died, her body was laid out on the dining room table in the house, and her only son, Ezra, watched as the people filed by. It is said the body was left there and turned with time to dust.

"The town fell into a slump, and it was a sad, sickly country that John and Ellen King of Philadelphia came to in 1946. Neither of them cared for the local lore and cults and pecking order. They paid the money-starved town handsomely for the old plantation and asked to be left to live quietly. They drove to church near Parker's Crossroads on Sunday, and they drove to the grocery store on Monday, and they gardened the rest of the week. But their bliss did not last long. No one is sure what happened, but it seems the house not only rejected them, but launched a full-scale assault against them. John wandered into town one autumn night asking for a doctor for his pregnant wife. The doctor returned with him to the island, but they found the house a roiling den of dust. John ran in to try to save Ellen. She had already succumbed while giving birth in the second bedroom on the second floor. John King emerged from the house a broken man. The doctor—he said out of mercy—took the poor man into the forest and helped him tie a noose and hang himself from an oak with a pit beneath it."

The man fell silent so long that Brad softly prompted, "Go on."

Hettinga bowed his head. "In the early fifties, Miriam's son, Ezra, finally sold off much of the land to the Middle Tennessee Mining Company. The Locust River Mine was developed across the bank and a few miles downstream of Three Summers. It became a mining town. The old plantation house sank into ruin, and Ezra resolved that the old place had outlived itself. It was time to board it up and put it in the past, where it belonged."

His head rose. His eyes had darkened to cave entrances. "But the house did not allow it, for the rituals surrounding it did not sink far from the surface. Again, fatigue crept like moss across the town. The sacrifices needed to experience the serenity brought by Martha and Magdalene and Miriam became more frequent. *Accidents* were frequent; lives were stolen from the mine. Ezra found the heat of scrutiny rising. And so, when a state prosecutor named Walter Collins came to investigate in early 1962, Ezra felt desperate for bargaining power. It arrived in the form of a woman named Missy, Mr. Collins's supposed wife. He discovered the truth of the man he was dealing with: a self-assured man easily enticed. One night, he took him to a town gathering, exposed him to the same presence that had brought peace to Darrin DeWitt more than a hundred years before: a dream, a different past, a different life. Together, they engineered a mutually beneficial plot that would disappear both of their problems. The case would be resolved in the town's favor, and the woman resolved in Collins's favor. The woman named Missy was buried. But Ezra did not keep his half of the bargain. He dug her up again. Adamah had a purpose for her."

The man's labored breathing stopped. He sat frozen, like a paused recording.

Brad stared at him as the effervescent hum of the sleeping city faded back into his ears. The battery icon on his phone was red. "Who were the sacrifice victims? After the slaves."

"Always the weak," Hettinga whispered. His thin cheeks were flushed. "The meek. The powerless. First the slave. Then the share-cropper. The ailing patient in the hospital. The wounded soldier. The lonely gypsy. The man who became lost looking for a shortcut. The woman with the flat tire. The teenager seeking thrills. The child running away from home. Compelled into the ground by the Queen of Hearts."

"Queen of Hearts," he said. "Is that where it comes in?"

"Queen of Hearts," Hettinga repeated. "The fulcrum."

"Martha, Magdalene, Miriam, Missy . . . " He stopped. One last name trembled on his lips.

"All broken vessels from which power spills."

"What is their power? What can they do?"

"They do what the first Queen did for DeWitt—bring peace. The past is the place where we dream of different lives. Where our faults can be forgiven. Where we can rest."

Brad . . .

He flinched at the voice in his head, a voice choked on smoke.

Stifling a cough, he said, "So how did they become Queens?"

Hettinga rose halfway and bent over, pressing his head between his knees. It was a discomfiting posture to see a man of his age assume, almost childlike. Then he straightened. "Would you like me to show you?"

"Certainly."

The man came across the tracks, motioning toward the parking lot. "Get in your car. Follow me."

The deep red taillights of Hettinga's car led the way along miles of dark roads until a very different part of Atlanta was passing outside my windows. Amber streetlights shone down on buckling sidewalks and overturned trash cans. When he turned onto a residential street, the headlights flashed across barred windows. The car stopped before one of the old houses.

—"The House of Dust"
Southern Gothic

IT CAME WHILE she was in the bathroom brushing her hair.

Sweetness. The faintest waft, like the wind from a butterfly wing. Immediately, her palm hardened against the brush handle. She completed the stroke, then raised the brush to her face and gingerly pressed her nose in among the bristles. Just the loamy smell of damp hair. Lowering the brush, she sucked deeply through her nose and caught the scent again.

Quickly, she turned toward the bathtub. All the water had drained away. No dirt ring on the porcelain. And the window was shut against mosquitoes. She sniffed again. Still there.

Her darting eyes went to the floor, then to her feet, then her legs, and the hem of the old white dress riding just above her knees.

It was the old thing she had found that first day, lying in the shadow of the door. Weeks ago, she had bundled it down into the basement. Today, he had come upstairs with it draped over his arm. "I want you to wear it. For tonight."

It had smelled like dust when she put it on. But now . . . she pressed her nose against her shoulder.

Yes. Buried below the layer of age, she could catch the itch of something else. Sugar. Daffodils.

The hairbrush clattered to the floor. Hands sprang to her neck as heavy coughing exploded from her throat. Her mouth became the hot pressure point as everything inside tried to escape. Blood stretched her face like an overfilled balloon, and she collapsed onto the tile.

Forcing her hands away from her throat, she clawed at the garment. The seam along the left shoulder tore. Then the bathroom door banged open and Ezra was beside her on the floor, yelling and grabbing her wrists.

"Missy! Missy! Stop it!"

As her lungs inflated, she shook her head and rasped, "I can't wear—it smells like . . . "

He led her into the bedroom and sat with her on the bed and waited for her blood pressure to equalize. One cool finger traced the rip on her shoulder. "Don't worry, it'll mend."

"I don't want to wear this."

"Just for tonight. You might even learn to like it. Now finish up. We can't be too late."

Just for tonight. Something Warren Dawson would whisper at HUG. Something the Boss would say at the Club. Something Walt would say on the phone when he wasn't coming home.

She got up from the bed and went to the dresser. She stretched a hair tie between her fingers before threading it into her hair.

"Did you see Roy today?"

He followed her to the dresser, fastening his black tie in the mirror.

"No."

Two weeks now. He wasn't coming back. And neither was *he*. She was alone. Like those days in the backyard after Grandmama died. Alone with the daffodils.

"Are you ready?" he asked.

"I don't want to see anyone."

"They want to see you."

Pounding, like a slow hammer, started inside her skull as they went down the steps and out to his car. Two weeks the boy had been gone and two weeks she had hunched in the corners of the house, waiting for something to happen. Ezra had told her to carry on with renovations, but what was the point? It wasn't her house. He was living there now: eating with her, sleeping with her, rocking on the porch in the evenings with her. She had been in limbo, watching him watch her. Until this morning, when he had announced a "community meeting." Until just now, when she smelled those flowers.

Long ago, they had come into the backyard in Atlanta and led her off to her new life. And now she was here, in this seat, in this dress. She was tired of being led. The hammer in her head thumped harder.

The car rumbled off down the driveway. She tried to breathe shallowly and through her mouth, but hints of the smell got through anyway and churned up her stomach.

It was near nine o'clock and the twilit country was very still—almost Sunday morning still. They bumped across the clay-stained bridge and entered the tunnel of trees. Fingers of light reached ahead from the car, feeling their way through the drowsing forest.

The quiet grew even more intense as they motored down an empty Adamah Road toward Three Summers. The houses that slipped past were curtained up for the first time she had seen; Grammy's Grocery and the Texaco station were closed. Only the DeWitt Cigarette lady's teeth were visible in the dusk.

As they drove into Three Summers, the lights at other establishments went out. Apartment windows went dark and streetlights waned to embers. Little creeks of lanterns flowed down the alleys as people came from the courts and stairwells behind buildings.

Lanterns. They were all carrying lanterns with ruby-colored globes. The orbs of scarlet light revealed tired faces. Sparks of eagerness, however, lit the eyes that turned toward the car. The crowd spilled out onto the pavement.

At the intersection, the headlights reached far enough down the road to reveal orange barricades on the bridge. The road had been closed.

They turned right onto Larkin Street. The old dress fabric rasped against Missy's skin as she twisted to watch the people follow them into the murky canyon of the cross street. "This is the usual procedure for a community meeting?"

"Very much so." Ezra smiled

The pounding inside her skull quickened. The smell again . . .

Bright flowers in the dark.

At the far end, they turned onto DeWitt and parked beside an overgrown field. Out in the grass, the shadowy block of a building loomed among the tenebrous trees and sky. Ezra came around and opened the door.

She shook her head. "No, I'm . . . this doesn't feel right."

"You won't be hurt," he assured her.

What Warren Dawson had said at HUG. What the Boss said at the Club. What Walt—

"No, this dress. This whole thing. You're trying to turn me into something."

He bent down, and she turned away from his too-smooth face. "Come on, Ms. Holiday. I'll hold your hand."

Inside her mouth, that broken tooth gnawed on her tongue. *You be good from here on,* Grandmama had said. *Now use that gum to hold your tooth in and don't try to get involved in stuff you don't understand.*

Turning back around, she faced the stale May evening.

The faces crossing the street, bloodred in the glow of their lifted lamps, were all turned to her. Each person had dressed to the nines, or as close as they could come to it. Polished shoes drummed the asphalt. She searched the crowd for familiar faces, but who did she really know? Not even those who sent the letters of welcome.

There was Mr. Irons, from the house on the hill, placidly smiling. There was the woman with thin dark hair who had skulked below the floor of the gray house. There was the gawky red-haired man who had led the men from Theater Grill to capture Roy and bury him. And there were hundreds more whom she had glimpsed in passing on the road, or in the lonely house on the hill, or at the diner. All silent. Respectful.

Ezra's fingers smothered her own. He drew her into the sea of grass, making toward the crumbling structure. The tangled blades swished around her unprotected legs. Startled grasshoppers launched themselves away from her intruding feet. From the trees bordering the lot and from the marshy riverbank, the insects stilled to witness their passage.

The brick wall blushed red as the collective tide of lantern light touched it. A little chink of a door appeared at its base. As they approached it, Missy gathered a good breath. Almost immediately, she choked it out again in the hot passageway that followed. The flower scent radiating from the dress was strengthening.

"Ezra." Her voice came back close in the corridor. "Ezra."

He didn't reply this time. His grip remained oppressive. Her shoulder jarred against the wall, and then he was leading her around a corner. Vastness opened against her face. Before she could hesitate, he led her into the void. Dry, packed earth scuffed beneath her sandals. Echoes came back from a distance. After perhaps fifty feet, they stopped.

Missy turned her head, eyes straining against the gloom. The occasional creak of timbers drifted from above. The sigh of falling dust. Craning around, she watched the little door they had come through brighten. With a sandy shuffling, the people filed in. As more came, flickering radiance melted across the sprawling room. Rafters and planks became visible above. The memory of a candle-light service at Grandmama's church jolted into her mind. Bile rose as the conjoined shadows of Ezra and herself flowed in black rivers from their feet.

He nudged her, and they started forward again. With a sound like showers of stones striking the earth, the people followed. The shadows and light reached ahead. They washed across a twisted mound at the center of the room. A pile of . . .

Sticks?

Bones?

Shovels.

And beside the mound of shovels, four white stakes protruding from the ground. Marking out a plot.

"No." She stopped. Quivering invaded her limbs as she remembered the binding, blinding void inside the coffin. The sound of dirt raining down. "No. You're going to do something bad."

The mound and stakes were thirty feet off. Ezra had stopped beside her. He did not compel her on. His grasp remained steady, even as she shook. The people flooded up behind them and passed around them and fanned out on either side of the ritual spot.

When everyone had stopped, they set their lanterns down and dimmed the flames. Hundreds of tired feet stood in dim, molten pools. An invisible line just beyond the mound seemed to stop both them and the light from venturing farther into the room. Darkness hung, an impenetrable deepness.

Quite spontaneously, everyone began moving, walking twisting patterns through the lanterns like a disturbed hive of ants, weaving in and out, never colliding. The crunch of a shovel biting into earth brought Missy's eyes to the center of the vortex. Six people were bending around the staked-off ground, scooping up the earth.

"*No.*" She turned on Ezra, dragged at his grip. "Let go. I'm leaving."

He did let go. But just as quickly his arm was across her shoulders, thrusting her forward, forcing her to face the shovels and stakes. "It's time to be quiet, Missy."

"If you *dare* try to put me down that—"

"I'm not, Missy. I told you—you're safe."

None of the tautness eased from her muscles, but she continued to watch.

A pattern had emerged from the swirling movement of the crowd. They were streaming toward the heap of shovels, picking them up, and proceeding to the rapidly forming hole. There they dug out a scoop of earth, flung it away, and then dropped the shovels in a second heap where a second procession picked them up to do the same.

The oldest members of the community filed through while the trough was shallow, and now the younger ones were at work, bending low, even jumping into the pit. And then the very youngest ones were passing: children. Missy searched their faces, but Roy was not among them. Adults who had remained by the hole lowered them in and handed down little shovels. They dumped the soil that was handed up and then pulled the grimy children from the hole. They threw the shovels in the heap and withdrew.

And the grave was complete.

Missy's eyes traveled across the gathering.

The people had resumed their places by their lanterns and stood still.

Then the murky-haired woman emerged from the softly glowing congregation. She paused by the digging and glanced back. Her gaze lingered on Missy as she nodded, eyelids rising and falling with the movement of her head. Then she passed over that invisible line beyond the grave, evaporating into the darkness.

Quiet rained down.

The hammering inside Missy's head intensified to the level of her heartbeat. The air was gelatinizing each second with the sucrose smell. It wasn't just coming from the dress anymore; it was radiating from that darkness. Daffodils were sprouting out there. Daffodils pushing up through the earth. Splitting open and oozing perfume. Binding her like sticky spider silk in the knowledge that she would never be free of what she was.

Ezra clutched her. He would not let go.

A smudge appeared in the darkness. The woman emerged from the veil. She was not alone. In her arms she clutched a small form. A body bound in white cloth strips that held the arms against its sides.

At the grave, she lay the body down and clambered into the hole. Hands protruded from the lip of the hole and drew the body in. The form did not stir as she crouched down, bearing it out of view. A moment later, she came up, arms empty. She climbed out and faced them. Another slow-blink nod. Then she withdrew.

Ezra's fingers tightened around Missy's shoulder. He propelled her toward the grave, speaking very low in her ear. "Missy, you will now complete the greatest act of love you can perform. It's an easy thing for a person to sacrifice himself for his friends, but to see yourself in another's face and still allow them to be offered, there is no higher devotion and no more binding tie. This act will prove your devotion to Adamah. It will solidify your bond as medium."

They were at the edge. At the bottom of the grave, in the dregs of flickering light, the body lay, small and still. Only the face was uncovered. It was discolored and bulging from the tightness of the cloth. But she knew it.

"Roy," she whimpered. "Oh God, please."

"With his breath," Ezra whispered, "you give breath."

He let go of her. Like amber, the sweet air held her in place above the brink. She stared down at that mashed little face. The closed eyes. Was he even still alive?

There was a soft clink, someone picking up a shovel. The gentle crunch of dirt being scooped.

Ezra was beside her again. She sagged against him. He put the shovel in her hands. It was laden at the end with a few ounces of earth. "It's a formality," he whispered. "A pure formality."

The shovel wobbled in her hands. The little pile of crumbles shifted on the edge of the blade. If even a few went in, would that be enough? She looked down again, at the boy wrapped up like a larva in the pit. He was disgusting. He had killed the cat. He hated her. He tried to leave her. He tried to stone her.

The shovel tilted.

The smell of daffodils stuffed up her nose. The pounding coming out of her skull like a brick. And that man close behind her, arms folded, breathing softly. Forcing her. Turning her into his tool, his *thing*. Promising her a place. Like Warren Dawson at HUG, promising her a family. Like the Boss at the Club, promising her security. Like Walt, promising her a home.

Missy's feet slipped on the brink. The shovel jolted in her hands. Scrambling backward, she spun. Dirt showered across the ground as the blade arched upward and flashed in the lantern light. Then—*thwack!*

Her arms jarred in their sockets as metal crunched through bone.

Ezra toppled. He sprawled onto his back. The right side of his head blossomed red.

Poor man. She moved forward swiftly even as shock reverberated up and down her body. He couldn't move, but his eyes rolled around as she stood over him. The orbs screamed louder than his mouth ever could as she drove the shovel point into his face. His skull broke apart with a sound like an eggshell splitting.

The pounding in her head was lost amid the slushy chopping around the shovel blade. The flower scent drowned amid a copper-smelling mist. When she dropped the shovel, her dress wasn't white anymore.

Missy drank in the air. She didn't look at the people. She turned and went back to the hole and slid clumsily inside. Dropping to her knees, she pulled Roy upright and cradled his head in her lap. She tried to loosen the cloths. It was tough, as her hands were shaking.

Still, she eventually got the fabric around his head and neck unbound. She massaged his throat and peeled his eyelids back. They stayed open. Slowly, they blinked. They focused on her and she smiled. Then they turned upward and she tilted her head to follow them.

The people had gathered around the grave. Their toes sent little cascades of earth down the walls. Their gazes were avalanches. She kept her head up and did not blink against the torrent. Then those in sight shifted. Mr. Irons emerged from their ranks. His hands were bloody, his face bloodless. He stood at the foot of the grave for a minute, staring down and rubbing his hands together, as if the blood would cleanse itself.

Quite abruptly, he squatted down and held out his hands. "Come out, Queen of Hearts."

She accepted the help and came out of the hole. The crowd moved back.

Rotating, holding Roy close, she looked at them. "Put him in." Her whisper carried in the quiet. They knew what she meant.

Two men grabbed Ezra and dragged him toward the hole. The remnants of his lips twitched. *Still breathing.* Her own breath lightened at that. Her heart, too. She held Roy close and watched the people begin to move once more in their twisting procession. Shovels crunched. Voices murmured, then melded into a chant as they refilled the grave. "Queen! Of! Hearts!"

A feeling like sinking carried up Missy's body, like water stroking away sand beneath her feet. Like standing in the shallows of a flat sea. An eternal feeling, filling her up. Smoothing away the tremors and tiredness. Calming. Vast. So vast it pushed at her seams, stretched her heart, throbbed through her veins. She looked at her hand resting on Roy's head and saw the skin flushed and full. Rippling, almost. It made her smile to remember it pinched and dry. That had been the call. This was the answer.

"Queen! Of! Hearts!"

Smiling still, she looked up and watched the burial and noticed the few who passed by without joining in the chant.

"You were that little boy?" I asked Hettinga.

"I was Roy. The Queen of Hearts raised me. And I raised her son, Sorrel. I wish I could have helped him escape that place."

—"The House of Dust"
Southern Gothic

THE CLOCK ON the dashboard said 3:01.

Brad killed the engine and dug an old flashlight from the trunk. Overhead, trees entangled the power lines, and thick leaves shredded the light from the streetlamps before it could reach the pavement. It was so late that even the bugs had gone to bed.

In the dimness, Hettinga was a black spidery figure unfolding from the door of his vehicle. When he slammed the door, Brad winced. The other houses, with their shuttered windows, seemed full of sleepers he did not wish to wake.

"This is where she grew up, isn't it?"

"Until she was ten," Hettinga replied. "Let's see if the door's unlocked."

Brown glass bottles and waxy fast-food wrappers clogged up the weedy lawn. Golden oak pollen carpeted the driveway. It hazed the windows of a green late-nineties model Toyota Camry parked up near the house. The vehicle sported expired Tennessee tags. Brad glanced between it and the house.

"The place isn't occupied," Hettinga assured him. "I was here just recently."

The house itself was a mildewed greenish-white. The gutters drooped from the low roofline. Hettinga opened the metal guard door and tried the handle of the warped wooden door. Brad's phone had recharged in the car, and he snapped a picture as the door *thunked* open.

"Ooh. They should get that carpet out." He coughed and stood aside to allow Brad first entrance.

The wet smell of a moldy washcloth slapped his face. Powering the flashlight, Brad panned it across a jumbled living room. A sagging couch along with pizza boxes, takeout bags, cups, clothes, blankets, plastic containers, and toys littered the spongy carpet. As he stepped deeper into the room, something split beneath his shoe. Flashing the light down, he scooted his foot off of a broken DVD.

"It's a mess," Hettinga breathed. "You might find something interesting in the bedroom on the left."

Brad stepped into a tiny hall and nudged open the door to the left, raising the light. A putrid mattress lay beneath a window masked by broken blinds. A pair of dimples in the wall beside the window. "Bullet holes," Brad said. They were like moon craters under the cold flashlight. "I wonder how many people have lived here since?"

"Many. But I think we can assume the environment was not so different when Missy Holiday grew up here."

Brad took a picture, then peered around the jumbled room.

Hettinga lingered in the doorway. "What will you do with all this?"

"Write it up. Publish it. With a healthy acknowledgment of your help."

A wheezing chuckle. "You're sure folks still read?"

Brad twisted out a smile.

"Where are you from?" Hettinga asked.

"Originally from Rhode Island."

"What brought you down here?"

Stepping past him, Brad crossed into the other bedroom. "School. Went to Poynter and published with the magazine shortly afterward."

This room was painted blue. A twin mattress sat on a low bed frame, and solar system stickers decorated the wall beside it. This was a child's room. This had been her room. But nothing distinctive remained. He took a picture anyway.

"Parents? Do they read your stuff?"

"I doubt it."

In the living room, he shone the light across a decaying couch and fallen box television.

"Do you know when she came here?"

"No. Mid-forties, most likely."

"And the neighborhood's condition at that time?"

"From what I have been able to learn, remarkably similar. Were the conditions you grew up in amicable?"

"Decent."

The man's interest in Brad's background had grown. Was he reconsidering the wisdom of handing over all this information for free?

The dark mouth of a doorway stood at the back of the living room. Stepping through, he advanced down a short hall. At the end, to his left, a heap of laundry festered in front of a washing machine. To his right was the kitchen. Green tile peeped through mushy newspapers, and insects clung to the slumping ceiling.

Straight ahead was another set of double doors, wood and plexiglass inside, metal guard door beyond. "She lived with her grandmother, you know," Hettinga called from behind. "Losing her was painful. But not having her parents during those formative years perhaps fractured her. I'm sure you can understand?"

Brad stepped toward the door and then caught himself short. The pointed nature of the man's words collided with a flare-up in his imagination. For an instant, the light burrowing through the dirty plexiglass revealed a person standing just outside. A grubby little girl with brown hair. She was gripping the rods of the guard door and screaming in at him.

"Missy!" Grandmama called. "I don't want you playin' out front tonight."

"You're not havin' another *visitor,* are you?"

She dragged her feet across the mangy lawn and looked up at Grandmama standing there, arm holding the door open.

"Just go round back, inside the fence." She grabbed Missy's topknot and tugged her inside.

"But I don't wanna play in the back!" Missy wailed as Grandmama trundled her across the living room and up the hall. "There's dog poop in the backyard."

"We'll have chicken noodle soup for dinner, if you're a good girl."

"You'll be in here a long time."

"Just a few minutes."

"Hours. Hours and hours!"

"Put your sandals on."

"They make blisters on my feet."

"You'll be fine." The back door whined open and Grandmama nudged her out.

On the back porch, Missy folded her arms.

It was always the same: lock Missy outside when a man comes over. As if she didn't know they were doing something dirty. As if she hadn't sat out here and listened to breathing and bellowing, 'cause the visitors never cared about being quiet. Not many people wanted to play with her, because of Grandmama; because she was dirty.

She decided to keep on crying. She pounded on the door until it rattled on its hinges. "Grandmama! Grandmama! It ain't fair!"

Grandmama came back into view. Missy took a step back when she saw her face. "What's wrong?"

Grandmama didn't say anything, just looked at her the way she looked at a big pile of dirty dishes. Then they both heard the front screen door squeak, and Grandmama went away.

Feeling suddenly very empty, Missy sat down on the warm, dirty patio and watched the ants detour around her. Mutt peered out of his doghouse across the yard, then slowly followed his well-worn path through the grass and sat down beside her. The locusts hissed in the trees, and a plane flew over, heading for the airport.

"Everyone's got somewhere to be," she muttered.

Mutt looked at her with gooey eyes, then licked her ear.

"Aw, yuck. Get off."

Mutt trudged back to his house.

When the concrete had cooled and her bottom had started aching, and the ants had gone to bed, and the first stars were peeping out, she trudged across the yard and picked some of the daffodils growing along the back fence. There was a big patch across from Mutt's house, so she carried them over to decorate his roof.

It was too late for proper dinner now, so there would be no storybooks afterward. Her mouth got that hot, tight feeling. Well, maybe she'd just stay out here tonight. She'd eaten Mutt's dog food plenty of times, and she could sleep in his house. Somewhere else in the neighborhood a dog was going off.

"That's the only good thing about you," she told Mutt. "You never make a racket like—"

The sound of a hand slapping a face. Again and again. A man yelling and Grandmama crying out.

Missy dropped the flowers and ran along Mutt's path to the back door. A greasy sort of satisfaction moved in her belly: *Too bad, that's what she gets for spending time with those men instead of her own granddaughter.*

But then the slapping started again, and all that feeling went away. With her tongue, she felt the place where her tooth had broken last year. Grandmama had told her never to get in the way again, but—

A thud inside, like something getting thrown.

That did it. She wasn't a baby.

She jammed her fingers against the top part of the door till the screen tore off and she could get her fingers around the little iron hook that held the door shut. It popped open.

As she slipped in, only the man was yelling; Grandmama was trying to yell but kept getting stuck on crying. Missy went into the kitchen, to the silverware drawer. Behind the plastic silver rack, hidden by the lip of the counter, she felt the gun. She held it carefully in both hands and went down the hall to the living room, then to Grandmama's room.

She stood outside the door. The gun was heavy, making her shake. And the words the man was yelling made her flinch. Grandmama's low, wrecked wail made her want to cry.

Why did Grandmama invite these people over? Why did she have to be locked outside? She wasn't a baby anymore. She'd show them she wasn't.

The door was slightly ajar. She used the end of the gun to push it open.

The floor lamp lay on the floor, casting light and shadow onto the ceiling. Grandmama lay slumped beneath the front window. She was only wearing her underwear. The man wore no shirt and the suspenders on his pants hung down. His hands were fists except for the finger he jabbed toward the floor.

They didn't notice Missy. They went on yelling and crying. She tried to say "Quiet!" but nothing came out because she was crying, too. So she pointed the gun at sort of where they were. She would fire a warning shot—they always did that in storybooks. That would get their attention.

That's when Grandmama saw her and began to stand up. When the man whipped his head around, she squeezed the trigger.

The sharp bang made Grandmama sit back down. It made a red dent in the wall where she had been getting up. It made the man yelp and stumble and fall down. It made Missy's hands and ears vibrate. She dropped the gun.

The man got up. Grandmama didn't. The man came over to where Missy stood. Through a blur, she saw him raise his hand. She tried to back away, but he hit her hard.

She fell against her bedroom door, and everything went out.

When the world came back, Mutt was barking. The overturned light in the bedroom glared in her face as she sat up. Then she remembered. Getting up, she went in and found Grandmama still sitting against the wall. Her head was down, her chest red. Missy squatted beside her. "Are you . . . I was just tryin' . . . "

Grandmama never cared about her excuses. Crying hard, Missy made her lie down so she could put her clothes back on her. Then she went into the bathroom and washed her hands and brushed her teeth while she was there, being careful around the broken one.

She went back to the bedroom. She sat across the room from Grandmama and said, "If I call anyone, they'll put me in jail."

She sat there until her bottom was sore again, and with the soreness came a realization. Not what she should do, but something she could do. She got up, and stripped the rumpled sheet off the bed and rolled Grandmama up inside it.

Tugging and sweating, she pulled her out of the bedroom, slid her down the hall, and dragged her outside onto the patio. Mutt quit barking, sniffed her once, and ran off to his house. Missy got the shovel lying by the patio and went out to the corner of the fence where the thick cluster of daffodils grew.

She began to dig a trench in the middle of the daffodils. The hot work and sweet smell made her stomach squeeze. Blisters formed and popped in her palms. The creek on the other side of the fence gurgled.

Finally, the scrape in the ground was maybe deep enough. She went back to the patio. Grandmama was stiff as she hauled her across the lawn. She didn't really fit in the hole, so she mounded the dirt up on top of her.

Wobbling all over, she sat down to rest. The daffodils lay around her, green ground fingers, their blossoms bright, full of warm scent. She picked up a handful of dirt and crumbled it over the mound.

Brad peered through the back door glass at the dark backyard. "So she buried her out there?"

"In the back right corner." Hettinga was behind him. "And I'll tell you, I had a time tracing down the police record from 1949. Apparently, no one checked in on Missy for over a week. Then someone got annoyed because that dog was barking nonstop, and called the police."

"And where was she?"

"Just sitting out there, alone with the body." A pause. "Were you all alone when you visited the house?"

"I actually lived there for a couple weeks."

A pause. "But alone, right?"

"Let's take a look out there." Brad used his shirttail to turn the doorknob. Outside, the gritty smell of dead cigarettes flavored the patio. More oak pollen mounded across the pavement.

Hettinga followed him out. "You were alone, though, right?"

Brad played the light through the deep grass beyond the patio. "No. My fiancée was with me."

The slender man held totally still. "You didn't leave here there alone."

He stayed quiet until he knew he could refrain from shouting, until he could speak evenly.

"As I said, all this will go into an article for a magazine called *Southern Gothic*. Once that article is published, I'm hopeful that it will dispel the myth around the place."

Drawing a breath, he raised the flashlight and looked out at the chain-link fence at the edge of its rays. "Now, you said the right corner?"

"*Myth*," Hettinga repeated in a smoky whisper. "You think Adamah's a myth?"

"You said the right corner." Stepping off the concrete, he waded across the yard, careful of broken glass among the weeds.

"Haven't you seen things to the contrary?" Hettinga was following without a rustle. "Isn't that why you left? Because you were afraid he might be real? Afraid he might bring up something from the past?"

Brad ignored him; he was ready to be rid of the man. Approaching the back of the yard, he neared a six-foot chain-link fence, braided with ivy and honeysuckle, obscuring whatever lay on the other side. He slowed. A pungent scent radiated from somewhere just ahead. Something dead lay in the weeds. He flashed the light around before proceeding cautiously. The fence drew together at the corner of the yard. Daffodils bent around his feet.

Then the light hit a black dress shoe.

Brad stopped.

The shoe was connected to a suited leg, and the leg was connected to a body.

"There's someone back here!" Clenching his nostrils, he moved around beside the corpse. The flashlight lens made rings on the back of the person's jacket. The arms stretched up from the shoulders, as if the man had been about to dive into a pond. The fingers were buried in the ground just short of the fence corner. The face was planted in the ground, white hair drooping down around the balding skull. The skin was gray. Days dead. No sign or injury.

"Did you not find this?" Brad asked him.

Hettinga stood utterly still, his grimy suit hanging from him loosely. His high forehead gleamed greasily, his white hair disheveled His eyes were staring, unresponsive.

Baring his teeth, Brad crouched and gripped the left arm and rolled the corpse over.

Dirt spilled from gaping jaws. Yellow eyes wept trails of scrambling ants. The face was that of an old man. A face with a high forehead and a white goatee. A face with gaunt cheeks. From weeks ago in a library picture and from tonight in the half-light. From behind him.

Richard Hettinga.

Springing up, he whipped around. The yard was empty. The man had vanished. Reeling, he turned back around. The body lay there still. Hettinga's body, undoubtedly. Impossibly.

Automatically, he reached for his phone. Had to get a picture. In the wavering light, he placed the head and shoulders in the viewfinder. The camera saw it too. It was real.

A tremor rattled along the fence.

It jarred him, and the picture smeared.

Turning, he listened as a strumming sound moved up the outside of the vine-wrapped fence, approaching. Raising the light, Brad tracked its movement by the shaking leaves. A person, running their hand along the wire barrier. They stopped, just parallel to him on the other side.

"Mr. Hettinga?"

No, Hettinga was lying dead in front of him. The thing he had spent the last several hours with was . . . what? A hallucination? His mind was glitching. He clawed for a memory of stopping by a pharmacy on the trip down, refilling his Prozac. But he hadn't. And he couldn't have imagined the detailed, almost encyclopedic history of Three Summers.

It wasn't a hallucination. It was the thing from the house. It had followed him. And now it was standing on the other side of the fence.

A greasy hand emerged from the leaves to press against the wire, sending another tremor along the fence. He held the flashlight beam on it.

"What do you want?" Brad whispered.

A newscaster's voice came from the other side, tinny sounding, perhaps from a radio. "Thirteen people died today following an explosion on an oil rig ninety miles off the Alabama coast."

Brad retreated a step. *I'm in a dream.*

The low, miserable chuckle that followed was very real.

The hand tightened against the fence. The skin creased around the wire. Then the palm broke through, splitting and reforming like gel, followed by burnt, glistening fingers. Next came an arm in an orange canvas suit. The stench from the body was borne away on a wind of black tar as a heat-shriveled man strained through the wire. Straightening, he grinned. Grass bent as he stalked toward Brad.

For a moment, an electric current from the ground held Brad quivering in place. The flashlight slid from his grip and with it plummeted any tenuous hope of standing his ground.

He fled. Flailing through the high grass, he pounded to the back door. He burst into the house and tumbled down the short hall, slamming into the doorframe at the end. In the living room, he tripped over an invisible stool and slammed against the front door.

Heavy feet came down the hall behind him. Breaths rattled in a paper-dry throat.

Wrestling the front door open, Brad tore across the lawn. Dead Hettinga's car still stood in the drive. The other was gone, the odd hybrid driven by . . .

I'm in a dream.

Ripping open his own car door, he fell inside, turned the key, and brought his foot to the gas pedal in a single motion. Squealing away from the curve, he glanced back. The man in orange bounded across the shaded lawn. He stopped in the middle of the street, in a pool of light. He reached after the speeding car.

Brad looked away from the rearview.

I'm in a dream.

Jamming his foot farther down, he quickly moved it to the brake as a stop sign loomed out of the darkness. The car bucked and slid to a stop. Slapping his face, he looked out. Barred-up houses set behind shaggy yards crowded with cars and fallen bicycles. The glow of TV screens in a few windows. Moths dancing in the halos around the streetlights.

It wasn't a dream. It was Atlanta at four in the morning.

The orange man walked up outside his window and rapped on the glass.

Barking, Brad kicked the accelerator. The engine roared with his heart. The needle climbed past thirty, forty, fifty. The intersection dwindled. Sweat bit his eyes. He glanced at the driver's-side window. Grimy marks from knuckles clung to the glass.

It wasn't a dream.

Just get out of here. Get out of the neighborhood. Away from the place where Hettinga had died and Missy had buried her grandmother. It couldn't follow him. Or could it?

It was not confined to the corner of a backyard fence or all the corners of the world. It had been with him in the Gulch. It was real. It was chasing him. His eyes flicked up to the mirror.

The man stood fifty feet behind. Motionless in the shadow of an overhanging tree. Reaching.

The vehicle swerved as he lost and regained control. A pile of brush protruded into the road. He whipped the wheel and narrowly missed two parked cars. He pushed the car past sixty. Yet when his eyes lifted to the rearview mirror, he saw the man in orange standing twenty feet behind him in the glow of a streetlight. How could that be?

Manically, his eyes flicked back and forth between the windshield and the rearview mirror. He had to watch for a place to turn; had to keep the man in sight. The road extended ahead forever: an endless stream of black-eyed houses and orange streetlights. And each time his eyes returned to the rearview mirror, the thing was a bit closer to the car. Inexorably, it closed the distance. The unwavering hand, sharp-tipped with blackened bone, floated toward the back glass.

Brad didn't realize he was yelling until the windshield began to fog-up with his breath. The car skidded as the orange man leaned across the trunk. His seared flesh swelled against the glass. His gravel eyes looked into Brad's pupils. Everything except the amber avenue of cars and pavement became a haze as his hands melded with the steering wheel.

He only fell silent when something touched him. A warm, heavy weight on his right arm. He looked down.

A claw hand folded around his forearm.

It was in the car.

Silently, frantically, Brad released the wheel. He writhed away from the grip, fighting it with his other hand, tearing at it. Grilled flesh came away beneath his nails.

Abruptly free, the vehicle veered.

At the edge of sight, a power pole rushed toward the hood of the car.

He had time to blink just once before everything shattered.

THE LONG HOME

For days, I swam through oil and cold water and fire. I wasn't swimming to escape the fire. I was swimming to escape the thing that followed me through it: a man made of fire.

—"The House of Dust"
Southern Gothic

MISSY WAS IN a dream.

The sky was golden. It had clouds painted on it—smooth, smeary ones. It was evening or morning, or maybe afternoon. The river was a flat expanse and golden, too. So was the grass. She was standing on the island, up by the old dock.

She looked at the pebbles beneath her feet and found dozens of tiny points of light glittering off each one. She was wearing the lacy white dress. Her feet were beautiful. When she turned her hands, they were smooth and flawless, tinged gold. *She* was beautiful.

When she spread her arms, everything around her opened up. She had been in a motionless painting and now the world was unrolling, inflating like a balloon. She walked up the old road as trees popped into fullness. Birds scurried through the air. Wind touched her face, bringing with it an entire landscape she could not see: the smell of earth, the hint of water that was cool and mossy.

The smell transported her. She was still walking up the road, but she was also by a creek. It was the creek behind the house, but different. An old boathouse was here, with a rowboat at the shoreline. She stepped in, and it glided away from the shore. She sat down, not bothering to touch the oars. She was borne along by water and time. Moss hung from arching branches. She lay back and the tips brushed around her, across her.

At the sensation, she found herself in the bedroom of the house, lying on moon-drenched sheets, tingling as a man's fingers trailed across her body. One finger was banded by a wedding ring. She turned her face toward the window, smiling dreamily, and listened to the chorus of the night insects.

A new window opened. She was on the front step of her old house in Atlanta, and the bugs were singing just as loudly, and it was evening. She was nine. But shouldn't she have the right to walk down the street without fear? There was a gun in her hand. And she so wanted to take a walk and enjoy the evening air. Her dog, Mutt, sat beside her, wagging his tail. She left the porch and started up the street. But the thump of a passing boombox sucked her off to . . .

The Club. She was dancing in pink light with all the men swilling cocktails, and she enjoyed it, until she saw the professor from Emory shake his head and get up from a table in the back, carrying away the latest volume of the encyclopedia. She ran after him.

But she soon found she wasn't running after him, but up the old road. She laughed as she realized she didn't need his books anymore: she had arrived. It was a golden summer on her golden island by the golden river. She lived here happily with a perfect husband and . . . yes, one adoring little boy. She knelt in the drive and held out her arms, and he ran to her through a yard that was a clean expanse of smooth grass and ancient trees while her husband, now faceless, stood on the front porch and clapped. He was sweaty and dirty from work. Missy walked with the boy toward the house, passing below a sturdy bough of the central oak where a man in a suit dangled. A handwritten sign strung around his neck said *Traitor*.

They went inside. As her husband's arm came around her, she was back in bed, tangled with him in the sheets.

She was also in the boat, voyaging down the twilit river.
She was also swaying in the Club.

And holding a pistol to blast the head off each person who had committed a crime in her neighborhood, all of them conveniently lined up along the evening sidewalk.

Everything melted into a collage. For the space of a held breath, she was hanging above the golden land, seeing and experiencing all of it. She was in the thick earth, and the humidity, and the boggy creeks, and the oppressive heat, and the cracked roads, and the silent afternoons. She was within them and above them, a participant and an observer.

Then, like the final humming note of a symphony, it faded.

She woke into a morning frisky with the scent of distant rain clouds. It was July now.

She sat up in the sheets and hugged her knees as a heavy chill swept her. It was always going to end this way. No shoulder to lean on. No hand to hold. Just dreams. Just her.

It was enough. The beautiful vastness from the night at the mill welled up through the mattress into her limbs and she grinned and stretched out her arms so her body could contain it.

Dressed in shorts and a green sleeveless top, she made oatmeal for herself and Roy and watched him while he ate. His appetite was good, and physically he seemed recovered. But his words, if he spoke, came singularly or in pairs, suggesting some interior damage that might never resolve. Still, she would do her best.

After breakfast, she went up to the study and got a piece of paper and a pen and wrote:

Dear Walt,
I am still alive. I think you should come see me. How about this Wednesday? I'm sure you can find the time. The house will be all fixed up.
Always yours,
Missy

Besides the town documents that Ezra had moved to the house, there were envelopes and stamps in the desk drawers. Walt's gun, she noticed, was gone. She wrote out the address of his Nashville office on an envelope, stamped it, then got her purse and the car keys from the bedroom. She went downstairs.

"Hey, Roy?" She rattled the keys. "Want to ride along?"

He shrugged and followed her out the door. The Three Summers sheriff's cruiser was parked out front. She frowned at the hazy windshield as they drove away, deciding the rain couldn't come soon enough.

As they approached Three Summers, she asked, "Where's the post office?"

He pointed to a squat little beige building on the left, first in line in the row of downtown structures. Parking at the curb, she told him to wait in the car, then she crossed the street and went inside the post office. Behind the counter stood the lanky red-haired man she remembered from the Theater Grill and the gray house. His head was down, hat brim hiding his face as the soft snap of playing cards punctuated the shallow stillness. Behind him, by a door leading to the rear room, a scruffy taxidermized eagle perched atop a dusty postage scale.

Missy moved past the cordoned waiting line and stopped before the counter. When the man's head did not rise, she cleared her throat. Looking up, he immediately began swaying and pushed his cap brim back. "Morning, ma'am."

Abe was his name. He had been at the cotton mill. He had not joined in the chanting as she came out of the grave.

"Good morning. I'd like to mail this?" She held out the envelope.

Plucking the letter from her fingers, he turned it over and over, not looking at it. "Okay. Just fine, just fine."

"The postage is okay?"

"Postage is just fine."

"Good." She hesitated. The envelope rotated. The man swayed. "One other thing. Is there any way I could . . . sort of get a message around without having to write a lot of letters?"

"Like maybe phone?"

"If I don't want to phone a lot of people, either."

His lips twisted doubtfully.

"See, I figured since you go around to all the houses already that you could spread the word."

"What word's that?"

"I'm throwing a party on the fourth. Everyone's invited."

"Oh." He stopped swaying. "No need for that, ma'am. We don't really make a big deal about the Fourth around here."

Missy let her eyes travel to the eagle. "That doesn't matter. It's not about the Fourth. It's just when I want the party to be. Tell everyone seven o'clock. And be sure that letter gets in the mail."

"Will do, ma'am."

Before leaving she said, "Where might I find floor shine?"

The man motioned vaguely. "Devin's Hardware. Three doors down."

"Thank you."

He touched his cap. "Yes, ma'am."

Outside, Roy was still sitting in the car. She waved to him and pointed down the sidewalk. He nodded. Then she went to Devin's and loaded a basket with brushes, sponges, industrial soap, and buckets of polyurethane. She smiled at the checkout man.

"You're Devin, aren't you? We're having a get-together at the house on Sunday. You'll be there?"

He fingered his beard. "Everyone else coming? Well, I guess so then."

The wind was picking up as she went back to the car and struggled to pack everything into the back seat. When she got in the driver's seat, the first drops were splattering down. She huffed and looked over to find Roy hunkered on the floorboard.

"What are you doing?"

He motioned at the door. Outside, a pair of men in overalls were passing.

"No need to be afraid of them," she said. "Or anyone else, either. We're going back to the house, and you can help me get everything cleaned up and sparkly. In a few days, we'll have a big party."

The boy gazed at her as she started the car; a smile of uncertain wonderment wandered across his face. She remembered sitting that way in the passenger seat of a car not so long ago, wearing that same sort of smile as the wind rushed in and the driver explained how he would take care of her and give her a real home and never let harm come to her.

Her nails bit into the vinyl wheel cover, but she looked over and met his smile.

"Don't worry. Everything will turn out just fine."

I resurfaced in Piedmont Atlanta Hospital on June 1. The nurse said a car accident had knocked me into a coma. I had been dehydrated, malnourished, and severely sleep deprived. And my fiancée had been calling.

"Who?"

"She said her name's Jennifer? She's been sending those every day."

A bouquet of daffodils graced my bedside table.

"When can I leave?" I asked.

They said Sunday. It was Friday. In the intervening time, I wrote most of this article. Heather, my editor, who is based in Atlanta and listed as an emergency contact, never bothered to come see me. I didn't care. This wasn't for her anymore, or *Southern Gothic*. It was about the thing that had chased me in circles for years. The thing that was manifest in that little town, inside that house, in the body of my fiancée.

I was released midafternoon on June 3. The rental car took the last of my money.

—"The House of Dust"
Southern Gothic

THE EXIT WAS just as dead as it had been back at the end of April. The sign for Three Summers was now invisible from the road, a drowning shape among the honeysuckle.

Clouds brought an early evening, filling the road through the ridge with muddy darkness. Brad listened to the tires on the ancient pavement. After hours on the interstates from Atlanta, the tenor of their thrumming changed. Deepened. As if the land had thinned and the hum were carrying down to a hollow place below the roots of the surrounding trees and below the approaching river. Alerting anything below of his arrival.

There's nothing . . .

But ever since waking in the hospital bed, that surety that had sustained him through his weeks in the house had been wavering. Those frantic minutes before the crash played again and again. That thing behind the car, drawing ever closer, appearing in the back seat, *touching* him.

As Brad crossed the Locust River, Three Summers appeared through a mist off the water. Within the town, all was still, gas station and grocery store abandoned, housefronts shut up and silent. Street signs leaned at intersections, heavy with the name *Adamah*.

His hands trembled as he twisted the wheel. His mind had been clear back on that dark street, and it was clear now. No drugs this time. No illusions. *Just what you asked for. The truth.*

Steam choked the forest road to Angel's Landing. The cicada songs were muted by the vapor. Deep Creek gurgled gently as the car bumped across the clay-stained bridge. The fields passing outside his window lay blanketed in half-light.

They buried people alive. That was the truth. For two hundred years at the house he was driving toward, they had laid the unneeded in the earth. And the men who established the Queen of Hearts had always been among those victims. Darrin DeWitt. Jerimiah McCloud. Rex Emil. The man who had brought Missy, who had disappeared without a trace, Walter Collins.

And Bradley Oswald Ellison.

His lips twitched. The somber kid from Rhode Island. The obscure crime writer. Lived with his girlfriend. Moved to an old house a month before he vanished. Last seen at a car rental booth in Atlanta. It had always been heading here, hadn't it? Lost beneath the gray earth of a river island in Tennessee.

The tires lurched through a pothole. Behind him, in the back seat, among the remains of his backpack, the Newton's cradle rattled.

Focus. Find her. Finish the article.

A few hundred yards from the house's driveway, the road was lined with dozens of cars. The same weary models that had made up the old woman's funeral procession. The drivers had obeyed four hand-painted signs commanding: *PARK HERE.*

Everyone was at the house.

The driveway was empty. Moss hung dripping from the drowsy oaks. As the car jounced along the gravel turns, he swayed in his seat. "Okay, Jen," he muttered. He repeated the name as the house neared, as if it might call her forth with open arms and beautifully, desperately barren eyes. *Brad, you came back!*

The last strands of moss slithered off the windshield. As the house came into view, his lips parted in awe.

The building was magnificent. The paint was pure white, and the vines were gone from the pillars. Buttery light poured from the windows. The rocking chairs gleamed, arranged neatly in front. The humid air hazed everything, adding a touch of soft-ness to the corners of the building and the point of the roof above the upper porch.

As he pulled up to the front steps, Brad's staring eyes returned to the clearing. He stomped on the brakes.

Sorrel stood near the steps, twenty feet from the car.

Instead of his uniform, the sheriff wore ragged jeans and heavy boots. A stained green T-shirt exposed his lean arms. His big hands were cocked on his hips and his steady gaze pierced the wind-shield without a trace of sentiment, as if surveying a building to be demolished.

Brad strangled the steering wheel. If Sorrel was waiting for him, then Jennifer must have been subdued. The flowers and phone calls had been a ploy. She was locked in the house somewhere, perhaps bound. He edged closer, until the bumper could not be more than two feet from the man's legs. He could easily run him over.

Sorrel didn't stir.

Brad put the car in park and let condensation gather across the windshield.

Abruptly, Sorrel rapped on the hood, then motioned.

"You showed up, Brad!" His voice was parched but full of false enthusiasm. "Come on out. There's something I want to show you."

Brad shook his head. The pistol was in the glove box.

Sorrel came around to the driver's side. The door was locked. Still, he should probably get the gun out.

"Come on," the man called, backing up a bit. "Just want to show you—"

Brad glimpsed a flurry of action before the heel of Sorrel's boot shattered the window and drove into his left temple.

Glass showered the front seat and his clothes. Through ringing ears, he heard the lock click and the door squeak open. His left eyelid twitched. His vision was hazy. Cold sweat was already welling across his skin.

Sorrel grabbed him by the collar and dragged him from the car.

"I had a feeling you'd be back, Brad. Let's take a walk."

The sheriff alternately dragged and shoved him away from the car, across the clearing, into the woods.

"You haven't published that magazine piece, have you? Answer me now, Brad." He shook him.

"N-n-no."

"Good deal."

He tried to move his feet to keep from falling, tried to keep his eyes open to see where he was being taken. Back toward the road, he thought. It was too dim to be sure. Soupy air was everywhere, and his brain wasn't firing properly. The blow had been powerful.

Still, he should probably try to get away. Yes, try to—

"That's real good." Panic rippled beneath the sheriff's easy tone. "That piece can't be published, you see? You're a part of it, Brad. I know I told you to write it, told you I didn't care, but I realized I was wrong. Sunlight won't disinfect anything here, only make it grow. Spread. And I can't take your word you won't publish it, 'cause I can't risk her getting to you. It's inside her now. I couldn't get rid of her. But you, that's a different matter."

What was he talking about?

Brad didn't try to ask. Instead he tried to breathe. Blood darted down the side of his face. The sound of cicadas reached a crescendo. They were in a clearing. The grip on his collar released and he slammed to his knees amid wet dirt.

"See?" Sorrel was kneeling beside him, voice rapid and miserable as his fingers searched Brad's pockets, found his phone. "You understand me? Every man who's brought a Queen of Hearts to this house has also built a monument to Adamah, a tool to extend his influence. For DeWitt it was the cotton mill down by the river. For Dr. McCloud it was the hospital. Rex Emil put up the theater for Miriam Larkin. Walt Collins gave us the mine back. And for you it's this article, Brad. This is your monument to Adamah. Only, there aren't going to be any more monuments."

His phone bent between the sheriff's powerful fingers.

Brad couldn't react. Was his skull fractured? The left side of his head felt dented somehow.

"Here we are," Sorrel continued, straightening up, voice hardening. "I'm sorry it's got to be this way. She took my gun, or I'd just shoot you. And believe it or not, no one else around here has one. Queens don't like them too much. And the Queens are strong, Brad, especially when they're new. I've never felt such power . . . "

What was happening? He felt something crawl up his nose. He blew out. *Blood.* Blood trickling down. He tried to move his hands. A shock to the head shouldn't immobilize a person this much, should it? His hands were against the dirt. He pressed down.

His body began to rise.

He was in a hunch, then on his knees.

He forced his head up, eyes open.

Sorrel was busily tying a noose at the end of a long, pale rope.

Brad's head lolled back, and he saw the rope snaking up to the bough of an ancient oak. The branches rose like supplicant hands. Around him, the large scarred roots plunged into the earth, piercing to the heart of the island. This was where . . . where . . . Jennifer . . .

As Sorrel worked on the knot, he casually offered, "Folks round here call this the Hanging Glen. Catchy name, huh? Many a Yankee and Rebel and slave and Klansman dangled right where you're 'bout to. John King, too, years before I was born. Yessir. Many a goodbye here. But they were all dropped down this hole. You won't be. I won't be part of that, and neither will you." He jerked the knot tight. "This way it won't spread."

Brad had to get away. Back to the car. The gun.

He trembled to his feet.

"That's right." Sorrel strode back over and grabbed his collar. "You'll need to be on your feet for this part. Up on your toes, in fact. Can you stand on your toes for me, Brad?"

"No-no . . . "

"I think you can."

The sheriff hauled him over beneath the noose and shoved him into position.

"Almost done. Just gotta get this loop—no, hold still—get this around your neck. There."

The man walked out of view.

Brad felt the noose around this neck. He found it with his hands. Rough rope, biting. He tried to pull it off and found his fingers drawn in toward his neck. Tightening. Then it was hard against his throat. Then it was strangling him. He gagged and started to slump but was jerked up by the pressure. Lifted. Looking down, he saw the black mouth of a narrow chasm below his swinging feet, a dark maw fitted between the fat lips of two tree roots.

Hungry. Waiting.

His vision started to phase out.

"Hold on, Brad," Sorrel called. "Up you go."

Bringing Jennifer to this quiet place had not helped banish the darkness from her. It had helped it metastasize.

—"The House of Dust"
Southern Gothic

"THIS IS MS. ABIGAIL BELKER," said Mr. Irons.

The little woman's shoulders bounced as she shook Missy's hand. Her face twitched and her fingers tightened, as if touched by a live wire.

Missy didn't blink. Every other guest had exhibited the same shock as they filed past. She knew what they felt. A tingle. A dry itch, like the one that had consumed her hands that first week in the house. An ache. Ms. Belker's smile phased, then returned as Missy released her.

"Ms. Belker and I are already acquainted," Missy said. "She came over earlier and helped me with the cooking."

They stood in the doorway of the house. A procession of guests stretched across the porch, down the steps, and across the clearing. It was only a little after seven, but a high, thin veil of evening had been drawn across the sky. None of the day's warmth had diminished, however, and the heat and smells from the field collided in the vestibule with the heat and aroma from the kitchen.

Missy had worked hard all day, flitting through the house's many rooms, polishing bannisters and mirrors, refolding a curtain to hide a tear, and oiling the carved fruits and vines that adorned the wooden doorframes in the hallway. All a welcome way to wind down the previous three days of mopping and scrubbing and vacuuming and painting.

At noon, Ms. Belker had arrived to aid in food preparation. Everyone had been asked to bring a side dish. Certain staples, however, such as pork and chicken, needed to be provided. Missy knew how to fry food and make sandwiches, but little else. So, at the suggestion of Mr. Irons, she had solicited Ms. Belker's help. Ms. Belker brought her friends, Mrs. Byrd and Mrs. Blyth, and the gentle ebb and flow of their conversation and the clatter of dishes worked through the walls and brought something deliciously homey into the house.

After bathing at six, Missy had put on the white dress. The torn shoulder was healed now, and the fabric clean. She smiled because she couldn't remember doing a thing to wash or mend it. Her smile departed as she stood before the mirror, smoothing down the dress and placing stock for the first time in the soreness that had plagued her breasts for the past few days. Her fingertips drifted across her stomach.

"Well," she said.

The women cooed with admiration when she came down the stairs, her hand gliding along the scarred banister. At 6:50, Mr. Irons had arrived to help her welcome guests. Her feet were bare, and she felt the endless thrumming through the boards as people came through the great front door; she remembered the house in Atlanta and being shooed away anytime a visitor came.

"This is Mr. Abe Daleder," Irons said.

Missy nodded. "How are you this evening?"

It was the spindly red-haired man from the post office.

"Evening, ma'am."

Daleder twisted his hands around themselves as she offered hers.

Missy hesitated, then withdrew her hands. "Well, why not head to the dining room? We've got some refreshments laid out."

The man traipsed up the hall. "A problem," Irons murmured.

"I wonder why?"

"Believe it or not, he was Ezra's right hand. He won't adjust. Just get bitter. Dangerous. There's always a few."

"What a shame." Missy looked after him. "Before you get started, I'd like a few minutes alone in the garden. To pick a spot."

"Of course."

She looked back at him quite suddenly. "And thank you, Mr. Irons. For all your help."

The frail man offered a fatherly smile that did not reach his eyes.

"Our family has been a friend of this house since we crossed the mountains with DeWitt." Then a quick rotation. "Ah! Mrs. McFee."

The final person in the procession was a ten-year-old girl with a blond pixie cut. Irons beamed as he bent to shake her hand. "And lastly, we have Ms. Jezebel Irons."

"Your daughter?" Missy crouched down, offering a hand. "How are you?"

The girl gripped it back, hard, barely flinching. She said in a bland little tone, "Very well, ma'am. I love your house."

"She's never gotten to see inside before," Irons explained.

"If you want," Missy said, "you can come over during the days. I wouldn't mind having you around at all. And Roy's around here someplace, if you want to play. He's not bratty like he used to be."

The girl smiled and nodded.

"Now, why don't you and your daddy go see the dance hall? It's my favorite part of the house."

Irons led her off through the bright doorway. Missy hung back a moment to look out at the evening.

He is coming.

The thought sent only the slightest ripple across her calm. He was the last wrinkle to be smoothed away.

She closed the door. She walked to the dance hall threshold and looked in at the roaring assembly. The Three Summers folks hadn't dressed up for the occasion. She was glad. They were comfortable in their shorts and sandals and T-shirts, sipping drinks in red plastic cups and eating food off paper plates.

Irons cut through the crowd in his conspicuous white suit and struck up a conversation with Abe Daleder, the problem man. Quickly, she averted her eyes. Instead, she watched a group of men with brass and a bass set up beside the piano and begin to plunk out the jazz tune "What a Little Moonlight Can Do."

The men who worked at the mine invited the women who worked in the town to dance. The hall became a hive of motion. The chandelier reflected in the—at *last*—spotless floor. Missy let her head prop against the door facing. She bathed her eyes in the grandeur of that cut-crystal fixture and the myriad slivers of motion it reflected.

Almost perfect. Almost home.

She left the door and stole quietly up the hall, past the kitchen, to the back door. Crossing the screened porch, she descended to the yard. There she found a shovel propped against the steps. She hefted it and walked on.

The garden beds were in sad shape. The liners had been scattered, and weeds had flooded in to choke the flowers. Her next challenge would be to refurbish this area: turn it into a real garden again.

Despite the bedlam, she was able to discern the original layout. A circle of outer beds ringing a larger central one. She waded into the central bed and planted the shovel against the dirt. How long since she had dug in the ground? Not since that night twelve years ago.

Always graves. It would be nice when she could plant flowers instead. A hint of yellow perfume rose out of the weeds. Narrowing her eyes, she discovered, crushed among the weeds, the dying stems and flabby trumpets of some daffodils. The last survivors from early summer.

Placing her foot on the blade, she bore down. The dryness persisted in her mouth as she dug a shallow trench. The earth was soft, parting easily before the probing shovel blade as she widened and deepened the hole. It rolled off the dress fabric without leaving a mark. As she worked, the sound of piano and brass came through the windows.

Once she was waist-deep, she decided the hole was deep enough. All the dirt had been piled on one side for easy replacement. Climbing out, she stabbed the shovel into the top of the heap. Then she went back up to the porch and through the back door.

In the empty kitchen, she washed her hands and sponged her damp forehead. As she passed back down the hall to the front of the house, a frantic knock leapt from the basement door. A muffled voice followed. Someone yelling, words distorted—by a gag, perhaps? Yes, gags were very unpleasant. Irons had been swift with him. She wondered if Dalaeer had scratched Irons like the cat had.

At the entrance to the dance hall, she paused again, examining the gathering. The eating was over. Couples swayed to the music. By the fireplace, Mr. Irons was speaking with the woman with drizzling black hair who had carried Roy's body. He glanced toward her, and a slightly pained expression crossed his face.

Yes, she thought. *Another problem. But it must be done if we're to have any kind of peace.*

A quick, brief rap came at the front door.

And here's the last one.

She went and opened the door. Walt stood there, carefully suited and shaved, mustache sharp. He looked her over. Taking his glasses off, he put them in his jacket, then placed a hand against the door-frame, as if bracing himself.

"Well, don't get all settled, darlin'," Missy said softly. "Come on in."

4 |

As I was lifted into the air, I saw an angel in a white garment step from the twilight. She held a gun.

—"The House of Dust"
Southern Gothic

THE GUNSHOT JOLTED Brad from his delirium.

The tension on the rope released. His elbows hit the roots bordering the chasm. His fingers closed even as pain reverberated up his arms. Lungs airless, he kicked at the wall of the pit, his legs flailing above the drop. How far down did it go? What lay at the bottom? Adrenaline fired through his veins. Arms heaving, he scrambled out over the root.

For a moment he lay wheezing. His nails felt bent from clawing. His neck burned from the rope. His stomach churned. He peeled the noose over his head and sat up.

Then he remembered. He was on his feet, searching the glen for the figure in white.

Sorrel lay twenty feet off at the base of the old oak. Brad approached cautiously.

The sheriff was sprawled on his back. There was a hole through his green shirt, the fabric rapidly staining darker just below his ribs. The rope had slipped from his hand and dangled above his body.

Brad turned slowly. Who would . . . ?

Jennifer stood at the edge of the glen, gripping a revolver. She wore the old woman's white dress. *It fits her so well,* he thought strangely. Her face was clean of dirt and her blond hair hung loose. Her gaze moved up from Sorrel's body.

"I'm glad you came back, Brad." She said it brightly, in a voice he'd never heard before. A twangy, childish voice that might have been hers in the years before addiction drowned her family. A calm voice.

"You're all right now," he said hoarsely. He staggered toward her, relief flooding through him.

"I know." The gun was pointed at Sorrel. "You're strong enough to carry him, you think?"

"Jennifer, what's—happening?"

"He's still breathing." She sighed. "We should hurry. Pick him up and follow me."

Fingering his throat, Brad studied the man for a second. Dizziness swayed him. There was the sheriff, bleeding out on the ground, bony face stretching as he struggled to drag in air. Why had he changed? Attacked him? What was it he had said? The reason he had given? *No more monuments to—*

"Brad!"

Nodding, he stumbled down beside the man. Her sudden appearance had somehow reduced the pulsating pain in the side of his head. He slid his hands under the man's back and bent, bracing to lift him. Wet, broken words came through the man's yellowed teeth.

"Brad, don't—touch. Don't move me. Leave me."

"You're shot. I'll take you inside." Brad's knees were watery as he tried to stand.

"No!" Panic sharpened the sheriff's voice. "Don't let her get to me. Don't let her put me in the ground!"

"She won't. We're going to help you."

Shaking, he stood.

Sorrel twitched but could not resist. His head wobbled as he tried to lift it. Their faces came into proximity, and Brad watched as life dimmed in his enlarged pupils. "No, Brad. You gotta run. I shoulda stopped you sooner. Shoulda . . . shoulda followed those tracks. Shoulda followed them and found my brother, Roy. Shoulda escaped like he did. 'Cause you can't fix it. Don't try to fix it. Don't publish it. It's in too deep. You gotta escape. I shoulda, like Roy did."

The eyes rolled back, exposing the whites, and his neck went lax.

Holding him close, Brad walked unsteadily toward Jennifer.

"We need to hurry." She led him back through the thicket to the gravel clearing. He was weak after the days in the hospital bed. He nearly fell while climbing the front porch steps. But she was safe, at least. In fact, she seemed totally composed.

It's inside her now.

He looked at the sheriff's lolling head, then at his fiancée.

Jennifer held open the door and nodded for him to enter. Just inside the vestibule, he stopped. She had transformed the old house into a palace. The floor shone. Light filtered cleanly through the ornate ceiling fixtures. The freshly polished banister of the great staircase glistened.

He wished now for a camera to capture the transformation. But his phone lay broken back among the trees. No way to call for help.

Music came from the door to his left. Unwittingly, he approached the dance hall.

"Don't go in there, Brad," Jennifer warned.

He stopped at the threshold. The weight of the man in his arms seemed to double.

Bodies were strewn across the floor. They wore Sunday clothes and writhed and twisted and arched against the boards, flopping like fish drowning in fresh air. Even Harlow was there, her long body arched, feet at one end, head of loose pale hair at the other, drilling her skull into the floor. Others he had seen—at the funeral, in the town, at the church—all tumbling, flipping over and over as if they were falling.

And Jezebel Irons was there, sunken on the bench before the piano, clumsily brushing the keys, her nose nearly touching them.

A blow to his shoulder made him jerk.

Turning, he found it hadn't been a blow at all. Jennifer had touched him lightly. "Come away, Brad." She stepped farther up the hall.

"Wait."

She looked back. Her eyes were far too reflective. As if the transparent membrane had been removed and the soft jelly inside were still hovering in place, ready to spill out. His hope that the sheriff might have been wrong began to dwindle.

It's inside her now.

"Jen, what's going on here?"

"Looks to me like they're settling in for a nap." The drawl that she had spoken with when they met, that she had worked so hard to lose during nursing school, was back.

"Now let's get him settled."

The lacquer smell of fresh paint pummeled him as he struggled up the hall behind her.

"Shouldn't we lay him down?"

"We are." She went to the back door. "Out here."

"Jen, he's bleeding a lot."

"So come on, huh?" She held the door wide. A hollow groan escaped Sorrel's lips as Brad maneuvered onto the porch.

Three men were slumped in wicker chairs, eyes closed. Air whistled dryly between their lips. Their skin clung closely to their bones. In the steamy evening light, they appeared almost skeletal.

Jennifer opened the screen door on the far side of the porch, pushing back a horde of mosquitoes. He kept his eyes on the steps as he descended, then followed his fiancée into the garden.

The grass had been recently cut. The dirt was churned up at the center of several beds, leaving a trampled outer ring of plants. Still stranger were the yellow blossoms rising from the large central bed, softening the air.

Daffodils don't flower this deep into summer.

"All right, lay him down," Jennifer said.

Brad slumped to his knees and rolled Sorrel in the grass beside the railroad ties bordering the bed. He stayed down, panting, recovering his strength.

"His breathing's really shallow, Jennifer."

Without responding, Jennifer stepped into the flower bed. At its center, she knelt.

For an instant, he saw the old woman lying there, earth raked up around her motionless body. He saw Hettinga in the backyard in Atlanta, mouth full of dirt.

It dragged them down. Now it's dragging her down.

"What are you doing, Jennifer?"

Jennifer stood up again. She held a shovel in her right hand.

"Here." She tossed it at him. He lurched away to avoid being hit. It fell across Sorrel, who twitched. "You strong enough to dig?"

"What are you doing?" he said again.

She shrugged, easy, casual.

"Helping people, like I promised. Now pick up that shovel and dig a hole for me right here in the middle. Don't worry, it's not for you."

"I can't do that."

Her fingers twitched, and then the gun came up.

"Come on, Brad."

"Jennifer." Cautiously, he sat up straighter on his knees. "You wouldn't do that."

Her reply was a kiddish grin.

Jennifer would never kill me. But the Queen of Hearts would.

—"The House of Dust"
Southern Gothic

"WELCOME HOME, BABY," Missy said.

She shut the door and smoothed the dress around her hips, her eyes climbing up him. "I see that gun under your jacket. And that collar looks awfully tight." Stepping toward him, she lifted her face. "What? No kiss?"

Walt's neck strained back, eyes darting around the hall.

"New varnish, new paint. Old place cleans up pretty nice, doesn't she?" Missy said. "And I know you always thought I was dirty, so I took a bath, too. Here, smell my hair."

He looked toward the dance hall. "What in God's name is going on in there?"

"Oh, that. You remember my silly idea of inviting folks over? Here they are. And you'll remember I wanted to make this hall a nice soft yellow. I think it turned out pretty good."

She tried to touch him, but his shoulder convulsed before her fingers could even brush the cloth. With long, scraping steps, he backed away. His eyes looked into hers and turned murky, trying to tease and taunt her in the way that used to make her laugh. He wanted her to smile and be silly, but her lips stayed flat as she slowly followed him.

A clunk came from farther up the hall, followed by a muted scream. Walt spun around, hand diving inside his jacket. They both watched as Mr. Irons appeared from behind the stairwell, dragging a bound, kicking figure toward the back door. Ezra's man, Abe Daleder.

The bouncy stream of jazz and the hum of conversation from the parlor and the dance hall were surprisingly effective in muting the struggle as the back door opened. They disappeared into the night. Going to the garden.

The vast calmness cloaking Missy remained even as Walt's hand reemerged with his snub-nosed .38. He didn't point it at anything. Instead, he turned back and said, "What are you doing?"

Studying her dusty toes on the clean floor, Missy wove toward him.

"That discoloration on your ring finger . . . you move fast. Or had you been seein' her while we were in Nashville?"

A huff. "I didn't come here to wrangle with you, Missy."

"Really? Then why did you? To use that, maybe?" Her gaze angled on the gun. "Don't act surprised. You already struck a deal once to get me put in the ground. I'm sure you'd be plenty capable of doing it yourself this time."

"I came because of your letter."

"Because it meant I'm alive. *That annoying thing is still alive.*"

He gestured with the gun. "Why'd you send it? What do you want?"

"You know already. I've never hid it."

"And you know how things are. You're not stupid, Missy."

"Oh, I am. Or I was. Because I *didn't* know how things were. I thought I'd found someone who would stay with me. I thought if I were quirky and silly and interesting enough, you might feel something for me besides . . . But what ambitious man wants to be anchored to a former whore and her bastard child?"

The flush left his flustered face. "Dear God," he said.

"Don't worry, it's not yours." A tiny bit of triumph in that, at least. "Doesn't a pregnant woman count as double homicide?"

"I didn't come to kill you, Missy."

They were close. She reached for the gun. It came up in a heartbeat and coldly kissed her left temple.

"But if you try anything, I'll blow your brains out."

She could feel her arteries throbbing against the muzzle. Throbbing with the sinking sense of tranquility bleeding up from the boards and drowning her mind. The music and voices in the adjacent rooms were slurring. The whole community packed inside the house was flowing rapidly toward the precipice of sleep. Mr. Irons must be doing his work in the garden.

Blinking, she found the metal had already warmed against her skin. She leaned her head against it, sniffing the nasal thrill of his fine cologne.

"We used to have such fun, didn't we? You said you could have no peace without me. And maybe that's true in reverse, too."

She tried to sway even as the gun bored against her skull.

"Hear that music, Walt? I wanted so much for me and you to be in there on that big open floor with all the people watching. When we came here I dreamed it. But we can dance out here."

"No, Missy."

Movement stirred near the top of the stairs.

Roy's pinched face withdrawing from between the leaf-work balusters. His tiny footsteps retreated to the upper floor. Leaving her.

"Please?" She let her eyes drift shut. "You're gonna have to shoot me, Walt. 'Cause you can't risk me writing pesky letters to other people. You'll have to shoot. So let's just dance for a bit first."

She moved gently, and he loosened just enough that they could sway in place, the pistol connecting them.

"In a few months, you'll marry that girl you're wearing the ring for," Missy murmured. "You'll start a little family together, and you'll be happy for a while. You'll become a DA, then state congressman, and you'll get to live in Nashville permanently. Sit in the fancy capital building and make laws. But you'll get tired of that. Eventually, you'll run for the big boys congress and go up to Washington. But that won't be enough. There's always a better club to join, isn't there? So, you'll come back home and campaign for senate. But something will happen. Your rival will find pictures from your old trips with me, and he'll say, *Hey! Anyone know who this girl is?* And someone else will say, *Hey! I found she used to work at a place near Atlanta called the Back Creek Club.* Well, that's bad, but maybe folks would understand."

Her feet were warm, her hands tingling. Their watercolor reflections moved on the gleaming floor.

"Political rivals, though—they would say, *Why not try to find that girl? She's probably livin' in a trailer park somewhere. Bet she could say some nasty things about him and maybe do some damage.* But they'd never find me. My body would have been dumped out in the river or thrown in the woods someplace. It would have rotted away long since. They'd never find any bills of sale or rent for this house, because you cleaned those out. But they would still ask questions. Too many questions. He was with a prostitute? He went on vacation with her to Mobile? Later she disappeared? No trace? And all while he was state prosecutor? Can he explain? You'd try. But they'd take a closer look at the mine case. Maybe ask more about all the people who supposedly died in there. You'd stay in the race, Walt, because a man like you doesn't quit. But you'd lose. And then it would all fall apart. Divorced by your wife, maybe estranged from your kids. Marked by the public like Cain was marked by God. You'd have to go back to the clubs to find company, back to those filthy places. And when you crept home before light, it would be to a quiet house full of dust."

They stopped swaying. The gun was shivering against her skull. It bit into her skin as Walt tried to stabilize it.

"Shut your mouth." He said it low, but it seemed loud. The music had stopped, and so had the voices. The house was still. "That's enough."

Missy lifted her right hand and held it toward his empty left one cinched tight beside his hip.

"*Please.* You'd have no peace. So stay."

A bit of that unbearable sympathy she remembered from the Club moved on his stern, clean face. Even as his trigger finger tightened, his other hand relaxed and reached to hold hers.

"No, Missy."

For just a moment, their hands slipped together. She felt that tingling, crumbling, endless sensation pass from her flesh into his. The gun jostled against the border of her eye socket as his fingers splayed open.

The weapon hit the boards and Walt reeled backward. "You're—"

Missy picked up the gun.

"Outside, then. That way. Back door."

Some of his carefully combed hair had fallen down, and as he turned automatically, hands up, she saw that the tight collar was chafing his neck, and a pulse of sorrow moved through her. Perhaps in some other life it would have worked. Or perhaps in a dream.

But then he began to speak very diplomatically as she pushed him up the hall and through the door and across the porch, down into the chirruping night garden where the house's yellow windows made prints on the grass.

"We can't stay, but we can certainly leave together, Missy, if that would satisfy you. You understand that this house is too remote for me to conduct a career from. I could find something closer to Nashville; though it might not be as grand as this, it would be better than our last apartment. I can sympathize with the dislike you had for—"

"It was you." She said it softly, but he quickly changed course.

"What was? Tell me what you want, Missy."

They were halfway toward the trees, at the center of the garden. The graves Irons had filled with Abe Daleder and the woman with dark hair stood mounded up in adjacent beds. Walt turned, and she forced her hand to tighten around the pistol grip.

"Tell me!" His raised hands were bloodless fists. "Tell me what you want. I'll do it."

"Nothing. It was always you, Walt." A final, tiny smile drifted across her lips. "Where we lived didn't matter. I didn't care if it was grand or not, but what's it worth if I'm alone? If we aren't together? If I'm *nothing* to you?"

"I'll stay!" he screamed.

Her smile dropped. "Yeah. Now you will."

She shot him in his right leg first, and when he fell, she shot his left leg just below the knee. Then she threw away the gun and got behind him and dragged him over the railroad tie. As he wailed and thrashed, she pulled him through the weeds, positioning him beside the hole. He tried to crawl away, but a quick shove rolled him into the grave.

She noticed that the dirt walls muffled his screams a bit. Blood was running freely from his wounds. She grabbed the shovel and started flinging clods from the mound into the trough. They sounded awful pattering across his suit fabric; she tried to remember the rain of dirt against her own coffin. It didn't help. She bashed his hands and his head with the shovel every time he tried to crawl out.

When she couldn't bear his roaring anymore, she dumped a large shovelful of dirt into his mouth. The cries changed to wet gagging and the burn of frantic breath through nasal passages.

Breathing failed as he became more deeply submerged. Then the dirt pile was diminished and the hole was filled and only his fingers were visible, pale stalks protruding from dark soil, squirming like unearthed worms.

Throwing away the shovel, she left the garden and went down the hillside and knelt by the bank and dipped two buckets of water from Deep Creek. She lugged them back up to the garden and wet down the grave until it was a smooth, glistening bed of mud. When the sun rose, it would dry out in no time, leaving a hard-packed surface, dry and dusty.

The fingers were motionless now. She lay down in the mud and gathered them together into two pinkish bouquets. Kissing the fingertips, she murmured, "Yes. Now you'll stay."

As I dug, I unearthed a skeleton. Scores of summers and winters had withered away features, hair, and clothes, but it was not hard to deduce whose body this must have been.

—"The House of Dust"
Southern Gothic

"ADAMAH," BRAD SAID.

He lifted his hand away from the skeleton's cavernous face. This wasn't a grave he was digging. It was a mouth being opened. Already he was waist-deep between its lips.

"Get the bones out," Jennifer said. The humid night deadened her voice. One arm was behind herself, the other pointing the gun at him. An old snub-nosed .38. Even a clumsy shot could kill.

"It's in this soil," he said. He extended both hands, feeling a bloodless chill sizzle through his nerves. "It drinks the air out of you."

"Fine. He can go on top of the bones. Get out." Backing away, she stepped out of the bed and bent down to grab the shoulders of Sorrel's shirt.

Brad's grip closed around the shovel shaft. Standing, he scrambled from the fresh hole. Jennifer noticed before he could reach her.

In an instant, she released the sheriff and was standing again, backing away, gun up. "Put the shovel down, Brad."

He took a half-step forward. Her arms stiffened and her lips rolled into a flat line. Another split second and she would do it.

"Put. It. Down."

One hand up, he dropped the shovel.

"Now get out of there. I'll do the rest myself."

He walked slowly, and so did she. Like objects locked in orbit of each other, they traded places. Once among the crushed daffodils, she crouched and tugged at the delirious man, an animal cautiously moving its prey.

"Adamah," Brad said again. "You know what that is?"

Wordless, she drew Sorrel toward the grave. His limbs flopped. If he wasn't dead already, he was hovering just above it. Only moments now.

Brad swallowed an unexpected tightness in his throat. "It's what these people are hooked on. Have been for two hundred years. It's living breath in exchange for false visions of fulfilment and glory. After what addiction did to your family, I thought you'd be stronger, Jen."

Sorrel's body slid into the grave. Jennifer looked up through slack hair, and her voice was low. "Be careful, Brad."

"I know you were hurt. I know it's hard to move on. And maybe these people don't have the greatest lives, either. But continuing *this* won't help anything. It won't fix anything."

She picked up the shovel.

"Come on, Jen. You became a nurse to help people escape this kind of thing."

She began heaving the dirt into the trench.

His voice hardened. "You're drowning them. You're a medium between here and down there, and you're pumping them full of something terrible. The latest dealer, overdosing them on—"

Jennifer's jaws twisted apart. She must have screamed, because her jaws gaped and he saw her teeth, but he heard no sound. Instead, he saw the shovel topple. He saw both of her arms come up, supporting the gun. He saw the muzzle bark yellow fire as she shot him.

On April 29, they sat in his car outside a little church in La Vergne. Jennifer shook.

Brad tried to crack the window to escape the sound of her panting. The driver's-side window wasn't working. She jolted when her window rolled down a bit. The hum of a distant lawn mower. And the sound of an organ playing a hymn. Muted by the church walls, but still recognizable: "The Old Rugged Cross."

"Sounds like they've started," he said. "We probably shouldn't intrude. "

"No." She sucked in loudly through her nose. Then she jerked the door handle. "Stay if you want."

He got out, tucked his black shirt into his black jeans, and accompanied her across the crowded parking lot. The church was on a little knoll. They had to climb three sets of steps to reach the front door.

Jennifer wrenched the door open and strode inside. He followed.

The transition from sun to shade placed him briefly in a spectral world. He stood looking across the backs of pews and the backs of heads while an organ played and voices sang. Jennifer, in her black dress and black jacket, walked ahead, directly up a river of scarlet carpet toward an open casket at the front of the sanctuary.

Panic sliced his chest. They should sit at the back. He hurried after her. Folks in their dark funeral garb became more distinctive, lit by dappled sunshine from colored windows.

About halfway up the aisle, he caught her and wrapped his arm through hers to slow her. The singing dropped off behind them as people looked up from their hymnals. Straining a smile at those nearest, he softly tried to coax Jennifer toward the rear. She shook her head. Her eyes were focused forward. Her hair was pulled so tightly back it seemed to extend her forehead across her scalp.

"Jennifer!" he hissed.

They were three-quarters of the way up the church's nave. Just six more pews. Still, she kept walking.

She wants to be near the family. Near the casket.

The body was clearly visible now. A teenage girl. Hair a loose, lush black. Face a contented smirk, slightly shrunken.

Three more pews.

Almost all the singing had stopped. Just the tremulous voices of the family in the front row remained. Quickly, they, too, faltered. Under the weight of silence, the boards beneath the red carpet creaked as Jennifer halted behind those hunched backs.

A woman at the end of the left-hand pew straightened. Her rigid spine leaned away from the back of the bench. Her hair was black, like the girl in the casket's, and cut at a slant from the back of her head down to a point below her chin. The hair swayed as the woman turned in her pew and faced them. Her raven hair split on her forehead, and the points came together below her chin, leaving a candle flame of face. The flame ripped open as she saw Jennifer. A scream—an icy gale—blasted from her parted jaws. Both hands rose, fingers rigid. "*You!* You killed my baby! You killed, you killed, you killed, you killed my *baby!*"

Outside the church, inside the car, the woman was still audible through the cracked window. By the time he got them out of the parking lot, Jennifer was screaming, too.

The bullet tore through his abdomen.

The pain didn't startle him. Shock must have done something to his brain because when he pressed his fingers against the wound, the blood oozing forth felt cold. He looked at Jennifer and tried consciously to calm his heartbeat. For an instant, she looked as shocked as he must. He thought about saying something consoling, like how it was okay, it wasn't her fault.

Rapidly, though, clouds formed across her face. She dropped the gun and shivered for a moment, head jerking, as if caught between two dragging forces. Then, almost in slow motion, she doubled over, fists clenching, eyes squeezing shut. She dragged air deep into her gut, more air than seemed possible, an endless, thirsty, ravenous gasp.

Adamah. It was filling her. Sorrel was dead in the hole, and the shovel used to bury him was lying at her feet.

For a few steps he went backward, trying to dredge up the courage to turn his back on the thing in the flower bed. Pain lit up his torso as he finally turned. He used the burst of adrenaline to charge across the garden. On the porch steps, he fell. As blood-slippery fingers fought with the screen door, a burst of footfalls broke out on the grass, rapid as galloping hooves. It had her fully now, and she was following. Fast.

As he tore across the porch, pounding feet sounded on the steps.

The back doorknob rattled inside his fist. It opened the next second and Brad burst through.

The lights were blinding. The piano music had stopped.

Flying feet clattered across the porch behind, and he turned and slammed the door. A frantic search revealed no lock. He knew that. He leaned against the door. For a couple heartbeats, the hall was still. Then rustling, like wind stirring treetops, came through the dining room, rasping his ears. The people in the dance hall, finally sleeping.

By his hip, the doorknob turned. Gradually, pressure built. He braced himself even as frosty weariness crawled up his legs. His splayed hands turned white. Lowering his head, he pressed his chin into his chest and felt sweat slide down his nose.

The pressure lifted for a moment. Then a blow struck the door. It vibrated through his frame. Then nothing.

Seconds dripped past. Blood seeped from his side, chilled his shirt, plummeted to the floor. Perspiration slicked his skin and his glasses slipped from his nose and clattered onto the floor.

In the split second before a blink, something dark darted from beneath the door and grabbed the glasses. It retracted with them until they bent and shattered against the threshold.

The saliva inside Brad's mouth dried. "Jennifer," he rasped.

A sigh came from the other side of the door. A deep current from an ancient cave. "Oh, Brad."

The darkness reappeared below the door. A silvery residue taking the form of two hands. Fuzzy, thin, impossibly long, they spread like a stain across the bright boards toward his feet.

Brad screamed.

He peeled away from the wood.

He hurtled down the hall.

Behind him, the door fell off its hinges. Her drumming feet quickly overtook his staggering legs. As he passed the foot of the staircase, her arms came around his neck, then her legs around his waist.

Brad stumbled. The front door was there, wide open. But all resiliency left his legs. They crumpled.

The door. Get through. To the car.

She lay on top of him, kneading his shoulder. His nerves were flakes of wood in the presence of a fire, glowing and curling up. She pulled her body up along his and bent down. Her hair piled on the floor beside his head.

"Shh, Brad. I know you want to rest."

He crawled, dragging them both by his fingernails.

Jennifer's right hand moved from his shoulder. It burrowed under his shirt and pressed against the wound in his side. The pain wasn't debilitating. But the black hole of despair that opened up inside of him was. The massive *weight*, like an anchor tied to his heart.

It was the same feeling he had experienced when she told him after the funeral to leave her forever, when she had pulled off the ring and thrown it onto the floor. The same feeling, cold and gray, that had flooded him so many times before that, ever since his father died. It snuffed out the light and will and purpose and strength in him. It inundated everything with a crushing emptiness that settled deep in his chest: no escape.

Murders. Memories. Unfinished business. The dead at Serene Flats in Mississippi, at the Martlet Mall in Louisiana, in the salt marshes in North Carolina, on the interstate near Jasper, and dozens more all across the South. They were his legacy. His life's work.

His hands lay on the threshold. His chin was propped on the floor. His veins were draining; his life was painted out behind him on the hall floor. He stared out at the ashen evening.

"Sleep," she whispered above him. Gentle. A healer's words. "Sleep well."

The softest rain fell beyond the porch: a coalescence of the rising mist.

"It's okay," she assured him. "You've wanted this for so long. Rest."

Rain. Back on that first day. Sorrel standing right out there. *Bury her before the rain comes.*

Muscles stiffened. Teeth ground together. Gagging in air, Brad dragged himself onto the porch. Her claws dug into his shoulder. She leaned down again. "It's time to stop, Brad."

The jutting nail heads tore his shirt. They gouged his flesh. He was at the edge of the porch. The car was pulled up before the steps.

Trembling, he reached out into the rain. He gripped the top step and hauled his body over the edge. As he tumbled down, she dislodged. They fell into the gravel together. She lay there quietly, watching him.

Wiggling toward the car, Brad gripped the door handle. He pulled himself up and the door opened. Behind, she climbed languidly to her feet. "You left me, Brad."

The glove box popped open. His hand strained inside and closed around the gun. As her feet crunched through the gravel, he hauled himself around to face her, pistol raised.

She stopped. "You abandoned me. We were supposed to support each other."

He held the gun still for a full minute as she stared at him, and then it began to tremble.

It was her. Blond hair, tired face, lonely eyes. Beautiful in the falling rain.

"Jennifer."

"Brad."

"Jennifer," he said again.

She stepped closer. "Yes."

"You . . . you told me to kill you if you ever became addicted."

Delicately, she pushed her loose hair behind her ears. "I'm fine, Brad."

"No." He braced the pistol with both hands. "Do you renounce the devil inside of you?"

"I . . . " She shook her head. Her lips bunched tight against tears. "I'm not strong enough. I need your help." Another step. "Help me get clean. Please."

Such a gentle voice. Without his glasses, and with the sweat in his eyes, and with the air itself sweating, she was blurry. A blurry shape motioning to him. Closing in. Reaching.

"Please help—"

Brad pulled the trigger. Her head split.

She pitched backward. There was no echo. The report vanished into the fog and into the glowing, staring house.

She lay prone in the gravel. Her reaching arm stayed sticking up. As he stood there, puddles formed in her eyes and in her open palm. It was raining. Returning to the car, he replaced the gun in the glove box and withdrew the other item stowed there. He took it back to the corpse.

He dropped the ring into Jennifer's hand.

The South is a ghost, and so am I.

—"The House of Dust"
Southern Gothic

FROM AMONG THE weeds, Missy plucked three daffodils.

The first she placed on Abe Daleder's grave. The second, on the grave of the woman with thin dark hair, the woman who had risen from the floor at the gray house, who oversaw the burial ceremony of Roy. Between their graves, in the central flower bed, she pressed the last daffodil into a little mound of mud covering Walt's hands. *There.*

Inside the house, she eased the back door shut. Repose was reigning. Enough rocks had been thrown into the pond to break open the surface, and now the earth was bleeding its vast tranquility up through the roots of the house, through every splinter of wood and sliver of glass, hazing the atmosphere in every room. The creak of her footsteps was wonderfully lonely as she stole across the dance hall, between the prostrate bodies, each paled just slightly by fine dust.

They slept in the parlor, too, and in the hall upstairs, and in the open bedrooms and in the study, and in the wicker chairs on the upper porch. On the front porch, they lay curled up by the columns and slumped in the rockers.

Only one chair had been left vacant. The central one.

Easing herself into it, Missy rocked slowly. She leaned her head back and drank in the reverie. Gradually, she became conscious of each sliver of silence and shiver of movement, each stitch in the tapestry of the dark country. Stillness in Three Summers and along the dark miles of the forest road. Silky water slipping below the clay-stained bridge. Cicadas in the trees, crickets in the fields, fireflies among the stars. Peace in the house at night. And then, before her closing eyes, the island morphed, melting into another place.

A golden land.

Wandering the ways of the night, we return and return to find the place where we died.

—"The House of Dust"
Southern Gothic

THE MCDONALD'S IN Lexington was crowded. Nine o'clock at night and people were shouldering through the glowing, greasy doors.

Brad found a place at the outskirts of the parking lot and eased his seat back. He couldn't feel his fingers anymore, but he managed to get the laptop open and navigate to the document containing the article he wrote from the Atlanta hospital bed. His eyes weren't working well, either, so he tripled the font size to examine the text.

It was a mess. Twisted histories. Ancient names. But always the same story. Always the same being looming behind the cycles, the same rituals.

Sorrel's words returned: *This is your monument to Adamah.*

Unbidden, he shivered. The dry scent of cooling pavement drifted in through the shattered window. And then the softer smell of the land beyond the lot. Mown grass. Dry, hardened earth. As the gentle current continued, the odors grew stronger.

Brad forced his fingers to move.

With clumsy swipes and clicks, he cut out most of the material, leaving only one history. His own. A story he'd never told before. The one that had followed him. The one he had hidden behind all the others. But even in that one, the specter remained, woven into his final month.

He leaned his head back. Chills needled every part of his body. He was almost over.

In the side mirror, people moved as dark outlines against the restaurant windows. Blinking heavily, he became aware of something beyond the windshield, standing beneath a light pole in the neighboring lot. A man with burnt, seeping arms folded across a blackened orange jumpsuit. Shriveled eye sockets gazing toward the car.

This is your monument to Adamah. Sunlight will make it grow.

Brad shut his eyes. He listened to the far-off tapping down a tunnel of his brain and found himself nodding faintly along with it as weight bore over him. It was time to let it out. To let it go. To trust the world with the truth.

But not all of it.

Words blurred as he altered the ending, deforming the truth of what had been present in Atlanta and tonight at Angel's Landing. What was closing in on him even now. He buried it in metaphor and myth. It was an ending to the cycles and the thing in the house. It was his ending.

When he was done, the article was still a chaotic collage. It didn't matter. His death would sanctify it in Heather's eyes. She would publish it. And people would read it. Marvel at it. And, eventually, forget it.

He typed "My last article" in the subject line and hit send.

Then he slouched over, head resting against the window frame. Out below the light pole, the figure had vanished.

He blew a long, painful breath.

Blood still trickled from his side, but much more slowly now.

The night sighed on his cheek, flavored thickly with the musk of earth. Not dry earth now, though. Damp, crumbly soil. Like the car had been transported to the center of a verdant field.

Movement outside the window, filling his periphery. A figure of raw darkness.

It leaned down. It reached for him. Its arms came through the razor fragments of the window and were everywhere, tingling, smothering, embracing him.

He couldn't move. His vision went. His feeling went. For a moment he was nothing but a thought: the word his dad had sworn to say before he died.

"Amen," Brad whispered.

THE HOUSE OF DUST

The day after Christmas of 1999, my dad called me out on the back patio. It was a Sunday morning and there was a church on the other side of the chain-link fence. We lived in Rhode Island, so it was cold, but my dad had been sitting out there for the last half hour, smoking and listening to the hymns.

"Hey, Brad," he said. "I didn't realize it was Christmas yesterday till I heard them singing over there last night. Sorry about that."

I shrugged.

"Don't worry, though, I got you something. Come here."

We sat in plastic lawn chairs by a wire table spray-painted yellow, and he opened a cardboard box.

"Instructions," he muttered, tossing a booklet aside. "Why would you need instructions for this?"

It was a Newton's cradle. He pulled back one of the beads, let it fall, and I watched the one on the far side of the row leap away. For a few seconds, they took turns tapping out their cadence. I huddled down in my chair, pressing my hands between my knees.

"You like it?" he said.

"How long does it go for?"

"Not forever, thank God. That'd be annoying. No, it stops after a bit. See?"

The jittering beads settled into stillness.

"I wish it would go on," I said.

"If it weren't for friction, they'd never stop," he said. "They'd go on forever. But the world's full of friction." He chuckled dryly. "Anyway, you can play with it after I'm gone."

He re-boxed it and sat back and kept smoking.

"Why do you listen to that stuff?" I asked, nodding toward the church.

My dad shrugged. "I'm grateful. Jesus rose from the dead so I won't have to." He grinned. "Go on now, I don't want you to breathe too much of this stuff."

"Why do you smoke?" I asked.

"They don't like it on the rig. Got to do it here."

"Why don't they like it on the rig?"

My dad let his head loll back. He looked at the sky, then over at me.

"Go back inside, Brad."

I obeyed and pretended to be asleep on the couch that afternoon when he came to say goodbye. He stood over me for a while, then went and got the cardboard box with the cradle in it. I heard the hiss of a Magic Marker across its surface. Then he left for the airport.

When I opened my eyes, the box sat on the coffee table. Written across the side were the words: *It can't go on forever.*

Five days later, on New Year's Eve, the New Horizon oil rig sixty-four miles off the Alabama coast caught fire. Twelve men died: Jacob Nilsen, Forrest Blakny, Earl Hoagland, Clifford Jones, Jason Gomez, Micah Dreyer, Daryl Farmer, Clive Kinsey, Warner Shultz, Tony Andre, Fenton Lee, Zed Lennon. And Martin Parker Ellison, who caused the explosion. I knew he hated the company. I knew he blamed my mom's departure on his brutal schedule. I knew it would happen.

I told no one. I did nothing. And afterward, I did worse than nothing. I tried to atone. I revealed the sins of others so I would never have to recount my own. I wrote articles for this magazine,

Southern Gothic; but what is the gothic if not rooted in denial and darkness? I must let in the light.

I met Jennifer in 2014.

She worked at a little diner in Marion County, in southern Tennessee. I was doing research there for "Scarlet Seven Miles" *(see Mar/Apr 2015 issue)* and used the spot as my office during the week I visited. I noticed that she did not go outside to smoke during her breaks like so many of the other workers.

Instead, since the place was usually crowded, she asked if it would be possible to sit at my table and study her medical books, because, well, that's where the light was best. Of course I said, "Of course," and then went back to writing the story of a monster who dragged a kidnapped family along a seven-mile stretch of local interstate behind his pickup, while she studied the anatomy of the brain. In that tense silence, a connection formed between us.

When I left town, I asked for her number. I called her, then I visited her, then I asked her to move to Nashville, where I would help pay her school bills. And then, in late October of 2017, I asked her to marry me because the rest of my life was looking pretty grim.

Heather at *Southern Gothic* was quite literally baying for blood. She asked me to present summaries of my upcoming stories; it was hard to admit that I didn't have any upcoming stories. I set out on a driving tour of the South, deciding I needed fuller immersion despite my almost ten years of residence.

I spent the early months of 2018 cruising through hundreds of miles of brown winter forests and gray winter fields and past blue winter oceans and rivers and lakes. My hopes of finding something unique to write about sank along with the balance in my bank account. But always behind me, around the last bend, was the idea of a man with a burned face, and a crime that might have been averted. That drove me more than my editor's shrill commands.

But nothing materialized in these months of wandering. I began to rely heavily on antidepressants, first prescribed after my dad's death to beat back the pursuing clouds. It seemed that if there was always another gruesome tragedy to expose, then my job was pointless. Nothing was changed by my reporting on the gory details. No lives were being healed, no progress was being made. I was recycling nightmares, and only people in faraway office buildings were collecting the treasure created by all this spilled blood.

In early February of 2018, my editor, Heather, called me from Atlanta to complain. She did it, however, in an unusually subtle way. Lily Verner, Heather explained, was a bright recent grad who was writing a series of five true crime articles set in an allegedly haunted oil field in Alabama. After reading the first one, Heather had bought the series. They would serve for almost a full year's worth of issues. She let an ensuing silence tell me the rest: after eight months of nothing from me, *Southern Gothic* was seeking fresh blood.

And then, on April 24, 2018, the final blow fell. My fiancée, interning at Nashville General, administered the wrong medication to a teenage girl named Lila Simmons. It was an accident. Lila needed an MRI. She was claustrophobic about the machine. Jennifer went to key in the sedative and selected the wrong autofill option.

It ended her career before it could begin, and it also ended our engagement because she insisted we attend Lila's funeral. The way her mother screamed when she saw Jennifer was a way I've never heard anyone scream. That scream made Jennifer scream, too. It made her say she was evil. It made her rip off her ring in the car and throw it onto the floor and say I needed to leave her.

Later that afternoon, far from Nashville, I got off the interstate to commit suicide.

I was supposed to interview a police chief in Jackson about a carjacking cold case, but my tire blew out with thirty miles to go. The delay killed the appointment, and the trouble I had swapping tires revealed my own inadequacy even more. The car rode unlevel on the spare, droning the prospect of another failed investigation into my bones. Heat pressed through the sunroof, pounding memories of my fiancée's screaming face through my sweaty scalp. Both of those pillars of my life—collapsing. When I saw the next off-ramp, I put on my signal.

It was one of those dead, pointless exits in rural Tennessee that serves perhaps a dozen people a day. Left was the interstate underpass. Right was blank road. I wanted a quiet place to do it. I went right, out into the wilderness, leaving the world and all its weight behind.

But the weight followed me.

It was the end of April, but outside the grimy glass, the afternoon trees wore the tired green of late summer. I searched for a shady gravel patch along the shoulder. The broken driver's-side window control clicked beneath my forefinger as the rising pressure crushed open a primal place in my brain filled with flames and billowing smoke and the searing smell of raw oil. My eyes watered. I tried to still my finger and couldn't.

The clicking only stopped when I saw the sign. It leaned drunkenly among thick honeysuckle at the left edge of the highway. My vision cleared. Buried beneath many spray-painted desecration attempts lay the official black lettering:

THREE SUMMERS—TWO MILES

Just beyond the sign, a leafy mouth opened in the wall of the woods, the shrouded access point to the forgotten town. It would do. I turned across the highway and stopped my car amid the brackish twilight.

An RIA .38 Special rode in the glove box. I took it out and braced it against my temple. The movements of my jaw, clenching and unclenching, translated along its length into my hand. I could already smell the sulfur, already feel the fiery track of the bullet through my brain. The window would shatter. The flies would come through the breach and settle on my body. Eventually, someone would happen down this road and find my car. Word would get out, swirl across local networks, then end up in Atlanta on the desk of my editor, Heather. My own death would be the last violent, meaningless story I provided to her. I might just as well have stepped out in traffic while changing the car tire back on the interstate.

No, I did not want a violent death.

I replaced the gun and picked up an orange canister from the passenger-side floorboard. Ten milligrams would buoy me up. Lift the weight. Bring me back to the surface. But there was fire on the surface. The endless fight to stay afloat. The story I could never tell.

I gripped the canister. It would take about a dozen pills to get sleepy, a dozen more to soar from my body for good. But I couldn't swallow one pill dry, let alone twenty-four.

"Some water," I said aloud. "I need a drink of water."

Stepping on the gas, I fled down the ancient road, crossed an ancient concrete span over a waterway called Locust River, and came to the town of Three Summers.

It was a place forgotten by our world, a place of early-twentieth-century brick buildings and dead neon signs. I stopped in at a Texaco station for a drink—one of the few places still open—and tried again to swallow the pills in the shade of the gas pump canopy. But a vision of a burnt man in an orange canvas suit welled up out of the heat and knocked on my window. It was by far the most vivid hallucination of my father I'd had since he died.

It resolved into a gray-colored old woman who insisted, in the mistaken belief that I was a doctor, that I visit a nearby residence. Apparently, a person of some local importance was ill.

I don't know why I answered yes. To ease the weight, perhaps, forestall the inevitable.

The town petered out into abandoned lawns and weed-cracked drives running up to ivy-shrouded houses. I turned left at the first road I came to, still in sight of the town, still with the gray woman visible in my rearview mirror. Some part of me already itched to pull this thread.

The road was straight, and the woods formed a green tunnel around it, diffusing the light to an even emerald gloaming. The hazy catacomb of forest absorbed the sound and motion of my car, adding to my delirium.

Three miles later, I passed back into the sun, crossing a little clay-stained bridge that spanned a dark creek. The road that followed was in bad shape. Thick, empty fields appeared on my left. The fields ran down a mile or so to the glimmering green line of the river. The heat and the pills and budding nausea blurred my vision.

I would have sped right past the old place if my gaze had not been suddenly pulled to the passenger-side window by that mysterious, magnetic presence possessed by things that wait. A murky drive led me up along through a twisting avenue of live oaks, and at its end I found a fine old plantation house, shrouded by woods and swamped by weeds, but beautifully preserved. And around back, in a verdant garden, I found the body of a woman. Like the house, she had been touched by many years, but remained beautiful.

The town sheriff, an antagonistic man who dressed in black, arrived at the house soon after I did, but in the company of a true doctor. Upon the pronouncement of death and the departure of the doctor, it was decided that my vehicle should act as hearse to the woman's body. My decision to linger had resulted in more than I had bargained for: and that excited me. So, I acquiesced, and we placed the body in the car.

After crossing the clay-stained bridge, the darkness in the tunnel of trees was made heavier by the approaching storm. I switched on the headlights and discovered dozens of cars parked along both sides of the road, sitting crookedly in the depression edging the woods. Under the passing headlight beams, solemn, staring faces faded in and out of existence behind the windshield of each vehicle. The people of Three Summers had come to pay their respects.

"We've been expecting this," the man in black said by way of explanation.

"Why didn't they come to the house?" I asked.

"That island was her ground," he replied. "Invitation only."

The sheriff refused to tell me the woman's name but seemed interested in my own romantic status. So, I mentioned Jennifer.

The community followed in procession through miles of road and rain to a shaggy graveyard on the banks of the river, near a kudzu-wrapped white church. I noticed that as the body was buried, the locals sank into a peculiar reverie. When I approached the grave, I also noticed that the woman had been laid in the ground without a coffin, and as I stared at her I imagined for an instant that her eyes opened, and she stared back.

This oddity only added to the intrigue of the place. I called Jennifer and asked her to come live with me there—please. For the summer, at least.

When I called Heather in May, asking for money and promising a blockbuster, it took an hour to convince her. I told her the story of a strange town in which the kudzu came only for the church. I painted a picture of decay, of rot. Of our times. In the end, it was reminiscing about my very first article that won her over. My fiancée took even more convincing. The prospect of a secluded life in western Tennessee did not initially appeal to her. But the financial and emotional extremes we were facing finally convinced her that a strategic withdrawal from the world might do us both good.

So on the first Saturday in May, we exited the I-40 ramp, she in her Chevy pickup and I in my Accord. We followed the curvy single-lane road from the state highway to Three Summers, and then the tree tunnel road from Three Summers to the island that Sorrel called Angel's Landing. It was a very quiet two o'clock when we passed beneath the live oaks along the drive. It only occurred to me then that the trees were hundreds of miles beyond their natural coastal habitat.

The house's layout was fairly simple. Both floors were split down the middle by high-ceilinged hallways. Rooms opened off these halls, ribs branching from a spine. On the first floor, as you crossed the threshold, the doorway to the dance hall stood to the left and the parlor to the right.

Down the first-floor hall, the staircase, ornately carved, rose like a cornucopia toward the second floor. Past that, doorways let off to the wide kitchen and the dining room, the latter of which connected back to the dance hall.

That first afternoon, I found Jennifer lying in there, curled in on herself. She was fine, she assured me. Fine.

Upstairs, a bathroom and three quiet bedrooms lined the western wing. The master bedroom and connecting master bathroom sprawled with royal abandon down the eastern side, capped near the front of the residence by a musty study and library. I set up base here, in the companionship of such titles as *The Coming Race*, *Justine*, and *Éloa*.

I waited out the afternoon eagerly anticipating darkness. This night's activities had been caged in my mind for the past two weeks, clawing to get out. Whether or not the move had been worth it, whether or not I had a story, whether or not I needed to even stay alive depended on what I found tonight.

I had, of course, conducted as much supplemental research as possible in the week before our arrival. It didn't result in much. No internet sites made reference to the town or the house. I located the practice of the doctor who had come to the house and pronounced the woman dead, but he refused to sway from the verdict. I also consulted the Register of Deeds at 17 Monroe Street in the county seat of Lexington. The last registered house owners were a couple named John and Ellen King, who purchased the property in 1946. After their abrupt demise, with no heirs and accumulating taxes due, the place fell to ownership by the town of Three Summers.

Finally, I went to the library in Lexington and asked for local records and writings about the community. But again, nothing was available. The woman who helped me, Brooke Carney, struck me as uncomfortable and slightly evasive. I left her my card and asked her to call should anything become available.

Thus, my initial knowledge was mainly geographical.

Three Summers lies a hundred miles west of Nashville, in the northwestern corner of Henderson County, lost amid the woodlands bordering State Route 104. At a width of approximately eight hundred feet, the Locust River flows flat and green past the settlement on its way toward the Mississippi. Due to the abundant distribution of sandy clay and gravelly silt loams, Henderson County has been described as inconducive to crop growth. This makes the plantation at Three Summers remarkable, not least because the quality of the soil is not discernibly superior to that of the surrounding county. On the contrary, it is gritty, crumbly, and quite gray in color.

After finding dirt in the master bedroom, in the bed, I was inspired to search the internet for a word I'd discovered in an old notebook lying in the basement of the house: *Adamah.* It was Hebrew for *earth.* Or *dust.*

The house was still when I finally departed, and midnight was approaching.

The graveyard by the Locust River was milky with moonlight and drenched in the smell of walnuts. As I dug down, shivers touched me, like fingers from the earth. And those same fingers, it seemed, had ground the woman to powder: I found no body. For a long moment, I crouched there. All around me in the churchyard the dead lay coldly, their presence seeping through the crumbling grave walls.

Someone had taken her.

Mind careening, I drove back to Three Summers and found the sheriff in a derelict cotton mill that haunted the edge of town, brooming water across the earthen floor by lantern light. I accompanied him back to the police station, a kudzu-swamped structure on the edge of a field where he evaded my questions. Instead, he asked after my own career. And to throw me off guard, he took me into a room at the rear of the building where a school lesson was taking place at 2:30 in the morning. The lights in the back half of the bleak room he led me to were burnt out. The walls were arrayed with posters of the state flag, state animal, state flower, and state motto; the floor was arrayed with school desks; the desks were arrayed with muddy-footed children. Under Sorrel's prompting, I told them the story of Serene Flats *(see Sep/Oct 2009 issue)* while rain fell outside. It was one of the most surreal things I've experienced.

I did not let this distract me, however. I had no doubt the body was still out there in some bedroom or basement or back-porch freezer. Stolen by some attendant of her curious funeral.

This suspicion was confirmed by a discovery I made that same night after seeing a trash collection truck at the plantation house, driven by the woman who had directed me to the house that first day. Inside, buried in the basement floor, among the decaying glory of past generations, I found a festering amputated hand.

The next day, I resolved to confront her, and drove the grisly package to town. Although I had taped wax paper around the hand, I had to stop halfway to town and wrap it in a Walgreens bag and put it in the trunk because of the smell.

The woman's name was Jezebel Irons, the proprietor of a waste disposal facility about five miles downriver, on the northern bank, at an abandoned mine facility: Adamah Mine.

During our interview, she confirmed her involvement with the hand, but deferred my questions on its significance, shutting down completely when I asked about two unusual titles I had become aware of in connection to the house: the name *Adamah* and the honorific "Queen of Hearts."

When I presented my findings to Sheriff Sorrel, his reaction was violent. When I pressed him about the connection of the house and the woman to the name Adamah, he dismissed it as angel worship gone awry. If I did not leave the town and its dealings alone, he threatened, I would be expelled from the house and my fiancée would suffer some nameless retribution.

That made me back off. But I was onto something, I could tell.

Something lay behind my simple dichotomy of whether the old woman had been loved or hated. Something that ran far deeper.

Brooke Carney from the Lexington Library called me that afternoon, and I drove to meet her. New artifacts had been delivered since my first visit there a week before. I reviewed them with her in the children's corner of the dim library. They revealed a rudimentary history of the house.

It was built in the 1830s by a shipping magnate who fled his responsibilities in Charleston with an alleged witch named Martha. After establishing the town of Three Summers nearby with the construction of a cotton mill dedicated to a being called Adamah, the man was killed by his own slaves. His wife, however, apparently loved, managed the plantation shrewdly until her disappearance in a raid during the Civil War.

In the late 1860s, a doctor named Jerimiah McCloud entered the region accompanied by a mute woman named Magdalene. He established a hospital in Three Summers, but was killed in 1877 by two patients on whom he was performing strange experiments: smearing mud across their bodies to heal their wounds and to contact the being called Adamah. His wife, Magdalene, survived until the First World War, when she vanished into the creek near the house.

In the 1920s, a gypsy leader named Rex Emil married a survivor of the Party Field Massacre, an ownership dispute over the plantation grounds and house. Her name was Miriam. Emil built a theater to the honor of the being called Adamah, but was killed by one of his circus animals at its inauguration. Miriam lived until the late thirties. When she died, she allegedly decayed in one afternoon on the house's dining room table.

In the forties, things changed a bit. A couple named John and Ellen King came to the house. They built nothing. They lived there a short time, and Ellen died in the winter while giving birth. Her husband, some say at the behest of the local doctor, hung himself from a great oak tree before the house.

Then in the early sixties, a couple named Missy Holiday and Walter Collins came. Walter, a state prosecutor, was investigating the recently constructed Adamah Mine for safety concerns. After swaying the case in the town's favor in the summer of '62, he disappeared. Missy stayed on and used the profits from the mine to fight legal ownership battles for decades. Missy, called Marilyn by some, was the one I found that day, the one I drove to her grave. She had occupied, it seemed, a role in the community called the "Queen of Hearts."

A different figure occupied my thoughts, one that was gradually emerging from the gloom. One that I could now give the name Adamah. For each building—the mill, the hospital, the theater—that had been built across the years, each was named for Adamah. It seemed to me then that if I understood what Adamah was, I would understand everything that sprung from this being. And so, initially, I paid little attention to the "Queen of Hearts" mythology. That was a mistake.

The man who had delivered these artifacts to the library was named Richard Hettinga, a regular patron of the library. He had left for Atlanta during the previous week, but Brooke Carney was kind enough to give me his number, despite the fact that he hadn't been answering her calls. In the car, I tried Richard Hettinga's phone. It went to voicemail, so I left him one. Then I drove back.

Adamah. That name. That thing that seemed to touch all the other things. That presence lurking around the house in symbols and clinging to Three Summers in street and building names. What was Adamah?

The woman at the mine, Jezebel Irons, had said Adamah was an angel. Outside of this Southern backwater, though, I had never heard the name, and my acquaintance with the major religious texts was sufficient to know that they contained no record of such a being.

This Adamah was depicted the same in all the artwork I came across: a human form with two legs and six arms spread-eagled.

Masculine language was used in reference, but the figure had no sexually defining characteristics. And no face.

For the next two days, I stayed in the study, patching together the scraps I had collected in a document titled, "The House of Dust." On the third day, Wednesday, I rolled out a photocopy of the town map, took a pen, and drew a line across Three Summers, connecting the old mill at the eastern edge, the theater in the center of town, and the old hospital at its western edge. If I wanted to learn about Adamah, the obvious way was to explore the shrines dedicated to it.

An exploration of Adamah Cotton Mill came first. Outside the great brick structure was a cornerstone, marking its completion date as 1842, and its builder as a man named Darrin DeWitt. Inside, a portion of the roof had fallen in, and clusters of human-size hollows pocked the dirt floor.

As I was exploring, a girl named Harlow entered the ruin. I had encountered her briefly the night I met Sorrel in this place, but I had never seen her face. She had blinded herself by cutting out her eyelids. Unknowingly under my gaze, she poured water on a central section of the floor and began caressing the earth. Then I spoke to her, and after an initial shock, she willingly conversed, telling how her father was buried in this place.

I drove away slightly enlightened on the town's curious burial practices, but anger smoldered inside me over the girl who had blinded herself. It was one thing to travel the underside of the South and see abused adults: Hilary Wegner from Serene Flats with her broken mind, the Tampa University hiking party's severed ears, even the burnt survivors of the New Horizon oil rig. But it was another thing to see a child in such condition. How had she been allowed to wander alone, to harm herself? I needed answers.

So I drove to the church and consulted the aged clergyman, Pastor Mark Burger. He was convinced that all of the bizarre customs in the town could be attributed to cycles in which the occupant of the house exercised a soothing influence on behalf of the Adamah being, and outside of which the land was gripped by a restless malaise.

Later, sitting at my desk in the house, I played the eyeless girl's words back. Out of everything she'd said, one phrase burrowed into my mind and lodged there: *shallow place*. Shallowness conjured something subterranean; from shallow places you could reach into the depths. And the depths could reach back. The house, she'd said, was one of these places.

Around midnight, Jennifer came into the study and asked if we could go for a walk. She hadn't slept since Saturday night, when she dreamed about the girl coming out of her casket. It showed in her eyes and translucent skin and slouching gait. She was fighting slumber and losing. I wanted her to lose. Even so, I agreed.

We went outside and down to the road. The cicada choruses rasped our ears as we walked up and down the island in the moonless night. I tried to speak about us. She cut me off: "Don't, Brad. Things are fine until we try to talk about them."

Sometime around dawn, we returned to the house. I waited up with her throughout the morning, until around ten, when she sat down in a dining room chair and didn't get up again. I carried her upstairs and put her in bed. Then I left. It was time to visit the second shrine.

Amid still noon heat, I made a similar search of the empty structure on the west edge of town: the Angel Adamah Hospital, built by the man named Jerimiah McCloud. Here, in the oxidized file cabinets, I discovered records chronicling the deaths of dozens of workers at the local mine, many due to suffocation.

On the second floor, something even more grisly: dozens of human bodies, coated in clay, lying beneath the bedsheets. And one living among the dead: the girl named Harlow, whose acquaintance I had made at the mill, tied to a bed in the empty ward, screaming. Her behavior discomfited me enough that I did not release her, but I walked directly to the sheriff's office to demand an explanation. He was not there. But as I stood irresolute, he called me on Jennifer's phone. He told me to come back to the house.

The cicadas were blaring when I leapt from my car in the house's clearing, and in that instant a question and realization collided in my mind and shook me. Dr. McDowell on that first day had said he never heard the insects sing out here. They had started the night we moved in. I found Jennifer in the forest before the house. A deep pit nestled between the roots of a large tree, and she was asleep down there on its floor, murmuring that she needed to "get closer." I feared that her remorse over the girl's death had finally pushed her off the brink. But when she woke, she said she felt much better.

Sorrel hung around to chastise me, to tell me to take better care of her. There was no need. I was shaken. And so, curiously enough, was he. He seemed deeply concerned with our relationship.

I stayed with her for ten days.

We went places in that time: down to Lexington, to the library, to eat at a little place called Dan's Café, to visit Pinoak Lake. About the middle of the following week, the seventeenth, I think, we drove west for about seventy miles, following the course of the Locust River. While we were out and the signal was strong, I tried again to call Richard Hettinga, but he didn't answer.

Jennifer took everything in stride. She was very quiet, and would smile occasionally, but always seemed slightly anxious to return to the house. When I tried to speak of the past, though, I detected ripples. She had not completely healed. Deeper currents flowed beneath her placid face. And deeper currents flowed beneath the things I had discovered—a connection I could feel but not yet express.

I stood in the dance hall several times during those days, looking at the shape on the mirror above the fireplace, at its many outstretched arms. What drove this cult? What happened to those who entered that embrace?

Jennifer slept at night, deeply, eerily. I did not. I sat in the study, computer open. Each time the chasm of sleep approached, a toppling, plummeting sensation jolted me awake and my eyes would land on the Newton's cradle at the edge of my desk. Silent. Urging action. One muggy morning, I jerked up in my chair to find her kneeling beside the desk. She hardly noticed me. She was going through the death notes retrieved from the hospital, nodding to herself, smiling softly.

This disturbed me. I consulted Pastor Burger at Simmons Creek and he advised us to depart immediately. I called Jennifer from the road. She sighed flatly when I asked if she was okay: "Brad. I'm fine." Still, I decided it was time to conclude the investigation. In Three Summers, I parked by the Theater Grill and went in and had chicken fingers and tater tots for lunch. I looked across the street at the arched cut-glass window above the marquee sign in the theater's limestone façade. The diner was empty besides a Stan Lee look-alike behind the counter. I asked him when the theater was last open, and he said, "I'm not giving any quotes," and went into the back. Before leaving, I took pictures of some photos hanging on the wall that showed people gathered around town, all with their eyes shut.

I got into the theater through the back door. Inside in the dark, in the dust, in the little projector room above the auditorium, I found an artifact that put all my other findings in place. A film, made by Miriam Larkin, which depicted the demise of a man who came to Three Summers one warm evening. He was welcomed at first, then led by a happy throng away from the town to the island where the house stood. And there, in the roots of a tree, he was buried alive.

I left the place reeling. Now I knew: the old woman who I had driven to the cemetery had been placed in her grave alive, as had hundreds of others through the long history of the house. The community had been consumed by a cult. Jennifer and I would leave today. There was just one last call to pay.

Jezebel Irons had said she was home during the midafternoon hours. So I went to see her. I drove back up Adamah Road and looked across the field at the house. Jezebel was home.

I followed her voice into a room where gaps had been cut in the boards so people could crawl into the gloom below. I went down there and found her sitting in the half-light, a hole dug between her heels, waiting for me. I knew what Adamah was, but I didn't know *why* he was, why this town was enthralled by a mythical being, why they buried living victims in his honor.

She showed me. She had preserved Missy's other severed hand. Burial, she said, imparted breath to Adamah, trapped in the ground. And as Queen of Hearts, Missy had breathed for Adamah and imparted his blessing: salvation in the past.

To learn this, Jezebel compelled me to participate in a ritual with her: the burial of this hand that had held so much significance. I complied. And then I hallucinated my father, burned, bloody, black with oil, crouching with me in the dark.

I fled.

Sorrel met me on the road. He had been out to the house again. He told me to be out of there by midnight. He said we were becoming part of the cycles that had gripped this place for centuries. Jennifer, he said, was in trouble. Premature evening fell as I drove back to the house.

From the records on my desk, Jennifer had discovered Jerimiah McCloud's ancient antidote. She had spread mud across her body. She was calm. Collected. More peaceful than at any point since before Lila Simmons's death.

She had become something.

She tried to share it with me, tried to smear dirt on my face. But I had seen the madness brought on by these rituals. And I saw now in her eyes not the loneliness I had come to love, but a contented companionship. I could not make her leave with me, and I could not make myself stay.

The whole land seemed to hold its breath as I drove away. That was Monday, May 22. My last day in Three Summers.

That evening, down in Lexington, disgusted in the face of my own cowardice, I received a call: Hettinga, returning my weeks-old voicemail. Through a cloak of static, he invited me to Atlanta, eager to share his knowledge. Believing he would know a way to extract Jennifer from the web of that place, I left at once.

The orange lights came out along the interstate, the clock climbed toward midnight, and Jennifer shadowed every thought. What was she doing back in that dark land, far from the city lights? I should have been more aware of her; aware of how we were slipping. But it happened during those ephemeral midweek days when I was unearthing the intergenerational connections between house and town. Before I realized we'd become a part of it.

It was midnight when I arrived in Atlanta. Down in the Gulch, down near the old Atlanta Constitution Building, I met the man I supposed to be Richard Hettinga. In the quiet of the night, he recounted the history of the house as a vast cycle of violent men and ethereal women. Each time a man brought a new Queen, the town was replenished and the cycle was sustained.

He told me about darkness that had possessed a young boy named Roy. He told of a Three Summers gathering in 1962, where burning cold had passed through the boy's body, and the endless void that had filled his chest, and he told how a woman named Missy had saved him from burial and absorbed the darkness; a woman who feared cruelty and longed for the peace that comes with utter silence. He told how she killed the town sheriff, a man named Ezra, and became Queen.

"You were that little boy?" I asked Hettinga.

"I was Roy. The Queen of Hearts raised me. And I raised her son, Sorrel. I wish I could have helped him escape that place."

I said, "Tell me how someone becomes a Queen of Hearts."

He told me to follow him. The deep red taillights of Hettinga's car led the way along miles of dark roads until a very different part of Atlanta was passing outside my windows. Amber streetlights shone down on buckling sidewalks and overturned trash cans. When he turned onto a residential street, the headlights flashed across barred windows. The car stopped before one of the old houses.

This was the childhood home of the old woman I had found, Missy. This was where she had, by accident one summer night in 1949, killed her grandmother, who was being abused by a visiting man. Hettinga directed me to the backyard to find the place where she laid the body. A bed of daffodils. A patch of earth where she had sat for days, mourning her accidental crime.

The scene triggered something in me. My own past broke open more vividly than it ever had before. It appeared again as my father. It pursued me down the dark neighborhood streets as I left. It drove me off the road and into darkness.

For days, I swam through oil and cold water and fire.

I wasn't swimming to escape the fire. I was swimming to escape the thing that followed me through it: a man made of fire.

I resurfaced in Piedmont Atlanta Hospital on June 1. The nurse said a car accident had knocked me into a coma. I had been dehydrated, malnourished, and severely sleep deprived. And my fiancée had been calling.

"Who?"

"She said her name's Jennifer? She's been sending those every day."

A bouquet of daffodils graced my bedside table.

"When can I leave?" I asked.

They said Sunday. That was Friday. In the intervening time, I wrote most of this article. Heather, my editor, who is based in Atlanta and listed as an emergency contact, never bothered to come see me. I didn't care. This wasn't for her anymore, or *Southern Gothic*. It was about the thing that had chased me in circles for years. The thing that was manifest in that little town, inside that house, in the body of my fiancée.

I was released midafternoon on June 3. The rental car took the last of my money.

I arrived at the house in the aftermath of a party. Sorrel was there. He attacked me. He broke my phone. He said I would never publish this article. In my weakened state, he dragged me into the woods and hung me from an oak. As I was lifted into the air, I saw an angel in a white garment step from the twilight. She held a gun.

It was Jennifer, saving me. She ordered me to bring Sorrel's body to the garden behind the house. Although he was not dead, she told me to bury him. And when I hesitated, she turned the gun on me.

As I dug, I unearthed a skeleton. Scores of summers and winters had withered away features, hair, and clothes, but it was not hard to deduce whose body this must have been. This was the previous cycle's version of me—the partner of the last Queen. This was Walt Collins. This was history coming back to claim the house and town for another generation.

Jennifer would never kill me. But the Queen of Hearts would. She had been changed not by a demon, but by the quiet land and the blemished community and the stagnant pull of old time. Someone of deep pain welcomed without spite into this fold, ready now to perform its deadly rites.

So, I killed the Queen of Hearts. And she killed me.

The South is a ghost, and so am I. Wandering the ways of the night, we return and return to find the place where we died. Walking circles, running cycles, never reaching beyond, never breaking free. Traveling through time, orbiting a black star.

It can't last. My dad tried to teach me this with his last Christmas gift. But I did not listen. I journeyed on, while the plantation houses became wedding venues, and the cotton fields became factory buildings, always searching . . . searching . . .

I'm going to send this to you now, Heather. Do what you want with it. This is my last article.

ACKNOWLEDGMENTS

A BOOK IS A HOUSE.

And a house starts with a dream. This dream began as a bicycle ride down a few quiet back roads in my native East Tennessee and a pondering on what might lie behind that quiet. What might stir in the green forest shadows? What might happen in the houses behind the trees? Who might come down these roads in the dead of afternoon? It began with stillness and sunlight and the name "Holiday" on a real estate sign and a few lines from the *Epic of Gilgamesh*.

But tools are needed to turn a dream into a plan. And for that I must thank my parents, who purchased that typewriter when I was fourteen, when I began writing seriously, and purchased a laptop soon after, and then another laptop, and put food on the table, and never pried into what was taking shape beneath the sound of those clattering keys.

And a plan needs encouragement to flourish, and for that I must thank my siblings—Ryan, Laura, Chris, Anna—who asked what I was writing now and when it would be done. And my siblings-in-law, Roger and Rose. And my friends, too, especially Luke and Rachel, who asked when I would finally publish something. And the professors of the Carson-Newman University English department, who were always enthusiastic about my pursuits, especially Dr.

Mraovic-O'Hare, and Dr. Underwood, and Dr. Sobiech, and Dr. McMasters (from whom I stole a line in this book). Thank you all.

But ultimately a plan needs an architect, and for that I must thank Adam Gomolin of Inkshares. He worked tirelessly with me, taking this book from its earliest state (through more drafts than I care to mention) until it reached its final form. Adam's ability to discern the proper threads to pull that will draw together the tapestry of a book is truly staggering. I could not ask for a better advisor or advocate.

And, of course, a house must have builders to make it take shape, and those builders were the wonderful readers and editors and designers who helped lay down the floors and nail on the roof and mix the proper color paint for each scene. Avalon Radys, who read the book and runs Inkshares and keeps us all on track. Kurt Mueller, Amanda Desiree, Chase Pletts, Laramie Dean, Grant Bayliss, and J-F. Dubeau, who all took time to read and consider and critique and encourage. And Sorcha Groundsell and Barnaby Conrad, both of whom brought their special talent to this story in its final days as a manuscript, honing, sharpening, taking it to a state I never could have. And Pam McElroy and Kaitlin Severini, whose meticulous care and attention to each page of this book during copyedit smoothed away my numerous errors and inconsistences of spelling and punctuation and setting and plot and much, much more. Thank you all.

But ultimately, a house needs inhabitants. And for that I must thank you, dear reader, for reading. For stepping through the door and sitting for a while and experiencing this story with me. Thank you.

And, finally, a house needs ghosts to haunt it, and for that I must thank those masters of the genre who inspired me. Edgar Allan Poe, who dreamed of a kingdom by the sea. Shirley Jackson, who invited us into the modern haunted house. William Faulkner, who made us reconsider time. Flannery O'Connor, who acquainted us with sublimity and absurdity. And Michael McDowell, who steeped us in atmosphere. All these luminaries contributed to dreams and ideas in deeper, more subliminal, and more profound ways than I can truly express. What is a writer without his forebearers?

And eternally, thanks be to God, without whom I can do nothing.

INKSHARES

INKSHARES is a reader-driven publisher and producer based in Oakland, California. Our books are selected not by a group of editors, but by readers worldwide.

While we've published books by established writers like *Big Fish* author Daniel Wallace and *Star Wars: Rogue One* scribe Gary Whitta, our aim remains surfacing and developing the new author voices of tomorrow.

Previously unknown Inkshares authors have received starred reviews and been featured in *The New York Times*. Their books are on the front tables of Barnes & Noble and hundreds of independents nationwide, and many have been licensed by publishers in other major markets. They are also being adapted by Oscar-winning screenwriters at the biggest studios and networks.

Interested in making your own story a reality? Visit Inkshares.com to start your own project or find other great books.